By

Pamela Hill

Published by Juliana Publishing

Book cover design by
Hillside Printing Services

Published by Juliana Publishing

British Library Cataloguing in Publishing Data.
A catalogue record is available from
the British Library.

All the characters in this book are fictitious
and any resemblance to actual persons living or
dead is purely coincidental.

Juliana Publishing
Highview Lodge
Oulder Hill Drive
Rochdale OL11 5LB

Printed and bound in Great Britain by
Hillside Printing Services, Rochdale.
Tel - 01706 711872
www.hillsidegroup.co.uk

ISBN 978-0-9559047-4-5

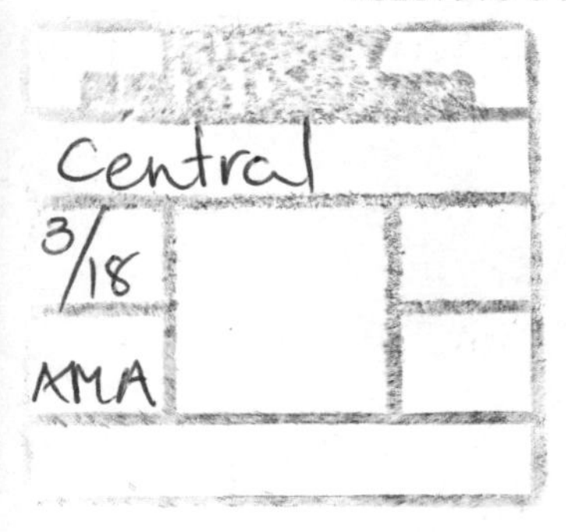

GOOD THINGS
DON'T HAPPEN TO ME

1

Infuriated, Paige glanced at the overcast sky. It was raining again. *'Terrific!'* she exclaimed, flicking the catch on her umbrella, causing it to fly open noisily.

When the Minister paused and frowned critically, his clear displcasure was met with a penitent smile, followed by a gesture for him to continue.

Reverently lowering his head, in barely a whisper he brought the committal proceedings to a close.

'Give him O Lord your peacc and let your eternal light shine upon him.'

There followed a hushed chorus of 'Amen' by the scattering of mourners in attendance.

She approached Reverend Thorne, shook his hand and thanked him for his heart-felt ministrations. He smiled, offering his condolences. 'Take it a day at a time,' he advised. 'You're a resolute young woman Paige. You'll come to terms with your grief before too long and meanwhile, should you need someone to talk to, my door is always open.'

As he moved away she stared at the coffin, strewn with red roses and arum lilies. 'I'll never forget you Grandad.' she sobbed. 'I love you.'

'It's time to go,' her best friend Emma murmured, tugging on her arm. 'Come on Paige; let's get away from here; you look shattered.'

'I'm alright,' she sniffled, wiping her tear-stained face. 'It wasn't as bad as I thought it'd be.' Turning to the others she continued, 'I take it you'll all be at the Rose and Crown for lunch. I've ordered lots of food and your drinks are on Grandad who insisted you raise a glass or two in celebration of his life.'

'Aye, that sounds just like him,' Bill, Paige's next door neighbour acknowledged with a loud sigh. His wife Ada nodded in accord. 'Bill will miss playing Dominoes with him; in fact everyone will miss him. Ted was such a likeable character, so witty and dry. Have you made any plans for the future yet Paige?'

She shook her head. 'Not really. I can't until I've found a job Ada. I'm twenty-seven now; I've never had a proper job since I left school. I had Mum and then Grandad to care for so I was needed at home. I have to work to put food on the table. I can't live on fresh air and I've a stack of bills to pay.'

As the drizzle turned to heavy rain, she quickened her pace with the others in hot pursuit.

'Flaming hell!' screeched Emma, anger ringing in her voice. 'I'm soaked to the skin. Can anybody tell me why it always rains at funerals?'

'To make the day more miserable,' Paige grunted, clambering into the car as tears clouded her vision.

Emma slipped an arm around her shoulder. 'Hey, pack it in. You're over the worst now.'

'I know; ignore me. It was the lovely flowers that set me off. I'm just feeling sorry for myself because now Grandad's gone I'm all alone. I have no one.'

'Not true. You'll always have *me* and we'll hang out more now you've no ties. It's time you started enjoying some social life again. Did your grandad leave you well provided for?'

She shook her head. 'There's not even enough to cover the funeral cost but Mum left me a bit. I need some decent new clothes though. I can't turn up for interviews wearing my shabby stuff. Still, it's not a problem because you promised to look out for me, so you can take me shopping for some proper gear. You know what's in fashion and where to go.'

She grinned from ear to ear. '*Wow*, retail therapy. Try keeping me away.'

Laden with bags they lumbered their way to the car. 'I'm having a massive clear-out when I get home,' Paige made known breathlessly. 'Out with the old and in with the new *and* I'm having my hair styled tomorrow. My first interview's on Friday.'

Emma was astounded. 'Paige Sheldon…you dark horse. I didn't know you'd applied for any jobs.'

'Call it putting out feelers at the moment. My CV leaves a lot to be desired. I'm just thankful I've got decent grades at A-level as my work experience is practically zilch. Apart from that three month spell in the office at M&S it's blank.'

'Er...that's not right. You've done voluntary work at the Hospice. Didn't you put that on your CV?'

'No, I didn't bother. That'll hardly help me in the workplace will it?'

'It shows you're compassionate so make sure you tell them. Where's your interview?'

'I've got two; one's at Dempster Brothers and the other's at Cavendish Engineering.'

'Doing what?'

'Secretarial work, though I haven't a cat in hell's chance of success at Cavendish Engineering. That's the interview on Friday. One of the Directors needs a Personal Assistant. They advertised for somebody with experience so I'm more than a little surprised I got an interview. Perhaps they're having a laugh.'

'Maybe they think they can mould you if you're a bit green. I can think of nothing worse than a *know all* who's forever saying, "Where I worked before, we didn't do it like that." I've worked with loads of folk like that. They drive you bonkers.'

Paige drove into the supermarket car park. 'I need to get something for my tea. You can wait for me in the car if you like. I'll not be long.'

Emma decided to join her and as they made their way into the checkout with their groceries, a young man pushed past Paige almost knocking her down. Without any apology, he held up a loaf. 'You don't mind if I go first do you? I'm in a hurry.'

After tossing his loaf on the conveyor he swiftly revealed a hand basket overflowing with groceries.

'You hard-faced bugger!' Emma hollered. 'How dare you shove other folk out of the way? Haven't you heard of an orderly queue, you moron?'

Curtly he snapped, 'I've told you I'm in a hurry.'

'Then you shouldn't have come shopping,' Paige said furiously. 'What gives *you* the right to priority treatment? You need to learn some manners.'

Glowering he quipped, 'Get a life; I didn't think you'd have a problem accommodating a handsome young guy in a hurry.'

Perhaps he imagined his hackneyed remark would raise a laugh but he was mistaken. Paige was livid. *'Handsome?'* she ridiculed at the top of her voice. 'I think *not.* You have a big nose, small ears and as for your manners, they're non-existent.'

Emma nudged her and laughed aloud, 'Well said. It's bloody typical of some folk...pig ignorant.'

There was no further exchange of dialogue and he left the store hurriedly without a backward glance after paying for his groceries.

'Can you believe that guy?' asked Emma as they were driving home. 'He deliberately hid that basket of stuff. What an arrogant...'

'Forget him; Tim was full of his own importance. Remember how he insisted I must choose when my grandad had a stroke? How could I have neglected a sick elderly man? Tim didn't care two hoots about me. I'm well rid. Who needs a bloke like that?'

'You're right and I don't suppose he got in touch when your grandad died.'

'No, not a word but he knew. A friend of his sent me a nice card but I heard nothing at all from Tim. I couldn't get through to him that I *had* no choice. I had to be there for Grandad.'

'You can do a lot better than Tim. There's loads of blokes looking for a girl like you so you'll soon find somebody else. Have you decided what you're wearing for your interview?'

She pondered. 'Probably that nice blue and white striped dress I bought in the sale.'

'Yes, excellent choice. You looked terrific in that, very chic. I can't wait to hear how you get on. You never know, maybe you'll end up with the job *and* marry the Director who needs a Personal Assistant.'

'Right, like that's going to happen. Anyway, I'm okay as I am. I need to unwind and I'd like to travel a bit. As an adult, I've never been anywhere outside UK so I've lots of places to visit.'

'Please, have a seat Miss Sheldon. I'm afraid all the interviews are running late. The Managing Director, Mr Cavendish Senior was supposed to be sitting on the panel but unfortunately he's been delayed. They had to start without him but hopefully he'll be here in time for yours,' the receptionist told her.

Paige smiled weakly and sat down. Her heart was beating rapidly and her palms clammy. Try to settle down, she chastised herself. It's a job interview, not a murder trial. All the same, she'd be relieved when it was over. It had been a ludicrous idea to apply for such a position. Who did she think she was? She'd be way out of her depth trying to compete alongside experienced candidates.

'I'm just getting a cup of coffee Miss Sheldon so do you want one? They won't want you for at least ten minutes. The last candidate's only just gone in.'

Her mouth was dry and she felt anxious. 'Thanks, that'd be nice. Milk and no sugar please.'

She flashed a friendly smile. 'Coming up.'

There was nobody else waiting in reception as she admired the décor. Her house looked really drab by comparison. Her house…that sounded so strange. It had been her grandfather's house for the duration of his marriage and her mother had given birth to her there, where she had been raised by her grandfather in the main until her mother had been forced to give up work as a nurse owing to severe illness.

Paige's mother, a single parent, had never married and she knew nothing about her father. That subject was taboo. She had raised it once as a child but her mother had made it clear she mustn't raise it again.

She had questioned her grandad about him soon after her mother's death, to no avail, because he had been just as evasive and tight-lipped.

Interrupting her thoughts, the door into reception was suddenly thrust open and a well dressed man in his mid-forties strolled in. He looked around before acknowledging her. 'Hello, is someone attending to you? Where's Mandy?'

She assumed he was referring to the receptionist. 'She's gone to make us a cup of coffee. I'm here for a job interview but the panel's running a bit late.'

'Rather inconsiderate of them wouldn't you say?'

'No, it's not a problem. They've been waiting for their Managing Director who's been delayed. If I'm honest, I'm glad he's not here. When I arrived I was really nervous, kind of anxious as I haven't worked for years so I've been dreading this interview. I've no idea what to expect. I just hope I don't make an absolute fool of myself.'

He smiled; it was a kindly reassuring smile. 'I'm sure you've nothing to worry about. Walk in boldly with your head held high. Show them what you're made of. That's the way to win them over. If it isn't too personal a question, why haven't you worked in a while? Have you been raising a family?'

‘No, nothing like that. Soon after I left school, my mother became ill. I had to give up my job to look after her and just before she died, my grandad had a massive stroke so I was needed again. I didn’t mind though. They were all the family I had. Two weeks ago my grandad died so now I can get on with my own life but it’s hard at my age starting afresh.’

He threw back his head and laughed. ‘Your age? You’re just a lass. I wish I were your age again. So, does that mean you have no family now?’

She nodded. ‘That’s right...no one.’

‘I’m very sorry for your loss. It takes a long time to come to terms with the loneliness; I know; I lost my wife five years ago in a car accident. I still miss her but one has to move on. Life’s for the living as they say, so come on, cheer up.’

As he smiled Paige recalled a brief memory of her childhood as she had hurried towards her mother in the school yard on her first day at school. She could scarcely wait to tell her about her kind teacher with the *scrunchy* eyes, referring as it turned out, to the deep laughter lines around his eyes.

Suddenly mindful she was staring at the stranger who regarded her quizzically with similar *scrunchy* eyes she flushed with embarrassment. ‘I’m sorry. I didn’t mean to stare. I was miles away.’

‘Worrying about your interview no doubt?’

On a short splutter of laughter she nodded. ‘I shall just have to bluff my way through. I’m rarely stuck for words though, so I’ll survive I expect.’

Mandy returned with two mugs of coffee. ‘Hello Mr Cavendish. You finally made it back then?’

'Aye, at long last. A lorry lost its load on the M6. There was nowhere to get off so I just had to sit and wait for a lane to reopen.'

Paige was dumbstruck to hear that. 'You...you're Mr Cavendish Senior?' she stuttered.

'I am, so now you know I don't bite you can stop worrying. I'll see you inside. Remember what I told you and not a word to the others that we've had this little chat.' With a wink and a smile he was gone.

Mandy's face lit up as she giggled. 'He's a proper joker, which is more than can be said for his ghastly son. He detests women. He looks at you like you're something horrible he trod in, so be ready for him. You'll be in for a hard time if you get this job, so I hope you have a broad back. He's the Director who needs a PA. They never last long working for him. I'm used to him so I answer him back.'

'Is *he* on the panel?' Paige enquired, inclining her head towards the interview room. 'The *son?*'

'He is, and Mrs Morris is too. She's the Company Secretary. She's nice; you'll like her. Remember to stand up to him if he starts. He can't cope with that. He expects women to be subservient and when they aren't, he doesn't know how to react.'

Paige would have liked to learn more but at that moment the previous candidate exited the interview room looking hot and flustered. She hurtled through the reception area like an Olympic heel-toe walker and shot through the door without a single word.

'That appeared to go well, I don't think,' Mandy chuckled. 'Sorry, I'm speaking out of turn but I've seen it so often.'

When Mandy's telephone gave one ring she stood up. 'Are you ready? Better not keep them waiting.'

With an apprehensive expression Paige leaped up and wobbled on her high-heeled shoes. Smoothing her hands down the front of her dress she emitted a heavy sigh. 'I'm a total wreck,' she told Mandy.

'You'll be fine,' she said reassuringly and opened the door announcing, 'Miss Sheldon.'

Paige heard the door close as she stepped into the room. She moved towards the desk in response to a sharp instruction to be seated. Glancing at the panel she recognised Mr Cavendish Senior, sitting on the right. He smiled pleasantly and gestured for her to take the seat facing them. The lady to the left of the desk smiled too but as Paige's eyes wandered to the central figure she emitted an audible gasp that she quickly attempted to disguise with a short cough.

'Have we met previously, er...Miss Sheldon?' he asked with a deep penetrating stare after consulting his paperwork.

As this interview was going nowhere she replied assertively, 'You're right; we have met before. You roughly elbowed me aside in the supermarket a few days ago when you jumped the queue. I gave you a piece of my mind.'

With contemptuous derision, he slouched back in his chair. 'Of course; you said I had a big nose.'

'*And* small ears,' she reminded him. 'I do believe I commented on your lack of manners too.'

She glanced at the others who were clearly enjoying the banter and Mr Cavendish Senior winked. 'In the absence of any introduction from the Chair, I'm the Managing Director, Richard Cavendish; this is Rosemary Morris and the young man with the large nose, small ears and appalling manners, who clearly needs no introduction, is my son, David.'

'Would you like me to leave now?' Paige asked.

'On the contrary Miss Sheldon,' Richard declared with a mischievous glint in his eye. 'So far, this has been the highlight of a most frustrating day for me.' He turned to the others. 'I suggest we dispense with the first three questions if you're both in agreement. I think Miss Sheldon has clearly demonstrated how skilfully she conducts herself under pressure.'

Rosemary nodded in accord, while David avoided all eye contact with Paige.

Richard continued, 'I note from your CV that you performed well at school and so I'm eager to learn why you didn't go to University.'

She collected her thoughts. 'I'd have loved to go to University but it wasn't possible. During my A-level exams my mother became ill with a degenerative condition. It meant she would soon be in need of day to day care that only I could provide so sadly that put an end to any aspirations I might previously have had about University.'

At that point David spoke. 'Did you not consider a nursing-home for your mother? Surely that would have been the easy option, allowing you to continue with your education?'

'That was never an option. As I explained, it was a degenerative disease, meaning she'd get progressively worse. Initially, she could do some things for herself but there was still the occasional day when she couldn't do much at all. She wasn't sick enough at the outset to require full-time care, besides which I wouldn't have sent her away from everything she held dear to her. I have strict moral principles; she was my mother, so I nursed her to the end by which time my grandad, who lived with us, had suffered a stroke, so he needed my care then until his death.'

Following a further disingenuous smile he asked, 'And how many interviews have you attended since your grandfather died?'

'This is my first.'

Apathetically, he made a note on his pad. 'I see.'

Paige felt a burning anger inside her. 'No, I don't think you see at all; you presume. It's less than two weeks since my grandfather's funeral and it took a full week for your company to set up my interview. *I* haven't wasted a moment's time. I applied for this position several days before his funeral took place.'

He paused momentarily. 'Nevertheless, you have no recent experience.'

'That depends on your definition of experience. I left school at eighteen. I immediately took a job for three months and when I had to leave I worked very hard, cooking, shopping, cleaning and also nursing. I dealt with the finances, struggling and juggling to buy food, pay all the bills and make ends meet with only the paltry state benefits at my disposal, yet not once have I ever been in debt or used a credit card. How's that for experience?'

David merely glared without response.

'Shall we move on to another question?' Richard promptly asked Rosemary.

There was a short pause before Rosemary spoke. 'Despite your busy life over the past few years, did you find time to pursue any hobbies?'

'I enjoy reading and I also help out at the Hospice regularly, though I don't class the latter as a hobby, more a calling. I like to read to patients and chat to them. It helps alleviate the pain of knowing death is just around the corner. I get so much satisfaction to see their smiling faces so it works well for all of us. It feels good to care about other people,' she stated, glancing pointedly at David.

'Quite the little Mother Teresa,' he countered in a disrespectful tone and Richard rolled his eyes.

'If you say so,' she was quick to rejoin.

Rosemary was clearly embarrassed and moved on swiftly. 'Let's discuss your office skills. I note you have no qualifications in typing. Can you type?'

'I'm self-taught but proficient. I did a correspondence course in shorthand too. I've submitted a few stories for women's magazines. They were typed.'

David looked at her scornfully. 'Well, submitting them is one thing but have any been published?'

She nodded. 'Yes, most of them.'

Displaying surprise he said with a sneer, 'They're simply aimed at *women* though?'

Calmly she stated, 'They're aimed at *anyone* who wishes to read them and as you would appear to be demeaning my achievements, may I ask if you've had anything published Mr Cavendish?'

He glared disapprovingly. 'No, you may not.'

Paige suppressed a giggle. At least she'd had the pleasure of humiliating him in front of the others.

Richard felt it was time to wind up the interview. 'Thank you very much Miss Sheldon. It's been an enlightening experience to hear something different and you certainly brought that to the table today. If you've any questions, please feel free to ask now.'

She shook her head. 'There's nothing thank you.'

'Once we've considered all applicants we'll make our decision and be in touch. Thanks for your time.'

'Thank *you* for affording me this opportunity.'

Mrs Morris smiled but David didn't raise his head and as Paige walked from the room feeling smugly satisfied at having stood her ground, her mind was already focused on her next interview which, hopefully, might prove less contentious.

Behind closed doors, battle commenced.

'You can't be serious Dad,' David gasped. 'That woman was rude and hateful throughout the entire interview. She showed no respect whatsoever.'

'You don't *demand* respect my boy; you *earn* it. You made it your business to provoke her and she responded accordingly so you deserved all you got. You were the one being disrespectful and as for the Mother Teresa quip, *that* was totally unjustified and bloody disgusting. If you weren't my son and heir I wouldn't employ you. You've lost four PAs in four months. This young woman is just what you need. She'll not tolerate your appalling behaviour, neither will she be forever in the ladies' toilet in tears like the last four were. What do you think Rosemary? I prefer to disregard David's input.'

'I think she has an old head on young shoulders. She might not have had a University education but what does that matter? She's bright, articulate and speaks her mind. I like her; I could work with her.'

'You can have her then, for I absolutely refuse to be humiliated by a subordinate,' David yelled.

'You just listen to me young man. There's going to be some major changes round here starting from now,' his father advised. 'You've had far too much of your own way since your mother died and while I must take full responsibility for that, it's time now for you to start acting like a man. You're overruled. I'll telephone Miss Sheldon and offer the job to her before she finds another position elsewhere though I very much doubt she'll relish the thought of working for an arrogant young upstart like you.'

David opened his mouth to protest once more but his father leaped up and silenced him. 'I'm warning you David. Don't cross me on this. Don't lose sight that *I'm* the Managing Director here. I worked my fingers to the bone to build this successful business whilst you, by accident of birth, stepped into it with little to offer and bringing me nothing but stress and aggravation. You made little contribution when you joined and your input is hardly worthy of mention now. Grow up boy. Someday you'll be running the factory. God help us when that day comes.'

After thanking Rosemary for her participation, he strode from the room shaking his head.

Paige opened the door and beamed. 'What a lovely surprise Emma. Come in. I'll stick the kettle on.'

'I can't stay long. I just wanted to hear about your interview and whether you'd got the job.'

'Come in the kitchen and I'll fill you in. I didn't get the job but I guarantee you'll love the story.'

She began with her initial encounter with the MD and after revealing the identity of the Chairman, his son, Emma screeched, 'No way…you're having me on. Tell me that cretin didn't recognise you.'

'He did, the second I walked in the room. He tried his damnedest to give me a hard time but since I'd nothing to lose, I made it my business to humiliate him in front of the other two. He's obnoxious, just a self-centred little jerk, full of his own importance.'

Emma shrieked with laughter to hear the big nose and small ears revelation. 'If only I could have been there to hear that. How embarrassing.'

Paige smirked. 'More so for him. He didn't even look at me most of the time. The others were okay though. I felt they enjoyed it when I talked back to him. The receptionist had warned me he was a right dork though I admit I'd never have guessed he'd be *that* particular dork. It seems he hates women and he made no attempt to hide his contempt.'

'So the interview was quite brief?'

Paige gave her a mug of coffee and they sat down at the kitchen table. 'No, it lasted quite a while. The other two seemed interested in what I had to say.'

'Did you mention your Hospice duties?'

She nodded. 'Do you want to know what the jerk said about that? With a sickening smarmy smile he said, "Quite the little Mother Teresa." Believe me; I could have slapped his arrogant face.'

Emma was shocked. 'The ignorant bugger! Well, I've got him weighed up. He hates women because he can't get one. Who in their right mind would put up with a moron like that?'

'I couldn't agree more. So, where are you off later as you're in such a rush? Have you got a hot date?'

'I wish. No, I'm just clubbing with the girls from work. Why not come too? We have such a laugh.'

She paused. 'Thanks for asking but it's not really my scene. I'd feel out of place.'

That wasn't what Emma wanted to hear. 'You're talking daft; you're coming so be ready at nine. It'll do you good to have a change and a few drinks.'

'But, I've nothing to wear,' she argued.

'No petty excuses. You're coming. Be ready.'

Despite her earlier reservations, Paige was enjoying her night out with the girls. She had met a couple of them previously and they were quick to offer their condolences for her recent loss. The other four girls were friendly too though it was difficult to hold any meaningful conversation above the loud music.

'We do this twice monthly,' one of the girls told her. 'They're a good crowd here. There's never any trouble, not since the police raid a few months ago.'

Quizzically Paige probed, 'Police raid?'

She nodded. 'I reckon somebody tipped them off that some scrotes were pushing drugs. They carted them off to the cop-shop and they got done for it so they never came back. Have you ever used drugs?'

Paige was horrified. 'No, never…have you?'

'I tried a joint once at a wedding of all places but I was throwing up all night when I got home so that taught me a lesson. I never did it again.'

Their brief conversation came to an end as Paige felt a hand on her shoulder. She turned to find Tim, her ex-boyfriend, looking down on her. 'Long time no see. Are we having a good time?'

For a moment she was shocked; she hadn't seen him for four years and the words tumbled from her lips before she had time to think of a suitable reply. 'I can't speak for you but I am.'

He pulled up a chair and moved close to her. 'I've really missed you Paige and I have to say you look stunning. I like your new hairstyle; it suits you. Can I get you a drink?'

She faked a smile. 'No thanks. I've had more than enough already.'

'I'm sure you can manage another,' Tim insisted. 'Besides, we've a lot of catching up to do. You've hardly been out of my thoughts.'

He stroked her face and she moved aside. 'What are you doing Tim? Do you think you can just pick up where you left off four years ago?'

Tim was perplexed. 'But things are different now and...'

'You're right about that,' she interrupted. 'Things *are* different. *I'm* different and I haven't the slightest interest in you anymore, so to save yourself any further embarrassment I suggest you leave.'

Tim wasn't ready to give up that easily. 'Come on Paige; lighten up. You know you don't mean that.'

She laughed scornfully. 'Oh but I do Tim. I know it must be a tremendous blow to your ego, but you must learn to live with it like I had to do when you walked out on me in my hour of need.'

Scraping his chair on the floor he stood up. 'Suit yourself; it's your loss,' he snorted. 'I was prepared to give you another chance but...'

Paige was furious. 'Get over yourself. You might think you're God's gift but believe me, you're not. I don't know what I ever saw in you. You're a small-minded self-centred boor with an oversized ego and I want you to leave me alone. Is that clear enough?'

As Tim sidled away feeling upset and humiliated, Emma approached. 'So what did the great Tim have to say for himself?'

'Not a lot. He was really considerate though. *He* offered to give *me* another chance.'

Emma howled with laughter. 'That's twice today I've missed out on you letting rip.'

Paige was rearranging her wardrobe when the door-bell rang. She ran downstairs and couldn't believe her eyes to find Richard Cavendish standing there.

'Hello again Miss Sheldon. I tried calling you but your phone seems to be out of order.'

'Is it? I didn't know. Please...come in. I'm having a clear out so I'm afraid it's rather untidy.'

Hastily she tossed a stack of magazines under the coffee table to make space on the sofa. 'Please, sit down. Can I get you a cup of coffee?'

'Er...I don't want to put you to any trouble but if you're having one I wouldn't say no; thank you.'

She smiled to herself. How different he was from David. He was such a gentleman. 'I'll not keep you a moment. Do you take sugar and milk?'

'Yes please. Two sugars.'

After filling the kettle she came back to check the telephone. 'You're right, it's dead but I've paid the bill so I don't know what's wrong. I'll call BT later. It was alright yesterday.'

When she returned with his coffee he told her he had fixed the telephone.

'That's great, thanks. What was the problem?'

'You've stacked some bags behind that chair and they were pressing against the phone socket. You'd loosened the contact, that's all, so I've stuck it back in. Keep an eye on that or it could happen again.'

She smiled in gratitude for his help. 'The sooner I get all this lot to the tip, the better. I'm clearing out Grandad's stuff. I'm normally a very tidy person.'

'Me too.' There was a brief pause as he sipped his coffee. 'I imagine you're wondering why I'm here.'

She nodded. 'Well, er...yes I am rather curious.'

'In that case I'll get straight to the point. I'm here to offer you the job. Before you say anything, I've talked to David and made it absolutely clear that he must behave properly. Without going into too much detail, he had a bad experience with a young lady a few years ago, shortly after he lost his mother. I'm not excusing his abominable behaviour; I'm merely pointing out there are mitigating factors but I won't lie to you. Working with David will present certain challenges but from an utterly selfish viewpoint, of all the candidates interviewed you're by far the best to keep him in line, so what do you say? Will you give it a go? It comes with a very attractive salary.'

Paige stared at him vacantly. 'This has come as a shock. Can I just say, I only acted defensively at the interview because I firmly believed I wouldn't get the job so I felt I'd nothing to lose. Believe me, I'm not normally so rude to people.'

Richard laughed. 'It was most entertaining if I'm honest. It's very rare for somebody to get one over on David. I especially enjoyed your eloquent reference to his nose and ears. Deep down he's not a bad lad so I repeat, will you give it a go?'

'I'm flattered you'd consider me and I'm tempted simply because of my circumstances. I need a job, there's no denying that, yet whilst I can promise to try and bite my tongue if provoked, I won't be your son's doormat. I'm worth much more than that.'

'I totally agree; you are. So, is that a *yes* then?' he asked with an optimistic smile.

With a beaming smile she nodded. 'It's a *yes* and thanks. When would you like me to start?'

'Monday?'

'Monday it is then,' she grinned.

'Report to Rosemary around nine o'clock; she'll show you what's what. You'll settle in within a day or two. Thank you for the coffee and apologies for my uninvited intrusion.' He stood up and shook her hand. 'This has gone much better than anticipated.'

Paige couldn't wait to call Emma to give her the news once Richard left.

'No way!' she shrieked. 'You can't work for *that* moron. You're wrong in the head.'

Paige laughed. 'It's a *challenge*. My whole life's been a challenge to date and I'd hate to settle for a dreary monotonous life in the future. This job will add a bit of colour to each day.'

'You can say that again, black and blue no doubt. Good luck to you. You're gonna need it.'

'Hello again Miss Sheldon,' Mandy chirped when Paige arrived on Monday. 'I heard you'd taken the job. Mrs Morris wants to see you when I've shown you to your office.'

Paige followed her through the general office to a room at the far end. 'This one's yours,' she told her. 'Mr David's office faces yours and Mr Richard's is next door to his on the left. Mrs Morris has the first one. Hang your coat over there and there's a lockable drawer in the desk for your personal stuff. The ladies' room is just beyond the general office.'

'What do I do when I want a drink?'

'Just give me a buzz on 44 and I'll make you one. You'll probably find one of the girls from general office will pop in a couple of times a day to ask if you need anything. It's very free and easy here. We all help each other. It's a really nice place to work. Right, shall we find Mrs Morris?'

Paige nodded. 'This place is so much bigger than I thought. I didn't realise there were so many staff.'

'Wait till you see the factory floor; it's enormous and we're always busy. You'll soon find your way around. Mrs Morris will show you everything.'

Mandy tapped on the door and walked in, closely followed by Paige.

Paige was greeted with a warm smile. 'It's nice to see you again Miss Sheldon. Please have a seat.'

As Mandy closed the door Paige sat down. 'Can we dispense with *Miss Sheldon* in favour of Paige please? I'd much rather be called by my first name, if that's alright.'

'Not a problem and I'm Rosemary, though David will likely insist you address him as Mr Cavendish. He's a rather pompous young man.'

Paige's lips curved into a broad smile. 'Fancy, I'd never have known.'

They laughed together and it lightened the mood.

Following a tour of the building Paige returned to her office. She needed to call Dempster Brothers at once to advise she had taken a position elsewhere.

'Personal call?' a voice asked and she looked up into the eyes of David, standing in the doorway.

'Good morning to you too Mr Cavendish. Yes, I was just cancelling a job interview for later today. It would have been rude to simply not turn up and I couldn't contact anyone over the weekend.'

'Whatever, who cares?' he grunted with a toss of the head. 'Are there any messages for me?'

'None I'm aware of. I've only just walked in here. Rosemary's been showing me round.'

'I need the file for Bland Construction. Will you bring it in?' After a short pause he added, 'Please?'

She nodded. 'I'll look for it right away.'

There were two tall filing cabinets, each with four drawers. Paige assumed everything would be filed alphabetically but there appeared to be no organised system in place. Rosemary had mentioned that during the absence of a PA, many client files had been kept on David's desk. That would no doubt account for the lack of orderly filing; they had simply been rammed into any available space.

As tidiness was of paramount importance in any well-run establishment, that would be her first job.

The moment she came across the file she knocked on David's door and walked straight in. 'The Bland Construction file Mr Cavendish. Is that how you'd prefer me to address you or do I call you David?'

Without looking up he stated, 'Mr Cavendish, and in future wait till I call you in before barging in my office. Understood?'

'Noted *Sir,*' she said with special emphasis. 'It's okay for you to call me Paige, in fact I prefer it.'

'Close the door on your way out Miss Sheldon,' he answered sharply.

Paige couldn't help but smile. David was such an arrogant jumped-up little tyke.

She had just finished reorganising the files when Richard edged in with a grin on his face. 'Do I need a hard-hat to come in here? How's it going?'

'Very well so far. I've just sorted out all the filing cabinets so I can find stuff.'

'Any run-in with David yet?'

She smiled. 'Nothing I can't handle.'

'Good. I'll no doubt see you later then.'

Earlier, Rosemary had introduced her to the girls in the general office and as Paige wandered through on her way to lunch she overheard a snippet of their conversation with two of the men from the factory as they huddled over a desk giggling.

'I've bet on two months,' the office junior said.

'No way Sue…three weeks maximum I say,' the wages clerk commented. 'Nobody human could last two months with him.'

'I'll give her a month and I bet she doesn't work her notice,' one of the two men stated confidently.

'Put your money where your mouth is, the lot of you,' Sue said. 'Here, jot down what you think and I want a quid each off you.'

'Can anyone play?' Paige butted in with a straight face. 'I bet she lasts for ages. She has a broad back and loads of stamina. Where do I write it down?'

Sue was mortified. 'I'm very sorry Miss Sheldon. We didn't hear you coming. It was just a bit of fun we were having. We meant no harm, honest.'

'It's fine Sue. Don't worry. I guess you've played this game before but take my advice and don't bet on me. I'm here for the long haul, believe me, and please call me Paige. Miss Sheldon sounds so stuffy and I'd really like us to be friends.'

Sue was horrified. 'We can't do that Miss. Young Mr Cavendish will do his nut if he hears us calling you Paige. You're his Personal Assistant.'

'All the more reason to do it,' she replied with a defiant grin. 'Refer him to me if he has a problem with that. It's my name; that makes it my decision. Right, now that's settled, can anyone tell me where I can get a decent sandwich round here?'

Following a flurry of advice, she left the group to reflect.

Whilst she was eating her sandwich, her intercom buzzed. 'I need you to take a letter Miss Sheldon.'

'Alright Mr Cavendish. I'll be with you in about ten minutes. I'm just on my lunch break.'

'Your lunch break's from one till two like mine,' he snapped. 'I need you now!'

'Strange, I didn't see that in my Contract. Perhaps it would have been pertinent to stipulate that but I'll know in future. I'll see you in ten minutes.'

Her office door was thrust open angrily by David. 'Are you deliberately trying to provoke me?'

She dabbed her lips with a tissue and smiled. 'On the contrary, I'm simply trying to please you. I said ten minutes by which time my lunchtime break will have lasted less than thirty minutes. Does yours?'

'In case you've conveniently forgotten, I happen to be a Director here. I don't answer to you.'

'Problem?' Richard asked, poking his head round the door. 'I thought I heard raised voices.'

Paige shook her head. 'No, everything's great Mr Cavendish. We're reconciling our lunch breaks.'

He nodded knowingly, smiled and left the room.

'I'm watching you,' David snorted. 'One wrong move...' He slammed the door on his way out thus obliterating the remainder of his outburst.

'That's just added a further five minutes to your waiting time,' she said superciliously, dabbing her lips once again. 'If this is to be a game of winners and losers, I'm a *very* worthy opponent.'

'How did it go?' Emma quizzed eagerly. 'I've tried twice already to call you and there was no answer.'

'Colourful,' Paige sniggered. 'He's such a ball of fun as you can imagine. I have to say it was pretty tame this afternoon though because he went out.'

'Can you cope? Is it hard work?'

'It's an absolute doddle. David doesn't do much so that means I don't either. I typed a few invoices for one of the office girls this afternoon to occupy my time. She had loads to do. They're all very nice, apart from David. Maybe it'll be busier tomorrow. I had a lengthy talk with the boss's PA just before I left and she's hoping to move to Australia soon so she'll be leaving. Her son and his family live there and they've asked her to join them. She's been trying to get a Visa for ages and has her confirmation now that she can go. She's worked there for years so the office girls are organising a leaving party.'

'Then why don't you offer to take *her* job?'

'What, and miss out on all the fun? Not on your nellie. Don't get me wrong, Mr Cavendish is a true gent but I prefer to keep my distance. He popped in twice today to check if there'd been any problems but I told him everything was fine. Besides, he only took me on because he thought I'd handle David. It appears no other PA could. I heard he'd lost four in the last four months,' she howled with laughter.

'Huh,' Emma snorted. 'Why am I not surprised to hear that? Right, enough about him. It's your birthday on Friday so what are we doing? Do you fancy going for a meal on Saturday?'

'Yes, that'd be great. Where?'

'It's your birthday; you choose.'

'You're having a laugh. I can't remember the last time I went out for a meal. You choose but nowhere expensive. I'm decorating the lounge so I'm skint.'

'Aren't you getting someone in? You don't know how to hang wallpaper.'

'No I don't but I can do all the preparatory work. I would sit for many an hour watching my grandad as he sanded the woodwork until it was as smooth as silk and he was as particular about the paintwork too. Plenty of patience, not skill was the only thing needed he would say so if that's the case I'll do that too. That way, I'll just have to pay someone to hang the paper. Do you know anyone?'

She thought for a moment. 'No but I'll ask around and you do the same at work.' She giggled. 'Maybe David will help you out as you reckon he does nowt much at work. Ask him; you're hard-faced enough.'

'You're such a clown Emma. Let me know about Saturday when you've arranged something. I'll fall in with your plans.'

It was a very apologetic Emma who called Paige on Thursday afternoon at work. In a rasping voice she told her she had laryngitis. 'I have to stay in bed for a few days so Saturday's off. I'm sorry.'

'It doesn't matter; we can go for a meal anytime. Try sipping icy cold water. That seemed to help me when I had it.'

'How's your stripping going?'

'I've nearly finished. I've a few holes and cracks to fill so I'm off to the DIY store tomorrow night to get some filler. I've measured up for the wallpaper.'

'Any more excitement at work?'

Paige giggled. 'Nothing that springs to mind *and* he's managing to choke out an occasional *"please"* and *"thank you"* would you believe? He still calls me Miss Sheldon though. He won't budge on that. He's okay in small doses and everyone else's camaraderie more than compensates for David's puerile shortcomings. I really like working here and I have a lovely sunny office overlooking the park.'

'So I take it he hasn't asked you out yet?'

Paige heard a throaty laugh. 'Get lost.'

The next day at work, Paige found a gift and a card on her desk. As she tore open the envelope, Mandy rushed in with a mug of coffee for her.

'Happy Birthday Paige. We keep a note of everyone's birthday, so the girls always chip in for a bit of something. We hope you like it.'

'Thank you Mandy. This is a very nice surprise.'

Paige read the card first and then opened her gift. 'What a beautiful scarf. I'll come out and thank the girls shortly. This has really brightened my day.'

Mandy beamed with delight. 'I chose the scarf.'

'I need you Miss Sheldon,' David cut in. 'I seem to have mislaid a quotation. I had it yesterday.'

Mandy headed for the door. 'Maybe we can all go out at lunchtime? I'll catch you later Paige.'

'Er...excuse me; aren't you forgetting yourself?' David asked Mandy pointedly.

She looked at him blankly. 'No, I don't think so. I'm Mandy. Don't tell me *you've* forgotten. I work on reception Mr Cavendish. You're having me on aren't you?' She flounced through the door without another word as Paige stifled a laugh.

It was so confusing. Paige scoured the shelves reading the small print on different types of fillers. She had no idea which one to buy and there was never a member of staff about when help was required. Just as she was about to seek assistance, someone asked, 'Are you alright?' and she turned to find Richard in her shadow. 'I thought it was you as I approached.'

She was glad to see him. 'Yes, I'm struggling but you'll know. I need filler for the walls I've stripped in my lounge. There's so many different brands and I don't want to buy the wrong stuff.'

'How much do you need? Is there a lot to do?'

'Not really. They're just little holes and cracks. I need a small trowel too. Once it's done, I'll look for someone to hang the wallpaper. When you called to offer me the job I could have died of shame. It was so shabby so I decided to redecorate. It's ages since any maintenance work was done. I remembered I'd to get undercoat as well as gloss paint as I used to watch my grandad. I've already bought the paint.'

'Did you get any spirit to clean the brushes?'

'Oh no; I never gave that a thought. I need a pack of sandpaper too. It's a good job you turned up.'

He walked round with her until she found everything. 'Are you buying your own wallpaper?'

She nodded. 'Yes, I know how much I need. I've already measured up.'

'Then don't forget adhesive too.'

'Are you decorating too Mr Cavendish?'

'No, I want protective wood-stain for my garden furniture. It's looking a bit sad but if I give it a coat or two it'll last a bit longer. It passes time when I'm alone. How are you coping on your own?'

She shrugged. 'I think I'm getting there slowly.'

'It's not easy; I know. What about your father? Is he not around anymore?'

She shook her head. 'I never had one...well, in the biological sense I did,' she acknowledged. 'What I mean is, Mum never married and I was never told anything about my father. I remember asking about him once but was quickly silenced.'

'That's a shame.'

'Maybe; maybe not. He might have been a rogue and what you've never had, you never miss.

Richard had to smile. She was very philosophical. Rosemary had been right to say she had an old head on young shoulders and she definitely seemed to be keeping David in check. That was no easy task.

She looked at him with beseeching eyes. 'Do you have time to look at wallpaper? I can't make up my mind between two I like. I'd value your opinion.'

Though displaying no emotion, he was delighted to advise her. She was a charismatic young creature and it was a pleasant change for him to be in female company. All he had to look forward to once home was an evening alone, falling asleep in front of the television. 'Alright young lady, you lead the way. I don't profess to be a connoisseur though.'

With a spring in her step she made her way to the next aisle and pointed out the two she liked. 'Please be honest. If you think they're terrible you must say so. I'm after a complete change of mood this time. I want something that'll make the lounge feel lighter and brighter.'

Richard studied them for a few moments. 'In my opinion this will make the room appear much more spacious. The pale background will reflect the light and brighten the room considerably. I think that one is rather too geometric in design. It won't look right unless you have completely straight walls and sharp corners. Any structural imperfections would be inconspicuous with this simpler design but noticeable with the geometric one but that's just my opinion.'

Paige smiled. 'Then I'll go with the expert. This one it is. I'm glad you turned up.'

He helped her load the rolls into her trolley. 'All I need now is a paperhanger. I'm doing the painting myself to keep the cost down. I don't suppose you know of anyone?'

'I might. I'll make a call when I get home. What you need is someone who does *foreigners*,' he told her. 'That'll work out much cheaper.'

'Foreigners?' she asked. 'What do you mean?'

'It's a slang term for a job done on the side by an employee of a company. I know just the lad if he's still doing it. He was saving to get married the last I heard so he might be glad of the money. He'd want paying in cash of course.'

'That's not a problem. Thanks Mr Cavendish.'

He collected his wood-stain en route to the checkout and helped load her car. 'Don't work too hard,' he cautioned. 'Take a short break from time to time. Have you anything exciting planned over the weekend?'

'No, I should have been going out for a meal with a friend tomorrow but she's cried off; she's ill.'

'That's a shame,' he stated, closing her boot. 'If I make contact with that young chap I'll call you.'

Paige gave him a cheerful smile. 'Thank you. I'm so grateful for your help. I'll see you Monday.'

Richard walked back to his car with a warm glow. He was pleased he had spotted her in the store and more so that he had been able to assist her. Though he knew very little about her he had learned enough to recognise that she'd had a challenging life to date and now she was alone, trying to pick up the pieces and rebuild her shattered life. Nobody knew better than he how difficult that could be, suppressing the tears and anguish and trying to come to terms with the solitude following the death of a loved one. His approach had been to throw himself into his work to the exclusion of everything else, including David and in so doing had omitted to recognise his son's grief. Most of all he had not provided the necessary love and care that he as a father should have given his son at that vulnerable time in his life. Instead he had given him a directorship; he had also given him money; he had bought him a fashionable apartment and an expensive sports car but he had failed in the fundamental requirements of parenthood to display how much he loved and needed his son, and now it was probably too late.

Richard was racked with remorse and bringing to mind the distinguished words of Omar Khayyam he sighed meditatively as he started up his car.

'The moving finger writes; and having writ,
Moves on: nor all thy Piety nor Wit
Shall lure it back to cancel half a Line
Nor all thy Tears wash out a Word of it.'

2

The moment he walked in the house, Richard called the decorator and explained what was required.

'No probs Guv,' he gushed eagerly. 'I'll go round tomorrow around fourish for a gander. I'll knock it off in a couple of days, easy. Gimme the address.'

'Let me call her first to check it's convenient. I'll call you straight back.'

Paige was thrilled to hear from Richard so soon. 'I'll be here all day. I'm so grateful. Thank you.'

'His name's Andy. He's a talkative young lad and does a cracking job. If you've noticed our reception area at work, he did that.'

'Yes, I admired it when I came for my interview. It looks really smart. Is he expensive?'

'I find him a few decorating jobs, so take it from me, the price will be right.'

'I can't wait to see it finished. I'll work very hard on the paintwork so I don't hold him up. I hope he can start soon,' she gabbled enthusiastically and he smiled at her exuberance. 'Thanks Mr Cavendish.'

Richard replaced the receiver and poured himself a drink. It had been an eventful week, a new PA for David and two lucrative contracts for the company, though they had been made to play a strategic game of cat and mouse to acquire the ship-yard contract.

They'd had to cut their price to the bone to compete for that but there'd still be a pretty penny in it, more than enough to meet the payroll cost and then some.

The boom of the 1990s was forecast to be coming to an end and there had been evidence of this at the turn of the millennium with a sharp decline in economic activity in several developed countries. The European Union had been badly hit and that in turn caused a knock-on effect in certain UK industries. Though it was a worrying time for Richard, he had to confess he was better placed than many competitors. He enjoyed repute for superb quality, meeting targets and competitive quotes, qualities fashioned over years of hard graft and sweat, as he constantly reminded David, although the latter had played his part. He excelled at maths and so was left in charge of quotations, relieving Richard of those duties. His role was to keep the factory active and trouble free. Raised from boyhood in engineering he had a vast knowledge of most aspects of manufacturing.

Richard reached for the photo of his late wife and sighed. If she were here now, she would be making their evening meal, the house would be spotless and she would be washed and changed. How lives could change in a single instant, he reflected.

His thoughts transferred to Paige. He understood her pain but if appearances were anything to go by, she had borne her grief and sadness with admirable stoicism seldom seen in someone so young.

Perhaps the time had come for him to do likewise. Life was too short to be full of self-pity and grief. It was then that Richard made a decision. It *was* time to move on with his life. By her actions and deeds, in the few short days he had known her, Paige had shown him that, and it wasn't beyond the realms of possibility that she would have a sobering influence on David too. He certainly hoped so.

Staring lovingly at the photograph clutched in his hand and with tears but a blink away he whispered, 'There'll always be a place in my heart for you Jan. As long as I draw breath that'll never change,' but as Richard closed his eyes that night it was Paige, not Jan, at the forefront of his thoughts.

Paige worked until midnight and crawled into bed feeling as if she had run a marathon but with a great sense of satisfaction that the preparatory work was now finished.

She set her alarm for an early start the next morning so she could undercoat the woodwork. According to the instructions on the tin, it would be dry in around six hours so she could then apply the gloss.

She was accustomed to setting herself targets. She had always been an organised individual, even as a child, but more so since her teenage years, brought about by her demanding role as a carer when there were rarely enough hours in the day to complete her numerous tasks, yet she had still made time to help out at the Hospice at least twice a week.

Paige believed she had inherited her late mother's devotion of caring for others. She had inherited her mother's looks too, with the same high cheek bones and expressive blue almond-shaped eyes…eyes that always spoke the truth.

She would often argue that she wasn't exhausted but her eyes would reveal otherwise; they revealed her every emotion from unhappiness to joy and her mother in particular could read them well but it was pointless to argue with Paige; her targets for the day were set and she never fell asleep before every item on her daily list was completed.

As promised, Andy arrived at four the next day.

Paige had already made a start on the final coat of paint and he commented that she was doing a good job. 'Yes, you can come and work for me anytime,' he told her with a broad grin.

She laughed. 'I had an excellent teacher. I used to watch my grandad painstakingly sanding the walls and woodwork for hours. He had loads of patience and repeatedly told me that over ninety per cent of the work was hidden when decorating a room.'

Andy looked round the room. 'He was right about that; it is. I can see he was meticulous. It's a grand house. Do you live here on your own?'

'Yes, my grandad died recently and as the whole place needed a makeover I decided I'd make a start. There'll be more rooms to do when I get round to it but it's a difficult balancing act when I'm working.'

'Where do you work?'

Paige was surprised. 'I thought you knew. I work for Mr Cavendish who contacted you about this job, well, for his son that is. I'm David's PA.'

He burst out laughing. 'You're joking. You work for *that* pig ignorant clown? He changes secretaries more often than I change my underpants.'

She giggled. 'Have you had a run-in with him?'

'I don't know of anyone who hasn't. He's a right arrogant little snot. He was telling me how to hang wallpaper the last time I worked there. I threatened to shove the paste brush up his...well...I'll leave that to your imagination.'

Paige wiped the laughter tears from her eyes. 'He does have a big opinion of himself but I can handle him. Having said that, I've only been there a week.'

'Early days...yes, early days,' he repeated. 'I can't see you working there much longer.'

'I hope you're wrong. I really need that job.'

'Any chance of a brew love? I could murder a pot of tea. Gimme your brush and I'll paint this casing. I think better with a pot of tea in my hand.'

She handed him the brush. 'Sugar and milk?'

'Aye, two sugars please.'

The casing was finished by the time she returned.

He made a loud slurping noise as he put the mug to his lips. 'You can't beat a gradely pot of tea. So, I'll come tomorrow, get that ceiling and a couple of walls knocked off and finish the rest Monday night. How's that? It'll give your paintwork time to dry.'

She could barely contain her joy. 'That's *brilliant* Andy. I was hoping you'd make a start tomorrow.'

'I'll see you about nine o'clock then. Okay?'

'Perfect. I'll make you some lunch.'

He grinned. 'Sounds good to me.'

Richard looked at his watch several times between four and five o'clock while pacing the floor. Paige had remained in his thoughts continuously since the previous evening. Finally, he grabbed the telephone and called her number.

'Hi...it's Richard...Richard Cavendish. I was just calling to ask if Andy had turned up today.'

Breezily she responded, 'Yes, he came at four and he's starting tomorrow so thanks for your help.'

'Don't mention it. Are you happy with his price?' he asked, trying to prolong the conversation.

'I didn't ask for one. He seems genuine and since he'd been recommended by you I didn't think he'd overcharge me. Besides, I told him I've some more rooms he can do when I've saved up.'

'Good move. It's always a good idea to dangle a carrot, as the old saying goes. I can see we'll make a business woman of you yet.'

'Listen, the way I've learned to juggle with pitiful handouts over the years I could teach *you* a thing or two. I never spend a halfpenny when a farthing will do, to coin an old phrase Grandad often used. You wouldn't believe how far I'd stretch half a pound of minced beef while waiting for the next Giro.'

This was an opportunity not to be missed. 'Then I suggest you teach me. I'm useless. I tend to live on takeaways and microwave dinners. Sometimes I go to a restaurant for a change of environment, though it's not much fun eating out alone.'

He regretted his words at once. What had he been thinking to make such a ridiculous remark? Had he expected her to say she'd be happy to join him?

'I can well imagine,' Paige sighed. 'I could never do it but it's different for a man I suppose. Men go in bars alone and it's accepted but women look out of place somehow, as if they're on the game if you know what I mean. That's how I'd feel anyway.'

Anxious to change topic he asked, 'Is your friend better now?'

'A bit. She hasn't been out yet but she might call tomorrow if she's up to it. I hope she is. I'm dying to show off my new wallpaper. I cleaned the carpet today and I'm going to clean the suite next week.'

'Don't you ever sit down and relax?'

'Yes, I sit down a lot but I don't relax in the way you mean. I'm always occupied. I enjoy writing so that's what I do. How do you fill your time?'

He pondered but could think of nothing. 'I watch TV and fall asleep in the main,' he chuckled.

'Mr Cavendish, that's a dreadful admission. You mustn't give up on life at your age. You should try to enjoy yourself. You'll be old soon enough.'

She hadn't intended to say that. The words simply tumbled from her lips and she apologised profusely. 'I didn't mean to imply you're getting old now. I'm sorry. I simply meant to say that life passes us by so quickly and that you should make the most of it.'

He laughed. 'No offence taken and you're right; I should be having a life outside the factory.'

His heart missed a beat when she replied chirpily, 'Well, I can help with that.' He was swiftly deflated however when she added, 'I can type a few recipes out for you. Once you master the basics, you'll find cooking a meal can be quite enjoyable...and easy.'

'Much as I hate to contradict you, I doubt it.'

'Trust me, there's nothing to it. It's really simple. I'll make them idiot proof, then you've no excuse.'

That was the second time she'd made an involuntary faux pas and she was horrified.

Richard howled with laughter. 'You seem to have me weighed up as a geriatric clown.'

'Oh no Mr Cavendish,' she gulped remorsefully. 'Please...don't think that. I'd better hang up before I say something else I'll regret. I don't know what's wrong with me today. I really didn't mean...'

'Forget it. I'd best let you get on with your work now. If I'm in the area tomorrow, is it alright to call and check how the work's going? I feel responsible, having recommended the young man,' he added to ward off any suspicion of his true motive.

'Yes, of course and I promise to watch what I say. Mouthing off has always been a problem of mine.'

Without reference to her forgoing remark and in a brighter tone he stated, 'I'll likely call round then.'

'Yes, that'd be nice,' she answered cheerily.

Richard settled down with a glass of whisky and reflected quietly on the dialogue with Paige. He had enjoyed those few minutes of gentle teasing and his lips broke into a wide smile, emphasising the laughter lines around his eyes. It was the first proper conversation they'd had. Though he had called into her office most days, barely more than a few words had passed their lips and very little had been said at the DIY store that didn't relate to decorating products.

As the evening progressed he became fidgety and uptight. They were emotions he hadn't experienced since his teenage years. Paige constantly returned to his thoughts and he was bewildered. He desperately needed a change of environment and decided to call

David. 'Have you anything planned this evening?' he asked cautiously.

As expected he received a curt response. 'I might have and then again I might not. Who's asking?'

'It's me...your dad.'

'Why, what's wrong?'

He sighed. 'Why should anything be wrong?'

'It's blatantly obvious because you never call me unless something's wrong so what's up? Come on, spit it out.'

'Nothing I tell you. I thought you might feel like going out somewhere for a meal or a drink together. We haven't been out for a while, so are you free?'

'Are you alright? Have you been on the bottle?'

'*No, I haven't*. Look, do you want to go out for an hour or so or not?' he repeated irritably. 'My treat.'

He paused. 'If you're paying, we'll have a meal.'

They chose a local pub with a reputation for good food and it certainly lived up to expectations, which was more than could be said for the sparse dialogue after David made it clear he wouldn't discuss anything work-related.

They ate their meal in silence and when Richard asked if David still enjoyed life in his ultra-modern apartment he was met with a monosyllabic, *'No!'*

'Then sell it and come home son,' he said. 'You and I used to get on well before Mum died. I know I haven't been very supportive in recognising your grief and pain. I was too busy dealing with my own to understand how her death had affected you.'

'Come home?' he cackled. *'Come home?* That's a laugh. You couldn't wait to be rid of me. It was bad enough knowing you blamed me for her death but I was barely twenty-one when you threw me out.'

He was horrified beyond belief. 'What the hell are you talking about David? I've never blamed you for your mother's death. It was nothing to do with you. You could have died as well in that accident. It was that drunk driver's fault and I didn't throw you out. I misguidedly thought you'd appreciate some space and independence. That's why I bought you the car and gave you a directorship. Would I have done all that had I blamed you? Why didn't you talk to me?'

'Why didn't *you* talk to *me* Dad? Why didn't you ask me what *I* wanted instead of making decisions for me? I was suicidal at times. I used to sit staring at four walls, week in week out. It was worse than the prison that drunken lout was sent to. At least he had folk to talk to. He appeared out of nowhere that night on the wrong side of the road. He crashed into me before I saw him coming. It wasn't my fault and when I learned Mum was dead, I wanted to die too. You let me down Dad. You turned your back on me when I needed you most. It was your job to be there for me. It was your job to spend time with me and talk to me and help me through my grief.'

David's eyes clouded with tears and other diners were turning round to eavesdrop.

'It's time to talk now son,' Richard remarked on a sigh. 'Let's get away from here and put things back on track. Christ, I wish I could turn the clock back.'

They talked well into the night. They had several drinks; they both shed tears and David revealed that when he returned to work, the girls who incessantly whispered would scatter as he approached and their eyes followed his every move.

'You know what girls are like,' Richard told him. 'They could have been tittle-tattling about anything, a raunchy night out, somebody's new boyfriend or repeating a joke they'd heard on the factory floor. It doesn't follow they were talking about you. Lots of folk find it impossible to express their condolences and they probably scattered when you approached to avoid embarrassment. I'm quite sure nobody was laying any blame at your door, so unless you know otherwise, I'd give them the benefit of the doubt.'

He snorted. 'Well, it's too late now. I've managed to alienate myself from the total workforce. I know they take bets about how long my PAs will stay.'

Richard laughed at that. 'Do they really? I reckon they'll be way out with their predictions about Miss Sheldon then. That young lady has staying power. How are you getting on with her?'

He shrugged. 'She's insolent.'

'Unprovoked?'

He hesitated. 'No, probably not but all the same I wish you'd get rid of her.'

'Not a chance David. I won't budge on that. That young lady's going nowhere so deal with it. She's efficient wouldn't you say?'

He pondered before answering, 'I suppose so.'

'Then give her a chance. She's had a bereavement too and she needs that job. So, do you want to move back here? You can hang on to your apartment for a while and see how things go. Looking at me has to be better than staring at four walls, surely?'

He smirked. 'I'll take that under advisement.'

Richard hugged him briefly. 'Go on, get yourself upstairs son. Your bed's made up. I don't want you rushing into anything. This time it's your decision.'

Richard felt a huge load had been lifted from his shoulders when he went upstairs to bed. Admittedly there were still mountains to climb but at least they had made progress in the right direction. For a first attempt, despite a shaky beginning, things had gone better than expected and now the two of them could build on the shallow foundations in place.

Paige awoke bright and early the next day; it was a beautiful spring morning.

By eight o'clock she was showered, dressed and had moved all the lounge furniture against the wall away from the window.

Bubbling with excitement she checked her watch repeatedly until Andy arrived.

'You shouldn't have shifted that furniture on your own,' he told her. 'I'd have done that.'

'I just thought it'd save time.'

'Your paintwork looks good. You'd be surprised at the mess I find in some houses. It looks like they daubed the paint on with a swill brush. Go on then, I'll have that brew you can't wait to make me.'

She laughed. 'Two sugars...coming up.'

By midday Andy had finished the ceiling and had also cut several lengths of wallpaper.

Paige beamed with delight. 'It looks terrific. You don't hang about do you?'

'Time's money,' he quipped.

'What time do you want to eat? One o'clock?'

'No, two o'clock. I'd like to wap a few lengths of paper on and I tend to slow down when I've eaten. I wouldn't mind another pot of tea though.'

As she brought his tea, Emma rang. 'I feel much better and as it's such a gorgeous day I thought I'd pop over with your birthday present. Is that okay?'

'Yes, fine. Have you eaten? I've got the decorator in and I'm making lunch for two o'clock so you can have some too if you like. There's plenty.'

'Yes please; I'm starving. How's he doing?'

'Fantastic…it's going to look brilliant. We'll chat once you're here. Don't be late.'

When the door bell rang a little while later, Paige expected to find Emma at the door but instead she was pleasantly surprised to see Richard Cavendish.

'I'm not staying long. I just thought I'd poke my head round the door to see how the job's going.'

'I'm glad you could make it. You'll be impressed. He really is a good decorator and I'm pleased I took your advice about the wallpaper. He's already hung a few lengths and it looks lovely.'

'How's it going Guv?' Andy asked with a cheeky grin. 'Are you checking up on me or is it this pretty young lass you're here to see?'

Richard was noticeably embarrassed and expelled a short burst of laughter. He made brief eye contact with Paige who giggled too. 'Can I make you a cup of coffee Mr Cavendish?' she offered in an attempt to call a halt to the mildly uncomfortable ambience.

'Er...yes, that would be nice,' he said.

The door bell rang again as she walked away.

'Would you get that please?' she yelled. 'That'll be Emma, my friend.'

Emma was surprised to be greeted by a tall well-dressed man. 'You must be Emma,' Richard stated with a gracious smile, revealing strong white teeth. 'You'll find Paige in the kitchen.'

It was the first time he had spoken Paige's name aloud, though in his private thoughts he had uttered her name a thousand times.

'Alright love?' Andy called to her. 'Are you here to give me a hand?'

'Yep, if you insist,' she winked, eyeing the trendy, good looking guy up and down.

Her reply brought forth a peel of laughter. 'I most certainly do.'

As she left the room, Richard perched on the arm of the settee. 'Are you keeping busy Andy?'

'I can't grumble. I get my fair share compared to other lads at ours who do foreigners. Are you keeping busy at work?'

'Tidy. We're still ticking over. It's more competitive these days but I'm lucky; I have a strong workforce. They give it all they've got when needed.'

'I think we've seen the last of the good old days.'

'I hope you're wrong lad. It's hard to cut corners in our kind of work. Still, time will tell. Right, I'd best be on my way. I thought I'd just call in and see how you were getting on.'

Richard made his way into the kitchen in time to observe Emma with a nudge and wink quiz, 'Right you dark horse. Come on, fill me in then; who's the dish with the cute bum?'

Paige incorrectly assumed Emma was referring to the decorator. 'His name's Andy and before you get any ideas, he's already spoken for so hands off.'

'Don't get your knickers in a twist. I only asked. So come on, out with it, how did you find him?'

'Through Mr Cavendish.'

'What, the *moron?'* she squealed open-mouthed.

Paige tittered. 'No, you daft bat, his dad.'

Richard cleared his throat and coughed noisily to make his presence known. 'I'd best be off now,' he told Paige.

She was mortified to think Richard had overheard and felt an apology was warranted. Before she had chance to speak, Emma cried, 'Don't go Andy. Stay for lunch. There's enough for Andy too isn't there?'

'Er...yes, there's plenty,' Paige stuttered with red cheeks, glancing at Richard ashamedly.

'Alright, you've persuaded me Emma but on one condition. You have to call me Richard. Andy's the decorator. I'm Richard Cavendish.'

Recalling her earlier quip to Paige she spluttered, *'Oh bugger!* What do I say to make amends?'

'It might be best to say nothing more, although I have to confess it's been a while since anyone made reference to me as a *dish* with a cute bum. Thanks.'

'Please, you must let me explain,' Paige insisted. 'Emma and I were together when David jumped the queue in the supermarket. He was rude to both of us so we both told him off and as for the other...'

'Quite right...such appalling behaviour,' he cut in. 'Can we try to forget about David now? Something smells good Paige. What are we having?'

'Just one of my many concoctions, nothing fancy. It was one of Grandad's favourites and it's easy to make, in fact I'll let you have the recipe if you like it. Will you see if Andy can break off now please?'

As Richard left the kitchen she turned to Emma. 'I could kill you, embarrassing me like that in front of my boss. I could have curled up and died.'

'Your boss? Don't make me laugh. He's not here as your boss. He's crazy about you, you dozy mare. It's written all over his face and don't try and crack on you didn't know.'

She was horrified. 'Don't talk so stupid and don't dare say anything like that in front of him. I mean it Emma; you can be such an idiot at times.'

'Well, if *you* don't fancy him I do. He's gorgeous. Of the two I prefer the decorator though; he's more my type, more outgoing...but spoken for, sadly.'

'Yes he is and let it drop now. I can't believe you invited my boss to lunch.'

With a snort she rejoined, 'You could easily have said *no* if you didn't want him to stay.'

'What? Embarrass the man further? Right, they're on their way in so keep it zipped. I'm warning you.'

'This looks cosy,' Andy remarked, sliding out his chair. 'I'm that hungry I could eat an elephant.'

'Please, sit here Mr Cavendish,' Paige said.

'I will if you call me Richard. We've named our firm *the family* because that's how we see ourselves and we always use Christian names. We don't stand on ceremony at Cavendish Engineering.'

With a glint of mischief in her eye Paige queried, 'Has anybody told David?'

He smiled. 'Ah well, David's the exception to the rule so I'm relying on you to sort him out Paige. If anyone can, you can.'

'Isn't that what they call the Mafia?' Emma piped up, trying to sound knowledgeable. '*The family?*'

He laughed. 'Yes, but *we* aren't criminals. We're peace-loving and work as a team. Right Paige?'

She nodded and began to serve up the food. 'Help yourselves to vegetables.'

'Excuse me a moment,' Richard said. He left the kitchen, hurried to his car and returned with a bottle of wine. 'This is far too good to eat without a glass of wine. It's lucky I went shopping before I called.'

Paige found him a corkscrew and put four glasses on the table. Richard half filled them saying, 'I take it we're all driving with the exception of Paige. It's a very pleasant Merlot but quite potent.'

'Cheers Guv,' Andy said taking a sip. 'Mmm, it's nice that. Great food too. Thanks Paige.'

'I'll second that,' Richard said and Emma agreed adding, 'She's a terrific cook and she makes lovely pastry too.'

Both Richard and Andy had a second helping and when Andy had cleared his plate he sighed heavily. 'I'm stuffed. I couldn't eat another morsel now.'

'Not even a slice of my homemade apple pie?'

He paused momentarily. 'Oh, go on if you insist.'

Richard topped up Paige's glass with more wine. 'That was superb, thank you. You do indeed make delicious light pastry.' When he winked and smiled, it didn't go unnoticed by her friend who was dying to declare, *'I told you so,'* but she held her tongue.

Paige's eyes were drawn to Emma who glanced at her and grinned mischievously.

Andy jumped up. 'Well, this isn't going to get the baby fed. I'd better get on or I'll be asleep.'

'How old is it?' asked Emma.

Paige and Richard shrieked with laughter. 'Don't tell me you've never heard that expression before,' Paige howled in disbelief.

'I don't know what you're talking about.'

'It's probably just a local saying...oh never mind.'

'Well, he could have had a baby. You said he was involved with someone.'

At that point Andy intervened, 'Who me? I'm not involved with anybody. I was until she emptied our joint bank account and buggered off to France with her mates for a fortnight! Good riddance to her.'

Emma's ears pricked up. 'So you're footloose and fancy free, like me?'

'I am that.'

She followed him from the kitchen saying, 'We'll have to do something about that then won't we?'

Paige shook her head. 'Talk about chucking yourself at someone. I can't believe that. I'm very sorry Richard; I can't imagine what you must think after what you've seen and heard in the past hour. I'm so embarrassed. I bet you wish you'd stayed at home.'

'Nonsense. I've had a great time, truly and a good laugh. Emma's a down to earth honest girl like you. She speaks her mind and I like that.'

'So you're not offended in any way?'

He smiled. 'Not at all. The food was great and the company's been great too. It's been such a pleasant change for me; I've enjoyed every minute. I'm glad you invited me to stay. Thank you Paige.'

Emma reappeared with a parcel. 'I forgot to give you your birthday present. Silly me. Open it now.'

'I didn't realise it was your birthday Paige. Many happy returns,' Richard said warmly.

'Thank you but it's not today; it was Friday,' she said as she tore the paper off Emma's gift. *'Wow,* is that the jumper I liked when we went shopping?'

'Yes, the one you couldn't afford. I went back for it the next day.'

'I *love* it. Thanks Emma. You're such a treasure.'

'I'd better get back to Andy. I'm helping him.'

Paige chuckled. 'She's such a nutter. Despite her runaway tongue her heart's in the right place. She's been so supportive since Grandad died. It's nice to have friends who really care.'

Richard nodded. 'I'll see you tomorrow then.'

'Yes, bright and early. I'm glad you came.'

'Me too,' he said softly. 'As I said, this has been a most pleasant diversion for me, to get out and enjoy myself, a rarity in fact.'

She walked him to the door. 'Doesn't the lounge look lovely now? There's not much left to do.'

'It'll be finished tomorrow night,' Andy chipped in. 'Nice to see you again Guv.'

'You too. 'Bye Emma. It was nice meeting you.'

'And you. I'll see you soon I hope. 'I'll keep my big gob zipped next time.'

As Richard made his way home full of the joys of spring, Paige had a heavy heart. She valued her job and wanted to hold on to it, but if Emma was right about Richard, and she *was* an admirable judge of character, her days at Cavendish Engineering could be numbered. Maybe she was worrying about nothing though. Maybe she had read too much into the weekend's events. The meeting had been accidental at the DIY store; his telephone calls were to arrange Andy's visit and his attendance today was simply to ask if she was pleased with Andy's work.

She cleared the table and tried to put it out of her mind but when Andy left shortly afterwards, Emma was determined to pick-up where she had left off.

'Right lady, how long has this been going on with the boss? I tell you all my secrets so spit it out.'

'Emma...there *are* no secrets, honestly. You'd be the first to know if there were. I've only been at the place a week. I've hardly seen the guy until today.'

'Well if you ask me, he's after you. It didn't take him long to get his feet under the table did it?'

'Er...thanks to you. He was ready to leave till you opened your rip and invited him to stay.'

'He didn't need much persuasion did he? What's your problem with the guy? He seems very nice, he has a keen sense of humour, he's good looking and better still he's filthy-rich.'

'Yes and he also has a pain of a son called David who *I* happen to work for in case you've forgotten.'

'Stuff David. What's it to do with David what his father does? You wouldn't be marrying David.'

She cackled with laughter. 'My God, we're all but married now. How many kids are we having?'

'You can scoff but I'm merely stating the facts as I see them. He's besotted; trust me; I know.'

Paige was becoming really exasperated. 'If you're so anxious to arrange somebody's love-life, might I suggest you concentrate on your own for I don't see hoards of guys lining up to get their feet under *your* table. I can't recall the last time *you* had a date.'

She smirked. 'Well, as a matter of fact I have one tonight. I'm seeing Andy later.'

'Is that right? Would it be correct to assume *you* propositioned *him*?'

'I might have given him a gentle push, that's all.'

Paige smiled. 'He's lovely. Have a great time but do me a favour. Don't go on about me and Richard. There *is* no me and Richard and there never will be. I've never been more certain about anything.'

Mandy looked up on hearing male laughter and was dumbstruck to witness the Cavendish father and son enjoying a joke as they ambled into work together. It was a rare occurrence to see David laugh.

'Good morning Mandy,' Richard said with a wide grin that was immediately echoed by a comparable greeting from David who added, 'What a nice dress you're wearing today Mandy. Very pretty.'

'Thank you,' she spluttered, unable to believe her ears. 'I hope you both had a good weekend.'

'We did,' Richard said. 'Any missed calls?'

'No, but Margaret wants to see you right away.'

'Sounds ominous. Nothing wrong I hope?'

'I'm guessing she's booked her flight to Australia because she seemed very excited.'

Richard exhaled noisily. 'I'm going to miss her so much. Ask her to come in right away please.'

Margaret's news was the bad news expected. She would be leaving in just a few days.

'I've called the Agency about a replacement,' she told Richard as his face dropped. 'I'm so sorry it's short notice but I've waited ages for clearance and now I have it, I want to be on my way.'

He walked round his desk and gave her a friendly hug. 'In your position Margaret I'd do the same. I'll miss your dry humour, your meticulous standard of work and above all your companionship. You were invaluable when I lost Jan and when David was ill. You kept me going from day to day and I thank you from the bottom of my heart for that. You get off to Australia. Enjoy your new and exciting life. It'll be unbelievable and please keep in touch with us all.'

With tears in her eyes she murmured, 'I will.'

David strolled into Paige's room. 'Good morning Miss Sheldon. Have you sorted my mail yet?'

'It's already on your desk Mr Cavendish.'

'Thank you. Any messages?'

'No, none.'

He breezed from the room without a further word only to be replaced by Richard who walked in and smiled. 'Good morning Paige. I've had a tad of bad news this morning. I'm going to need your help but first, I'd like to thank you again for yesterday.'

He sat down with a worried expression. 'I take it you've heard Margaret's leaving us in a few days.'

'So soon? I knew her departure was imminent but I hadn't heard of any final arrangements.'

'She's finishing Friday week so that presents me with two problems. I need a replacement PA and I need Margaret to arrange interviews. The trouble is Rosemary's away this week so how would you feel about participating on the Interview Board? I prefer to have a female present.'

'It'd be alright I suppose. I can't imagine it'd be too difficult.' She smiled mischievously.

'What?'

'As long as the candidates aren't as argumentative as I was.'

'You have a point. However, I'm quite sure you'll handle anything they throw at you. I'd hate you to be interviewing me.'

She looked surprised. 'Why do you say that?'

'Because you never miss a trick. No one gets one over on you.'

'Thanks. I'll take that as a compliment.'

He looked relieved. 'So that's a *yes* then?'

'It is. Was there a second problem did you say?'

Richard cleared his throat. 'Yes, there is actually. How busy are you, working for David?'

She looked concerned. 'That's a loaded question. I need to be careful how I answer that. I often have time on my hands but I put it to good use.'

'Paige, this is not criticism of your work. Let me explain. I can't manage without a PA. Margaret has been invaluable to me but she's leaving soon. I've no doubt I'll find someone equally efficient but it'll take time. Meanwhile, I need to have somebody to reach and fetch for me. Do you think you can learn her work and take over in the short term until somebody else can be appointed? As you know only too well, the last thing I want is to take you away from

David because you're good for him but I can't see any other way round it in the short term.'

'And what does David say?'

'I came to you first. What do *you* think?'

'I know Margaret has a more demanding job than I have and I'm willing to do my very best but with the best will in the world I can't do two jobs. David does *some* work and he needs me too so I'll agree if I can get help with some of the typing.'

'I can organise a temp if that'd suffice.'

'Yes, it would but let's see how it goes first.'

He breathed a sigh of relief. 'I knew I could count on you.'

'Hey, don't get excited. I'm not Superwoman.'

He winked at her. 'I happen to think you are.'

From there he went to talk to David.

Paige didn't have long to wait before David came thundering into her office. 'Trust you to agree to his hare-brained scheme. What about *my* work? I said what about *my* work?'

'I heard you the first time and I made it perfectly clear to your father that I work for you and that any work of yours takes priority. I have a lot of time on my hands and I happen to think it's logical to pull together. Your needs won't be adversely affected in any way but you might have to walk a bit further to find me. You've time to though. You're not exactly pulled out with work are you?'

'How dare you speak to me like that when you're just an employee? I could sack you for that.'

'And who'd do all your typing and run around for you then?' she questioned flippantly.

He glowered, turned on his heels and bolted from the room. Within minutes he stormed in again, eyes blazing. 'Have you seen my father?'

'Not since earlier. Hang on.' She called Mandy's extension. 'Do you know where Mr Richard is?'

'He went out a short while ago.'

'Did he say where he was going?'

'No Paige. He just walked by and went out.'

'Thanks.' She turned to David. 'He's gone out but Mandy doesn't know where he's gone or how long he'll be. Can I help with anything?'

'No, you can't!' he snapped. 'Just tell him I need to talk to him urgently if or when you see him.'

It was almost lunch time when Richard returned. Paige opened her office door marginally on hearing a heated exchange on the corridor.

'*Deal with it!*' Richard told David. 'How will you ever learn to make decisions when you persistently refuse to commit? Arrange the interviews whenever you want or talk to Margaret or Paige about it. I've more important things to worry about than trivia.'

'Tomorrow then?'

Richard sighed. 'Yes dammit, tomorrow's fine if they can attend then. The sooner the better. I fail to see what all the fuss is about. There's nothing needs organising apart from a table, four chairs and a jug of water for Christ's sake. Even *you* should be able to manage something as simple as that. Just get on with it David. I despair...I really do.'

Paige giggled and closed the door quietly.

It transpired that the Agency had a couple of well-qualified candidates, both of whom were available immediately. One had been a PA for many years to the MD of a nearby company that had recently gone into liquidation. The other, a younger woman, had a degree in law, together with an impressive CV that the Agency had faxed to Margaret earlier that day.

She gave the details to Paige. 'As you're going to be interviewing, you need to take a look at these. If possible try to get telephone references although the young one mentions no recent employment history on her CV. That's an issue you must investigate at the interview. It requires a satisfactory explanation.'

Paige sifted through both applicants' details very carefully. The older one, Patricia had been provided with a first class testimonial by her boss for whom she had worked for seventeen years. She presented no problem on paper but Paige was less enthusiastic about the younger candidate, Susan. Although only twenty-six she had listed numerous employers and there were lengthy periods unaccounted for. One of her earlier employers was Sampson's where Emma was employed and so Paige decided to call her.

Emma had no recollection of anyone of that name but promised to make some enquiries and call back but when Paige was ready to leave the office Emma still hadn't contacted her.

It was just after five when David stormed in with a heap of letters to type. 'I'd like these first thing in the morning...please,' he advised her curtly.

She looked up from the keyboard. 'Certainly.'

'What are you typing now? I wasn't aware I was waiting for anything.'

'You're not; it's personal. I've almost finished.'

'You're doing personal work in office time?'

'Nope. I finish at five. It's turned five.'

He checked his watch. 'You're supposed to be off the premises by five o'clock.'

'It doesn't state that in my Contract of Service. It merely stipulates my hours of employment.'

Determined to have the last word he asked, 'Have you signed off?'

'Of course. Don't question my integrity David.'

'It's Mr Cavendish to you. Remember your place and don't be so arrogant.'

She stopped typing and glared at him. 'Why don't you get off home and stick your head down the loo or whatever you do for entertainment? I'm answerable to you during working hours, that's all. Get off my back. You're like a bear with a sore arse today!'

Neither had heard Richard on the corridor until he expelled a raucous laugh. 'What the hell am I going to do with the pair of you? Is it always like this?'

'It's only a spot of friendly banter Richard. David tries it on knowing I'll stand my ground, isn't that right David? It's just a battle of wits. I usually come out on top though,' she smirked.

'Come on son. Let's get off home. We've all had a trying day.'

Paige walked to the printer and removed a couple of documents for Richard. 'You've no excuse now.'

He glanced at the top copy and laughed. 'Thanks for that Paige. Idiot proof of course?'

She giggled. 'Of course. I'm off home now.'

Richard handed the car keys to David. 'I'll catch up with you in a mo. I just need a word with Paige.'

When David left, Richard removed a packet from his coat pocket and gave it to her. 'Happy Birthday Paige. I'm sorry it's rather late.'

'What's this? I don't understand.'

'Open it. I think you'll like it. I owe you a lot and I wanted to show my appreciation.'

She caught her breath when she looked inside the box and found a solid gold bangle. 'Oh no Richard, I can't possibly accept this. It's beautiful but far too expensive a gift.'

'Answer me...do you like it?'

'I love it; it's gorgeous but it doesn't feel right.'

'It feels right to me Paige. Please accept it in the spirit in which it's given. As I said, it's to show my appreciation for your support because you're in for a rocky ride over the next few weeks.'

'I don't know what to say.'

He smiled affably. 'How about "goodnight"?'

She sighed. 'Thank you. I've never seen anything as beautiful in my entire life.'

He'd have liked to respond, 'Neither have I,' but resisted the urge.

With a wave of the hand he was gone, leaving her mind in a state of turmoil.

As soon as she got home Paige telephoned Emma for any information about Susan, the job applicant.

'I was just about to call you. I couldn't really talk in front of the others at work but yes, I found something out if it's true. It seems your young lady has a habit of suing firms for sexual harassment. According to one of the supervisors, she tried it on here but got nowhere and at her next job, she went before a tribunal claiming constructive dismissal, saying that she'd had to leave because the boss came on to her. Apparently it was in the local rag and she got a load of compensation out of them. I bet she's tried it on at other places too. She sounds a right dirty slut.'

Paige was horrified. 'I knew there was something; I had a gut feeling about her. Do you know which firm made the payout? I'd like to give them a call.'

'Yes, Harrison Plastics in Oldham. Don't mention my name though. I'm simply repeating what I heard and it might not be true.'

'I wouldn't mind betting it is but I'll let you know what I find out. How did your date go incidentally? Did Andy turn up?'

'I thought you'd never ask. We had a great time and then we came back here. That's when it really got hot. *Wow.*'

She groaned. 'Spare me the details...please.'

'You asked,' she said on a ripple of laughter. 'I'm seeing him again on Friday. How are things going with you and your MD? Has he asked you out yet?'

Adrenaline rushed through her body. 'I've something to tell you Emma He bought me an expensive gold bangle today...for my birthday he said.'

'Oh my God. He's got it bad. What did you say?'

'I was shocked. I said I couldn't possibly accept it as it was far too expensive a gift.'

'Huh. I bet you kept it all the same. Is it nice?'

'Yes, it's really beautiful.'

Emma giggled. 'I've got it. He's starting from the top and working down.'

Paige was baffled. 'What do you mean by that?'

‘It’s obvious. First a gold bangle for your arm and next it’ll be a gold ring for your finger. It might not be a bad idea to have a word with Susan about how to file a claim for sexual harassment. You play your cards right and he could have his leg over by weekend and you could make a fortune,’ she guffawed.

She burst into tears. *‘Stop it!* I wish I’d never told you about the gift. Everything’s a big joke to you. My job’s on the line and I can’t afford to be out of work. I could understand it if I’d given Richard the slightest encouragement. I’m at my wits end and on top of everything else I have his blasted son griping at me every few minutes. I should never have taken the job. *Big* mistake.’

‘Calm down Paige. I’m sorry. I was just having a laugh. I should have been more considerate. I didn’t mean to upset you. Do you really dislike Richard?’

‘It’s not about liking or *dis*liking him. It’s about the position I’m in, working for his son. In different circumstances it wouldn’t be a problem. He’s a nice guy, very nice in fact but if he’s getting any ideas it has to stop, but how do I tell him? What do I say?’

‘Leave it to work itself out. He’s not the forceful type and he’ll soon get the message. Trust me.’

Paige wanted to end the discussion. Her head was bouncing and everything around her was spiralling out of control. She felt very vulnerable and close to tears again. As luck would have it the chime of her doorbell came to her rescue.

‘I have to go,’ she told Emma. ‘Andy’s here. I’ll talk to you tomorrow.’

3

'Good Morning. I'd like to speak with the person in charge please, preferably your Managing Director.'

'Who's calling?'

'Paige Sheldon, Cavendish Engineering.'

'One moment please.'

She drummed her fingers on her desk impatiently until the receptionist said, 'Putting you through.'

In a thick Lancashire dialect he announced, 'This is Frank Jessop. What can I do for you?'

'Good morning Mr Jessop. Thanks for your time. I'd like some information about a former employee who's applied for a secretarial post here. She's due to attend for an interview this morning. Her name's Susan Martin.'

Without a moment's hesitation he shouted, 'Shoot her between the eyes and make sure you don't miss the scheming bitch. Do us all a favour. That's what I should have done. She'll take you to the cleaners, mark my words.'

'So it's true what I heard then? Rumour has it this young lady makes a habit of claiming compensation for alleged sexual harassment in the workplace.'

'It's no rumour lass; it's flaming true and *she's* no lady. She's a lying trollop. It nearly finished us here and it was all a pack of bloody lies. I didn't find out until later that she'd done it before somewhere else and she's done it again only recently. It cost a small fortune defending ourselves and then she won, so to add insult to injury we had to cough up compensation. It was *me* she accused you know...said I'd had my hand up her skirt. I'd have it round her bloody throat if I got half a chance. You should talk to Bob Shipley at Thompson's. I'll give you the number if you hang on a minute. His case is still ongoing and you couldn't wish to meet a nicer bloke. He never touched her either but I'll be going to court to give evidence about his character. They reckon I won't be able to mention what happened to me but I will, even if they end up sending me down for contempt. Lasses like that ought to be drowned at birth.'

'Quite. I can understand your irritation.'

'Irritation? I'm flaming livid! Do you want me to barge in on her interview? I will do; I've nowt to be ashamed of; I've done nowt wrong.'

'That won't be necessary. I'll handle it Mr Jessop. If you give me Mr Shipley's phone number I'll call him too. The more information I have, the better.'

She jotted down the number, thanked him for his help and promptly called Bob Shipley.

'Mr Shipley hasn't arrived yet,' his secretary told her. 'Can I help with anything?'

'You could ask him to call me back very urgently. I need to speak to him before ten o'clock.'

'In connection with...?'

'Sorry. I prefer not to discuss it with anyone else.'

'Okey-dokey. Give me your name and number. I expect him in shortly. I'll pass on your message.'

Paige checked her watch every few minutes until almost ten o'clock. She would have liked additional information but couldn't keep the candidates waiting. Susan Martin was due in first at ten and there hadn't even been time to alert Richard and David.

She called Mandy. 'I'm expecting an urgent call from a Mr Shipley. Will you find me the instant he calls please? I'll be in the interview room.'

She darted down the corridor to Rosemary's room where David was sitting stony-faced. 'You've cut it fine. We usually discuss the candidates' CVs before they come in,' he grunted.

'We'll have to dispense with that. Good morning Paige,' Richard said with a pleasant smile.

He picked up the telephone and asked Mandy to bring in the first candidate.

'I'm so sorry I'm late. I've been trying to contact Miss Martin's last employer,' Paige explained.

'You should have tried sooner,' David snorted.

'Alright David, drop it now. That's quite enough. There's no harm done.'

Mandy flung open the door and bounded towards Paige announcing, 'That bloke's on the phone.'

Much to David and Richard's surprise Paige leapt to her feet. 'I'm sorry. I have to take this call.'

As she ran out saying, 'Tell Miss Martin there's a slight delay Mandy,' David emitted an audible gasp of disbelief. 'That woman's worked here little over a week and she's already running the factory. Why you don't get rid of her is a mystery to me.'

It was a good ten minutes later when she returned looking flustered. 'I'm sorry, I'll explain later.'

David was fuming. 'It'd better be good.'
There was a sharp knock on the door and Mandy announced, 'Miss Martin.'

There was no denying she was an elegant young woman as she strode confidently into the room. She brought to mind in Paige an image of a gazelle with head held high. Long shapely legs, barely covered by her micro skirt, appeared endless. In her peripheral vision Paige saw the men glance at each other.

'Er...please have a seat Miss Martin. I apologise for the delay in calling you,' Richard stated. 'We've arranged the interviews at rather short notice so we needed a little time to check through your CV.'

He smiled and she returned his smile.

'Introductions first. I'm Richard Cavendish, this is Paige Sheldon and on my left, my son David.'

'I'm delighted to meet you,' she gushed as Paige squirmed in her seat at her audacity.

'Would you like to start first Paige?'

'No, I prefer to go last please if that's alright,' she remarked assertively.

'David, would you start then please?'

When the questions began, Paige paid little attention, being far too engrossed in devising her own in the light of Bob Shipley's revelations.

Finally Richard turned to her. 'Paige?'

She looked up from her papers. 'I note you have a law degree Miss Martin. In what aspect of law did you specialise?'

'We had to cover the whole spectrum but I guess I had more of a leaning towards civil law. I wasn't that interested in criminal law, murder and the like.'

'But surely criminal law covers a wider field? I'd have thought it much more interesting. I took law at A-level where we covered many aspects of criminal law from petty crimes like shoplifting and burglary to the more serious offences like blackmail, murder and obtaining money by deception and extortion.'

She shook her head. 'No, that wasn't for me.'

'I see. Looking at your CV, I notice there are gaps in your employment history so may I ask what you were doing during those periods?'

Without flinching she remarked, 'I just explained to Mr Cavendish that I was abroad a lot.'

Persistent as ever she continued, 'Doing what?'

'Working, casual work, you know what I mean.'

'No, I don't. Enlighten me please.'

'Well er...bar work, er...jobs like that.'

'Really, with a law degree? That's rather a waste, not working to your full potential. Let's move on. As you have a leaning towards civil law, let me ask what guidance you'd extend to somebody who had encountered sexual harassment in the workplace?'

Without hesitation she replied, 'I'd inform them to seek the advice of a solicitor right away.'

'You mean like *you* did when you were working at Sampson's, Harrison Plastics and Thompson's to name but three employers, two of which you failed to mention on your CV? Why was that may I ask?'

Richard sat bolt upright awaiting her response.

'Well...er...would *you* want your new employer to know something like that had happened to you?'

'But it was in all the newspapers. The whole town was aware of your lurid explicit allegations against

Mr Jessop at Harrison Plastics but that didn't seem to concern you did it?'

'Well…er…yes, of course it did but...'

'But the award you received more than compensated for your embarrassment. Am I right?'

'If you're suggesting I was lying, I'll...'

Paige held up her hands. 'I'm not suggesting anything; I'm merely stating facts. You won your case, so surely you're not disputing the accuracy of those facts as reported? What *am* I to deduce however if you omit to show vital information on your CV?'

She shuffled nervously in her chair and uncrossed her legs, revealing her black panties.

'I have one more question. If your date of birth is correct as shown on your application form, according to my calculation, you were only nineteen when you joined Sampson's, based on employment dates provided by them, so I'm a little confused. At what age did you obtain your law degree?'

For the first time she stared ahead blankly in total silence. 'Alright, I didn't actually finish the course. It *was* a law degree course though and I *would* have got a first had I continued. I'm very astute.'

'I wouldn't disagree with that. I don't think I have any further questions Miss Martin. Thank you.'

'Anything else from you David?' Richard asked.

He shook his head and turned away.

Richard thanked Miss Martin for her attendance and she flounced from the room, head held high.

'I need the loo,' David said jumping up.

'Then make sure your zip's fastened till *she's* off the premises,' Richard cautioned and Paige giggled.

He swung back on two legs of his chair, ruffling his thick dark hair with his hands. 'Christ, that was bloody torture! How the hell did you find that out?'

'Women's intuition. There were too many blanks on her CV for my liking. Emma helped too.'

'Oh? How did she help?'

'She works at Sampson's so I called and got her to do some digging. The scheming opportunist lost that case but was awarded a tidy sum from Harrison Plastics according to Frank Jessop, their Managing Director who was livid when I spoke to him earlier. She could come unstuck with her current claim too. That was the call I had to take when we were due to start but unfortunately I couldn't disclose anything during the interview. She's made similar allegations about their MD too, specifying dates and times in a sworn affidavit yet on two of those dates he was out of the country, but that's confidential.'

'You've saved me from a fate worse than death. I'll never be out of your debt. I owe you Paige.'

'You owe me nothing. You offered me a job at a very low point in my life when I was desperate.'

David returned and took his seat. 'Right, call the next one in and let's get it over.' Turning to Paige he said, 'Have you finished preening yourself now? That's a few more Brownie points you've earned to add to your ever-growing list of accolades.'

Richard was furious. 'Shut up or get out David. I won't allow you to speak to Paige like that. If you'd displayed a little intuition maybe *you'd* have picked up on something so don't blame other folk for your own incompetence.'

He rang Mandy and asked her to bring in the final candidate and with a sigh remarked, 'Let's pray she isn't hell-bent on making sexual harassment claims. I don't think I could stomach another interview like the last one, albeit you did all the probing Paige.'

He needn't have worried for Patricia Winters was a plain middle-aged widow, who, with an infectious smile, bounded into the room and flopped down on the chair facing them without any invitation.

Richard heaved a loud sigh of relief causing Paige to fight desperately to contain her amusement.

It soon became apparent they need look no further and Richard offered her the post without consulting the other two members when the interview ended.

She was ecstatic and agreed to start the next day.

Paige escorted her to Margaret's office where she would be working and on her way back she bumped into Richard who asked, 'Do you still have Frank's phone number? I haven't heard from him in years. A while back, he was a fellow Rotarian.'

'Yes, on my pad.' He followed her to her office.

'There you go,' she said passing him the number.

'Is it okay to use your phone?'

She nodded. 'Help yourself.'

Frank was pleased to hear from him after so long. 'Are you after more information on that woman?'

'No no, it's all done and dusted and one interview *she'll* not forget in a hurry. Miss Sheldon, who you spoke to earlier, wiped the floor with her.'

'Good on her. Nothing's too bad for that slag. By the way you'll never guess who waltzed in here ten minutes ago.'

‘Who’s that then?’

‘Hang on a tick; have a word with him and see if you can recognise the voice.’

Despite a few clues Richard had no idea until the speaker revealed his identity. ‘Jake Allcock. I don’t believe it. What are you doing in these parts?’

‘I’m here for a retirement do.’

‘I wish I’d known. How long are you here? Can we get together for a drink?’

‘Sorry, not unless you want to join us for lunch. I have to leave tomorrow. I don’t know where we’re going for lunch. I’ll get Frank to tell you. Hang on.’

There was a muted discussion in the background before Frank said, ‘We’re off to the Anchor shortly; you’re welcome to join us. We’ve a lot of catching up to do. Fetch that nice young woman as well so I can shake her hand. They do a decent pie and chips there, plenty of other stuff too.’

‘Cheers, I’ll ask her but I’ll definitely be there.’

He turned to Paige saying, ‘Frank’s invited us to lunch. He wants to shake your hand. Okay?’

This was an awkward situation. To refuse would be impolite, yet were she to accept, what message would that convey? A tad of strategic thought was called for. ‘David will probably need me. I think I’d better stay here in case anything urgent crops up.’

Richard wasn’t having that. ‘You leave David to me. Nothing will arise that can’t wait an hour or so. We’ll be back in the office by two; I have a meeting at three. Alright?’

She could hardly refuse. ‘Alright...I’ll ask Mandy to refer David’s calls straight through to him then.’

'Do that and then get your war-paint on or whatever girls call it these days. We'll be away in ten to fifteen minutes. Besides, we both need a drink after that debacle. I'll be having nightmares for a week.'

The unrivalled smell of leather permeated the air as she opened the car door. 'Fantastic car,' she said.

Dispassionately he replied, 'It does its job. It gets me from A to B. It's reliable.'

The engine purred like a kitten as the car moved forward, most definitely in a different league from her old battered banger that not only creaked like an old tank but ran like one too. Still, it had served its purpose over the years, owing her nothing should it disintegrate tomorrow.

'Where are we going?'

'The Anchor. It's not far. It used to be a good pub but I've not been for a while. An old pal's going to be there too. He's up north for a retirement party.'

'Where's he from?'

'Here originally. He took a promotion and moved away nearly thirty years ago. He's in Warwick now I think. It'll be nice to catch up. He was in his late thirties when I last saw him on a fleeting visit. I'm glad you came along,' he added softly and smiled.

'Did David have anything derogatory to say about my extended lunch break?'

'He shot me one of his legendary black looks. I'd have asked him to join us but didn't want to afford him the satisfaction of refusing or tagging along to spoil our lunch.'

She hesitated. 'Forgive me for asking but why is David always so angry?'

'I wish I knew Paige. It started after his accident.'
'Accident?'
'When his mother died. He was at the wheel.'
She was shocked. 'Oh no, I didn't know he was in the car too. I assumed...'
'It wasn't David's fault in any way. A guy went down for causing the accident. He was drunk and it wasn't the first time he'd caused a fatal accident.'
'So David walked away unscathed?'
Richard shook his head. 'Not at all. He was badly injured. He was in hospital for a month with a head injury. When he came home he was depressed and disagreeable. I was grieving for my wife and David was grieving for his mother. In addition I was doing my best to keep the business running. Thank God I had two dedicated foremen who worked their butts off at that time or we'd have folded.'
'What was David like before the accident?'
'Immature and sullen like most twenty-one-year-olds but rarely angry though, not as he is now. I've often thought the head injury might be responsible.'
'Has he ever seen anyone about it?'
'At the time yes, but not since. He doesn't accept that anything's wrong. David's very pig-headed and as he's a grown man now, I can't make him see the doctor. Hopefully he'll sort himself out in time.'
He swung into the car park. 'Everybody out.'
The other two were standing at the bar when they walked in. 'Over here Richard,' Frank called. 'Glad you could make it. Long time no see. I've got us a table. Would you have recognised Jake? He's aged a bit wouldn't you say?'

Jake laughed. 'In twenty years it's to be expected. *You* don't have your boyish good looks any longer Frank Jessop so you can zip it. How are you doing Richard? I'm pleased to see you again.'

Richard shook his hand. 'Great to see you again too Jake. You're looking well for an old codger.'

'It takes one to know one,' he laughed.

'Hang on; you can give me ten years. Seriously, how old are you now Jake?'

'Fifty-six,' he whispered.

'Really? I'm shocked. I'm a baby by comparison. I'm forty-four.'

Jake turned to Paige. 'We haven't been formally introduced by your sugar-daddy yet but take it from me, Richard hasn't seen forty-four for a while. He's having you on but I must say he looks damn good.'

She was clearly embarrassed as Richard glared at him. 'For the record, Paige is my son's PA, so less of your smutty innuendo and I *am* forty-four. Don't judge other folk by *your* immoral standards Jake.'

'Come on ladies; put your handbags away,' Frank intervened. 'You're as old as you feel. I invited this delightful young lady here today to shake her hand. She did me a great favour earlier. I've had a spot of trouble you see Jake. A lass at work brought a case of sexual harassment against me and before you say owt I never touched her nor did I say owt suggestive. She's been doing the rounds making a fortune out of unsuspecting folk like me. She's an evil so-and-so. Anyway, she applied for a job with Richard and when this young woman called me about her, I explained what she'd done here, so at the interview she gave her a hard time. That's the measure of it. Right young lady, what would you like to drink?'

'This round's on me,' Richard insisted. 'You've saved me a fortune Frank. I'm indebted to you.'

They went to sit down with their drinks and Jake made a point of sitting next to Paige. 'I'm so sorry for my earlier remark. I meant no offence. It was a stupid thing to say. Am I forgiven?'

'Of course,' she said and smiled.

Jake stared into her eyes until her embarrassment forced her to look away. She didn't like that man at all; there was something odd about him. She would have much preferred to sit next to Richard or Frank.

'I'm sorry,' he said. 'I was staring at you. I'm not normally so rude, please believe me. As you looked up at me, you reminded me very much of someone from my past, someone I loved but lost.'

Paige chuckled to herself. Of all the corny chat-up lines she'd heard over the years, without doubt that was the least original. Sarcastically she commented, 'I imagine I wasn't even born then.'

Jake nodded. 'You're probably right Paige. It was almost thirty years ago.'

Richard caught her attention. 'Another drink?'

'No thanks. I've work to do when I get back. It'd be foolhardy to upset my boss.'

Richard threw back his head and laughed. 'Have you decided what you're eating?'

'Steak pie sounds good. What do you fancy?'

He looked into her clear sparkling blue eyes and with an inward sigh replied, 'That'll do me fine.'

'Make that three,' Jake added.

'No four,' Frank chipped in. 'They make a damn good pie here.'

Their earlier altercation was soon forgotten as the three men chatted about old times, relating amusing anecdotes to Paige.

The next time Richard checked his watch it was two-thirty. He leaped up. 'I'm sorry to break up the party but I have a meeting in half an hour.'

'If you'd like to stay, I'll run you back later,' Jake offered as Paige stood up.

Without a sideways glance in his direction, Paige picked up her shoulder bag. 'I have to leave too.'

'It was nice meeting you Paige,' Frank said.

She smiled cordially. 'You too and I'm very sorry about what happened with Susan Martin.'

'Worry not lass,' he beamed. 'It's in the past. I'll be more careful about who I take on in future.'

Once alone with Paige, Richard could hardly wait to express his regret for her earlier embarrassment.

'Forget it Richard; I'm a big girl. I'm used to men hitting on me. Have you known Jake a long time?'

'Yes, since I was about seventeen. He was always a lecher if you get my drift...always had an eye for the ladies.' He laughed. 'He turned up for work one day with two cracking shiners, according to one of his work colleagues.'

'A jealous husband or boyfriend presumably?'

'The girl's father I believe. Rumour has it she was pregnant but it was never confirmed. It might have been speculation. You know how folk embellish the tale to make it more interesting. Soon afterwards he moved to Warwick with his wife.'

Paige was shocked. 'He was married?

'Oh yes. Jake married very young as he'd got her pregnant too but she lost it. She had a miscarriage a week or two after they got married. That was such a shame because I don't think she got pregnant again. A year or two later somebody told me they'd parted company.' He laughed again.

'What? What's funny?'

'His proper name's Jacob...Jacob Allcock but his pals call him Jake when they're not referring to him as, *Allcock by name and Allcock by nature*.'

She giggled at that. 'I must admit I took an instant dislike to the man. He wouldn't stop staring at me. I felt so uncomfortable and then he offered to run me back to work later. Did he work at your place?'

'No, he worked at the local hospital. I was only a lad when I first met him. We had a big job on there that lasted for weeks and Jake and I often took our lunch breaks together in the canteen. He's a doctor.'

Paige froze before expelling a loud gasp.

'What? Is something wrong?' he asked.

'No...*no!* I mean er...he doesn't seem the type to be a doctor. I don't know what I mean. I don't want to talk about him.'

He pulled up by the kerb. 'Speak to me Paige. It's pretty obvious something's upset you. Did Jake say something else to offend you?'

Her head was spinning as she associated the little she'd gleaned about her background with the recent revelations. That awful man...that ghastly lecherous individual could be her father. Unable to control her emotions a moment longer she burst into tears.

Richard was devastated. 'For heaven's sake Paige tell me what's wrong,' he implored.

'It's nothing, really. I don't know what came over me. We'd better get back or you'll be late for your meeting. I'm alright now, honestly.'

Richard shook his head in total bewilderment. He would never understand women.

It was Margaret Cooper's final day at the office and she'd been in floods of tears all day.

'You wouldn't catch me skriking my eyes out if I were leaving this place,' Sue remarked, attempting to cheer her up. 'I wish *I* were going to Australia.'

Margaret dabbed her puffy eyes. 'I've been here such a long time,' she sighed. 'I hope I'm doing the right thing, going to the other side of the world. Do you think I'm making a big mistake at my age?'

Sue gave her a reassuring hug. 'Of course not.'

The entire workforce had gathered in the general office awaiting Richard's presence and the moment he approached everyone fell silent. With a smile he kissed Margaret's cheek and then, slipping his arm around her shoulder, he talked emotively about the many years they had worked together.

'I'm not the only one who's going to miss you,' he told her. 'Over the years, everyone here at some point has come to you for help and advice. You will be greatly missed by all of us and as you embark on your new and exciting adventure, our thoughts and best wishes go with you.'

There followed a further flood of tears and Paige swiftly handed her a box of tissues.

'As a token of our appreciation for your undying loyalty, not only to Cavendish Engineering but also to each and every one of us, we'd like you to accept this gift. As you're going away in a couple of days we didn't buy flowers; call this a *get out of jail* gift. There's more than enough here for a one-way ticket home if you really dislike Australia,' he told her.

'All that remains now is for me to wish you a safe and pleasant journey and all the best for the future. Everybody here will be at your party tonight.'

Margaret was overcome with emotion. 'I'd like to thank you all very much,' she blubbered. 'I'll never forget any of you. You've been such good friends.'

Everyone joined in the round of applause.

'I'll pick you up tonight,' Richard told Paige. 'It could be in the early hours when we leave the party and I don't like the idea of you hanging around the city centre waiting for a taxi.'

'Don't worry. I intend taking my car and...'

'Why do that? That means you can't have a drink. I insist. It's a party.'

Though feeling ill-at-ease she faked a weak smile. 'Alright, you've persuaded me. Seven o'clock?'

'Perfect,' he nodded.

The meal, at a new Chinese restaurant in the city, was booked for eight o'clock. Including Margaret's friends, more than sixty people would be there, and Paige had been looking forward to the outing until Richard had offered to take her. Recalling Emma's earlier comments she felt troubled.

Paige hadn't been home long when Emma called. 'I want to know all about that restaurant tomorrow.

We still haven't been out for your birthday so if it's a nice place, the two of us could go there.'

'It's a thought I suppose,' she said disinterestedly.

Emma sensed something was wrong. 'Er...what's up with you, misery guts?'

'Ignore me. It's just my mind working overtime. Richard's offered to pick me up and bring me home tonight so I'm a bit edgy.'

'I can't think why. You don't have to do owt you don't want. We've had this conversation once. Why you let that moron David rule your life beats me. Is it David that bothers you or something else like the *age* thing with Richard?'

'The *age* thing? What are you talking about?'

'You know, the age gap. How old is Richard?'

'He's forty-four that's all.'

Emma scoffed. 'And some.'

'No, that's right. I overheard him telling someone the other day.'

'So how old is David then?'

'Twenty-six.'

Emma did a quick calculation. 'So that means the randy old sod must have only been seventeen when he got David's mother pregnant. No wonder you're anxious. Kick him in the nuts if he tries owt.'

'Stop! Stop right there! You can't resist can you? Don't forget I've been out of the playing field for a few years. I don't know what goes on these days. I just feel like crying off and staying at home.'

'Don't be daft. You won't come to any harm with Richard. I still think he's after you but he'll wait for a sign before making a move. Trust me.'

'I hope you're right Emma. How's it going with Andy?' she asked, changing topic.

'Great. We get along really well. We have a lot in common. He's coming round later but he's working all weekend. He's a grafter. We might go away next weekend though. He says he needs a break.'

'Me too. Listen, I'll call you tomorrow. I want to be ready when Richard arrives, then I don't have to ask him in.'

She chuckled. 'Get ready then. Enjoy your party.'

The moment the car pulled up outside, Paige shot through the door and was taken aback when David stepped from the car.

'Do you want the front or back seat?' he asked.

'The back seat's alright for me. Thanks.'

He held the door for her until she was seated and then joined Richard in the front.

'Someone smells nice,' Richard commented.

'Thank you. It was a birthday present.'

'By the way, I forgot to mention earlier, David's got something to tell you.'

'Have I?'

'The meal...yesterday,' he prompted him.

'Right. Yes, Dad cooked one of your recipes last night. Very successful it was too. What was it?'

'Beef hot-pot. I'll definitely make that again.'

'Be honest. It was easy, wasn't it?' said Paige.

'Yes, you were right. It's just a matter of having the confidence. It's called fear of the unknown.'

'Listen, if you can read, you can cook. I'll type a few more out when I've time. Do you like fish?'

Eagerly David cut in, 'I do. I prefer fish to meat.'

'Then fish it'll be next time. You should try your hand at cooking too David. If you can boil a kettle, you can make a tasty meal and fish is very easy and quick. The important thing is hygiene, so wash your hands regularly. I'm looking forward to the meal. I feel quite hungry now,' she said perkily, her earlier fears dispelled.

After hanging her coat in the cloakroom she made her way to the table where Richard had saved her a seat next to him.

'You look really pretty tonight,' he said quietly. 'I like your gold bangle too.'

'Thank you. A friend bought it for my birthday.'

He looked around to ensure no one was listening. 'I'm pleased you think of me as a friend. These past few years it's been difficult making friends. My old friends are couples and though I often get an invite to dinner or a night at the theatre, I feel I'm intruding so I tend to make an excuse. When my wife was alive it was different. I can't reciprocate and invite them back like she used to do. Can you understand what I mean?'

'I...I think so. I've never been married nor have I been in a long-term relationship so it's different for me I suppose.'

'I don't want you get the wrong idea Paige. The last thing I'm seeking is a romantic involvement. It would be good to have a female friend, someone to join me for dinner at a restaurant from time to time, a friend I could call on for a chat, just for a change of environment. Everyone needs a friend.'

'I agree. Have you no male friends?'

‘Yes, but they’re all married. Besides, it’s nice to have female company.’ He topped up her glass with wine and decided to change topic. He’d planted the seed so that would suffice for now. ‘How’s Emma? Is she still seeing Andy?’

‘Oh yes. They seem well-matched. They might be off somewhere together for the weekend, next week I mean. He’s working this weekend.’

‘He works most weekends but then so did I at his age. I hardly saw David when he was young. I was busy touting for work and planning our future but sadly life doesn’t work out the way you expect.’

‘You can say that again. I was looking forward to going to University until my whole world suddenly fell apart but I don’t dwell on the past. I did what I had to do and did it willingly. I look at life now as having changed direction. I’d like to see a bit of the world and I’m old enough now to take care of myself. I’m very independent.’

‘That hadn’t escaped my notice. How long have you known Emma?’

‘We were at school together. She left before I did though. She couldn’t wait to start work; she wanted her own flat. It’s in a very nice area overlooking the river.’

‘Rented?’

‘No, she’s buying it. It’s beautiful. She has an eye for nice things but my house will be lovely as well once I’ve finished all the work I intend doing. My mother’s bedroom is next on the list. It’s very dated so I’ll be calling Andy again before long to paper it. He only charged me eighty pounds for papering the lounge. I gave him extra though; I was very pleased with his work.'

'I haven't seen it finished yet but I can visualise the end result. He's very professional isn't he?'

She nodded. 'Here comes the food. I'm starving.'

David, who had been chatting to Rosemary, took his seat facing Paige. He glanced at her and smiled. 'I hope the food tonight is as tasty as your beef hot-pot.'

She took that as a compliment and was more than a little surprised at his pleasant demeanour. It was so out of character and as the evening progressed he became even more sociable and witty, much to the surprise of everyone else too.

Paige turned to Richard asking, 'Has David been on the happy pills?' to which he replied on a laugh, 'Search me. It happens sometimes, not often mind you. He's a bit of a Jekyll and Hyde.'

'Just a bit,' she giggled.

'I suggest you make the most of it because I can't see it lasting too long. It never does.'

On this occasion however, he was wrong. David's behaviour was impeccable throughout the evening and it didn't end there. Over the next few weeks he continued in similar vein but Paige was becoming concerned. She would often walk into his office to find him in what was best described as a trance. He was oblivious of her presence and on one occasion she sat down facing him in silence, waiting at least two minutes before he acknowledged her presence.

That day she left the room clutching the unsigned letters that she signed on his behalf.

She made Richard aware of her concerns and he promised to raise the issue with David, but as usual, David insisted he was fit and well and again refused to see his doctor.

Shortly afterwards the mood swings returned with a vengeance. Paige had been working there for four months when an argument developed between one of the foremen and David on the shop floor. Before Richard could be summoned to arbitrate, David had struck the foreman, knocking him to the floor. By the time Richard arrived on the scene it was mayhem with David kicking and yelling as some of the workers restrained him while Eric, the foreman, lay prostrate and dazed with a bloody nose.

'What the hell's going on?' Richard demanded to know.

Breathlessly one of the lads gabbled, '*He* started it, coming down here shouting and hurling abuse at Eric. It's summat to do with a quote that's gone out wrong. He was like a madman. Eric just stood there trying to explain he'd done the job proper, and then that nutter clocked him one right in the chops.'

'Let's get Eric into a chair,' Richard said.

'I'm alright, really,' Eric insisted. 'It was a simple misunderstanding that's all. Tempers just got a bit frayed. There's no harm done, honestly; nothing's broken. I don't want to lose my job over this.'

'You won't be losing your job Eric. I'll speak to you shortly. I'm sorry about this.' Turning to David he snarled, 'You, upstairs now...my office.'

David shrugged himself from his restrainers' grip and headed upstairs two at a time.

Richard slammed the door as he walked into his office. 'What the bloody hell's wrong with you? Do you think you can go round thumping folk when it takes your fancy? We could end up with a law suit on our hands, thanks to you, you daft bugger. What the hell got into you?'

David shrugged. 'Eric wouldn't stop arguing. He swore he'd given me the proper information but he hadn't Dad. Thanks to his incompetence the quote's gone out wrong. The entire job's been underpriced.'

'And that's it? You thumped him for that? You're not right in the head. The man hasn't been born that doesn't make mistakes and you ought to know that better than anybody; you make your fair share with your foul temper. It's your job to check it properly, so why didn't you?'

'I *did* check it. There were two pages missing and when I came across them, they'd not been included in the totals. I reckon he dropped them on my desk after he found them.'

Richard shook his head. 'Eric's not devious. He'd never do a trick like that. Don't you photocopy the pages and then number them?'

'Yes, you know I do.'

'Show me then; show me what was missing.'

David opened the file and passed the pages to his father. 'There are seven pages now but there were definitely only five when I did the quote.'

'You're sure about that?'

'I'm positive. These two turned up later.'

There was a tap on the door and Paige walked in. 'Is Eric alright? I heard about what happened.'

'You just keep your interfering nose out,' David snapped. 'I don't answer to you.'

'Well, maybe you should. If this is about a couple of extra pages you found, I left those on your desk. They were simply duplicates of pages four and five. I left them for you to see and destroy.'

'So the quote was correct then?' Richard asked.

'As far as I'm aware,' Paige confirmed. 'David's calculations were spot on.'

'So it's *your* fault then,' David snarled at Paige.

'No, it's *your* fault,' Paige snapped back. 'Don't attempt to lay blame at my door. You should have checked the pages carefully in the first place; then when you found two further pages, you should have checked those extra carefully. It was obvious to me they were duplicates so why not to you?'

With a theatrical flick of the wrist David sneered. 'Whatever, it matters not. There's no harm done.'

Paige and Richard exchanged glances. 'No harm done? *It matters not?*' Richard bellowed furiously. 'You thump the foreman who just happens to be the shop steward and who, it transpires, did nothing at all wrong and you believe that's okay? Well, let me put you right. If I can smooth this over with a bonus payment deducted from *your* salary I hasten to add, I will, but if I can't resolve it satisfactorily, I'll sack you because *you* matter not. Every day you become more of a liability than an asset David and I'm sick of clearing up after you. End of.'

He stormed from the room without another word closely followed by Paige, leaving David to reflect on his earlier actions.

Richard remained on the factory floor all morning after speaking to Eric who was more than happy to put the earlier issue to rest when Richard explained he was concerned about his son's health. By way of apology, he offered Eric a sum of money which he reluctantly accepted when Richard insisted.

When Paige passed through the general office at lunchtime, Richard was walking towards her looking tense. 'Is everything alright now?' she asked.

'Thankfully, yes. If you're off to the shop would you get me a sandwich please?'

'Any preference?'

'No, just choose what you think. I'm going to see the bane of my life now. Who'd have kids? Thank God I only have the one.'

'Don't be too hard on him. Whatever he does he's still your son and family is very important. I'm sure it's a medical problem that triggers his erratic mood swings. No one would behave like he does without good cause.'

'I couldn't agree more but I can't allow David to run my business into the ground. If he won't see his doctor I can't make him. We'll discuss it when you get back.'

David looked up sheepishly when Richard walked in his room. 'I'm sorry Dad. Is everything alright?'

'No thanks to you. You owe me a hundred quid. I wasn't prepared to insult the guy by offering less. It would have cost more for half an hour with a solicitor to defend your actions only to be told there *was* no defence. This is your last warning David; I mean it. If you refuse to seek medical advice I can't make you but this is *my* company and I won't allow anyone, especially a family member, to pose a threat to any of my employees. Is that clear?'

'It is and I'll get the money from the ATM later.'

'I should have been in York for a meeting at one o'clock. I've had to rearrange that for Saturday now after I've worked all week. I can do without all this aggravation. We need to sit down together and talk about your problems calmly, man to man. The way you behave isn't normal and needs to be addressed. I can't face it tonight though; I'm going out. I need to put some space between us for an hour or so.'

David remained silent as his father left the room.

Richard sighed despondently and flopped down in the chair facing Paige. 'What am I to do with him? He's as quiet as a lamb now and very contrite.'

'That's how he is Richard. I never know what to expect when I go in his room. I can understand why his other PAs didn't stay long. Eat your sandwiches and try to put him out of your mind for a while. It's been a trying day. It'll blow over.'

'I need to distance myself from him so I intend to eat out this evening. I was wondering if you'd care to join me. You understand David's problems better than I do and I'd value your advice. I'd also enjoy your company.'

He expected a refusal so was pleasantly surprised when she replied, 'I have a better idea. Come round to mine instead. I'll rustle something up. We won't be disturbed there.'

'That's very kind of you if you're sure. I wouldn't want to put you to any trouble.'

'It's no trouble. Besides I'm celebrating; I've sold another short story; I got my cheque today so I can decorate another room now.'

Richard was impressed. 'That's very good news. Well done. Do they pay well?'

Paige smiled. 'I wish, but it'll cover Andy's cost. The main thing is I love writing and the satisfaction of seeing one's efforts in print is immense.'

She went on to explain those feelings of euphoria, punctuating her words with the occasional giggle as he studied her closely. She had so little of material value yet she was always happy. Nothing fazed her, not even the exasperating behaviour of his son who would try the patience of a saint.

'Seven-thirty alright then?' she suggested.

He nodded. 'Perfect. I'll bring a bottle.'

As he reached the door he halted. 'I haven't paid you for the sandwiches.'

'My treat. Try to unwind now. It'll all be resolved in the fullness of time. Trust me.'

Richard arrived punctually with a bottle of red wine and a bunch of flowers.

As Paige went to hang up his coat he admired the décor. 'Andy definitely does a good job. It doesn't look like the same room. It's a good solid house.'

'Grandad used to say that but I always felt it was cold and impersonal before the double glazing was installed. That made a big difference to the gas bills too. It's a nice neighbourhood. I guess I'm lucky to own my own house at my age with no mortgage'

'I'm sure you earned it.'

Modestly she replied, 'I just did what I had to do.'
'Can I do anything to help?'
'You can open the bottle and put it on the table.'
He wandered into the kitchen. 'Corkscrew?'
'Try the top drawer. We'll be eating in the dining room. It's through there. It hardly gets used.'
'I didn't realise you had a dining room. We ate in the kitchen last time I called round.'
'Yes, out of necessity as the dining room was full of stuff from the lounge. I tend to eat in the kitchen when I'm on my own.'
He chuckled. 'I eat my TV dinners on my lap. It's not much fun eating alone is it? Having said that, I have David staying at my place presently as you're aware, though I don't know how long that'll last.'
'Has he gone out tonight?'
'I don't know and I don't much care. He kept out of my way when we got home. I'm at my wits end with him Paige, I really am.'
'Let's enjoy our meal and talk about him later.'
After removing a hot baguette from the oven she proceeded to slice it. 'Will you put that on the table please with the salad? I need to keep an eye on the grill. I can serve up in a minute. Are you hungry?'
'I'm starving and I do appreciate your kindness. I also enjoy your company,' he said tenderly.
Although Paige offered no response, inwardly she echoed his words but she had to resist him, charming as he was. It would be very easy to fall in love with Richard but there were too many reasons why she shouldn't. She had to remain resolute, keep her distance and offer no encouragement whatsoever.

The cheese topping on the salmon and pasta bake was golden brown and sizzling.

'Wow, I'll do that justice,' Richard said hungrily. 'It smells absolutely delicious.'

'It's a quick easy meal you could make if you like it. It takes half an hour, that's all. Why don't you go and sit down and I'll bring it through in a minute. I thought I heard somebody at the door.' She hurried away to check and was surprised to see David.

'I'm so sorry for intruding but I've brought you a box of chocolates by way of apology. I didn't know Dad would be here but as he is, would you give him this please?' He held out a wad of notes.

'Why not give it him yourself? Come in David. I offered to make him a bite to eat. He's very worried about you. Have you eaten yet?'

He stepped inside. 'No, I was going to get...'

'Then you can eat here. There's plenty for three.'

'I don't think Dad would be too keen on that. He went out to get out of my sight.'

'No, he just wanted to give you a little space but as this is my house, I decide who'll eat at my table. Give me your jacket. I was about to dish up so your timing's perfect. Let's sit down to a meal together and see how things go. It's something you'll like.'

With a forced smile he nodded. 'If you're sure.'

'Of course I'm sure David. Come on, follow me.' Paige led him into the dining room where Richard looked up in surprise. 'Look who I've just found on my doorstep. As they say, *there's no show without Punch*, no pun intended. I've invited David to join us for dinner.'

Before he could stop himself Richard asked, 'Did you follow me?'

Paige laughed whilst flashing a threatening glance at Richard. 'He's here to see *me* actually. He came to apologise for earlier. He only realised you were here when he saw your car outside. Not many have the registration RWC 1. I've been meaning to ask, what does the 'W' stand for?'

Awkwardly he replied, 'If you don't mind I prefer not to say.'

David shrieked with laughter. '*Wilbert!* The 'W' stands for *Wilbert*,' he squealed even louder.

'*Wilbert,*' Paige chuckled. 'I'm not surprised you kept that quiet. Right, sit down there David next to *Wilbert* and I'll lay another place.'

'That's for you,' David said quietly, handing him the money. 'I spoke to Eric and apologised. He was alright about it. It won't happen again.'

David's eyes lit up when Paige placed the plate of food in front of him. 'That looks delicious. Thanks. I love salmon. It's my favourite.'

'Don't wait for me. Help yourself to salad. That's yours Richard. Enjoy. I'll just pour the wine.'

'Allow me,' Richard said, filling Paige's glass to the rim. 'You're driving David so go easy.'

Barely a word was spoken as the two hungry men devoured their food and polished off the final two chunks of bread.

'Superb,' Richard said, scraping his plate clean.

'Is it okay if I finish off the salad?' David asked.

'Don't show me up son,' Richard cautioned.

'Er...you can talk. Who ate most of the bread?'

Paige smiled to see father and son sharing affable banter as she spooned the remaining contents of the savoury dish on to their respective plates. She was glad she had asked David to stay for dinner following their earlier dispute at the factory. At least they were speaking again now.

'I'd never be able to make a meal as good as this,' said Richard. 'It's the coordination I find difficult.'

'It's easy,' Paige argued but Richard was far from convinced as he sighed with utter contentment.

'I'll tell you what would go down a treat now...a big fat cigar.'

Paige was surprised. 'I didn't know you smoked.'

He laughed. 'I don't...I never have...but it always looks very agreeable in films.'

David shook his head. 'Dad's such a nutter.'

'Well, it takes one to know one David,' his father mocked. 'How do you feel now?'

'Alright but I'd rather not talk about it here.'

Richard sighed. 'I'm sure you wouldn't but it has to be faced. We can't keep ignoring your behaviour. You must learn to control your aggression because if you don't it'll get you in a lot of trouble.'

'I know. It wasn't my proudest moment but none of us is perfect. I bet there have been instances you weren't proud of if the truth were known.'

'Indeed there have David. My worst moment ever was having to inform your Grandad Thomas when I was barely seventeen that I'd got his daughter, your mum, up the duff.'

'*Up the duff?*' he shrieked and Paige howled with laughter.

'Oh aye, I was *Jack-the-Lad* back then. I'll never forget that look of loathing in his eyes as long as I live. I thought he was going to kill me and he made damn sure I did the right thing by her; we were wed three weeks later but things were different then. He was very old school but once you were born he was never away. You were his blue-eyed baby boy. He absolutely worshipped you.'

'So didn't you want to marry Mum?'

'I'd never thought about marriage; we were skint. We were just two teenagers very much in love but I imagine we'd have got married eventually. Grandad Thomas was very generous as were my parents too. They helped us financially and offered their support but I won't deny it was really tough at first.'

It was time for Paige to leave them alone. She left the room inconspicuously and closed the door.

'Did you resent me for causing such heartache?'

'Resent *you*? It wasn't *your* fault son. I resented myself for not being there, for not hearing your first word or seeing your first step, for missing your first day at school and for all the other important things I missed but I never stopped loving you, not for one single moment and I still do. Despite our occasional altercations, you're still my flesh and blood and I'll never stop worrying about you. That's what parents do as I'm sure you'll discover in time.'

'Can I ask you a personal question Dad?'

'Certainly...what's on your mind?'

'What's with you and Paige?'

'She's a good listener and before you jump to any conclusions, the last time I came here was over four months ago to introduce her to Andy, the decorator, when she wanted her lounge papered. She's a good person David and you'd do well to remember that. I enjoy her company. I often chat to her at work but more importantly, she keeps *you* under control most of the time which is of great comfort to me.'

'Point taken. She's a good cook too.'

'Yes and I'm sure she mentioned dessert. I'll pop in the kitchen and see what she's doing.'

Paige looked round and smiled as he wandered in. 'Is everything going okay?'

He wanted to give her a hug but resisted the urge. 'Everything's perfect. Thank you Paige and thanks for your diplomacy. I'll be honest. I wasn't pleased when David turned up here but I have to hand it to you; you think on your feet. We've talked a lot and so it's a move in the right direction. I came in here to help with the dishes but I see everything's done.'

'You're a guest. So, are you ready for blackberry crumble and custard now? I've put the coffee on.'

Richard was ready for much more than that but he had to keep such emotions hidden. 'Yes please,' he replied keenly, picking up two bowls to carry in.

He halted briefly. 'I'm off to York on Saturday to a meeting. There are some nice shops there if you'd care to join me. We could meet up later and have a spot of lunch. It's a charming city. Have you been?'

'No I haven't but I'm at the Hospice on Saturday. I'll try and swap it to Sunday. Can I let you know?'

'Certainly. I hope you can. If you haven't visited The Shambles you haven't lived. You'll love it. It's the most visited place in Europe I've heard.'

'Oh? Why is that?'

He grinned. 'You'll have to come with me to find out but I guarantee you won't be disappointed. I've another trip planned next month, to New York. It's for three days. I could take you along as my PA and put it through the books. That's definitely a place to see if you've never been.'

'I've never been anywhere apart from Spain when I was a child. I'd love to go to New York but I can imagine how David would react. He'd be ripping.'

'Let me worry about David. Everybody's entitled to time off. We'll discuss it nearer the time.'

It was approaching midnight when they left and as Paige closed the door she held diverse feelings of apprehension and jubilation. She could hardly wait to tell Emma about Richard's proposal and seek her advice but it was far too late to call her now.

That night she couldn't sleep; so many questions occupied her mind. If Richard made a move, would she be able to resist him? Had she the willpower to say *no* to a man so considerate and handsome with the most beguiling eyes she'd ever seen? They had similar tastes and shared a parallel sense of humour but there was David to consider, a greatly troubled and impulsive young man who stood between them like a concrete stanchion.

Finally she fell into a deep and welcome sleep.

'Tell me what you *want* to do,' Emma said frankly.

There was a short pause. 'What I *want* to do and what I *should* do are two very different things,' she sighed ambivalently. 'Of course I'd like to go with him but I need somebody level-headed like you to advise me. I can trust you to be honest.'

Paige heard a short chuckle at the other end of the telephone. 'Me, level-headed? I'll tell you what I'd do if I fancied him like you do and don't deny that. I'd be off like a shot and we'd only need one room, but that's me. I'm not level-headed; I'm impulsive. If you can't bring yourself to jump in bed with him, stay away from New York because that's definitely where it'll happen. That's why he invited you. I'm sorry but you wanted the truth.'

That wasn't what she wanted to hear. 'Everybody isn't sex-mad like you and you're merely surmising Richard is. I told you what he said, that he wanted a friend, not a romantic involvement and I happen to believe him.'

'More fool you. Just go Paige. Enjoy the amazing experience and if it happens, it happens. You asked for the truth and I've given it to you.'

Argumentatively she countered, 'Right I *will* go if only to prove you wrong. I should never have asked for your advice. What the hell do you know about platonic relationships? You've never had one.'

4

Paige took her seat by the window and fastened her seat belt. 'I can't believe I'm actually going to New York,' she gabbled excitedly.

'Just remember it's only a few days so you'll find it tiring. We've made an early start today; this is an eight hour flight and New York is five hours behind us so effectively it'll be a very late night tonight. At midnight there your body-clock will be five o'clock tomorrow morning and you won't get an early night as I've booked us an evening sightseeing trip.'

'Really? That's fantastic, thank you. I'll definitely stay awake for that. I just hope you don't fall asleep at your meeting tomorrow. What time does it start?'

'Nine o'clock but I'd like to arrive by eight-thirty so I get a decent seat. I'll meet you back at the hotel at two o'clock and we'll grab some lunch then. You can sleep in for a while in the morning if you stick the *do not disturb* sign on your doorknob.'

'Not likely. I'm looking round the shops. I'll ask at reception where the best ones are and then I'll try to get round every one.'

He laughed. 'What is it with women and shops?'

'It's the same with men and cars I suppose,' she replied pragmatically. 'Do you recall what *you* did in York? Three showrooms you tramped me round and not one car you raved about was half as classy as the one you drive now.'

'I was only *looking*,' he remonstrated.

'And that's all I'll be doing at the shops, looking.'

He grinned sceptically. 'I'll have you a small bet you buy something.'

'Maybe, maybe not but I'll enjoy looking. I only buy stuff that's value for money. Will there be time to have a last look round on Wednesday morning?'

'We leave at nine so I'm afraid not and don't forget to add five hours to the flight time, so we arrive home late evening. If you enjoy New York we can come again and stay longer. I'm glad you're here. I enjoyed our day out in York very much.'

She smiled. 'I did too, apart from those boring car showrooms. You were right about The Shambles as well. I've never seen anything like it before. I'd like to go there again. It was like stepping back in time and looking at a former life.'

'There are lots of places I'd like to take you. Paris is lovely in the springtime, Monte Carlo too.'

'Slow down, I'm not made of money. I know this trip was put through the company books but it still has to be paid for; I'm not stupid. If we go places as friends then I have to pay my corner.'

He gave her words some thought. 'So, does that mean I pay half to the food when I eat at yours?'

'No, of course not; now you're being silly. I like to make you a meal. Besides, it's company for me.'

He looked at her coyly. 'Is this our first quarrel?'

She laughed. 'No, whatever gave you that idea? I need to be careful with money, that's all. I've bills to pay and I can't spend what I don't have. I'd love to go to all those exotic places with you and when I can afford to I will, so can we leave it at that?'

There was a slight judder as the plane eased away from the gate and she grabbed his hand. 'I'm sorry; I can't remember going on a plane before and I'm a bit scared,' she confessed looking embarrassed, but when she tried to remove her hand he held on to it to offer reassurance.

'It's okay to be nervous. Everyone's apprehensive at first. You'll feel calm very soon. Put your trust in the Captain. He'll take good care of his passengers. The weather forecast is quite good so it should be a smooth flight.'

Half an hour into the flight she was enjoying her breakfast and chattering excitedly about New York but nothing could have prepared her for their scenic taxi drive to their hotel in Manhattan.

Thirty minutes after check-in they were back out, showered and changed and Paige was raring to see the sights. He directed her to the Rockefeller Centre first where they soared the seventy floors to the Top of the Rock Observation Deck to see the panoramic views of the city. On such a beautiful day it was the perfect vantage point to see the thrilling skyline and Richard was on hand to point out Central Park and many other places of special interest.

It was turned two o'clock and Richard suggested they ought to grab a quick snack as he had booked a three hour sightseeing cruise for later. 'There's such a lot to see when we're only here two days. I have a surprise planned for tomorrow that you'll enjoy.'

Sighing silently, Paige looked up into his smiling eyes. He was such a thoughtful person. 'Didn't you say we had an evening trip too?'

'That's right. I don't know if or when we'll fit in a meal but we can take sandwiches on the boat and we'll be able to get drinks on there.'

Again Paige was excited. 'I'm looking forward to the boat trip. I've never been on a boat that I recall.'

Back in the street they wandered past Saks, Fifth Avenue. 'I'm definitely looking in there tomorrow and in Bloomingdales. It's an amazing city Richard. You were right. Thanks again for inviting me.'

It was turned midnight when they arrived back at their hotel. 'Do you feel tired now?' he asked.

'Not at all. I did earlier but I'm wide awake now. I can't recall ever having had such an action-packed day and the cruise was fantastic. That was the highlight of the day for me and our evening sightseeing trip was great too. Everything looks totally different when illuminated; it takes your breath away. I bet I don't sleep a wink tonight.'

They stepped from the lift and walked slowly towards their rooms, halting at Paige's door. 'I'd like to thank you again Richard. Without doubt, today's been the best day of my life. It'll take me forever to write my diary. Everything I've seen and done has exceeded all expectations and I don't want this day to end.'

Was that the cue he'd been waiting for so long he wondered. He moved closer until he could feel her warm breath on his face. His body was quivering, his eyes smouldering with need for her. 'It doesn't have to end yet,' he murmured softly. 'Just say the word Paige.'

His eyes searched hers, awaiting her answer. 'Am I making a terrible mistake here? If so, I apologise.'

As a rush of adrenaline shot through her body she answered, 'There's no mistake. I can't and I won't resist you a moment longer. I can't go on fighting my feelings. Is that what you wanted to hear?'

Richard smiled and took her in his arms, holding her silently for what seemed an eternity before asking, 'Are you really sure about this Paige?'

She smiled back at him with a mischievous glint in her eye. 'You can be such an old fuddy-duddy at times. Getting me between the sheets has been your top priority since the first day we met so don't deny that. Even Andy and Emma had *that* sussed. We're both adults. Seize the day Richard. What happened to that teenage *Jack-the-Lad?'*

He laughed awkwardly. 'He grew up I'm afraid.'

'Then we'll just have to find him again won't we? Right, decision time, your place or mine?'

He took the key-card from her hand, opened her door and with an evocative smile whispered, 'I can guarantee *this* will be the highlight of *my* day.'

When Paige awoke at eight o'clock she was alone. Richard had obviously returned to his room to get ready for his meeting.

In response to a tap on the door, she leapt out of bed and as expected, it was Richard.

'Did I wake you? I didn't want to shoot off without seeing you.'

‘I was already awake.’ Clasping both arms around his neck she brushed her lips against his. ‘I’m going to miss you so much,’ she said straightening his tie.

‘Same here. You look very sexy. See you at two.’

With a roguish grin she winked. ‘It’s a date.’

As she closed the door something caught her eye on the bedside table and she smiled. There wasn’t a man alive who could have got away with that apart from Richard she told herself as she approached to find two hundred-dollar bills and his hand-written note. ‘Treat yourself to something extravagant that you wouldn’t otherwise buy. Love you,’ it said.

With a straight face she would reprimand Richard about that later...the nerve of the man, to spend the night with her and leave money by her bedside. She giggled knowing he would be mortified to think he had offended her in any way.

She made a start on her diary entries whilst all the events were still fresh in her mind. She had kept a page-a-day diary since her teenage years and often looked back over previous years’ entries to refresh her mind about things from the past so her favourite memories would never be forgotten.

As she was writing her diary, Richard was hailing a Yellow Cab outside their hotel to take him to the World Trade Centre.

Surprisingly it didn’t take long to fill the page and as she began to describe what happened later at the hotel, she paused to delete those lines. As they had returned after midnight, the unforgettable bedroom antics related to Tuesday the eleventh, not Monday the tenth of September.

Paige sighed as she reflected on their first night of passion, a date she would never forget, but little did she know that the whole world would never forget that date either for the unspeakable atrocities which, in the next hour or two, would bring absolute terror to the United States of America and cause countless unsuspecting men, women and children to lose their lives as the world famous Twin Towers were razed to the ground by an horrific and unprecedented act of terrorism.

Oblivious of the mayhem outside, Paige picked up her bag and hurried towards the lift. There wasn't a moment to lose if she was to visit every shop she'd been longing to see.

Saks was at the top of her list but as she exited the hotel something was clearly wrong. The traffic was jammed bumper to bumper and the wailing noise of ambulances and police cars was unbearable as each struggled to weave its way through the congestion. This was much more than a traffic accident.

People were gathered together in groups, pointing and talking. Some were weeping; while others with vacant expressions hovered like ghosts, refusing to believe what was happening in their city.

Paige approached a cluster of women asking, 'Do you know what's wrong?'

'Haven't you heard?' one replied. 'They're saying it's a terrorist attack. Two planes have crashed into the Twin Towers. The North and South Towers are ablaze and thousands of people work there.'

She was horrified. 'Has that just happened?'

'Yes, in the past hour. The first hit at eight-forty-five and the second about twenty minutes later.'

Paige suddenly felt clammy and nauseous. 'Is that anywhere near the World Trade Centre?'

'It *is* the World Trade Centre,' another answered.

Trembling with fear, Paige grabbed the woman's arm to steady herself. 'My God! My boss went to a meeting there this morning.'

'And my husband works there,' the first one said. 'I've tried his cell-phone and there's no answer but I'm trying to remain positive. Apparently the phone lines are jammed. I know they've led lots of people out already but they've got to use the stairs because the lifts aren't working. The thing is, you can't get near enough to find out what's going on. If you try, the authorities order you away. It's worse further up the street but if you've got access to a television, all news channels are covering it.'

Paige had to get away. 'I hope your husband gets out safely,' she said, her face as white as a sheet.

'Thank you. I hope your boss does too.'

'Thanks. I can't believe this is happening.'

With tears in her eyes she agreed. 'No one can.'

'Good luck,' Paige said, squeezing her hand.

She hurried back to her hotel and took the lift to her room where the full reality of the situation only dawned when she switched on the television. Tears flooded uncontrollably from her eyes as she thought of Richard who could still be trapped in one of the burning buildings and there was nothing she could do but await the final outcome. There was so much to take in and she sobbed broken-heartedly to watch the horror unfold. People were jumping from office windows to their deaths and then when she believed it could get no worse, in seemingly slow motion the Twin Towers were individually razed to the ground taking with them thousands of innocent people who had been unable to escape and leaving behind nothing but gigantic clouds of dust, concrete and debris. This was a catastrophe of unbelievable magnitude.

Suddenly, people began to emerge from the thick, billowing, choking dust; some were walking, some were running. Emergency workers were on hand to assist the elderly and infirm to safety. Those people were the lucky ones who had made it into the street prior to the collapse of the North Tower. There was little likelihood of many survivors now.

With her eyes glued to the screen Paige absorbed every minute detail, checking the faces of everyone and praying she'd catch a brief glimpse of Richard, but he was nowhere to be seen amongst the scared, grim-faced, dusty people caught on camera.

With heavy heart she sighed. She had to face the agonizing truth that the odds were heavily stacked against his having survived.

Bordering on hysteria, she buried her head in her pillow, weeping bitterly for the man she loved.

David drummed his fingers on the table irritably as he tried again to contact the hotel in New York. He had made a dozen or more attempts already without success. He was at screaming pitch when suddenly the number was ringing. *'Yes!'* he yelled as his call was answered. 'Do *not* disconnect me, *please!* I'm trying to contact my father who's booked into your hotel with a member of staff and I'd like you to try to connect me to both rooms please. My father had a meeting at the World Trade Centre this morning and I need to know he's safe. I live in UK and I've just heard what's happened.'

David provided both names and the receptionist came back to him shortly afterwards. 'I'm afraid I can't contact Mr Cavendish so I'll try Miss Sheldon now. One moment please.'

Paige snatched at the receiver, her heart missing a beat when the telephone rang and burst into tears on hearing David's voice.

His heart sank. 'I know about the terrorist attack. Have you heard anything about Dad? Has anybody been in touch with you about him?'

Her words were almost incomprehensible. 'I only know what I've seen on TV. I couldn't get through to the local hospitals; I tried to ring you at work and I couldn't get through to UK either. All the phone lines are jammed. It's a nightmare from hell.'

'Slow down. What time did he go, do you know?'

'Yes, he knocked at my door around eight o'clock saying he'd meet me here at two. I was going shopping and we were meeting up for lunch. I've neither seen nor spoken to him since then. I only found out about the attack when I went out but you can't get near enough to enquire. It's absolute pandemonium outside. You've no idea what it's like David.'

'I'm going to try and get a flight to New York.'

'That's impossible. The receptionist enquired and all international flights at JFK are cancelled. I can't get back tomorrow but I don't want to leave until I know what's happened. I waited in because I knew you'd call me but now I want to find out where the hospitals are and I'm going to take a cab to check if your dad's been admitted. I'm sure he'd have contacted me or come back had it been possible. I can't stop crying. I just want to know he's safe.'

'I know. I do too. He's very resourceful so try not to worry. Are you leaving now?'

'Yes, then I've time to check them all. Someone might have a casualty list but I won't find anything out hanging around here. Besides, there's a messaging facility if someone rings me. When I have some news I'll try to call you. Will you be on your dad's number all night?'

'I will and if I haven't heard from you by eleven o'clock, I'll try to call you again. It might be easier to get through from this end. Good luck. If anyone can find Dad, you can Paige.'

'The New York Presbyterian Hospital would be the best place to start,' the taxi driver said when Paige explained the state of affairs. 'Many casualties were taken to their burns unit earlier today.'

That revelation did little to calm her nerves. 'Will you wait for me when I go inside to enquire please? If there's no record of him there, I want you to take me to other hospitals.'

'No problem. Have you any idea which floor your boss's meeting was on?'

She shrugged. 'No, he didn't say though I hope it was one of the lower ones. He'd have stood more of a chance of getting out then. He might have tried to call me but I heard the phone lines were very busy.'

'Yes Ma'am, they sure are. New York has never seen the likes of this before. People are calling from all over the world. The authorities believe that six thousand or more people could have been killed.'

Paige shuddered. 'I'd rather not think about that if you don't mind. I had to turn the news channel off. I couldn't bear to watch it any longer.'

They made the rest of the journey in silence until he stopped outside the main entrance. 'I'll wait over there for you. Good luck.'

She was quaking as she stepped from the taxi and in tears as she approached the reception desk. The receptionist looked up compassionately. 'How may I help you Ma'am?'

'I'm trying to find someone. I came from England yesterday with my boss. He had to attend a meeting this morning at the World Trade Centre. I haven't heard from him since he left at eight o'clock and I don't know if he managed to get out. Can you help me please? Do you have the names of the casualties who were brought here?'

'We do and we also have a list of the people who were taken to our associated hospitals. Give me his name and I'll see what I can find.'

'Richard Cavendish'

'Date of birth?'

'I don't know. He's forty-four; that's all I know.'

'Don't worry. It only matters where there are two or more people with the same name. Just take a seat Ma'am. I'll make some enquiries.'

Paige waited what appeared an eternity for her to return and when, with a smile, she gestured for her to step forward, Paige ran to the desk optimistically crying, 'Have you found him? Is he alive?'

'Yes, a British patient named Richard Cavendish *is* listed. He's gone down to OR for treatment for a broken arm. It appears he has no other injuries so it looks like your boss has had a very lucky escape.'

Beaming with delight she gabbled, 'Oh my God, you're sure it's him? You're *really* sure?'

'As sure as I can be Ma'am. If you'd like to wait, you can see him when he comes back.'

'Oh yes please. I can't believe it. Thank you. It's such a relief to know he's safe. His son's calling me later to find out if I've heard anything. We've been absolutely frantic. Do I wait here?'

She nodded. 'Yes, take a seat Ma'am. It could be a while but there's a vending machine at the end of the corridor if you need a drink or snack.'

Paige had forgotten the cab was still outside until the driver poked his head round the door. 'Is there any news yet?' he called to her.

She jumped up right away. 'I'm *so* sorry. With all the excitement I completely forgot about you. He's fine; he's broken his arm, that's all. I'm waiting for him to return from OR. What do I owe you?'

He was genuinely delighted. 'It's so good to hear happy news. Believe me, there hasn't been much of that today. It's twenty dollars please and here's my card. If you want me to collect you later give me a call.'

She gave him twenty-five and thanked him.

Paige could hardly sit still. It was nothing less than a miracle that Richard was alive. She couldn't wait to see him and after pacing the floor for a while she approached the receptionist. 'I'm going for a cup of coffee; would you like one too? I've just realised, I haven't had anything to eat or drink all day.'

'I'm fine thanks. I've just had a drink.'

'Has it been really horrible here today?'

With a nod of the head she said, 'It was very busy earlier. There were some terrible burn victims but it seems like we're over the worst now. The numbers have eased off a little over the past hour. I won't be sorry when it's time to go home. It's been a trying day. Is this your first trip to New York?'

'Yes it is. We arrived yesterday and we should be going home in the morning but I don't think there are any flights in and out of JFK. I was really looking forward to this visit. I must say though, we had an amazing day yesterday. My boss has been many times so he took me to see some of the sights.'

'I'm so sorry your trip's been ruined.'

She sighed. 'It could have been much worse. I'm just thankful Richard's alright. His broken arm will mend. Hundreds if not thousands of other folk will have a lot more to contend with.'

As Paige returned with her coffee the receptionist informed her Richard was back. She held her breath when she entered his room, tears coursing down her cheeks. Softly she asked the nurse, 'Is he asleep?'

'No, he's just resting. Go ahead; talk to him.'

Richard opened his eyes as she clasped his hand. 'Hey, stop it. What's all the fuss about? I've broken my arm, that's all,' he told her. 'Don't worry; it'll soon heal.'

'Press the button if you need me,' the nurse said.

The second she left the room, Paige wrapped her arms around Richard and sobbed. 'I thought I'd lost you. This has been the worst day of my life.'

He stroked her hair. 'Yes but wasn't yesterday the best day of your life?' he reminded her. 'I'm alright Paige so please stop crying. It's only a broken arm.'

'Have you any idea what happened today?'

'Of course. I tripped and fell. I'm a clumsy oaf.'

'Don't joke about it Richard. It's horrible. David called. I said I'd call him back when I had news.'

He looked surprised. 'David called? How on earth did *David* know I'd fallen? More to the point, how did *you* know? Did someone contact you?'

She was about to say that the terrorist attack had been broadcast on world-wide television but instead she hesitated; she was confused. 'Tell me what you were doing when you fell.'

'We'd been told to evacuate the building because there was a problem. They didn't say what but there was evidently a badly fractured water main as water was cascading down the stairwells. Everybody was pushing and shoving as we hurried down and then suddenly I was on the floor yelling; I'd twisted my ankle and my left arm was painful. I also felt dazed but recall there was loads of debris flying around. A paramedic appeared; he helped me up and stuck me in an ambulance. That's it. That's all I know.'

'When you got here, did no one tell you what had happened at the World Trade Centre?'

He shook his head. 'Not a word. I'm just annoyed I missed my meeting. I tried calling you at the hotel a few times but I couldn't get through so I gave up. I imagined you'd have gone shopping by then and I expected being back at the hotel by two o'clock but they couldn't take me to theatre when I got here as there was a big emergency of some kind. Everyone was rushing around so I got into bed and fell asleep until they came for me. It was a tiring day yesterday and I hardly got a wink of sleep last night, thanks to you. You were *extremely* demanding,' he guffawed with a roguish glint in his eye.

That remark brought a smile to her lips. 'Strange, that's not the way I remember it.'

He stroked her arm. 'I'm so sorry I messed up our last day. I wanted everything to be perfect.'

'It isn't your fault. You're lucky to be alive. You obviously have no idea what happened earlier at the World Trade Centre.'

'Apparently not. Enlighten me.'

Richard listened ashen-faced as Paige related the morning's events with tears flowing from her eyes. 'That's the reason David called, to find out if you'd escaped from the building but I couldn't tell him as I didn't know. I found you by chance. I hailed a cab with the intention of visiting every hospital in New York. While there was still a glimmer of hope, no matter how slight, I wouldn't give up. I was frantic. As luck would have it, the cabbie suggested we try here first. I can't believe you didn't know about the terrorist attack when the entire world knows about it. Incidentally, we can't leave New York for a day or two. I must contact the airline as all international flights appear to be grounded at JFK.'

'That's the least of my worries. Eric's running the factory and David will just have to step up his game and keep things ticking over. I'll talk to him.'

'When are they discharging you?'

'Shortly I hope. If that's coffee you've got there, I wouldn't mind a drink please. My mouth's so dry.'

'Mine too.' She passed him the plastic cup. 'I've had nothing to eat or drink all day.'

Following a short sharp tap on the door the doctor entered accompanied by the nurse who was present earlier. He glanced at the notes. 'How are you now, Mr Cavendish? Are you still feeling groggy?'

'No, I'm fine. Are you discharging me?'

He checked Richard's cast and looked carefully at his fingers. 'Everything appears to be alright. Your circulation is fine so yes, I think we can let you go now but get back in touch at once if you have any problems. When are you returning to UK?'

'I'm not sure. We should have been flying back tomorrow morning but I've heard all flights at JFK are grounded.'

'Yes, I heard that too. You can collect the paperwork when you leave and make arrangements to see your doctor as soon as possible and give him the X-rays. The cast should stay on for five or six weeks and if there are no complications, your arm should be back to normal by then. Any questions?'

He shook his head. 'Everything's fine thank you.'

'Good and I'm sorry about the long delay earlier. I'm sure you understand we had to prioritise.'

Richard shook his hand. 'I do and thanks again.'

Paige collected the documents from reception and called the cab driver. It was almost five o'clock and David would be calling her shortly hoping for good news. She imagined he would be frantic but at least they had good news to impart unlike many, whose lives would be in turmoil for days, weeks, months or possibly years as the recovery process continued in the search for loved ones.

'First things first, I must call David,' Richard said.

'Yes, and then we can get you out of those filthy clothes.'

'What I wouldn't give for a nice hot shower,' he sighed. 'I'll be back when I've spoken to David.'

He returned a short while later looking frustrated. 'It's no use. I can't get through.'

'I'll keep trying for you. Meanwhile, I had this in my wardrobe. It's a plastic dry-cleaning bag and if I cut it, you can wrap it around your cast and have a shower. I'm sure you'll feel better then. If we take it off carefully afterwards, you can use it again. Can you manage to get undressed?'

'I can but try. I'd better use your shower in case I need any help.'

She helped remove his shirt and skilfully wrapped the plastic over the cast, tucking it in securely at top and bottom. 'Just be careful. Yell if you need me.'

He claimed to feel ten years younger when he reappeared with a broad smile, wearing her polka-dot robe. 'What would I do without you?' He gave her a quick kiss. 'Did you get through to David?'

‘No, I’ve been waiting for you. I’ll try now.’

At the third attempt she was successful and as he took the phone from her, David picked up.

‘It’s me son,’ he said quietly. After a brief pause he spoke again. ‘There’s really no need to get upset. I’m fine apart from a broken arm, that is.’

Paige went into the bathroom, allowing father and son some privacy and on her return it was apparent it had been an emotional conversation.

She held him in her arms and for the first time she saw him cry. ‘It’s good to let it out,’ she whispered. ‘It’s been an appalling day for everyone but you’re safe now and David knows you’re safe. How about we go out, get a breath of air and find two of those New York steaks you told me about? We can come straight back afterwards and have an early night.’

He smiled and hugged her tight. She always knew how to react in a crisis. ‘Slight problem Paige. How do I eat a New York steak with one arm?’

‘Simple, I cut it up for you. Get dressed. I won’t be long. See if a sweater will slip over your arm.’

Out of the blue he asked, ‘Do you love me?’

Richard’s question took her by surprise and when she didn’t answer he kissed her. ‘*I* love *you* and I’m terrified of losing you. I wish you’d stop agonizing about who I am, what I am or that I’ve a few bob in the bank. I’m just a normal average guy who loves you. Nothing else matters so, do *you* love *me*?’

Though her lips remained silent her truthful eyes and smile answered his question and he sighed with utter contentment. ‘It might be wise to keep this to ourselves for the time being Paige. There’ll be time enough for David to be told when things improve. What do you think?'

She nodded. She wouldn't argue with that. David had been the major stumbling block from the outset when she first realised she had feelings for Richard. Warily she asked, 'How do you think he'll react?'

'Now there's a question…petulantly, angrily and with a vast array of acerbic comments no doubt but I have a broad back and I know you have too.'

'I'd like to make a suggestion Richard. Let's not worry or even think about the future. Let's just live for today. I've had so many bitter disappointments in my life and none of us can predict what's lurking around the corner. You only have to imagine what *could* have happened today and...'

'You're a strange creature at times,' he cut in.

There followed a high-pitched ripple of laughter. 'That's rich coming from a guy dressed in a polka-dot robe with everything on display. Do you intend to walk to your room dressed like that?'

'Doesn't everybody?' he quipped with a quizzical smile. 'In case it's escaped your notice, that brown rectangle over there is a connecting door from your room to mine.'

'Oh, so you've unlocked your side have you?'

He laughed. 'That's a point; no, I haven't. I guess it's a quick dash down the corridor then.'

'Unless you give me your key and I unlock it.'

He shook his head. 'Why didn't I think of that?'

She poked him in the chest. 'Because *you're* not as smart as I am. You're just a normal average guy, remember?'

Her words cheered him. They had turned another corner.

'Do you realise, this is the first decent meal we've had since we left England. Wow, I can't wait to get my gnashers into that,' Richard panted hungrily as the waiter placed their sizzling steaks on the table.

Paige was equally impressed and hurriedly cut up half of Richard's steak. 'It's very tender.'

At the end of the meal he sighed contentedly. 'It's the first time I've eaten here but I'll definitely come again. I enjoyed that very much.'

'Me too but I'm absolutely shattered now. I think the late nights have caught up with me.'

They wandered back to the hotel hand in hand.

'Do you mind if I sleep in my own room tonight? I'd hate to keep you awake if I'm restless.'

That was the perfect opportunity for a wind-up.

'Not at all,' she stated straight-faced. 'At least I'll be spared the indignity of having my fee tossed on my bedside table in the morning.'

His reaction was worse than expected. 'Oh God, I didn't give it a thought. I'm *so* sorry. I wanted you to have a great day and buy something special you couldn't otherwise afford. Can you forgive me?'

'I'm working on it, like I'm working on trying to understand why you can't see through me when I'm winding you up. You're *so* gullible Richard.'

He sighed with relief. 'You're not angry then?'

'Of course not, it was a very kind gesture. Thank you. I wouldn't have spent it though but I think you know that if you're honest with yourself. I'm rather odd where money's concerned. It comes from never having had much I guess. I did fork out fifty dollars on the combined taxi fares however so don't expect to get *that* back,' she made known demonstratively.

He threw back his head and laughed. 'I'm so glad I met you Paige. You're such a remarkable girl. I'll make sure you enjoy the next few days here.'

Outside her door he kissed her goodnight.

'Leave your inner door unlocked Richard in case you need me. I'll leave mine unlocked too.'

Once in the confines of his room, Richard turned on the television to view the day's horrific events as the world had seen them earlier. Selecting CNN, he perched on the edge of his bed, his eyes riveted to the screen. To say he was traumatized didn't even come close. How terrifying it would have been for Paige and David, watching the day's events unfold, knowing he was in one of those buildings. All that remained now of each majestic edifice was a titanic mass of tangled metal and structural debris, strewn across a site that for many unfortunate souls would undoubtedly remain their burial ground forever.

Richard couldn't settle. He had to see the horrific event with his own eyes. Draping a jacket over his shoulders he left the hotel and headed towards the Twin Towers. As he drew closer, the overpowering stench suffocated him, bringing tears to his eyes. It was far worse than he could have imagined.

Some people were standing in silence as cameras flashed. Other dismayed onlookers wondered at the mass destruction, many in tears...many too shocked to weep. He moved closer, stepping into a doorway out of sight whilst listening to the ghostly creaking symphony of twisted metal swaying in the evening breeze, intermittently punctuated by the shrill cries of rescue workers as they went about their business of recovery. It was all too unbelievable to take in.

Paige made Richard a cup of coffee and took it to his room but he wasn't there. His television was on, tuned to the terrorist attack. With no response when she called him she knew where she would find him.

She made her way down the street where she had first learned of the disaster from the lips of the girl whose husband worked at the World Trade Centre. Paige had prayed for her all day...prayed that there would be a happy outcome for her as well.

The closer she got, the more hectic it became and it was a devastating spectacle she beheld when she reached the point where she could go no further.

There was still no sign of Richard, secreted in the doorway, and she paused a while, her head bowed, praying for the souls of those who had perished.

Only when returning did she notice Richard in the doorway and she crossed the street to go to him. As she drew close she looked at his eyes...eyes swollen with tears and filled with sorrow and disbelief.

Taking him by the hand she asked, 'Do you want to head back?'

He emitted a deep sigh. 'This is unbelievable. It's truly unbelievable; it's a total war zone; it's nothing less.' He cupped his arm round her shoulder, taking a final look before they walked back together. 'I'm glad you came. How did you know I'd gone out and where to find me?'

‘I brought you a cup of coffee. I wanted to check you were okay. When you weren’t there I assumed you’d be here. Where else would you have gone?’

He stopped and pulled her towards him. ‘I could never put into words how much I love you Paige. It scares me at times. I don’t ever want to lose you.’

She frowned. ‘Didn’t we agree to live for today?’

‘We did but it’s not enough for me.’ He searched her eyes. ‘I can fix things with David. I know he’s holding you back. Be patient; give me a little time.’ He kissed her tenderly. ‘We’ve been given a second chance today Paige, a whole new beginning.’

As they were about to move on a figure appeared beside them. ‘Excuse me,’ the girl said. ‘Aren’t you the British girl I spoke to this morning, the one who was looking for her boss?’

Paige shrieked with delight to see her again. ‘I’ve been praying for you all day. Please tell me you’ve found your husband.’

With a beaming smile she pointed to a man across the street. ‘Your prayers were obviously answered. He got out safe and well and I take it your *boss* did too,’ she added with a wink of the eye.

‘Yes and I think you know he’s a little more than my boss. He escaped with just a broken arm.’

She beckoned her husband to join them and as the two men wandered off together, exchanging details of their bitter experiences, Paige explained how she had found Richard at the hospital as Laura, her new friend, listened eagerly.

‘We’re so lucky,’ Laura sighed. ‘Brad ran all the way home when he reached the exit but I’d already dashed down here to look for him. Finally we found each other. So, how did Richard break his arm?'

'He was rather vague about that. As far as he can recall he stumbled when he reached the bottom of the stairs and would you believe he knew nothing at all about the terrorist attack until I told him when I found him at the hospital?'

'Never!' she exclaimed in disbelief.

'I'm telling you Laura; no one mentioned a word about that in front of him. He believed a burst water pipe was the cause of the evacuation as water was cascading down the stairs.'

'How strange. Listen, could you manage a cup of coffee or a milk-shake? There's a coffee shop at the end of the block. I've a horrible taste in my mouth.'

'Mmm sounds good to me; I'm nearly choking on this thick dust that's floating around.' She called to Richard who, engrossed in conversation with Brad about his IT work, nodded in accord.

It was eleven o'clock when the four finally parted company. The girls had exchanged email addresses and telephone numbers and there had been mention of a meal out together if Paige and Richard were to remain in New York for several more days.

When they exited the lift Paige was concerned, 'Is something wrong Richard? You've hardly spoken a word since we left Laura and Brad.'

He kissed her lovingly. 'Sorry, I was miles away. I was just wondering, as it's a woman's prerogative to change her mind, can that apply to men too?'

'In these times of sexual equality I don't see why not. What's on your mind as if I didn't know?'

On a short burst of laughter he said, 'I'll assume that's a *yes*. How about my place this time?'

'Is Sunday okay Richard?' she called to him. 'They have a huge backlog of passengers.'

'If it suits you it suits me. It gives us a few more days together.'

'Yes, that's fine,' she told the agent. 'I don't need to contact you again do I?'

The agent reconfirmed the details. 'No you don't Ma'am. You must check in three hours before your departure time and collect your tickets at the desk.'

Paige stuffed her notes in her bag. 'I have to book the rooms for four more nights now.'

'Do we really need both rooms?' Richard asked.

Paige shook her head in disbelief. 'Much as I hate to waste one cent, just *think* Richard. If you hand a receipted invoice to your finance department showing two rooms for two nights and one room for the rest, can you imagine the tittle-tattle? You might as well swan into work on Monday with, "We've been at it all week," tattooed across your forehead.'

Laughing heartily he took Paige in his arms. 'The problem is I *can't* think when you're around. That's the effect you have on me.'

She rested her head against him, glad to be in his arms and referring to his broken arm enquired, 'Did you sleep alright last night?'

'I did, once you left me alone,' he spluttered with laughter, anticipating her reaction.

'*Stop saying that!*' she protested. '*You're* the one with the insatiable appetite for...'

'I never heard you complain,' he cut in dryly.

With a broad grin she collected her bag and coat. 'I'm ravenous. I want my breakfast; I need to book these rooms for the extra nights and then I want to look round the shops. I've bought nothing yet.'

'Great…what could be more enjoyable than that?' Richard huffed with irony. 'Hey, hang on for me,' he hollered as she walked from the room.

It was anything *but* an enjoyable day out, the sole topic of conversation being the terrorist attack. That was only to be expected though as broadcasters updated the horrendous details of the ever increasing number of fatalities. The one thing that struck Paige however was the steadfast stoicism of the American people who, in the face of adversity, were there for each other, complete strangers giving and receiving comfort and support, regardless of race or creed.

Within the space of twenty-four hours, they had become one great family, an entire nation united in their determination to stand together against acts of fear and oppression.

'Are you calling David again?' asked Paige. 'I must call Emma. I'm on duty at the Hospice on Saturday so they'll have to be told I won't be available.'

Richard checked the time. 'If we make our way to the hotel now I can call Eric at work for an update, and I can have a quick word with David too.'

'Where are we eating later? What do you fancy?'

He winked at her provocatively. 'You.'

'Just for once can you be serious?'

'I am. Don't you fancy me?'

'Too much,' she sighed. 'That's the problem. I'm forever telling myself this is too good to last. Good things don't happen to me. That's why I feared for your life yesterday. Whatever happens in the future, I want you to know I love you more than you could ever know Richard. I'll be honest; I didn't intend to fall in love with you and did my utmost to avoid it, in the mistaken belief that by treating you solely as a friend you'd get the message and tire of me. One day however, I awoke to the reality that my feeling of friendship was something totally different, something much deeper. The only person I'd succeeded in fooling was me. Does that answer your question satisfactorily?'

He looked at her with misty eyes. 'Yes darling, it does and trust me; nothing will stand in our way.'

They ambled back to the hotel, each with a warm glow.

Emma was delighted to hear from her. 'I knew you were both alright. I phoned David at the office this morning. Imagine such a tragedy happening the day after you got there. It's never been off the TV here. How's Richard's arm? I suppose that put paid to all your intended shenanigans,' she cackled raucously, pausing in anticipation of an answer.

Paige ignored Emma's intrusive question. 'How *was* David?'

'Very polite would you believe but then he didn't know who I was. I just said I was a friend. He said his dad had called him and that you were stranded in New York. Do you know when you'll be back?'

'Sunday, unless anything else goes wrong. Would you do me a big favour? I'm on duty at the Hospice on Saturday so would you call them please and say I can't make it?'

'Leave it to me. I'll sort it. Apart from the horror, are you having a good time?'

'Brilliant,' she gushed. 'This is an amazing place. We've done so many things. We're both shattered.'

It was worth another attempt. 'Shattered because of your bedroom antics or shattered because of your sight-seeing?'

Determined to ignore the inquisition she replied, 'There's so much to take in. Everywhere you look, it's absolutely unbelievable. I'll fill you in with all the details once we're home.'

In a petulant tone she grunted, 'Fine, don't tell me then though it's pretty obvious. If there was nothing to tell you'd be only too quick to deny it.'

Richard walked in the room as she said, 'If there was anything to tell, not that there is, you'd be the *last* to find out. You're not fit to know *anything* so let's leave it at that shall we?'

'Fair enough. I won't tell *you* anything in future.'

She hooted with laughter. 'Like I believe that, the way *you* run off at the mouth.'

Richard was perturbed when she hung up. 'What was all that about? Were you arguing with Emma?'

Paige giggled. 'Not really. She was having a strop because I wouldn't tell her if your broken arm had affected your sexual aptitude.'

'Oh right,' he muttered, wishing he hadn't asked. 'Do you always discuss everything with Emma?'

'*No*. I told her *nothing*. You heard what I said.'

Taking her in his arms he quizzed flippantly, 'So *has* my broken arm affected my sexual aptitude?'

She giggled once more. 'Ask me again when your plaster cast comes off. I'll be better placed to make an informed decision then. I have to say though, it certainly hasn't affected your sexual *appetite*.'

'Like I said earlier, I've not heard you complain.'

'Shut up. So, how was David?'

'He's fine. He appeared to have everything under control and a few more jobs have come in. He said there was no need to rush back.'

'So does that mean we can stay another week?'

He stroked her hair. 'Would you like that?'

Sighing happily, she buried her head in his chest. 'I love every minute of the time we spend together.'

'I do too,' he told her softly. 'How about we walk to Times Square and grab something to eat? I think you'd like it down there at night. Incidentally, have you called Laura yet about an evening out?'

'No I haven't, but either Friday or Saturday was okay for them. Do you have a preference?'

He shook his head. 'As long as it isn't tomorrow. I have something planned I'm sure you'll enjoy.'

At that she pricked up her ears. 'What's that?'

'A night on Broadway. You can't visit New York without seeing a Broadway show so I've got us two tickets for Phantom of the Opera.'

'*Richard*...I *love* that music. It's fantastic and you are too. You're *so* good to me.' She pranced around the room like an excited school-girl. 'I can't wait. I'll go mad before tomorrow. I've never been inside a theatre in my entire life. I bet I don't sleep a wink tonight.'

With a droll expression he commented, 'Gawd, is that another night you're keeping me awake? I'll be leaving the hotel in a wooden box at this rate.'

'Shut up you clown,' she tittered.

Paige couldn't sit still. Her eyes were everywhere, trying to take everything in.

Hand in hand they had walked the short distance from the hotel to the Majestic Theatre. Once inside they had climbed a flight of stairs where they were shown to their seats on the front row of the circle. Only then did Paige appreciate the grandeur as she looked around.

'Look at all those musicians in the orchestra,' she said, nudging Richard. 'And doesn't it smell nice in here? Look at the beautiful lights and the décor. I'm struggling to find a suitable adjective to describe it.'

'Majestic?' he prompted on a laugh.

'Perfect. They certainly chose a fitting name.'

Shortly afterwards, the lights grew dim and a loud blast of music shook the theatre. Paige was on the edge of her seat when the curtains parted, scrutinising every minute detail as Richard took hold of her hand. She glanced at him fleetingly, a broad smile illuminating her face. The waiting was finally over. From that moment until the interval, her eyes were riveted to the stage, her hand clasped tightly in his, watching a performance she would never forget.

'Right, if we look slippy we can get a drink now,' Richard said jumping up.

‘Will we get back in time?’ she asked anxiously.

He nodded. ‘They ring a bell when it’s time for us to return to our seats. Help me with the drinks.’

She carried the drinks outside where many people were standing on the sidewalk. ‘So what’s your first impression of Broadway? Impressed?’

‘Fantastic. I can’t wait to tell Emma abou everything. It’s all so...so *resplendent*. To think I almost didn’t come to New York.’

He looked puzzled. ‘What do you mean?’

She giggled. ‘It was Emma. She said *this* was the place where I’d end up in bed with you, so I lost my rag and told her I *would* come if only to prove her wrong.’

‘But Emma wasn’t wrong; she was right. It’s little wonder men never understand women. So what will you say when you get home? Will you apologise?’

She laughed. ‘Are you for real? I’ll say nothing at all. I wouldn’t give her the satisfaction. It’s none of her business.’

‘You mean you’d lie to her?’

Without hesitation she answered, ‘Yes if I had to. Right, if David asks you, will you speak the truth or lie to him? Didn’t we agree to keep it to ourselves?’

He had to admit she had a point. ‘Okay, I’d lie as well I suppose if I were put on the spot. Come on, I think the bell’s gone. Everyone’s making a move.’

He smiled to himself. Women were such complex creatures. Nothing was ever straightforward.

Paige was equally spellbound by the second half, and at the end of the production, when the audience leapt to their feet to join the theatre cast in a display of solidarity as they sang, 'God Bless America', she wept openly for every victim of the terrorist attack.

Richard and Brad were in deep discussion about the aftermath of the attack on the World Trade Centre. The lucky ones who had survived had no jobs to go to until new premises could be found Brad told him so they could do nothing but await a communiqué with advice and there was no indication as to when that would be received.

Out of earshot, Laura quizzed, 'Is Richard really your boss Paige?'

'He owns the company. I actually work for David his son; he's a Director. I'm David's PA. Richard's a widower. His wife died five years ago so I'm not stealing another woman's husband. It's complicated because neither of us wants his son to find out. Our *intimate* relationship only began here in New York. It was never my intent for that to happen although I guess Richard had other ideas. I'm not complaining though because I love him very much. Between you and I Laura, I've loved him for some time but I was too stupid to admit it to myself. He's a great bloke with a big heart.'

'So you think David would have issues about the two of you being together?'

'We both *know* he would. He can be very hostile. When David's mother was killed in a car crash, he was driving and he suffered a serious head injury. He was in hospital for several weeks and Richard's convinced there's still an underlying problem that causes his mood swings but he won't seek medical help. He's really stubborn and that's very worrying for Richard.'

'I can well imagine. What a mess.'

'Who's ready for another drink?' Richard asked.

'I'm ready for something to eat,' Laura groaned. 'I keep seeing plates of food flashing past my eyes but they always end up on other tables.'

Paige smiled. 'It's worth the wait, you'll see and everything's freshly cooked and hot. We waited for twenty minutes last time so it should be here soon.'

She had barely uttered the words when the server appeared, apologising profusely for the delay but as the four pairs of ravenous eyes scoured their plates, their wait was quickly forgotten. 'This is a veritable feast,' Brad commented with a broad smile. 'I can't believe I didn't know about this place.'

'I've been coming here for years,' Richard made known. 'I've yet to be disappointed. To friendship,' he stated, lifting his glass and the others echoed his words.

'How far do you live from here?' asked Paige.

'Just a couple of blocks...walking distance,' Laura said. 'It's an apartment overlooking Central Park.'

'Sounds lovely,' she sighed enviously, imagining the view. 'So what kind of work do you do Laura?'

'I'm a dentist but I'm not working at the moment. We want to start a family so I'm trying to adhere to a strict routine of calm though I must say these last few days haven't helped. What time are you flying to UK tomorrow?'

'Around nine. I've done our packing but I seem to have a lot more to take back than I came with.'

On a laugh Laura nodded. 'That's New York for you. No one can resist our elegant shops and I hear they're cheaper than London shops. Is that right?'

'Much cheaper. Haven't you been to London?'

'No, I think we're coming to England early next year. If we get the opportunity it'd be great to meet up again.'

Paige jotted down her surname, telephone number and home address and Laura did likewise. 'I'm glad I met you Laura albeit in such tragic circumstances. We must be thankful we were lucky though unlike so many others.'

Sighing deeply, Laura nodded. 'Several of Brad's friends and acquaintances have still to be found and every day they remain missing makes it less likely they'll be found alive but in these troubled times we have to learn to embrace the concept of change. The world has become a different world of late...an evil world. We've no idea what will happen next, where the next disaster will occur and how many innocent victims will perish next time but the one sure thing is that something else like this or even worse maybe *will* take place again and soon.'

Paige shuddered. 'I'm not looking forward to the flight tomorrow after what happened on Tuesday.'

'I think that's the least of your worries,' she told her reassuringly. 'Security will be stepped up at all airports now.'

Although Paige smiled she remained unconvinced and jittery, for no matter how thorough the security proved to be she wouldn't feel safe until she arrived home on British soil once more with Richard.

5

With a broad beaming smile David hurried towards his father and Paige as they appeared in the arrivals hall. He hugged Richard warmly before turning his attention to Paige. 'Thank you for taking care of my dad. It must have been horrendous to go through all that…such a tragedy on your first visit.'

'It wasn't all bad,' Richard said with an evocative wink and smile when his son bent down to pick up the bags.

'Pack it in,' she mouthed with a guilty expression, giggling as Richard took hold of her hand.

She strode ahead and caught up with David. 'We saw some amazing sights, albeit the trip was marred by the appalling terrorist attack that overshadowed everything. No doubt you saw most of it on TV?'

'It's never been off the telly because there's never been anything like it before. It's hard to believe that Dad escaped with just a broken arm.'

With a smirk Richard remarked, 'I'm not ready to let *you* take over yet. That must be what drove me to get out quick. Is everything okay at the factory?'

'Of course,' he said with irony. 'I doubt anybody even noticed you weren't there.'

'Good, as I'm somewhat restricted with a broken arm. It means I'm going to need a bit of help. God,

I'm knackered. I won't need rocking tonight. What about you Paige? You don't have to rush in early in the morning. Just take your time and come in when you're ready. Today's been a long and tiring day.'

'Thanks. I'll see how I feel when I wake up.'

When they reached Paige's house, David jumped out of the car. 'I'll fetch your bags in Paige.'

'Not even a goodnight kiss,' sighed Richard out of earshot of David. 'Sleep well darling. I'm going to miss you so much.'

'Same here. I've had an amazing time. Thank you for everything Richard.'

There were three messages from Emma on Paige's answer-phone, all begging her to make contact the minute she arrived home and when Paige called her she burst into tears. 'I've been so worried about you in case something happened on your flight. Weren't you scared about getting on another plane?'

'I was but the security was rigorous at the airport. I was relieved though when we touched down.'

'I bet. Poor you…your first holiday abroad and it was totally ruined. I'm so sorry.'

Paige was quick to correct her. 'Listen to me; I've had a fabulous time. New York's an amazing city. I was scared until I knew Richard was okay and then we made the most of our time there.'

'Oh wow, are you saying he came on to you?'

'For heaven's sake, is *that* all you think about?'

Emma chuckled. 'I like to be kept in the loop.'

'Sorry to disappoint you then Emma. There *is* no loop. As I've told you many times, he's a real gent.'

Disheartened she said, ‘So nothing happened?’

Paige hated lying to Emma but it was a necessary evil. ‘Nothing, so can we drop it now please? Buy a magazine if you want to read smut.’

‘I’m only interested in *your* smut. I really thought it’d have happened in New York and I’m generally spot on with my predictions,’ she grunted tetchily. ‘He’s obviously not up to it...his age I suppose.’

She allowed the remark to pass without response and changing topic asked Emma if she’d contacted the Hospice about her absence on Saturday.

‘I did and they were all concerned for you.’

‘Yes, they’re a lovely crowd. I’m going to unpack now. I just wanted you to know I was home. I’ll tell you more about the holiday later in the week.’

Paige flopped down in an armchair, Richard very much in her thoughts. She was missing him already after spending almost a week in his company, night and day. She couldn’t begin to imagine what would happen now they were home and there were bound to be whispered comments at work about the two of them having been together. No doubt Sue would be running a *book* about that now, taking bets from the workforce, not that Paige was concerned as long as David didn’t get wind of it. That would be all.

Her telephone rang again and it was Richard. ‘I’m missing you already. I’ve just come up to bed with a hot drink and realised for the first time what a big, cold, empty bed it is. I wish you could be here with me now Paige. How about we go somewhere at the weekend and stay overnight? We could go to York again. I know you liked it there, or to Chester. What do you think? You'll have to drive my car though. I can't drive with my arm in a cast.'

She was overjoyed. 'I'd really like that Richard if you feel David won't kick off about it.'

'Don't fret about David. I'll work it into the conversation somehow and make it okay. I tried calling when I got home but your line was busy. Were you talking to Emma?'

She giggled. 'Yes, I was getting the third degree.'

That amused him. 'I did wonder. So what did you say? Did you tell her about us?'

'*No,* I promised I wouldn't and I didn't. I lied.'

She heard a raucous laugh. 'What is it about girls that they have to know all the minutiae?'

'Er...and blokes don't? You lot are worse than us and don't deny it. With blokes if there's nothing to tell they'll concoct something melodramatic simply to keep face with their mates. *Locker room talk* it's called isn't it?'

'You're probably right,' he sniggered.

'I *know* I am. Before I forget, how's your arm?'

'It aches a bit but I doubt it'll keep me awake.'

'You mean like I allegedly do?'

He sighed. 'I wish you were here now keeping me awake. I've got used to having you around.'

'I know. It's the same for me. Try and get a good night's sleep and I'll see you tomorrow.'

She heard another deep sigh before he murmured, 'I can't wait. Goodnight darling. I love you.'

'What's wrong with the bloke?' Andy said. 'Fancy being in New York with a ravishing young creature like Paige and not capitalising on the situation. If I were in Richard's shoes you'd not find me hovering in the shadows. The man must be off his rocker.'

She poked him hard in the ribs. 'Is that right? So how long have you had your beady eye on Paige?'

There was a short pause followed by his stuttered apology, 'I didn't mean *me,* Emma. I was referring to *Richard.* He had every opportunity to...well...'

'Shut up Andy,' she interrupted. 'You're all alike. Men never think about anything else.'

On a laugh he rejoined, 'Well, Richard obviously does and *you* can't talk...I heard *you* quizzing her.'

Andy was right; Emma couldn't argue about that. Grabbing her magazine she began to turn the pages as he smiled superciliously. It was extremely rare to get one over on Emma but on this occasion she was totally lost for words. That was one to chalk up.

It was turned ten o'clock the next day before Paige caught sight of Richard and her heart missed a beat when he wandered into her office smiling lovingly. He leaned against the closed door, beckoning her to come to him and when she did, he kissed her with passion. 'You have no idea how much I've missed you. I've wanted to do that since last night.'

She nuzzled his neck. 'I've missed you too but we must be careful or tongues will start wagging.'

He kissed her again. 'We're doing nothing wrong. I was thinking, how about we go out for lunch? It'd give us a bit of time alone.'

With a glint in her eye she nodded. 'Yes, I'd like that. Meet me near the Post Office at five-past-one.'

Over the following weeks Richard and Paige saw each other whenever possible. Occasionally Paige would invite Richard and David to her house for an evening meal. That was meant to pave the way for when the time was right to make their relationship common knowledge though they felt that would be in the distant future.

David's relationship with his father continued to thrive following Richard's return from New York, presumably due to a combination of factors, namely his relief that his father had miraculously survived the terrorist attack and was, as a result of his injury, dependent on David whilst hampered by the plaster cast on his arm.

It had been very busy at the factory. Several new commissions had recently materialized, initiated by factory closures in the vicinity, and whilst Richard was delighted to have acquired the work he derived little satisfaction from the fact his good fortune had resulted from somebody else's adversity. A fair and principled man, he felt compassion for those whose businesses had been forced into administration after many years of success and even more sympathy for the workers at this inopportune time with Christmas fast approaching. When hearing of another factory closure he was frequently heard to comment, 'There but for the grace of God go I,' followed by a deep and meaningful sigh.

Paige's life had not been uneventful either. It had been her intent for some time to redecorate her late mother's bedroom and she had already finished the preparatory work and all the paintwork.

She had given Andy a key so he could call round to hang the wallpaper when he had some free time.

Paige was rarely around at the weekend. She had changed her rota at the Hospice to spend time with Richard. David was aware his father enjoyed spending time with her and although he hadn't been made aware of anything other than a platonic friendship, he believed it was rather more than that.

No doubt his father would tell him at some point.

David's former aggression had disappeared over recent weeks. His offensive jibes had been replaced by complimentary remarks and humorous quips. He worked as part of the team and he had regained the respect of the entire workforce, but on occasions he was the cause of concern to both Richard and Paige when he appeared to slip into a trance or daydream, oblivious of anyone's presence. It had to be said he remained in control of his duties however.

Whilst Richard preferred to believe that the recent change in nature resulted from the renewed camaraderie between father and son, Paige was far from convinced and her intuition was soon to be proved correct.

It was at the end of November when matters came to a head. It had been a particularly busy day on the shop floor where a huge consignment of parts was being despatched by road. Everybody was involved at the loading bay including Richard and David and as one of the components was swung into position to be loaded, it caught one man on the shoulder. He was shunted into another who in turn bumped into David, pushing him against a stanchion. Thankfully no one was injured, in fact they all laughed about it and the loading continued.

Following the departure of the vehicles, everyone went back to his place of duty following a job well done and David returned to his office.

It was late afternoon when Paige took in David's mail for his signature. She made a comment about the weather, how sunny it had been for November and when he didn't reply she looked at him closely and was shocked.

There was stark deathly pallor about his face and he was staring ahead blankly as if in a trance. Paige was concerned and walked round his desk.

She touched his arm. 'David, do you feel okay?' When he didn't reply she prodded him. '*David!* Are you ill? Answer me.'

He began to shake as if he was having a seizure or fit and as she tried to control the movement, he fell to the floor still shaking.

She grabbed the telephone, dialled 999, requested an ambulance and called Mandy on reception. 'Get in here quick. I'm in David's room. Talk to no one.'

No sooner had Paige hung up than the door was flung open and Mandy dashed in. She was shocked to see David lying prostrate on the floor. 'What on earth's happened?' she cried.

'He's had a fit and fallen off his chair. Help me to get him into the recovery position and then find his father. I've called for an ambulance.'

She was scared. 'But I don't know what to do.'

'I do. We need to keep his airway open. Pull him over onto his side and help me bend this leg. Thank

God he's still breathing. I can manage myself now. Find Richard. Don't alarm him and say nothing in front of the others. We don't want the entire work-force in here.'

As Mandy disappeared to look for Richard, Paige spoke quietly to David, stroking his hair as she tried to keep him calm and allay any fears. 'You're doing fine. Try not to move. Help's on its way.'

His eyelids flickered as he tried to open his eyes. Her words were soothing and he tried to speak.

'Just lie quietly. Don't talk. We'll soon have you well again.'

Sensing there was a problem when summoned to David's room, Richard thrust open the office door and was devastated to find his son semi-conscious on the floor. He immediately dropped to his knees beside him.

'Don't move him. He has blood oozing from his left ear. I've called for an ambulance. He had a kind of seizure when I brought his letters in to sign.'

'What happened? Were you arguing?'

Defensively she countered, '*No!* He looked to be in a trance when I walked in and then he started to shake. We never spoke at all beforehand.'

'Sorry Paige. I didn't mean to imply...'

'Then *don't*.'

'Come to think of it, there was an incident earlier on the loading bay. He fell against a stanchion.'

David tried to move again and Paige took hold of his hand. 'You haven't to move David...not till the paramedics get here. They'll tell you what you can and can't do. Stay calm. Your dad's here now.'

Richard fought back tears as he clung to his son's hand. 'You're going to be fine son. Don't worry.'

'Go and check out the ambulance Mandy,' Paige said. 'I'm sure it'll be here now. Fetch them straight in and say nothing to anyone else.'

As Mandy hurried towards the reception area, two paramedics appeared at the main entrance.

'Follow me please,' she said, leading the way.

Paige outlined what she had seen and done, while Richard gave a brief account of the earlier accident.

'Is there previous history of serious head trauma, any accidents you're aware of?' asked one of them.

Paige looked to Richard to answer that question.

'Yes, he was in a bad car crash several years ago and was hospitalised for seven or eight weeks with a severe head injury. I don't think he ever recovered from that. He's been temperamental and aggressive ever since. By comparison, that incident today was negligible. He made no reference to it afterwards.'

The paramedics lifted him onto a stretcher saying a thorough examination would be carried out at the hospital.

Richard went for his coat and car key so he could follow the ambulance.

'Call me at home later. Good luck,' said Paige.

It was after nine o'clock when Richard turned up at her house.

'I've been on tenterhooks since you left,' she told him. 'How's David?'

'Not good,' he reported. 'He has to have surgery. They're monitoring him at the moment but should he deteriorate they'll take him to theatre right away.

He's had a brain haemorrhage. He went for a scan a few hours ago that identified a foreign object, either a shard of glass or sliver of metal. The Consultant said it could have been circulating round his system since the car accident until it eventually got caught in an artery and then a blow to the head could have caused it to perforate the artery wall. That would be the most likely scenario he told me but they'll know more once they operate.'

Paige sighed deeply. 'Poor David. I wonder if that was the cause of the aggression. Did he complain of headaches following the car crash?'

'He never complained at all. If he did have headaches, he kept it quiet. Perhaps he was afraid he'd need further surgery. You couldn't blame him if he was scared of that. I wouldn't relish the thought of someone drilling holes in my head.'

Paige shuddered at the thought. 'I agree but now he's in hospital he'll receive proper care. Have you eaten? Can I get you something?'

'Please...a coffee and a cuddle. I'm very weepy at the moment. Lots of memories keep flooding back, memories of all the times I've yelled at David and criticised him and now it seems it wasn't his fault.'

She wrapped her arms around him. 'Don't blame yourself. You did what anyone would have done. I said my piece too more times than I care to recall. Let's just look to the future, to a swift and complete recovery. Can you do that?'

Richard nodded. 'I can but try. God, I feel utterly depressed. I'm so glad you're here for me Paige. If anything were to happen to David I'd...' Unable to finish his sentence his bottom lip started to quiver and he broke down and sobbed.

Holding him tight Paige murmured, 'Everything's going to be alright. Have faith in the professionals. David's otherwise fit and healthy so everything's in his favour He'll come through this. I know he will.'

He wanted to believe Paige's words. Racked with guilt he vowed there and then to be a better father if only he could be given one more chance.

David was taken to theatre the next morning and it turned out to be a lengthy and complex procedure.

Grim-faced, the Consultant explained that David had suffered a subdural haematoma as a result of a bleed, probably caused by bone fragments he found embedded in a blood vessel. He went on to say the procedure appeared to have gone very well and as a precautionary measure to control the pressure in his brain David would remain in an induced coma for a few days.

There was just one question on Richard's lips. 'Is he going to make a complete recovery?'

'It's too early to say I'm afraid. There can never be guarantees with this type of surgery,' he voiced compassionately. 'We have to see how he responds. He'll remain on Intensive Care for now where he'll be closely monitored. We'll know more in a couple of days. In the meantime, try not to worry.'

'*Try not to worry,*' the Consultant had said. Those words resounded in Richard's head like a clanging bell. David had suffered a brain haemorrhage; he'd undergone surgery and was in a coma. Richard was frantic with worry. Would David wake up? Would the same thing happen again in the future? Would he be permanently brain damaged when he regained consciousness and would he always need care?

That was just a sample of the questions for which he needed answers, but with no one there to provide the answers he could do nothing but wait anxiously, hope and pray.

Richard had telephoned his mother following his conversation with the Consultant and she had been equally distraught. She had insisted on accompanying him to the hospital later to see her grandson.

He had also relayed the information to Paige who was just as keen to see David. Perhaps this was an opportune time for Paige to finally meet his mother. He couldn't continue to defer the inevitable and he knew his mother would be delighted to learn he had finally met someone. She had badgered him for the past two years to get a life outside the factory.

His major concern however was her exuberance. Though his mother meant well, he would hate Paige to feel pressured were she to have them heading up the aisle together at their first meeting. It was early days in their relationship and the last thing Richard wanted was to scare Paige away. The timing was of paramount importance because he needed her now more than he'd ever needed anyone or anything in his entire life. Paige had already made it clear that she wasn't looking for long-term commitment, that she wanted to live for today and a tactless comment from his mother, albeit innocent, could drive Paige away. He had to talk to his mother. It was the only course of action for damage limitation. In the nicest possible way he had to try to persuade her to watch her tongue. He would tell Paige too that she mustn't be offended by anything his mother might say.

At the prospect of meeting his mother, Paige felt apprehensive. Would she think her suitable? In her mind's eye she had an image of Richard's late wife, a genteel kind of lady, capable and elegant and who could wine, dine and entertain affluent guests while feeling self-assured in anyone's presence but what perception had *she* of such a way of life? Although caring of others and devoted to Richard, she lacked those finer qualities of breeding as the illegitimate daughter of a single mother.

She stared at her reflection in the mirror until her tears blurred her vision but she had seen enough of the drab cotton print dress to realise it was a far cry from a stylish outfit likely to impress a refined lady like Mrs Cavendish.

Fingering through the rail of her wardrobe Paige sighed heavily. Richard would be arriving soon and she still wasn't ready. Finally she settled on a blue and white suit she'd bought from a charity shop the previous spring when a friend from her schooldays was getting married. Emma had helped her choose it and the admiring glances from many of the guests hadn't gone unnoticed. Yes, that would do nicely.

Rummaging through her wardrobe she found her shoes and bag and after applying her make-up she ran downstairs as Richard was ringing her doorbell.

His face was alight with a glowing smile when he saw her. 'Wow, you look amazing. New outfit?'

Paige was delighted. Richard clearly approved of her choice. 'I bought it for a friend's wedding last year. I thought I'd better make an effort as I was to meet your mother. Will she approve do you think?'

He took her in his arms. 'Don't worry about my mother; she'll adore you. She's a sweet lady who's dying to meet you. I have to tell you though, she's rather capricious. She has a terrible habit of speaking out before giving thought to what she's about to say, so, if she says anything that embarrasses you, trust me, there's no malicious intent whatsoever.'

Paige felt more at ease to hear that. 'Is there any further news on David?'

'He's about the same so I suppose it's good news. Am I allowed a kiss or will it spoil your make-up?'

'I'll be disappointed if you don't.'

'You're the best thing that's happened to me in a long time. Everything will be perfect if David fully recovers. I love and need you so much Paige.'

She smiled contentedly and hugged him. 'I love you just as much. Come on, it's time for me to meet your mum and then we can all visit David.'

Surprisingly, it wasn't a large ostentatious house as Paige had imagined. Secreted at the top of a rural cul-de-sac it was a neat early post-war bungalow set in a delightful landscaped garden. Although winter, when all the flowers had long since died, there was an abundance of colour from the winter flowering shrubs, planted throughout the borders.

'Lovely garden,' Paige said stepping from the car.

Richard nodded in accord. 'Mum has an excellent gardener. He's been with her for years and when he finally retired he continued to do it after Dad died. I suppose it supplements his pension and it certainly keeps him fit and active. The back garden's much bigger, enormous in fact as they were in those days. Ask her to show you round; she'd be delighted.'

'*Richard,* you don't walk in someone's home and ask to be shown round. That's *very* rude.'

'Why? I'd show you round mine if you asked.'

With raised eyebrows she said, 'Would you now? It might surprise you to know I have no idea where you live, so it might be a good idea to tell me since it appears to be the world's best kept secret.'

He looked at her aghast. 'It's not a secret darling. I suppose it's never come up in conversation. I just assumed you knew. The only reason I haven't taken you there is because David's always around. I'm so sorry and I'll rectify it later. We can go to my place after I've dropped Mum back home. Alright?'

At that point Richard's mother appeared, beaming broadly. 'It's Paige isn't it? What an unusual name. Did your mother read a lot?' she asked quizzically.

Richard howled with laughter when Paige looked at her mystified.

'She did but it's nothing to do with my name; she had a friend called Paige.'

'Mum's name is Eleanor,' Richard interposed on a grin. 'She prefers to be called *Nellie* though.'

'I do *not*,' she protested, annoyance resounding in her tone. 'I absolutely detest that name. You're not too big for a clip round the ear you know.'

Paige shrieked with laughter at the thought. 'Why is it that certain names are regarded as *nice* whilst others aren't? After all, it's merely a word, a sound that escapes your lips. That's always puzzled me.'

'It's all a question of association my dear. I once knew a woman called Nellie.' She chuckled before continuing, 'I was only a young lass then and Nellie was a down-trodden type, perpetually pregnant who already had half a dozen kids before she moved to our neighbourhood. She'd spend every day washing and pegging her laundry on the line that ran across the entry but everything still looked grimy after it'd been washed. The kids always looked grubby; she looked grubby too and their house was the dreariest place. She was never seen without a headscarf, tied tight and knotted at the front like a turban. Locks of greasy straggly hair forever fell across her face; she wore a crossover pinafore that had seen better days and clogs over her thick, matted, grey socks.'

'Tell her the best bit,' Richard said nudging her.

Looking puzzled Eleanor asked, 'What's that?'

He spluttered with laughter before revealing, *'She skenned lahk a basket o' whelks too.'*

'Oh yes,' she chortled. 'I'd forgotten about that. I bet Paige has never heard that expression.'

'Oh but I have,' she chuckled. 'My grandad was always spouting colourful expressions like that. He would have me in stitches; he was a real character.'

'I think you should know Mum that Paige is very knowledgeable, well-read and famous,' he declared proudly. 'She writes stories for magazines.'

Eleanor was impressed. 'Do you my dear? That's wonderful. We'll discuss that in more detail when we've the time. So, tell me, how old are you?'

'I'm twenty-eight.'

She nodded. 'I thought you looked young. When Richard told me earlier today that he'd met someone, I hoped it'd be someone young so that maybe, before too long, I might hear the patter of tiny feet again. I do so love having children around.'

As Paige recovered from Eleanor's shock remark, Richard was quick to intervene. '*Mother!* Paige and I have only known each other for a few months and as for pattering feet, unless you have rats or birds in your rafters you're going to be bitterly disappointed because it ain't going to happen at my age. I've had more than enough truck with David.' He glanced at his watch. 'Right, it's time we were heading off to the hospital. Ready?'

He snatched his keys off the hall stand and rushed through the door without another word.

The two women looked at each other with raised eyebrows before following Richard to the car.

Eleanor held her tongue throughout their journey, conscious she had spoken out of turn. As for Paige, she was near to tears as she recalled Richard's cruel words. In moments of former contemplation, when she had dared glance into the future, she had visualised a panorama of happy family life, interspersed with children's laughter. Sadly, it now appeared her reverie would never become reality though this was neither the time nor place to raise her concerns with Richard.

'I'll see you two shortly in Intensive Care. I want to slip in the office first for an update,' Richard said.

Eleanor couldn't wait to apologise once they were alone. 'Me and my runaway tongue. I'm very sorry Paige. I didn't mean any harm when I said....'

'It's alright Eleanor. Don't worry. At least I know how he feels now. His remark was as big a shock to me as it was to you. I'd no idea he felt that way.'

'He'll come round in time I'm sure. All the upset with David is weighing heavily on him. First he lost his wife; he almost lost his son too and when things are beginning to improve, there's another problem. He's a good man but I'm sure you know that and he really loves you. I know my son. When he called to tell me about you earlier, he couldn't stand still. He paced round the room till I felt dizzy. He has a great deal on his mind at the moment, the poor lamb. Be patient and I'm sure everything will work out fine. He relies on you for support so keep reassuring him that David will recover. I assume you and Richard sleep together. I know that's the norm nowadays.'

Paige was shocked once again but Eleanor merely tittered at her facial expression. 'There I go again; I always manage to put my big foot in it don't I?'

'Eleanor, you're such a lovely lady that I couldn't take offence at anything you said. Yes, we do sleep together but only occasionally as David's generally around and we don't want him to find out. David's my boss as you probably know and he's definitely not the easiest of people to work for so that's why we've kept our relationship quiet.'

'I understand. Your secret's safe with me. Despite my loquacious tongue I'm good at keeping secrets and I hope we can be the best of friends.'

She smiled at the petite smartly dressed lady who looked at her optimistically. 'I was about to say the selfsame thing. Yes, we'll always be good friends.'

As Eleanor squeezed Paige's hand affectionately, Richard returned looking less harassed.

'There's still no change in David's condition,' he reported. 'That's a positive sign I'm told, so we can see him now.'

As they approached his bed, David appeared to be sleeping peacefully and there was a serene smile on his face. Although it was distressing to see his head so heavily bandaged, it was a relief to note that his breathing was quiet and regular.

'He's not in any pain,' the nurse made known.

Eleanor leaned over and kissed him on the cheek. Wiping tears from her eyes she said, 'Life can be so cruel...as if the poor boy hasn't suffered enough.'

Richard moved two chairs into position and stood at the opposite side of the bed staring at his son.

Paige took hold of David's hand. 'I know you'll pull through and we're all here for you David.' She looked up at Richard who was red-eyed and tearful. 'Talk to him Richard. Say something reassuring.'

Richard placed a hand on his son's shoulder. 'It'll be good to have you back son and whatever it takes we'll get you right, don't worry.'

Paige walked towards him and held him. 'You're not alone Richard. You'll have my full support.'

They left shortly afterwards and Richard, in deep thought, barely spoke throughout the journey.

As Paige walked Eleanor to the door and saw her safely inside, Richard turned the car round.

When she returned he told her he was taking her straight home as he'd decided to continue to his in-laws' house to give them an update on David.

They had planned to visit David the next day and as Albert Thomas was not a healthy man, if Richard could prime him first, it could save much heartache. Albert idolised David and was totally devastated by his further admission to hospital.

Paige was thankful she was going straight home. Following Richard's outburst, she had given serious thought to her future needs as the same distressing question tormented her. Would a childless life with Richard satisfy her needs and be preferable to a life with someone else who wanted children as much as she did?

She didn't think it unreasonable to want children of her own, of her own flesh and blood particularly when she no longer had any known living relatives. Granted, she might have a living father. God forbid, it could be Jake Allcock; it certainly wasn't beyond the realms of possibility, but there was definitely no likelihood of a happy family reunion there.

Richard's insensitive words had hurt Paige deeply and the heart-rending question she'd been unable to rid from her mind still remained unanswered as she cried herself to sleep that night. It turned out to be a disturbed and erratic sleep however as she awoke at frequent intervals feeling afraid, nauseous and very much alone.

At seven o'clock Paige went downstairs for a hot drink. She had a blinding headache, had barely had any sleep and she was due at the Hospice at ten.

Climbing the stairs on her way back to her room she likened to climbing Everest. She felt exhausted. Before she reached the top the nausea had increased tenfold and she just made it to the bathroom before she was violently sick three times. Making her way along the landing she paused when the water in the cistern stopped filling. She was sure she'd heard a noise downstairs. Suddenly there was another. She froze, fear emanating from every fibre of her being as she heard footsteps on the stairs. She hadn't the strength to fight and although attempting to scream, no sound escaped her lips. Fumbling her way to her bedroom she peered through the crack at the side of the door. Her heart was pounding so loudly she felt the intruder would hear it too. Suddenly there was a deafening crash followed by a piercing cry, 'Stupid sod, my blasted foot!' in a voice she recognised. It was Andy who had let himself in to hang the wall-paper in the upstairs bedroom.

Half laughing half crying and with a sudden burst of energy she ran out onto the landing scaring Andy rigid. He bellowed at the top of his voice, *'Christ,* I wasn't expecting to see you Paige. I thought you'd gone away for the weekend. Sorry if I scared you.'

They laughed about it later over a mug of tea.

Andy was still working when Paige returned from the Hospice mid-afternoon. 'Richard rang not long after you left. He said he'd call you back later and I found this letter when I was humping that flaming dresser away from the wall. It must weigh a ton.'

'I know. I didn't even attempt to shift it so there's still some skirting to paint behind there.'

'It's done. There were no cracks to fill in the wall so I papered it and gave the skirting a quick undercoat. Later I glossed it too. I didn't want you daubing my newly papered wall,' he laughed.

Slanting her gaze in his direction she snarled, 'I'll have you know I'm not a cowboy. I'm meticulous like Grandad used to be. I do *not* daub.'

He grinned. 'No, I must agree; you *are* careful.'

'Praise indeed from a true professional,' she said. 'So where did you find this letter?'

'I had to take the drawers out of the dresser. That was jammed in the back of one of the drawers. I bet it's been there for ages because the envelope looks old. It's very discoloured.'

Scrutinising the faded writing on the front of the envelope, Paige made out her name, written in her mother's hand.

She opted to read it downstairs for whenever she came across photos and other items of memorabilia she usually ended up in tears.

Paige removed the neatly written pages from the envelope that had lain undetected in that drawer for almost five years and read her mother's words.

'Darling Paige, I'm sorry I've been a burden for so long and I'm grateful for the help you've given me. My life is drawing to a close now and there are things I need to explain while I still can. You must believe, hard as it might seem, that both I and your grandad acted with good intent when we decided to withhold the identity of your father from you.

Things were so different back then. Your grandad was a very strict man and when he discovered that I was pregnant, I was ordered to get a termination at once. Your father was married, you see.

Naturally I refused. I threatened to run away with him as I wanted to keep you. We argued a lot and in the end Dad agreed the pregnancy could continue if I agreed to give you up for adoption.

I had to agree or I'd have lost you there and then and I prayed Dad would reconsider once you were born and he did. It was stipulated though that your father's name must never be mentioned again and it never was. I also promised I would never reveal the identity of your father but you're old enough now to make your own decisions. You have a right to know what I can tell you though it isn't much.

We'd met at the hospital where I worked and yes, he was married but they weren't happy. When I told him I was pregnant, he wanted me to go away with him. He'd get a divorce so we could get married, he said. He applied for a post in the Midlands where we could make a new start. It all sounded fantastic, romantic and exhilarating but when I told Dad he went mad, stating any man who'd treat his wife that way would likely do the same thing again.

I didn't know what to do. I was afraid. If I turned my back on Mum and Dad and things didn't work out I'd be all alone with a child, though deep down I knew I loved him far too much to let him go alone.

Things happened very quickly after that. I'd had a few days off work with tonsillitis and only found out later that your father turned up here to ask where I was. Your grandad answered the door and I heard there'd been a quarrel and when I returned to work your father had already left and I never heard from him again but I believed he was a decent man who would never have deserted us without threats from your grandad. I suppose I could have been wrong.

The last thing I want is to drive a wedge between you and your grandad, especially now Paige when he relies on your help. His crime was to do what he thought was the right thing. He always adored you and still does so please don't be too hard on him.

All I can tell you is that your father was a doctor. The position he applied for was as a Consultant in the Midlands. His name is Jake Allcock.

Despite my best efforts, I failed to find him. They closed ranks at work, claiming they knew nothing of his whereabouts but I didn't believe them.

If you decide to try, please don't walk out on your grandad. You've waited until now so please wait a while longer and if you do find Jake, please tell him I never stopped loving him for a single moment.

You've been an amazing daughter Paige. I am so very proud of you. All my love, Mum xx

Two or three times Paige paused to dry her tears as she absorbed her mother's poignant words. She reflected on what might have been had her mother left with Jake or found him after he'd disappeared.

With a sigh she returned the letter to its envelope, aware her worst fears had now become reality.

'What now?' she murmured. 'Do I make contact or do I simply forget about Jake Allcock?'

Paige's decision would for the time being, have to be deferred. It was clearly not a decision to be taken without due consideration.

6

The following Wednesday, after his medication was withdrawn, David regained consciousness. A doctor and nurse were by his bedside when he opened his eyes. Although somewhat confused, he was able to engage in a brief exchange with the doctor.

With no recollection of what had occurred at the factory, he couldn't understand why he was in hospital and persistently asked why he was there.

Richard had been informed that David was awake and that provided a much needed fillip after several days of anxiety. He couldn't wait to share the news.

Paige too was delighted to hear David was awake and agreed to accompany Richard to see him.

Since Richard's tactless remark to his mother the previous Saturday, Paige hadn't been out with him. He correctly deduced he had offended her in some way. All week he had experienced what could only be described as the cold shoulder treatment. He had intended to take her for a meal on Sunday to thank her for her help and rapid response when David had been taken ill but she had refused his offer, claiming to feel out of sorts in addition to having work to do in the bedroom that had been redecorated. Apart from requesting updates on David's health, she had restricted her dialogue to work-related matters.

Richard knew enough about women not to probe, aware of what the response would be. There would be a quick flick of the hair followed by *'Nothing!'* in a high-handed despotic way meaning plenty was wrong. Women were all made in the same mould.

Thinking of his late wife Jan, Richard smiled. On a regular basis he would arrive home late, his meal completely ruined and although she rarely censured him, her displeasure never went unnoticed. Initially she'd bang and clang a pan or two in the kitchen as she attended to the dishes and afterwards she would sidle off quietly to the living room to telephone one of her friends. Following her lengthy conversation, if he happened to ask to whom she had been talking her curt response would be, *'Nobody.'*

That never ceased to amuse him and he'd expel a raucous burst of laughter, thus bringing her anger to a swift end as she laughed with him.

Richard looked at his watch. It was time to leave, but still with heavy heart. Although the earlier news had raised his spirits somewhat, it hadn't dismissed his concerns. David still had a long way to go.

Surprisingly David looked quite perky as the two of them approached and when Richard took hold of David's hand he attempted to smile before transferring his gaze to Paige.

With concern Richard asked, 'How do you feel?'

There was a lengthy pause before he answered in a quiet voice, 'Alright...yes I'm alright.'

'Are you in any pain?' asked Paige.

Again he paused. 'Pain? I don't think so. You're Paige aren't you? Miss Sheldon...that's your name.'

‘That’s right David. I work for you at Cavendish Engineering. Do you remember?’

He grinned and nodded. ‘I think so.’

Paige removed a tissue from her bag and wiped a few beads of perspiration from his brow. She imagined the thick heavy bandage would make him feel hot. Within seconds several more appeared and she summoned a passing nurse.

‘I’ll fetch a fan. It’s hot in here,’ she stated. ‘He’ll adjust to his surroundings quite soon. Don’t worry.’

She returned moments later, plugged in a fan and gave him a few sips of water. After plumping up his pillows she dabbed his forehead and moved away.

‘Maybe we shouldn’t stay long,’ Paige suggested.

‘Just a bit longer,’ Richard rejoined. ‘It’s a shame there’s no doctor around. I’ll see if I can find one.’

David’s eyes followed the staff going about their business which meant he was alert. That had to be a good sign, Paige felt.

Suddenly David asked, ‘Where am I?’

‘In hospital. You’re going to be fine though.’

That seemed to pacify him and he closed his eyes, still with the same serene expression on his face.

Paige felt Richard’s angst. It must be devastating, to see his son so ill, surrounded by equipment with countless tubes and drips attached to his body.

The nurse reappeared and checked the monitors.

‘Is everything alright?’ asked Paige.

She smiled reassuringly. ‘Let’s say that if David’s stable tomorrow, he might be moved to a ward. The Consultant’s very pleased with his progress. He has some way to go yet but it looks promising.’

On hearing voices the nurse turned round. 'Looks like the Consultant's on his way now. I haven't told you anything, okay?'

'What about?' Paige smirked.

David opened his eyes when the Consultant spoke to Richard. 'Early indications are quite promising,' he advised. 'It's too soon yet to say anything more. He's rather confused and until the swelling subsides we won't know if there's any permanent damage. I might move him to a ward tomorrow if I see further improvement today. You're smiling David. That's a positive sign. I like it when patients are happy.'

'Should we come back this evening or would it be better not to disturb him again?' Richard asked.

'A short visit might be beneficial to assist David's memory. Familiar faces aid cognisance and in a day or so I suggest you bring some photos of people he knows. That often helps.'

Richard felt more relaxed as he drove Paige back to work. 'Will you come with me tonight please? If we just have a few minutes, I'll feel so much better. I could take you to dinner later if you like.'

He was surprised when she agreed without hesitation. 'I'll pick you up at seven then if that's okay.'

Adding to his surprise she said, 'I'll look forward to that. It seems ages since we went out together.'

Armed with a large bunch of flowers Richard rang the doorbell and much to his relief, received a warm reception. Handing her the flowers he looked at her apologetically. 'These are to say *sorry*. I don't want to dwell on it. I've so much on my mind at present that I can't think straight. I love you darling and I'd never knowingly say or do anything to hurt you.'

'They're lovely, thank you,' she murmured softly. She clasped both arms around his neck, kissing him fondly. 'Everything will turn out right Richard. I'm sure of it. I can understand why you're so tense.'

David seemed more alert than at their earlier visit and had been given a bowl of soup earlier. The duty nurse advised he had eaten it eagerly.

That snippet of information pleased Richard as it was another move in the right direction but he was disturbed by his son's continuing lack of perception when he turned to Paige asking, 'Where am I?'

'You're in hospital but don't fret because you're in excellent hands and you're doing fine.' Changing topic she asked, 'Did you enjoy your soup?'

'Soup?' he repeated. He continued to stare at her for several moments and then grinned. 'Yes, it was fish soup. I like fish. That's my favourite, Paige.'

Richard squeezed her hand. She always knew the right thing to say. David's recollection was a major step forward, a further milestone he had passed. He had recalled something significant from the past.

Intent on prolonging the discussion Richard said, 'You've always liked fish haven't you David?'

He turned to face him. 'I have Dad, cod and chips with a pint of Boddies. Do you remember going to Harry Ramsden's chippy? I think it was last week. I got a *massive* fillet of fish hanging off both sides of the plate.'

Richard's eyes welled with tears. Although it was at least a year since their visit to Harry Ramsden's,

David had remembered that too. 'Aye, I can see it now son and we'll go again when you feel up to it.'

That was the night Richard sobbed with relief as they left the hospital. There had been so much emotion stirred by David's few words. For the first time in his life Richard firmly believed in the power of prayer. He had prayed incessantly over the past few days and his prayers had been answered.

It was turned eleven when Richard dropped Paige at home. He waited until she unlocked the door and was safely inside the house before driving away. He had desperately wanted to accompany her inside to ask if he might stay over but afraid to be met with a refusal, he had held his tongue. The restaurant had been especially nice, the company even better, and whatever had caused Paige to be distant for the past week appeared to have been resolved. In the car she had kissed him lovingly after reiterating once more that she thought David would make a full recovery.

Richard couldn't hear those heartening words too often.

No sooner had she walked through the door than the telephone rang. It was her friend Laura calling from New York. She was bubbling with excitement as she shrieked, 'I've been trying to get through for ages with the most incredible news; I'm *pregnant!*'

Paige was speechless. Collecting her thoughts she squealed, 'That's *wonderful* news. I'm so happy for you both. When did you find out?'

'Today. I did a test and when it showed positive I shot off to see my gynaecologist for confirmation.'

'How's Brad taken the news?'

Laura giggled. 'I thought he'd passed out. He just stood there open-mouthed with a bizarre expression on his face unable to believe I was serious. Now it's sunk in he's deliriously happy. He's already talking about baby names and he's looked on a comparison site and downloaded a list of all the best schools in New York State. He's an absolute headcase.'

'I'm so happy for you both. I can't imagine how relieved you must feel after the worry and waiting. I can't wait to tell Richard the news.'

'Has he had better news about his son since your email yesterday?'

'David's awake. He's talking but rather confused. His Consultant seems happy enough though. Maybe it's to be expected following a brain haemorrhage. Richard's very emotional. We went for a meal after we'd visited David. He needed some company.'

Laura felt there was something she wasn't telling her. 'Is everything alright between you two?'

She hesitated. 'No Laura, it's not.' She described how he'd reacted to his mother's remark and Laura was horrified.

'I can't believe he said that in front of his mother. I bet you were astounded. Had he never discussed it with you prior to that? It's only natural you'd want children. What's wrong with the guy?'

'He feels too old to start again but I don't know if I want to spend the rest of my life without children. I have no family and I feel the need for someone of my own flesh and blood. Does that sound selfish?'

'No Paige, it doesn't sound selfish but before you say or do something you'll regret, have you thought you might be over-reacting? He's going through a bad patch with David, his only child. He's probably afraid he'll lose him. Have you considered that?'

'I've thought of little else of late. It's not the first time Laura. I paid no regard to his initial comment when he remarked he was thankful to have had just the one child as he was such a handful. I ignored...'

'Listen,' she interrupted. 'We all say stupid things when we're cross or upset. You should talk to him.'

'Perhaps I will when David's better but now isn't a good time. He apologised for what he said at his mother's but he didn't retract it and so I don't know if he still means it but it's created a barrier between us. Anyway, forget it. You're calling with fantastic news and I'm spoiling it by being despondent. Have you any preference for a boy or girl?'

'None whatsoever. As long as it's a healthy baby that's all that matters. I'm still hoping to get over to UK in the New Year with Brad. I should be okay to fly as the baby isn't due until early June.'

'What will you do about your job now?'

She laughed. 'What job? Ask again when Junior's at school. No way would I go back to my job now. Seriously it can be quite strenuous pulling teeth and I'm doing nothing that could endanger my unborn baby. Luckily, I don't have to work because Brad's an excellent provider and I happen to enjoy being at home. It's weird isn't it, the way things work out?'

'How do you mean, weird?'

'Ten weeks ago, when I couldn't track Brad down following the terrorist attack I felt so alone and yet now, in such a short period of time, we're going to be a family of three. Life's so unpredictable, that's my point but I don't expect you to understand.'

'But I do. In my case we *were* a family of three. I lost Mum then Grandad. *That* left me alone. I have no one now, so that's why I'd like to have children. I don't like the idea of spending the rest of my life alone so that's something I must resolve to *my* best advantage, not someone else's. When I've reached a decision I'll let you know. Meanwhile, you enjoy your pregnancy and take care of yourself.'

Laura tittered. 'I fully intend to. Give Richard our best wishes and keep your emails coming. We both love hearing from you with all the news.'

Paige sighed as she reflected on Laura's exciting news. Her meditation was soon interrupted however when Richard rang her. He spoke quietly. 'I wanted to hear your voice. I miss you when we're apart. Do you miss me?'

'You know I do, even at this unearthly hour. You do know I have work tomorrow don't you?'

Ignoring her remark he continued, 'I almost came back to your door. I wanted to stay over tonight but thought better about pushing my luck. We'd had a really nice evening and I didn't want to spoil it. Am I forgiven now for whatever I did to annoy you?'

She paused. 'I suppose so. I meant to ask if you'd like to stay over tomorrow. You could come to me for a meal after you've been to see David.'

His tone swiftly changed. 'Oh yes I'd love that.'

'Me too. By the way, I got a call from Laura as I walked through the door. You'll *never* guess what she told me,' she taunted in a high-pitched voice.

He pondered but a moment. 'Er...she's pregnant.'

'Richard!' she screeched in utter disbelief. 'How did you work *that* out?'

He laughed audibly. 'Listening to your excitable tone of voice, it doesn't need a Philadelphia lawyer to work that out Paige. What is it about women that the mere *thought* of babies causes mass hysteria?'

The effrontery of that man, she snorted inwardly. 'Er...don't crack on you weren't ecstatic when you discovered Jan was pregnant with David.'

'Ecstatic? I was bloody *suicidal* till I'd faced her tyrannical father but yes, I take your point. After I'd talked to him and my folks I was delighted and I'm pleased for Laura and Brad too.'

Paige sighed. 'Same here. They still hope to visit UK in the New Year. It'd be nice if we could meet up. I hold such fond memories of that trip.'

'It'd be *very* nice,' he said thoughtfully. 'I have a great deal to thank New York for.'

She giggled. 'Yes, your broken arm, missing your meeting...'

Softly he interposed, 'Getting to know you.'

'But you knew me before we went to New York.'

'Yes I did but not in the biblical sense. God, how amazing was that? I wish we were there now.'

She had to agree. 'You and me both Richard.'

She had been wide awake all night, sighing, tossing and turning as the same agonizing thought returned to the forefront of her mind. Though Paige had tried hard to clear Jake Allcock from her memory, it was proving impossible. She felt guilt and resentment in equal measure, guilt that she was denying his very existence yet resentment that he had abandoned her and her mother. She was constantly reminded that he was her only blood relative, so wasn't it her duty to confront the man face to face, if only to tell him what she thought of him? It had been a despicable act for him to turn his back on his child. It wouldn't be difficult to make contact. Frank Jessop would be only too happy to provide the necessary details.

She checked the time again on her alarm clock. It was almost five o'clock and she still hadn't had one wink of sleep. If only her mother hadn't written that letter, she sighed. If only...but she had.

Paige imagined too how horrified she would have felt had she come across her mother's letter sooner, before meeting Jake on that fateful day. She cringed as a cold shiver ran down her spine, for how would she have reacted when introduced to Jake, knowing a man with the same unusual name was her father? But why deliberate over what *might* have been, she chastised herself. Reminded of a famous quotation by Benjamin Disraeli she had read in school, *'All is mystery; but he is a slave who will not struggle to penetrate the dark veil,'* Paige reached her decision. At some point, maybe soon or maybe not so soon, she *would* find her father. When the right time presented, she would know; there would be no turning back, and if only to seek retribution for her mother, she would track him down. Paige would be a slave to no man. She would penetrate the dark veil.

7

It was the first week of December when Paige consulted her never ending list of things to do. She still had lots of presents to buy and many people to visit. It had been over a month since she had seen Emma and more than two months since her latest night out with the girls. Christmas was fast approaching and as yet she hadn't written a single card.

The previous Saturday, after they had seen David in the rehabilitation unit, Richard took her on a surprise visit to his house.

She stepped into the spacious entrance hall wide-eyed. Never had she seen such beautiful décor. 'No prizes for guessing whose handiwork this is,' Paige remarked, knowing what the answer would be.

He nodded. 'Jan always gave Andy a free hand to experiment and surprise her. Not once did he fail to impress us. He even recommended which wallpaper we should choose.'

'It's superb. I can't wait to see the rest.'

'In that case, I'll be proud to show you round and then we'll have a quick drink before we go out. As a matter of fact I'd like your advice. I'm thinking of fetching David home and employing a nurse and a physiotherapist to attend to him here. Tell me what you think when you've had time to look around.'

'Won't he need lots of equipment?'

With a nod he explained, 'There's plenty of room upstairs so I was thinking we could maybe utilise a bedroom. We only use two presently.'

'Have you spoken to a physiotherapist about it?'

'No, but the one I went to privately when my cast came off my arm is excellent so I'm going to seek her advice. She got my arm right in no time.'

There was an empty spacious bedroom at the rear of the house that David had used when, as a young boy, his rowdy friends came round to play music.

'I was thinking of this room,' Richard said. 'What do you think?'

'I think you should ask your physiotherapist first. It's definitely viable but you shouldn't rush to bring him home before he's ready. That's my opinion for what it's worth. This is a beautiful house. I love it.'

'It's rather big for two of us and I'm sure at some point David will want to return to his flat. I employ a cleaner and gardener or I'd never cope.'

They made their way downstairs and went in the lounge where Richard poured them both a drink. 'I was thinking you might like to come back here after we've been to the restaurant. We could relax with a drink, enjoy some music and you could stay over.'

Without hesitation she replied, 'No, I'd rather not, thanks all the same. I don't want to stay over in the house you shared with your wife.'

'I don't understand. It's well off the beaten track,' he argued. 'No one would know you were here.'

'*I'd* know and I wouldn't feel comfortable. That's my point and I'm sorry. You come back to mine.'

He decided not to labour the point.

Over recent days there had been one or two issues where they hadn't seen eye to eye. Notwithstanding David's earlier abrasive treatment of Paige, the two of them, since his illness, appeared to have bonded. There was no doubt in David's mind that had Paige not been present when he collapsed, he could have died and he owed her a huge debt of gratitude. Also she had the patience of a saint. She had helped him to eat when his lack of hand to mouth coordination had so required; she had wiped a damp cloth across his face to cool him down; she had combed his hair from his sticky brow and these deeds were followed by a warm smile and an indebted beam from David that hadn't gone unnoticed by Richard.

In David's presence, Richard had spoken to Paige on more than one occasion about this. In confrontational terms, he had accused her of mollycoddling him. He felt his son should learn from his mistakes but Paige had been quick to counter that dribbling food down his clothes could hardly be regarded as a mistake, considering the trauma he had suffered.

It was then that he arranged to take David home, stating his convalescence was lasting too long.

After speaking to the Consultant the wheels were put in motion but Paige felt Richard was misguided. She envisaged there'd be ructions should David not respond at the speed his father expected.

She was soon to be proved right.

'Come on David, make the effort. Give it one more try,' Richard said in an impatient tone.

'For God's sake can't you leave me alone? I can't do any more; I'm knackered,' he snapped. 'I'll try later when I've rested. I'm getting back in bed.'

Sensing a row could be brewing Paige intervened, 'Go and make your phone call Richard and I'll see to him. His physiotherapist said it'd take a while.'

Richard grumbled, 'A while, *yes*, forever, *no*. We seem to have been at this stage for months.'

Paige laughed. 'What are you like Richard? He's only been home for a few days. He's doing his best. Try having a bit of patience.'

'Patience isn't one of his virtues,' David scoffed. 'Never has been...not where I'm concerned.'

'Phone call,' Paige repeated as Richard turned to face his son with an angry expression. *'Just go.'*

As Richard strode from the room, Paige perched on the edge of the bed. 'He's worried. Try to see it from his perspective. He wants you fit and well.'

'Huh, right. Dad wants me back at work earning my keep more like.'

'Don't be daft.' She pulled the bedclothes up and wiped the beads of perspiration from his brow. 'It's strange how the left leg won't function yet but your physiotherapist is optimistic. She's good at her job and as you've no doubt noticed, very pretty too.'

For the first time he chuckled. 'Why do you think I'm not trying too hard? I'm not completely stupid. I want to keep her here as long as I can. Penny's an absolute doll. Boy, what I wouldn't give to...'

'Alright David, I get the picture,' she cut in on a laugh. 'Seriously though, all her patients must find her attractive so I wouldn't pin too many hopes on having a romantic involvement with her. She has a job to do and part of that is being nice to everyone.'

With a pensive nod David agreed. 'She's lovely. That's the one thing Dad got right, finding Penny.'

'That's rather unfair. Your dad would do anything for you. They'd have kept you in rehab longer but he wanted you here with one to one care and Penny certainly doesn't come cheap, nor does your nurse.'

'I know; I'm being spiteful. I keep thinking, why me? I get so frustrated but it isn't Dad's fault.'

'You have to try and set yourself targets. Physio's painful, I know, but it'll be worth all the effort soon and once you're fully mobile you'll be able to drive again. That'll really restore your independence.'

'I'd like to get back to my flat. I feel to be playing gooseberry when I'm here with you and Dad.'

That was the first reference David had ever made about there being anything other than a professional working relationship between the two of them and she winced as her blushes emblazoned her cheeks.

She was about to protest when David winked and laughed saying, 'Don't worry on my account Paige. I'm happy for you both.'

When she stared at him sceptically, he nodded his head. 'I'm okay about it, honestly. You're good for Dad. There's been nobody else since we lost Mum. It's five years since she died so it's time he got on with his life again and I know he thinks a lot about you.'

She felt some explanation was warranted. 'We're simply good friends David. It's nothing serious. We enjoy each other's company, that's all.'

‘If you say so,’ was his glib reply but the satirical smile told her he didn’t believe a word of it.

He threw back the bedclothes. ‘I need a pee. Will you help me to the bathroom please?’

‘Can’t you wait till your dad gets back?’

He tried to stand. ‘No, I need to go now, sorry.’

She took his arm as he half walked, half hopped across the bedroom to the landing and reaching the bathroom, she opened the door and called Richard. Steadying David from behind she slowly edged forward and Richard appeared.

‘What’s going on?’

‘David needed the loo. Can you take over now?’

He glowered at her as they swapped places. ‘Why didn’t he use his walking frame?’

‘Cos *you’ve* shifted it,’ David snorted in Paige’s defence. ‘You said I had to manage without it.’

Paige went downstairs to check on the casserole in the oven. After giving it a gentle stir she turned off the gas. It was ready to serve.

No sooner had Richard walked in the kitchen than he verbally attacked her, eyes full of venom. ‘Has it escaped your notice that David happens to be your boss? As his PA, it doesn’t fall within your scope of duties to take him to the bathroom. I can’t...’

Paige was infuriated and interrupted vociferously, ‘Don’t you *ever* raise your voice at me, Richard. If you’d been around he’d have asked *you*. He said he couldn’t wait so what was I supposed to do, let him wet the bed? That *would* have looked impressive in front of his PA. Or perhaps I ought to have let him struggle alone and then you could have yelled even louder had he fallen and banged his head. Yes, that would have really assisted his recovery wouldn't it? I give up all my evenings and weekends to offer my support and I make you several meals a week at my own expense I hasten to add, and that's the thanks I get. You've been itching for a barney all day. David *needs* you. You're his father and that makes *you* the adult so try acting like a bloody adult and grow up. In addition while we're on the subject of employers and employees, remember I work for *you* as well as *David,* so as from now, I do *nothing* that isn't in my Job Description. Understood? I have rights as well! Your meal's ready to eat. I'm off home.'

Paige snatched up her bag and car keys from the table, snorted and stormed from the kitchen without a backward glance, leaving Richard lost for words.

'Nice one Dad,' David, who had overheard every word, shouted downstairs. 'You've just managed to alienate yourself from the one person who cares the most about both of us, so ten out of ten for that. I'll have my meal in my room if you'd care to fetch it up now Paige isn't here to mollycoddle me.'

Paige drove to Emma's place, screeching to a halt outside her door. She hoped Emma would be home. It had been a while since they'd had a girly chat.

Emma was delighted to see her. 'Andy's gone for a takeaway so he'll not be back for a while. There'll be enough for three though, in fact I'll call him and ask him to bring extra.'

'There's no need Emma. I've eaten,' she lied. The last thing on her mind was food. 'Actually I'm here for a change of environment. I've just had a hell of a row with Richard. I really put myself out for him and David. I've done their ironing and cooked their evening meal, as well as helping with David and all day Richard's been nit-picking and building up to an argument. He can be really obnoxious at times.'

'Everyone argues Paige. It'll blow over. The poor man must be half out of his mind with David. He's probably regretting it now whatever he said or did.'

'I don't know about that. After all his tears and all his promises to be a better father he snipes at David at every opportunity. I feel really sorry for David. I know he used to be a pain in the butt but he's really polite now and appreciative of all the things I do for him. It's like they've swapped roles. Don't get me wrong; when we're alone Richard is charming. He spends a fortune taking me out for meals. It's when David's present that he kicks off. I don't understand him. He took David's walking frame away, arguing he should be able to manage without it but no way can he walk without help. He does some really daft things but what can I say or do? I merely work for them. If I interfere or try to smooth things over, I'm forgetting my *place*, as he was quick to point out to me. That's when I lost my temper, bellowed at him and stormed from the house absolutely furious.

'Ouch!' Emma cried. 'I bet that shocked him.'

'It certainly did. I never lose my rag as you know. I swore at him too and that's not like me.'

Emma discharged a loud raucous laugh. 'I bet the answer-phone's full when you get home.'

'Well I won't be returning any of his calls if it is.'

Emma stood up. 'Let me get you a drink.'

'No, I'm fine honestly. Besides I'm driving. I've loads to do when I get home. I want to write all my Christmas cards and I've a few presents to wrap.'

'Have you wrapped mine yet?' she queried with a mischievous grin.

'I haven't bought anything for you yet. That's the trouble. I give up all my free time to help them but then things at home don't get done, and am I shown the slightest gratitude? Am I hell as like.'

'Listen, you know you don't do it for gratitude. I bet he turns up tomorrow with a bunch of flowers.'

That remark was met with a disinterested, 'Huh.'

'So how's David doing now?'

'Better than he was but he's a long way to go yet. He can hold a brief conversation but he's forgetful. His short-term memory is abysmal; he has a limited attention span and quickly gets bored and confused. His right leg's fine but his left leg barely functions. That's why he needs his walking frame.'

'Did he hurt that leg when he collapsed?'

'No, it's because of the blood clot and bleed from what I can gather. He still lacks proper coordination in his hands and often slops food down his clothes. When I'm around I help him but Richard's stance is to let him get on with it until he learns to eat without spilling and I can't make him see how heartless that is. Physiotherapy will presumably help his lack of coordination but meanwhile he gets upset when he makes a mess.' She shook her head. 'It really is a ridiculous state of affairs. You have to be there to see and believe it.'

The headlamps on Andy's car flashed across the front window and Paige jumped up. 'Right, I'm off. I haven't a clue when I'll see you again but I'll call you and keep you posted.'

Although unaware of it then, Paige would in fact see Emma again the very next day and the news she would impart at that meeting would not only reduce Emma to tears, it would shake her to the core.

There was one message when Paige arrived home. As expected it was from Richard who stated tersely, 'We'll talk tomorrow.'

She deleted it and went upstairs with her laptop. Maybe, just maybe she might reach the end of the chapter she'd been working on conscientiously for the past few days. Her Christmas cards could wait.

Following her success with short stories, she had embarked on a full-length novel and was enjoying the challenge of creating something unique. There was no denying this task was more difficult but she had always thrived in difficult situations.

By ten-thirty she had attained her goal, albeit she had only produced an initial draft. There remained a vast amount of research to be done and many more chapters still to write but lethargy had never been a trait of her character. If there was work to be done, it had to be done properly as second best had never been an option to Paige.

Pleased with her progress she went to bed.

During the night she awoke feeling nauseous and in the morning she was violently sick when she got out of bed.

Convinced it would pass, she quickly got washed and dressed and drove to work where she was met on the car park by Mandy.

Showing concern she said, 'Are you okay Paige? You look terrible. Don't you feel well?'

'I felt tired when I woke up. I've been having too many late nights,' she prevaricated. 'I'm fine now.'

'I'll fetch you a nice cup of tea as soon as I can,' she said affably. 'How's Mr David?'

'He's improving gradually but he has a long way to go yet.'

'The girls were thinking of sending some flowers if he's up to receiving them. What do you think?'

'That's a lovely idea Mandy and I'm sure David would appreciate the thought.'

There was a sudden flash of lightening followed by a loud thunderclap and it began to rain. Giggling they hurried indoors, trying to avoid the downpour.

Rosemary was in the cloakroom when Paige went in to comb her hair and she too was anxious for any update on David. 'It's been such a stressful time for Richard. How is he coping at home?'

'There are still problems but I'm pleased to report David's making reasonable progress. He's certainly much better than he was before the operation.'

'It's starting to tell on Richard. He's aged terribly these past few weeks. The thing is you don't know what to say do you? He came into work early today and he looks dreadful. Keep me posted if you hear anything as I'm reluctant to ask him.'

After agreeing to keep her updated Paige went to her office where Richard was waiting for her.

Their eyes met briefly before he spoke. 'First, I'd like to apologise Paige. I should never have reacted the way I did and I'm sorry for...'

'Then why react like that?' she cut in impatiently.

He shrugged. 'Things had been getting me down all day and suddenly it peaked and I lost it. I'd give anything to retract the things I said. I value everything you do; I have enormous respect for you and I love you more than you could ever know, but after many hours of soul-searching I've made a decision. I have to let you go. No, allow me to finish,' he said as she was about to interrupt.

'Coming to terms with David's illness might well take me down but I won't take you down with me. I have to face facts. You once told me you'd never be anyone's doormat, that you were worth much more than that and I agreed with you unequivocally. You are and always will be. You might interpret this as arrogance when I say it's not open to negotiation. I have made my decision. We're over Paige, much as it tears out my heart to say so. Since the outset I've been aware of the age difference but I was arrogant about that too. I made a play for you from day one, but you knew that. Who knows, maybe we'd have made it work if David hadn't fallen ill again. Then again, perhaps it was doomed from the outset.'

He stood up and moved to the door. 'Since your teenage years you've been a carer and that's no life for a young woman. Out of need you cared for your mother and grandad but David isn't your responsibility and I have to look to the future. I'm forty-five now. In fifteen years I'll be sixty. *I* might need help then. It might transpire that David needs continuous care. If so, that's *my* responsibility. I'm so sorry for leading you on, giving you false hope but I trust we can at least remain civil with each other. I want you to know you still have a job here for as long as you wish to stay on.'

There was a tap at the door and Mandy hurried in with Paige's tea. 'It was going cold so I thought I'd best fetch it in. Sorry, Mr Cavendish. I didn't mean to interrupt,' she said making for the door.

'I was just leaving Mandy.' Turning to face Paige he forced a smile. 'I'll never find anybody else like you but I hope you'll find someone worthy of your special qualities. I'll always love you.'

'You haven't said why you shouted at me. Don't you have the moral fibre to be honest with me?'

Their eyes met once more but instead of replying he left, closing the door behind him. Moments later he opened it again and strode across the room. 'You want the *truth?* You really want to hear the *truth?*'

'Yes, I do Richard. I think you owe me that.'

'Okay, here's the truth. It was jealousy, plain and simple. Happy now?' he said angrily.

'Jealousy? I don't understand what...'

'Oh but I think you do...the way you look at each other, the body language, the little asides, the way you're always there at his beck and call, hanging on his every word. I can't tolerate it any longer.'

Paige shook her head in total disbelief. 'Are you referring to *David?*'

When he didn't respond she cackled, 'You foolish man. *Nothing* could be further from the truth.'

She sighed heavily once more. 'All I ever wanted was to help alleviate the burden placed on you...to try and make things better in some small way but I would *never* come between father and son. I wish I'd never asked you to explain because I intended to try and talk you round, but I won't now Richard. If the trust between us no longer exists, I'm afraid we have nothing worth saving, nothing at all.'

Turning to face the window to hide her suffering she added, 'If you don't mind I'd like you to leave.'

Without a word Richard headed for the door and once he closed it she knew he would never open it again. Not only had he closed the door, he had also closed a memorable chapter of her life.

She hovered by the window, her eyes filling with tears as she watched the raindrops rolling down the pane of glass. There was no synchronised harmony. Many descended rapidly and were gone in a flash, whereas some meandered painstakingly in different directions, like little people who had somehow lost their way.

Soon the tears were tumbling down her cheeks in rivulets, obscuring her sight. She could taste the salt and she wanted so much to cry out. Everything had seemed perfect until a few short hours ago yet now all that remained was a sense of emptiness, save for the living foetus developing within her that would now have to be aborted. She must move away from here; she must look for some distant location to lay down her roots and then go on to bury the past once and for all before attempting to rebuild her painful and shattered life.

After clearing the items on her desk, Paige typed out her letter of resignation, requesting that her last month's salary be retained in lieu of notice.

She marked the envelope 'Confidential' and left it in Richard's pigeonhole.

It didn't take long to pack her belongings and as soon as Mandy left the reception desk at lunchtime, Paige made her escape by a side door.

Once away from the car park she stopped in a lay-by to make out a list of things she must do. She was grateful to Andy for having smartened up her house as that would enable her to find a respectable tenant more swiftly. A former school friend was employed as a letting agent with a local company that enjoyed a good reputation and Paige needed somebody she could trust to secure a reliable tenant and handle the management side as she wouldn't be around to deal with it. With no income now and little likelihood of finding work soon, she had to find a tenant as soon as possible. She also had to find a place to live.

It suddenly came to her as she recalled her former thoughts, *when the right time presented, she would know.* There could be no better time than now when she needed help. The time to penetrate the dark veil had arrived. Whatever the outcome Paige would try to find Jake Allcock and with her determination she would succeed. Failure was not an option...but the nagging question on her lips was, would her father acknowledge her or abandon her for a second time?

Edgily, she scraped her feet along the floor, waiting for the surgery door to open. Twice she'd been on the verge of leaping up to run in but someone else's name had been called, adding to her anxiety.

She knew Dr Stephenson well. He had been their family practitioner for many a year and was the one who had prescribed what he'd portrayed as the new innovative contraceptive pill in advance of her visit to New York, a very reliable one, he had expressed. A fat lot of use that had been, she snorted to herself. A cough drop would have proved equally effective.

His door opened once more and with an agreeable smile he beckoned her to his room.

'It's good to see you Paige. How are you today?'

'Rather pregnant!' she answered in a disrespectful tone. 'I can't say I'm impressed with the *innovative* contraceptive pill you prescribed.'

He looked shocked. 'Oh dear. You did remember to take it as instructed, didn't you?'

'Of course I remembered. I never missed taking it once. You said it should be effective after a week.'

He nodded. 'I do recall, although having said that, it's probably more reliable if you've been taking it a bit longer before having unprotected sex. Are you booked in for an antenatal check yet?'

'I won't be having an antenatal check. I want an abortion. I'm in no position, financial or otherwise, to raise a child so I want it done as soon as possible. That's why I came to you for the contraceptive pill. I've spent the whole of my adult life to date looking after other people and now I want a life of my own, at least for the next few years. I don't think that's unreasonable, selfish as it might seem to other folk with no concept of everything I've had to contend with since my teenage years, so please don't lecture me about available help. My mind is made up and I won't be dissuaded by you or anyone else. I believe I can get an abortion on the National Health and I'd like to get it done as soon as possible.'

Gesturing for her to move to the examination bed he performed an external examination. 'Yes, there's no doubt you're pregnant,' he confirmed.

Avoiding her gaze he tapped the keys on his keyboard. 'Your initial appointment date should arrive in around three days.'

She nodded. 'Good, the sooner the better.'

'I have to ask you Paige, what about the father? Is he of the same mind? This is a very big step to take and I've known women spend a lifetime regretting their decision.'

'He doesn't know; I didn't tell him and we're not together now. Besides he didn't want children.'

'Then I'm sorry it worked out the way it did. No contraceptive pill is a hundred per cent guaranteed. It seems you were one of the unlucky ones but let's hope this is soon over. Meanwhile, you can call and see me anytime you need help or advice.'

Though Paige smiled sweetly, her inner voice was screaming, *'Like hell I will.'*

With utter foreboding she thought of the next few weeks, wishing it were all be behind her. Christmas was looming and she had to sort out the house and pack her personal belongings; she had to tell Emma and she had to find her father; she had to look for a place to live and instruct the letting agent to find a suitable tenant; she had to suffer a termination and then come to terms with her decision whilst dealing with all the hormonal changes that ensued.

From the surgery she drove to the letting agent to set things in motion. Her friend Annette was happy to see her again after so many years.

Without reference to her pregnancy, Paige stated she was making a fresh start in pastures new.

'I envy you,' Annette sighed. 'The trouble is, you get stuck in a rut and by the time you realise, it's far too late to get out of it. I've had a rough time. Jason and I split up six months ago. I should have seen it coming when we began to have a few problems but I allowed myself to believe it'd sort itself out. Sadly it didn't. I have a tough balancing act now but luckily my boss is considerate about my hours. I have a four-year-old girl who's at nursery and Jason helps a bit. At least we parted friends. This is Bethany.'

Proudly, Annette showed her the photograph.

'She's adorable,' said Paige. 'What beautiful hair. It's so thick and curly and she has a gorgeous smile. Does she have much contact with her father?'

'Thankfully yes or I wouldn't cope. I could *never* be a single mother like those poor women who have to manage completely alone. It's so difficult raising a child, expensive as well and the child must suffer when there's only the one parent.'

Had there been any earlier doubt in Paige's mind those sober words provided the reassurance that she was doing the right thing while conveniently forgetting her mother had been one of those *poor women* with no help whatsoever from the man responsible, yet who had fought tirelessly to keep *her* baby.

'So you're not with anyone else then?' she asked.

'God no,' Annette cried. 'I've had enough of men to last a lifetime the way I feel now. Besides I don't have time. I heard Jason was seeing someone but I don't know if it's serious or even true.'

After taking down the details of Paige's property, Annette said she'd take some photographs the next day and also contact suitable prospective tenants on her mailing list. 'I'll really push yours,' she told her quietly. 'I'll hopefully have a tenant for you within a couple of weeks and I'll reduce the fee as agreed,' she added in a louder voice with a nod and a wink.

Paige looked puzzled. 'But I...'

'Shut up,' she said in a whisper. 'If anybody asks, you haggled over the fee. Every landlord tries to get the cost down. If I can't help a friend...'

Paige was grateful. 'Thank you Annette. I'll need you to manage it too as I won't be around.'

'We'll discuss it when we're alone. *Off the record* I can do it myself for a lower fee but you can't tell anyone. It has to be our secret...right?'

Paige certainly wouldn't argue with that. With no money coming in, she needed to save every penny and was sure Annette could make use of extra cash with a child and the added expense of Christmas.

She smiled and nodded. 'That'll be fine.'

With a loud sharp knock on Richard's door, Patricia Winters hurried in with his afternoon mail. 'I've not opened this one as it's marked "Confidential" so if it's something I need to deal with, let me know.'

'Thank you,' he mumbled distantly.

Richard waited until she'd closed the door before opening the letter and as anticipated, it was Paige's letter of resignation. He read through it once more, sighing heavily, in part an expression of sorrow, yet one of relief too. Had someone told him it would all end like this he would have laughed in that person's face but it had been right to end it and to do so now because Paige deserved better. It would have been easier, had he been a selfish man, to continue in the same manner day after day, taking advantage of her charitable nature but it would have been wrong. She was young, bright and high-spirited and it was time she enjoyed a fun-filled uncomplicated life.

Transferring his thoughts from Paige to David he expelled another loud sigh. David, with good cause, had reacted furiously to his father's unexpected outburst the previous evening and had lost no time in pointing out that Paige, after a day's hard work, had prepared and cooked the evening meal two or three times a week; she had also played cards and various board games with him by way of occupational therapy whilst his father had shown his appreciation by expressing insulting remarks and virtually throwing her out. It had been their first heated argument for a while and had ended in tears for David.

Richard had found himself in an unenviable position with only one outcome, to give Paige up before his son became even more dependent on her. It had been a colossal personal sacrifice but Paige's future happiness had to come first, irrespective of David's feelings on the matter and hopefully, in time, David would learn to live with his father's decision.

Paige strived to recall the dialogue with Richard about her father. The letter her mother had written was at best vague about his whereabouts. It merely made reference in non-specific terms to somewhere in the Midlands and *that* being a vast area would call for a concerted effort on her part to track Jake down, assuming he was still in the vicinity.

She felt sure Richard had mentioned *Warwick* the day she had met Frank Jessop so it might be worth making initial enquiries at a hospital there, she felt, after deciding not to contact Frank who might then notify Jake she was seeking information about him.

She went online and found the telephone number for the main Warwick Hospital. With shaky fingers she called the number clearing her throat repeatedly while waiting for somebody to answer. It was a far cry from her usual self-assured approach.

'Warwick Hospital,' a female announced.

'Er...yes...er...' she stuttered. 'I'm so sorry, please forgive me. Could you tell me if there's a doctor by the name of Allcock at your hospital?'

'Putting you through now,' she said hurriedly.

Before Paige had time to explain, another female, this time in a high-pitched tone stated, 'Paediatrics Dr Allcock's secretary. Can I help you?'

'Oh...I'm really sorry,' Paige stuttered once more. 'Your switchboard operator put me through before I could explain what I wanted.'

'Sounds about right,' she laughed. 'She operates a very busy switchboard but don't worry; I'm sure I can help you. Are you a new or existing patient at Dr Allcock's clinic?'

Paige was becoming increasingly flustered. 'No, I wanted to be sure I'd found the right hospital for Dr Allcock. It isn't a medical matter at all.'

'Oh…then I don't understand.'

'Let me start from the beginning. Dr Allcock is an acquaintance. As I'm driving to Warwick tomorrow I was hoping to meet up with him if he had...'

She interrupted her. 'Before you go any further, it appears you *have* rung the wrong hospital. Our Dr Allcock is female, Dr *Miriam* Allcock. It's quite a common error since there are two in Warwick. The one you want will be Mr Jacob Allcock, yes?'

'Er...yes, though I know him as Jake.'

'That's right; he goes by the name of Jake. He's at St Michael's Hospital of the South Warwickshire Mental Health Services NHS Trust. He's the Senior Psychiatric Consultant. I'll just find the number.'

Appreciative of her help, Paige thanked her.

'You're welcome,' she said. 'I hope you manage to catch up with him. Watch how you drive though. They've forecast snow in these parts for tomorrow.'

Paige sat down and collected her thoughts. Would it be wiser to simply turn up at the hospital or ought she to call him first? The latter was a silly idea she quickly told herself. What reason could she give for calling him? She could hardly exclaim, 'Hello Dad, I'm your daughter!' No, it had to be a face to face disclosure where she could observe his reaction.

Bringing to mind he was a Psychiatric Consultant, Paige laughed scornfully, wondering just how much self-analysis there would have been at the time he abandoned the two of them. Perhaps there had been none. Maybe he was just a cold-hearted individual who could shirk his responsibilities without even a thought.

She lay back and closed her eyes, thinking of all the men in her life, Tim her ex-boyfriend who had turned his back on her, her grandad who had been adamant her mother must seek an abortion, David, who as an employer had made her life hell, Richard who had callously ended their relationship and then there was Jake, the father she had never known, for he too had shirked his paternal duties. What was it about men that they had to be so devious and cruel?

Shaking her head in dismay, Paige picked up her bag and headed off to see Emma.

The moment Emma opened the door, Paige burst into tears and dashed inside where she poured out the entire story about Richard and David. Purposely she omitted to make reference to her father and by the time she reached the end of her revelations, her best friend was in tears too.

'I can't believe you're moving away from everyone you know. If you're hell-bent on going through with the abortion, you could stay exactly where you are. Why let Richard rule your life? And where on earth do you intend going? You don't know anyone who doesn't live round here so you'd be making a new life in unfamiliar surroundings. It'd be terrible. You've not thought this through. Where would you find work? Listen, it's a cowardly act run away and hide. You should face up to what's happened, deal with it and move on. You'd be the first to preach at me were our roles reversed. Well, *wouldn't* you?'

With a noncommittal shrug and raised eyebrows she looked away. 'That's purely hypothetical since *you* aren't the one pregnant with Richard's baby.'

'No, and I'm flaming gobsmacked you are when, according to your relentless protestations, you'd not slept with him. I can't believe you lied about that.'

'Needs must. You have a loose tongue and that's why I lied as I had to make sure it didn't get back to David. I haven't even told Richard I'm pregnant.'

'Why protect Richard now? I think you should let him know. Why should you have to shoulder all the responsibility on your own? It's not right.'

Paige sniggered. 'What useful purpose would that serve? I've finished with men. They're all the same, full of their own importance, selfish and underhand. Remember Tim? I've had a right bellyful of men.'

'Can't argue with that, kid. That's quite a bellyful you've got there,' she hooted with laughter.

Paige looked shocked. 'Are you saying it shows?'

'Are you for real? Of course it does. I'm surprised you're only three months or so. It's obvious. I can't believe Richard hasn't seen it. I knew yesterday but I thought I'd better keep my gob shut. I bet the girls at Cavendish Engineering know. When was the first time you had sex with Richard?'

'Do you mind?' Paige cried in disgust. 'I refuse to discuss such personal matters with you.'

'You'll be discussing them with all and sundry at the clinic and it's not like folk don't know how the baby got there. Protest all you want but it definitely isn't an immaculate conception.'

She'd heard enough. 'I'm off,' she said furiously.

'That's right Paige, run away again. You have to start facing the truth. You're pregnant; you've two choices, keep it or don't keep it. It doesn't matter to me what you do. I won't like you any less whatever you decide. You've had a hard life and it'll get even harder raising a baby alone. It's a lousy decision for you to make but do what you think is right for you. It's nowt to do with anybody else so don't feel you have to run away. Are you staying for tea?'

'Thanks but no. I've loads to do. I need to tidy up. I've got an agent coming round tomorrow to look at my house I intend to rent out. You'll remember her, Annette Bradley from our school. She married a lad called Jason and they have a little girl. They split up though so she's raising the child on her own.'

'I remember. Does *she* know you're pregnant?'

'*No,* no one knows but you, and I want to keep it that way so please promise me you won't tell a soul because it'd be awful if Richard found out, not that he'd find me where I'm going.'

'Where *are* you going?'

'I can't tell you; besides I'm not sure yet. I won't disappear forever without giving you a new phone number and you have my mobile number so we can keep in touch. I intend being here for your wedding. I'm not missing that. Is it still on for next year?'

That brought a beaming smile to Emma's face. 'It is and I'm counting the days, not that we've fixed a date yet. We're saving like mad at the moment.'

'You've got a good bloke there. Andy's a star.'

Emma nodded. 'He is. I'm just sorry things didn't work out for you Paige.'

Paige forced a laugh. 'Nothing ever works out for me does it? In a former life I must have done something really terrible and now I'm paying the price.'

She headed for the door. 'I recall telling Richard that good things don't happen to me. I'm just glad I have a broad back. I must dash. I'll see you soon.'

As Emma waved goodbye she felt a huge pang of sadness. They had been the best of friends for many years and that was soon to end because of Richard Cavendish. How she despised that man.

'Are you on your own?' asked David when Richard arrived home. 'I thought or should I say hoped that Paige might be with you. Have you squared things with her? Is she okay now?'

Richard threw down his briefcase. 'She won't be coming here again. Furthermore she resigned today; she's already left and taken all her things with her.'

David was horror-struck. 'Didn't you try and stop her? Didn't you go after her? Why did she do that?'

Richard sat down beside him. 'It's better this way as you'll realise in time. You've got all the help you need during the day and I'm here at night. We don't need anyone else, not when we have each other.'

He shook his head in disbelief. 'I thought the two of you were...'

Richard cut in immediately, 'No, we were friends, that's all and I don't have time for friends now. It's my place to attend to your needs until you're fit and well. So, how's it gone today?' he queried changing topic. 'Did you manage all your exercises? Did you do different things with Penny?'

Fighting back tears of anger David yelled, *'Go to hell. Mind your own bloody business.* God, I wish I could walk without help but mark my words, once I'm mobile again I'll be away from here in a flash. I refuse to spend one second longer than I have to in your company. You're nothing but a bloody tyrant who derives pleasure from spoiling everything.'

In an attempt to smooth things over Richard said, 'Let me get you a drink. I can see you're upset. You were becoming too dependent on Paige. She has her own life to lead.'

'You're talking crap. *Paige* never said that. It was *you*. You deliberately stopped her coming here and don't deny it. Don't bother making me any tea. I'm going upstairs and don't try to help me. I'll manage on my own if it kills me. I don't need your help.'

Clinging to the furniture he made his way to the stairs and hauled himself up. His anger provided an inner strength, making him all the more determined to be independent. By the time he reached the bedroom he was exhausted but smugly satisfied. Penny had told him he could do better if only he'd try and she'd been right. From now on he would do all his exercises without a word of complaint. His useless left leg would improve in no time and meanwhile, his father mustn't know how he felt about Penny or he'd no doubt send her away too.

He thought about Penny as he lay on his bed. She was like Paige in many ways with the patience of a saint. He liked how her auburn shoulder length hair curled under, how her hazel eyes sparkled when she was pleased with his efforts and above all her quiet persuasive manner when she coaxed him into trying once more to do something he found demanding.

Penny remained active in his thoughts, leaving a broad smile on his face until he fell asleep.

Distraught, Richard sat with his head in his hands, his whole world collapsing around him. He had lost Paige and now he was losing David again too.

For a man whose business was flourishing when dozens of other firms were failing, why couldn't he be likewise successful with the people he loved? He hadn't meant to upset anybody. He had been trying to protect Paige and David, firstly by offering Paige the chance of a better life and secondly by offering his only son his love and wholehearted support.

He sighed heavily, poured a stiff whisky followed by another after gulping down the first. His appetite for food had disappeared. He wondered what Paige would be doing, whether she felt as miserable as he did. Already regretting his actions, he was wishing he'd been less impulsive. She was a grown woman capable of making her own decisions and he should at least have afforded her an opportunity to contribute to and comment on his concerns before rushing headlong into such an irresponsible decision.

Shortly afterwards Richard went upstairs to check on David but finding him asleep, he felt it better not to disturb him.

He covered him with a spare duvet, turned out his light and made his way to his room, hoping the next day would prove more agreeable.

8

Paige was waiting outside the letting agent's office when Annette arrived just before nine o'clock.

'Are you popping in for a coffee?' Annette asked.

Paige shook her head as she handed her the house keys and alarm details. 'No, I need to get off now. I want to look at rental prices, view a few properties and get a feel for the place where I might finish up. Do what you think is best with my house. Use your discretion. I need a good reliable tenant, one who'll pay the rent and look after the place. You can get in touch with me on my mobile if needs be. The house will be available in a week's time. That's my plan. I want to be away from here before Christmas.'

'Will you be back later today?'

'I don't know yet.'

'So where are you off to?'

Turning away shiftily she prevaricated, 'I haven't a clue. I don't care where I finish up as long as it's well away from this place.'

Annette sensed she was running away from someone and didn't wish to pry. 'Well, the best of luck. I hope you end up somewhere really nice.'

Annette's suspicions were confirmed when Paige remarked, 'I'm sure I will and if anybody asks, you have no idea where I am, okay?'

She grinned. 'That'd be hard to let slip. I haven't a clue whether you're travelling north or south.'

'Could even be east or west,' Paige laughed on a wave as she headed for her car. 'Talk soon.'

Armed with details of the journey she headed for the M6. With one hundred and twenty-five miles to travel it would take in excess of two hours and she wanted to arrive at the hospital by midday. With no plan as to how she might orchestrate a meeting with Jake once there, she would play it by ear. There was no guarantee he'd even be there that day. He might be on holiday but Paige's journey would definitely not be in vain. She would ask questions about him and try to piece together what Jake had achieved in life since abandoning her mother.

She wondered about the other Dr Allcock, if they were related. It wasn't beyond the realms of possibility that she was his wife. He had been working in Warwick for a very long time, almost thirty years. She knew nothing about Jake apart from Richard's exposé that he was a womaniser and her mother had merely advised her that he had disappeared without trace, leaving no explanation for his actions.

There was no doubt in her mind that she'd catch up with him at some point and she wasn't averse to expressing her views in the strongest possible way when that time presented. He might well be the 'oh so omnipotent' Senior Consultant at the hospital but she would soon bring him down to earth. She'd met his kind before.

Paige was so engrossed in her thoughts about the things she would say to that egotistical creature that she became overwrought and without realising, her speed had reached eighty miles an hour. When she caught sight of her speedometer she was horrified. Her heart pounding, she shot towards the slow lane.

By eleven-thirty she had reached her destination where snow had clearly been falling for some time. Stepping carefully from the car she shivered as the sharp biting wind stung her cheeks.

With diverse emotions of disquiet and trepidation at the imminent prospect of making herself known as Jake Allcock's daughter, she trod warily towards the main entrance, shaking the snowflakes from her hair as she entered the reception area.

'Oh dear, is it snowing heavily?' the elderly lady behind the desk said with a look of concern. 'I'm so afraid of slipping when it snows. I'm due to retire at Christmas and believe me, my final day can't come quick enough. I really hate winter.'

'It's just a quick flurry I think so don't worry. It's not sticking much on the main roads. It might have cleared by the time you finish today,' Paige said.

The lady seemed heartened by her response. 'I do hope so. Can I help you with something?'

'Yes please. Can you direct me to the Psychiatric Department please?'

She nodded and smiled. 'Follow that corridor and it's clearly signposted so you can't miss it. Are you here for an appointment?'

'Er no...not really. I'm hoping to see Mr Allcock. I'm an acquaintance of his and I just called on spec hoping he might be around today.'

'In that case you're in luck,' someone remarked.

Stunned, Paige spun round and came face to face with Jake. Caught off guard she couldn't think of a single thing to say.

He laughed. 'Sorry if I startled you. I guess Frank gave you my particulars. So, what are you doing in these parts Paige? You see, I've remembered your name. I *never* forget a pretty face.'

He was doing it again...womanising...and she was absolutely furious. He couldn't even wait to get her away from the reception area before he started.

'How about a cup of coffee? My last appointment of the morning has cancelled so I've no patients till two. It's so good to see you again.'

Before she had chance to respond he whisked her away. 'It'd be nice to take you to lunch if you have time to spare. I'm glad I didn't miss you.'

'I am too,' she murmured. 'I really wanted to talk to you, in private if possible.'

'That sounds ominous. Is something wrong?'

'I'll let you decide when you've listened to what I have to say.'

He searched her eyes for a clue as to the purpose of her visit but could see neither a smile nor frown.

'Right, let's go to my consulting room. We won't be disturbed there. My secretary will bring us some coffee. Will it be six months since I last saw you?'

'No, a little longer. It was around April or May.'

'Tempus fugit,' he remarked analytically. 'I don't know where the time goes, I really don't.'

'Yes, life slips by so quickly,' she concurred.

He gestured for her to go first through his waiting room and when they entered his consulting room he asked Marjorie, his medical secretary, to bring them some coffee.

Offering her a seat, he sat beside her, rather than behind his desk. 'I must confess I'm intrigued Paige so will you please enlighten me as to why you have travelled all this way to talk to me as I'm assuming you have no other business in the area, right?'

She opened her bag, removed her mother's letter and gave it to him. 'I came to you because I didn't know where else to go. I need your help but first I'd like your observations on that letter.'

He looked puzzled. 'Forgive my asking but would this have anything to do with your being pregnant?'

First Emma and now Jake had commented on her pregnancy. Was it really so obvious, she asked herself; did everyone know?

When Paige didn't answer he was more confused. 'Forgive me. You're evidently finding this difficult to talk about so please, just take your time and tell me how I can help. What is it Paige?'

His tone was gentle and caring and not at all what she had expected. She had gone to the hospital with the sole intent of humiliating him in front of everyone. This was the man who had heartlessly walked away. He deserved nothing less than her contempt but he was making it difficult for her to hate him.

Finally, she pulled herself together and keeping it brief said, 'You're right. I *am* pregnant and I'd like you to help me get an abortion.'

Only for a split second did his eyes reveal he was shocked and then he spoke softly again. 'Have you undergone counselling about this?'

'Not really. My GP tried but my mind was made up. He referred me to a clinic but I've not been yet. I didn't know until yesterday that people could tell, so I had to get away before the father found out as we no longer see each other.'

'Would he not support you? Does he not have the means or is it something else? Is he married?'

That infuriated her. 'Why? Would being married exonerate him from paternal responsibilities? Is that the male viewpoint? Would that be *your* viewpoint if you'd fathered a bastard child whilst married?'

'Please, I'm simply trying to establish why you'd choose not to tell him. He has a right to be told and you have a right to expect his support.'

'God, that's rich coming from you,' she snorted.

He totally misread the undertone in her words and carried on, 'I'd like to tell you about something that happened to me many years ago. I was married to a lovely young woman. We were so happy when she became pregnant. It was an exciting time, planning for the new baby to arrive but tragically something went wrong; she had a miscarriage. It was no one's fault. It just happened but it drove us apart. It was more than she could bear. She grew temperamental and couldn't bear to be near me. I tried very hard to make it work but she wouldn't seek counselling and repeatedly yelled that she wanted a divorce. After a while I met somebody else and we fell in love. She became pregnant too and I was happy again but...'

'While you were still married?' she cut him short.

'Yes, but our marriage had been over for a while; we hardly spoke. I was certain she was seeing other men. She went out most nights until the early hours so in the end I agreed to the divorce.'

'So, this girl you met...did you marry her then?'

'Alas no, but I *would* have married her. I wanted to take her away but things didn't work out.'

'Why was that?'

'She suddenly changed and she broke my heart. I thought she loved me as much as I loved her. When she found she was pregnant we were elated. That's when we planned to go away, to begin a new life. I wanted that baby so much. I'd lost all hope of ever having children after my wife's tragic miscarriage, yet it was happening again, I'd been given a second chance and I was ecstatic.'

'Then I don't understand. What went wrong?'

'She had a termination, that's what went wrong. I called at her house to check everything was alright when she hadn't turned up at work for several days. Stony-faced, her father came to the door. He didn't even invite me in like he'd done before and then he told me she'd had an abortion. I was distraught. He said she'd changed her mind and that she was ill in bed following the termination. I didn't see her then, nor did I ever see her again. She broke my heart and that's why I'm asking if you are absolutely certain it's the right course of action, as there's no turning back once it's done; you've got to live with it. I'm not speaking to you as a professional; I'm speaking as someone with experience of the agony caused by such a decision, especially when I was there for her. I never got over losing my child though I appreciate your circumstances might warrant such a decision.'

Paige was distraught. Her mother wasn't a liar so if anyone had lied, assuming Jake was speaking the truth, it had to be her grandad.

Tears gushed from her eyes and Jake handed her a tissue. 'Paige, please...I'm not asking you to change your mind. It's *your* decision and you must do what you believe is right. I don't know why I mentioned my past. It's not a topic I've discussed before. I've tried to store those agonizing memories at the back of my mind. I found it too painful to discuss and I a psychiatrist, encouraging patients to face up to their problems. Rather incongruous, wouldn't you agree? Where *is* that coffee Marjorie was making for us?'

Impatiently Jake rang her extension but there was no reply. 'I bet she's forgotten and gone for lunch. Do you still want me to read this?'

She nodded. 'More than ever now.'

'I don't understand...'

Paige smiled through her tears. 'Oh you will Jake. Trust me, you will.'

Not once did he raise his head as he studied those three pages and Paige observed every facial movement, each twitch of the nose, each blink of the eye and she listened to each and every agonizing sigh as he absorbed her mother's poignant words. He was breathless with tears welling in his eyes by the end. *'Oh my God!'* he cried. 'Oh my God! It wasn't like that Paige. I *swear* it wasn't like that. I loved her so much. You must have really despised me when you read this letter. How long have you known?'

'Not long; I found it recently after Grandad died although I had my suspicions that you might be my father after we'd been for lunch with Frank Jessop. You made a corny comment that I reminded you of somebody you'd loved and lost. I thought you were coming on to me so that's why I was rude. Then, on my way back to the office, Richard said you were a womaniser, a doctor who'd turned up at the hospital one day with a cracking pair of shiners after a girl's father had hit you for allegedly getting his daughter pregnant. That's when I first suspected and Mum's letter merely confirmed those suspicions.'

'I never abandoned you Paige. Your grandfather's to blame. He lied to me *and* your mother but we've found each other now thank God. Would it be overstepping the mark were I to give you a hug? I can't believe I have such a lovely daughter and I'd like to hold you. May I, please?'

Tears coursed down her cheeks as she admitted, 'I came today hating you. I'm so sorry. You suffered more than any of us. At least Mum had me but you ended up with nobody. I shouldn't have judged you before hearing your version of events and yes Jake, I'd really like to hug you too.'

He stepped towards her. It was probably the most exciting moment of his life, hers too, as she melted in his arms. He was her biological father. His heart was pounding rapidly; his strong arms were holding her close and now that she'd found him she wanted to hold him forever. Those tender, caring moments would never cease to be the highlight of her life.

A noisy rattling of crockery preceded Marjorie as she backed into the room with a tray bearing coffee cups, sugar, cream and a large coffee pot.

She was somewhat surprised to find Jake with his arms wrapped around the young woman he'd taken to his room earlier especially as he made no attempt to release her.

Ever the gentleman, Jake relieved her of the tray. 'Don't look so shocked Marjorie. This is not what it seems. This is my daughter, Paige.'

'Oh, I didn't know you had a daughter Jake. I'm sure you've not mentioned her before.'

'That's because I didn't know myself, until now. It's a long story and when I've time, I'll enlighten you. Meanwhile, as an independent authority who's known me for many years, would you ever describe me as a womaniser? Please, be honest.'

She expelled an infectious ripple of laughter. 'Are you for real? *You, a womaniser?* I've never known you have a woman at all.'

'Alright, point made, so drop the melodrama,' he protested. 'I could easily pull a bird if I wanted to.'

Turning to Paige she cackled noisily and winked. 'Maybe a barnyard rooster but that's about all.'

Paige howled with laughter as Marjorie shot from the room. 'She certainly has *you* weighed up.'

'Maybe, but now you know I'm not nor ever have been a womaniser. I'll give Richard an earful when I next see him. How is the old clown? Has he said anything unfavourable about you being pregnant?'

Swallowing hard, Paige avoided eye contact with him. She hadn't come prepared to answer questions about Richard. She had turned up expecting a brief confrontational encounter with Jake that would no doubt end with his refusal to assist her in her plight.

Sensing something was amiss, he held her at arms length, searching her eyes for the truth. 'Talk to me Paige. Is Richard the father of your child?'

Paige had to admire his perception but that's what Jake had been taught to do, to seek out the truth.

With a nod of the head she answered his question.

He gathered her in his arms. 'I'm so sorry darling. It would appear *he's* the womaniser.'

As he wasn't there to defend himself, she felt the need to do so. 'It wasn't like that,' she explained. 'I entered the relationship with my eyes wide open. It lasted several months and every day was amazing, that was until Richard's son suffered a severe brain haemorrhage. He's out of hospital now but still has a way to go. He's at his dad's house where a nurse attends daily and he has regular physio too. Things became too complicated for Richard. He said I was helping out too much, wasting my young life, as he put it and I couldn't convince him I was doing what I wanted. I didn't feel pressured or obligated. When you love someone you do all you can to make life easier, so I helped round the house and made them the occasional meal but he was obviously clocking all the things I was doing. When he ended it, I was gutted. He said he was ending it for my sake but I didn't want him to. I didn't tell him I was pregnant so it's not like he sent me away when he found out. Besides, it's of no importance as I intend having the termination as soon as possible if you're able to put me in touch with someone who can help.'

He handed her a cup of coffee. 'I've a lot to make up for and whilst I'm not happy with your decision,

I have to respect your wishes.' Sitting down beside her he added, 'I would never judge you and you can count on my whole-hearted support; I won't let you down. There is one point I'd like to make though. If this is a question of the expense involved in raising the child, then let me make it clear that I'll offer all the financial support you need. Don't lose sight that we're talking about my grandchild but I'm not saying that to influence you Paige. When you've drunk your coffee, I suggest we go for lunch. Okay?'

She smiled. 'That sounds like a great idea. I seem to have an appetite all of a sudden.'

They covered a lot of ground in the next hour, by which time she felt as if they'd been acquainted for some time. Jake was easy to talk to which made her feel secure. 'I'm so glad I came,' she said. 'I didn't know what to do at first. I was at a low point in my life. I've had a few tough years taking care of Mum till she died and then Grandad needed my help too.'

'What was the cause of your mum's death?'

'Multiple system atrophy, for which there was no effective treatment or cure as you probably know. I made sure Mum had a decent quality of life within her limitations and I did the same for Grandad too, so I've nothing to reproach myself for.'

Jake smiled proudly. 'I'm sure you did your best. So, are you planning to return home later today?'

'Er...I was going to look round for a place to rent. Obviously I'll have to go back to sort out my house but I was hoping I'd find an inexpensive motel for tonight and then drive home tomorrow if the roads aren't thick with snow.'

Instantly he offered, 'You can stay at my place. I have a five-bedroom house and live alone so there's plenty of room. You can take a look when we leave here. It's just a couple of miles away. I regularly eat here as it saves cooking for one. I'm finding it hard to believe this is happening Paige. I keep thinking I'll wake up to find none of it's true.'

He pointed to his crooked nose and grinned. 'Can you see that? That's where your grandad whacked me. He broke my bloody nose.'

She laughed. 'He did have a temper but after he'd had the stroke, he mellowed a lot.'

'He needed your help,' he stated pragmatically.

'You're probably right. There's something else I need to ask, purely out of interest because it doesn't bother me, truly, but am I half Jewish?'

He looked surprised. 'What's brought that on?'

'Your name, Jacob. That's a Jewish name; at least it would have been at the time you were born.'

With raised eyebrows and a humorous expression he rejoined, 'Back in biblical times you mean?'

She giggled. *'No,* I didn't mean that. It's become popular again recently but in your day, surely it was a name given to men of Jewish faith, no?'

'I'll have to pass on that because I don't know but I can assure you I'm not Jewish Paige. I was named after my grandad. I don't think he had any belief at all as he did more than his fair share of blasphem-ing. I hated my name as a child and became known as Jake. Speaking of grandads, my dad is still alive. He's in a nursing home just a few miles from here. He's poor at walking but has all his other faculties.

He'd be delighted to learn he had a beautiful granddaughter, so would you like to meet him?'

She beamed with delight. Everything was getting better by the minute. 'Yes, if you're sure the shock won't upset him. Are there any other relatives?'

'Sadly not. I was an only child. I just have Dad.'

'Please don't tell him I'm pregnant when we visit him. I'm so ashamed. I wish it was all over.'

'I'll have a word with a colleague and start things moving when I get back. He might have a slot later today to discuss it with you. Meanwhile there's no cause to be ashamed. Have you had enough to eat?'

'Plenty thanks and it was lovely. This is a really nice place with a great atmosphere and that log fire is so calming; I'm almost asleep. It's nice staring at those crackling embers and I love the smell. I can't begin to describe how happy I feel. I didn't expect anything like this. I was certain you'd reject me as you'd allegedly done before.'

'Thus verifying one must never presume,' he said satirically. 'Let's make a move. I've patients to see. We'll stop off at my place so I can show you what's what and then I'll take you back to collect your car and give you a door key. If there's no pressing need to go home tomorrow, you can stay here with me as long as you like.'

'Sounds good to me,' she said with a broad smile.

9

Rosemary poked her head around the door. 'Do you have a minute to spare Richard?'

With a vacant expression he asked, 'Problem?'

'Er...no. Well, yes, I suppose it is, though it's not of my making I hasten to add but I think you should be made aware of what's being said.'

'Being said?' he enquired quizzically. 'Being said about what, by whom?'

She wrung her hands nervously. 'I know you've a lot of stress at the moment with David's issues and Paige's sudden resignation and I hate to add to your troubles but...' Her voice trailed off.

Irritably he said, 'For God's sake, get to the point if there is one; this isn't at all like you Rosemary. If you've something to say then say it; spit it out.'

She halted to gather her thoughts. 'I've overheard the office girls gossiping. They're all aware Paige is pregnant; they're saying you're the father and that's why you sacked her.'

For several seconds he didn't speak. He was too shocked to speak. Arising from his chair, he walked across the room and opened the door. 'You can get back and inform that motley crew that Paige is *not* pregnant; that means I'm *not* the father, and for the record I did *not* sack her. She resigned of her own volition and if they'd like to appoint a spokesperson to face me with these lewd allegations, I'll be only too happy to deal with that person in the same way I allegedly dealt with Paige. *Is that everything?'*

Rosemary had never seen Richard so angry but it couldn't be left like this. 'I'm not trying to pry,' she told him. 'I'm trying to protect your reputation and shouting and bawling won't help.' Closing the door again she walked back to her chair and sat down.

'I understand it's no one's business but yours and Paige's but I'm concerned as the finger's pointing at you. Everyone knows you were, how shall I say, *friendly*. Even I knew that, and I don't make a point of sticking my nose where it's not wanted but when the girl suddenly ups and vanishes, they're bound to suspect *you* when she's clearly pregnant.'

He stared in utter disbelief as she continued, 'I've heard her being sick a couple of times in the ladies' toilets and though I kept quiet, I had my suspicions but over the past couple of weeks it's become quite noticeable. Girls will be girls; they'll talk Richard, especially when the girl's involved with the boss so how do you want me to handle it? I'll deal with it.'

He emitted a pained sigh. 'There's no doubt she's pregnant?'

'None whatsoever. I'm so sorry your name's been dragged into it. Some folk thrive on tittle-tattle and creating a scandal out of nothing.'

There was no point in trying to disguise the facts. Eventually everything would come out. 'If indeed, Paige *is* pregnant, I'm responsible. It *is* mine, but I knew nothing about it. I ended our relationship the day she walked out of here. It was a selfless act; I thought she could do better. She helped with David, she cooked our meals and I felt very guilty. Paige is a delightful creature with an enormous heart and I thought she deserved better but unable to offer any guarantee that David would make a total recovery, I couldn't allow her to continue as a nursemaid at her age and so, painful as my decision was, I ended it.'

He paused. 'Shortly after, I received her letter of resignation. She had already packed her belongings and left the premises. I swear to you, I didn't know she was pregnant. I would never have sent her away shirking my responsibilities. God only knows how I can make amends now but I must try, so thank you for telling me and please, keep it to yourself.'

Sidling to the door to make her exit she nodded. 'I won't breathe a word to anyone.'

After she left, Richard sat quietly with his head in his hands. If Paige was pregnant, he must go to her. Whatever his reasons for ending their relationship, there was now a child involved, his child but the all important question was, would she forgive him?

There was only one way to find out.

He asked Eric to assume responsibility for the rest of the day and hurried to his car.

To discover the *To Let* board displayed in Paige's garden came as a shock to him.

He had already rehearsed what he would say, how he would plead for her forgiveness. He would make no initial reference to the pregnancy. If everything appeared to be going well he could then pretend to notice and express delight.

He rang the doorbell and waited but there was no answer. He tried her mobile too but that was dead. As he was about to walk round the house, Bill from next door came out. 'Can I help you mate? If you're here about the house for rent you'd best talk to the agent. The owner's not here.'

'Do you know when she'll be back?'

He shook his head. 'I don't know if she's coming back. If she gets fixed up with summat where she's gone, she reckons she won't be back at all.'

He was frantic. *'Just listen.* I need to get in touch with her urgently. You must know something.'

Bill eyed him up suspiciously. 'Sorry, I can't help you chum. I know nowt, nowt at all.'

This was simply wasting time, he concluded. The man had obviously been primed to keep quiet about Paige's whereabouts but where did he go now? No doubt the agent had been told to keep quiet too but he couldn't sit back and do nothing. He had to find her to put things right. He sighed in desperation as he drove to town to see the letting agent.

That visit proved fruitless too although there was a certain credibility about that young lady's account that Paige had left with no firm destination in mind.

There was only one more person he could ask and that was Emma but he doubted he'd receive a warm reception there. She was his one remaining hope.

Making his way to Sampson's where she worked, he checked his watch. It was four-fifteen. He turned into the car park and parked at a good vantage point to see staff leaving the premises. Before long a few women appeared in view, one of whom was Emma.

She left the group and as she made her way through the car park, Richard approached, calling her name.

With a smile she turned her head but the moment she saw him, her face altered. *'My God, you've got some bloody nerve coming here,'* she hollered, eyes blazing with fury. 'Do you know what you are? Let me tell you. You're a jumped up nowt, Mr bloody high-and-mighty Cavendish.'

He took another step towards her and at that point Andy stepped from his car calling her name.

'I haven't finished with this toe-rag yet,' she told Andy, turning to face Richard again. 'You're all the same you well-to-do folk. You think it's alright to have no regard for a girl's feelings, to crack on you like her then chuck her aside once you've had your leg over, leaving her to pick up the pieces. I really thought you were different but you're not; you're a pile of scum, that's what you are, bloody scum.'

Ignoring her acerbic comments he pleaded, 'Tell me where she is, please. I want to make amends. I didn't know she was pregnant. I've just found out. I was simply trying to protect her, that's the truth.'

'Trying to protect her?' she cackled. 'You dump a pregnant girl, leaving her with no alternative but to give up her job too, so that she has *nothing, nothing* at all to live on. Tell me, why did *she* deserve that?'

'Believe me Emma, please; I'd no idea Paige was pregnant then. I only found out today when...'

Emma sneered scornfully. 'You could have saved yourself the trouble coming here because she isn't pregnant now. She's gone far away from here, away from you and all you stand for. She's gone to get an abortion because she couldn't cope. I tried talking to her but she wouldn't listen. So, are you proud of yourself now? I've ended up losing my best friend thanks to you. I'll most likely never see her again.'

Tears filled Emma's eyes as she glowered at him. 'I don't ever want to see you again do you hear? If I did know where she was I'd never tell *you*. You've caused nothing but heartache to a loving and caring girl who wouldn't harm a fly. She'd have done anything for you and David and this is how you repay her loyalty and devotion. Now she has to live with that agonizing decision to end her pregnancy.'

In desperation he turned to Andy with beseeching eyes. 'I don't suppose you know where she's gone.'

Before he could respond Emma yelled, *'Get away from him.* Andy detests you as much as I do. If you were on fire he wouldn't piss on you. Is *that* clear enough for you to understand? Go on, crawl back to your swine-mobile and sod off.'

Suddenly conscious of spectators eavesdropping he backed off. With all known avenues of enquiry now exhausted there was no other way to find her.

Emma's words tormented him. Paige was having an abortion; maybe she'd had it already. It was too much to bear and he couldn't contain his feelings a moment longer as he wept for Paige, the love of his life and likewise for the loss of his child.

'Do you fancy a cup of tea love?' Andy asked.

'Not for me thanks. I want summat stronger. Pour me a vodka and lemon please. I could kill Richard. Fancy that hard-faced sod asking me for help. Then he has the nerve to ask you. He's no better than that pig ignorant son of his. I think *you* could have been more supportive as well. Instead of gawping around saying nowt you could have backed me up.'

'It's more awkward for me Emma. I don't want to fall out with him because he puts a lot of work my way. Most of my foreigners come from him; I earn plenty of brass thanks to Richard. Besides, the way you were mouthing off you didn't need my help.'

'Flaming typical that, sitting on the fence. It's the *Old Boys' Club* isn't it? Just forget it Andy. You're all the bloody same.'

Changing topic to circumvent a heated argument that was brewing he asked, 'What's for tea?'

'Potato pie I made yesterday. It needs reheating.'

'Can I do owt to help?'

Emma shook her head. 'No, I'm just having a few minutes and then I'll get on with it. I wonder where Paige is and whether she's scared. I know I would be. There's no end to that poor girl's misery.'

'Have you still heard nothing from her?'

'Not a word. I suppose she'll get in touch with me when she's found somewhere to get her head down. I still can't believe the effrontery of that man.'

Risking life and limb, he dared to contradict her. 'He seemed genuine to me when he said he wanted to make amends. Maybe you should have heard him out, listened to what he had to say and then passed on a message. It wasn't your place to interfere.'

'He's not fit to lick her sodding boots,' she cried. 'Let it drop Andy. Paige is *my* friend, not yours and he's really hurt her. It's best she forgets him.'

With a toss of her hair she headed for the kitchen to prepare their tea.

She was clearing away the dishes and tidying up when the telephone rang. It was Paige. Emma cried with joy, 'I'm so pleased to hear from you. Where are you? Are you okay and is your car holding up?'

'Stop worrying,' she laughed. 'I'm fine; the car's fine and I'm at a friend's house for the night, someone my mum knew a long time ago. Make a note of this number. I could be here a few days; it's snowing heavily. My mobile's flat but I intend changing my number so if you need to get in touch, call this landline number until I give you another.'

She jotted the number down on her pad. 'So, does that mean you haven't made any arrangements for the *you-know-what* yet?'

'Yes I have. I saw a doctor this afternoon and it'll be sorted in the next day or two.'

There was a brief pause before Emma remarked, 'You haven't had a change of heart then?'

'And why would I do that?' asked Paige.

'No particular reason. I was just wondering, that's all. Are you scared?'

'Let's just say I'll feel a lot better when it's over. Right, I'm off as this isn't my phone. I'll call again tomorrow, hopefully.'

'Good luck with the...well...'

'Thanks Emma and don't worry; I'll be fine.'

As Emma hung up, Andy remarked, 'You didn't mention Richard,'

She slanted her eyes in his direction. 'Your point being...?'

As he picked up the Evening News and proceeded to read it, Emma yawned sleepily. 'I think I'll turn in early tonight. I'll see how I feel after my bath.'

'Yell if you need owt,' he called to her. He waited until he heard her bath filling before he jumped up. Moving to the telephone table he inspected the pad and at first was disappointed as she had torn off the top page, but as he tilted the pad towards the light, there was a faint impression of Paige's number that he swiftly copied.

Needs must, he told himself as he ran upstairs two at a time. 'Can you hear me?' he called to Emma.

'Yes, what's up?'

'I have to nip out for half an hour to price a job. I just remembered I promised to be there for half-past seven. See you later.'

As he turned into the avenue he saw Richard's car on the drive. It hadn't been a wasted journey.

When Richard opened the door he was surprised to see Andy. 'Come in lad,' he greeted him warmly.

'I can't stop Guv. I daren't hang about. It's more than my life's worth, coming round here, but I had to speak to you. I'm caught up in the middle as you know so you must promise you haven't seen me.'

'Don't worry; I understand the position you're in. I created this problem and that means I have to deal with it. The sad thing is I've exhausted all options. I have nowhere else to go now.'

He led Andy to the lounge and gestured to him to sit down. 'How come you were at Sampson's when I called to see Emma?'

'Her car's in dock. She gets it back tomorrow so I took her to work and picked her up. I stay at hers a few nights a week and fortunately I was there when Paige called half an hour ago.'

Following that disclosure, Richard's ears pricked up. 'So she *does* know where Paige is then and...?'

'No, she doesn't,' he interrupted. 'When she left, Paige didn't know where she'd end up. She wanted to find a suitable place to rent in a good area where she could start over. She could be anywhere.'

Richard's head flopped into his hands. 'I've made such a bloody mess of things. I was trying to do the right thing, to give Paige the chance of a decent life with someone her own age. I have all this baggage with David. It simply wasn't fair that she'd become embroiled in my troubles. I hadn't a clue Paige was pregnant, I swear. I'd never have ended things had I known and now I can't find her to make amends.'

'Listen, I don't want to get your hopes up but this might help. When Paige phoned Emma earlier, she gave her this number. I got it from the impression it left on the pad. If you manage to make contact with her, you mustn't say how you found her number. If Emma knew I'd told you it'd be curtains for me.'

'Aye, you're not wrong there lad. She has a bit of a temper though I can't blame her for the things she said. If they presented an academy award for being the world's biggest pillock, I'd win hands down.'

Andy tittered. 'I'm saying nowt. I've done what I came to do so I'm off now. Good luck.'

Richard shook his hand. 'Thanks Andy. You're a good mate. I'll not let you down. I'll keep schtum.'

Following a sleepless night, Richard went to work at seven the next day. He had thought long and hard about how to use the valuable information supplied by his friend. As discretion was paramount, he was struggling to find a way to avoid implicating Andy if Emma happened to be the one and only recipient of the telephone number and Richard had to assume she was in the absence of evidence to the contrary.

He placed Eric in charge during his absence, saying he had an urgent matter to attend to out of town and went to his office to attack the ever increasing mountain of paperwork on his desk while awaiting Rosemary's arrival.

She looked up and smiled as he entered her room. 'You look worn out Richard. Is everything alright? Has there been a development?'

'Yes, kind of,' he answered. 'The thing is, I need your help but I don't want anyone's job on the line. I don't know where Paige went but I've managed to find a phone number. She's somewhere out of town according to my source.'

'So how can I be of help?'

He glanced at her apologetically. 'This is a liberty I know, but don't you have a relative who works for Directory Enquiries? I was hoping she'd get me the address for this phone number.'

'It's my sister who works there but the operators are constantly monitored. I can put it to her but I'm afraid I can't promise she'll be able to help.'

He made for the door. 'I wouldn't ask if there was any other way to find Paige but I don't want to get anyone in trouble. If it's too risky, tell her it's fine.'

When Richard returned from the sandwich shop at lunchtime, he found a folded typewritten sheet on his desk with an address in Royal Leamington Spa. He couldn't imagine why Paige had ended up there but hopefully all would be revealed before too long.

He went home first to attend to David's needs and after speaking to the nurse, he set off on his journey to find Paige, praying he wouldn't arrive too late to persuade her not to have the abortion..

It was just after four o'clock when he approached the house in a pleasant tree-lined avenue with well spaced architecturally designed detached houses of early post-war era where even the bungalows were huge, indicating it was an affluent area. Remnants of a heavy fall of snow were piled against the kerbs, making it difficult for Richard to see house names and numbers until suddenly his heart missed a beat as he approached Paige's familiar old and battered car. Stopping behind it, he switched off the ignition and sighed, afraid of the reception he might receive.

He stepped from the car and made his way to the front door, clearing his throat nervously. After ringing the bell he waited in trepidation like a naughty schoolboy would wait by the Headmaster's door for his punishment, then suddenly she was there, standing before him with a look of utter disbelief in her bright blue eyes.

In a weak voice he spoke her name. 'Paige...I had to see you. Please don't turn me away.'

She answered with a question. 'How did you find me when no one knows where I am? Did you speak to Emma?'

'No...er...well yes I tried but she wouldn't tell me anything. I met her on the car park at work and she was very angry and verbally abusive.'

His answer didn't suffice. 'So if Emma didn't tell you how did you find me then?'

'That's not important. What matters is I did. I had to talk to you Paige, to explain I'd made a terrible mistake. I'd like you to come home, please. It was all my fault. I wasn't thinking straight. I've been so uptight about David but it won't happen again. This is the worst decision I've ever made in my life.'

His plea found no sympathy. 'You'll get over it. We all learn to live with life's disappointments so try and live with yours. Don't imagine for a minute that I moved a hundred miles away on a whim. You gave me good cause and I won't ever come back.'

He couldn't leave it at that. 'Can't we talk about it? I don't want to lose you; I can't lose you; I love you. Just tell me what I can do to make amends.'

His words tormented her and she wanted to throw herself into his arms but she resisted and stood her ground. Squaring her shoulders she met his earnest gaze. 'We're finished. You really hurt me Richard. You made me feel cheap and worthless and nothing you say will change my mind…ever.'

His next words shook her to the core. 'Have you had the abortion yet? I know you're pregnant and I don't want you to have a termination. It's my baby too so I think I'm entitled to have my say.'

Her mind was in turmoil. Who was feeding him such information? He knew she was pregnant and where he would find her. There could only be one person responsible. Nobody else knew, so it had to be Jake, but why? 'It's too late,' she replied coldly. 'The procedure's booked in for tomorrow and as a single person, it's my decision and mine alone.'

He pleaded again. 'Please don't do it. I'll provide financial support and anything else you might need. I know it's not easy raising a child on your own but if you're determined it's over for us, I'd hate you to spend the rest of your life regretting your decision. Think of that friend I told about, Jake. His wife lost her baby and then she couldn't have any more.'

Richard had confirmed her suspicions. It was too much of a coincidence for him to have mentioned Jake's name had he not been instrumental in setting up Richard's visit. She was outraged. 'Is that it?'

He sighed heavily. 'I suppose it is. Whatever you think of me, I'll always love you. It was never my intent to hurt you and I'm sorry for what I said.'

He turned and walked up the path without looking back, and with a heavy heart Paige closed the door. Had she been right to send him away? Should she proceed with the termination? Only she could find the answers to those questions.

She watched through the window as he drove past the house. 'I'll always love you too,' she murmured through choking tears, 'It would never have worked out though. I told you once before that good things don't happen to me. It's for the best.'

As she returned to the kitchen to proceed with the meal she was making, Richard paused at the end of the avenue to give way to a car indicating to enter. The other driver reduced speed, acknowledging the courteous act and as their eyes met simultaneously, there was instant recognition by both parties.

Richard stamped on his accelerator and drove off at speed with fury and frustration raging inside him. 'I don't believe it. *Jake Allcock,*' he bellowed. 'The lecherous swine that never misses an opportunity. I could kill him; I could kill the bloody pair of them.'

Jake threw his car keys on the hallstand and made his way to the kitchen to find Paige. 'I'm sure I've just seen Richard. If not, it was his double.'

When she didn't respond he moved closer. 'Your silence would appear to confirm my suspicion. Has he been here?'

She turned to him with bloodshot eyes, her thick dark lashes saturated with tears. 'Don't you play the innocent with me Jake Allcock. If you wanted me to leave you only had to say. You didn't have to get in touch with Richard. I've never found one man in my entire life that I could trust.' Expelling a short derisive cackle she went on, 'Shall I tell you something? For a brief moment I truly believed you were different. I really thought you cared. Have you any idea how it feels to know I've been betrayed by my own flesh and blood? I can't describe how demoralised and stupid I feel for having trusted you.'

He continued to gaze at her silently until she spat, 'So? Aren't you even going to deny it?'

He leaned against the counter-top. 'This would be the point at which I would say to my patient, "And how did that make you feel?" but as you've clearly stated how it made you feel, you've pre-empted my question. However, before we continue, I'd like to answer *your* question and yes Paige, I am going to deny it because I haven't seen or spoken to Richard since our meeting with Frank. I know you're upset. I would be too in your position but I'm not the one to blame, I swear, and I find it hard to believe you show such little faith in me after our discussion last night when the two of us opened up our hearts. So, as it isn't me, who else knew about your plans?'

'That's the whole point Jake, *nobody* does and I still think it coincidental that at the precise moment he leaves this house, you just happen to walk in.'

'And did you seek the source of his information?' he asked without reference to her accusations.

She nodded. 'He wouldn't tell me.'

'I can't make you believe me Paige. I offered you my support and that alone should make you realise I wasn't the cause of Richard's sudden appearance.' He stared deeply into her eyes and she knew he was speaking the truth.

'I couldn't believe it when I went to the door and saw him standing there. I didn't tell a soul where I was going, not even my best friend so it appeared to be the only possible explanation...that *you* had told him. I'm sorry I yelled at you. I'm overwrought.'

Jake smiled. 'Then how about a hug? I'm thrilled to have you here Paige and I want you to stay.'

She cried as he held her. 'It'll turn out alright,' he said. 'I see patients with seemingly insurmountable problems who recover. Things *will* get better.'

'I wish I shared your confidence. I'm very tense at the moment. I lost my family, first my mum and then my grandad and when I began to think things couldn't get any worse my entire world fell apart. I then lost my job, my home and on top of that I've left my friends behind too. I've also lost the man I loved, I'm pregnant and I've a termination to face as well now. Add to that the shock I had today seeing Richard and even you in your job will admit it's a lot to deal with but you're right I suppose; I *will* bounce back because that is what I do best. I've had lots of practice in standing my ground and fighting the authorities for welfare entitlements. As I made clear earlier, I didn't drive all the way down here to play happy families. I came because I was angry, so I could tell you to your face that you were another disappointment in my life and give you the chance to reject me once again.'

Releasing her grip Paige stepped back and looked into his eyes. 'I'm pleased I did come though and it was great to meet Grandad. He's a sweet old man. I've been such a liability since I turned up here but once I've had the termination, I'll quickly come to terms with everything. I promise I'll give it my best shot anyway. I can't say fairer than that.'

He gave her a squeeze. 'That's the spirit,' he told her though he was deeply saddened by her decision to go ahead with the termination.

'You're shaking,' Jake said stroking her hand.

'I know. I can't bear the smell of clinics. They all smell the same, so...er...'

'*Clinical?*' he smiled. 'I can't say I ever notice.'

Paige let out a sigh. 'I'll be glad when it's over.'

'I know. Try to be positive. I'm here for you.'

She wrung her clammy hands, conscious she was panting heavily; her heart was pounding too. 'Am I doing the right thing?' she questioned nervously.

Though he understood her indecision and felt her pain there were simply no words of comfort to offer her. 'I can't advise you I'm afraid. It has to be your decision but if you're having second thoughts I can ask to defer it for a few days until you're absolutely sure. Dr Ainsworth will understand. It's a difficult decision; you wouldn't be the first to have doubts.'

Her mind was in turmoil. Thinking of what might have been, in her mind's eye she could see Richard standing by a crib, looking down and smiling. She tried to peer into it too but it was empty. What did these thoughts and visions mean? Her images were instantly curtailed when the nurse in a sympathetic tone asked, 'Would you like to come in now?'

Jake stood up. 'Shall I come in with you?'

She tried to stand and wobbled. 'Yes please.'

Jake took her arm and led her into the consulting room where she burst into tears.

Dr Ainsworth passed her a handful of tissues and smiled, waiting for her to compose herself.

Tearfully she snivelled, 'Sorry, I'm a bit upset.'

'It's not too late to have a change of heart. You'd not be the first,' he told her compassionately. 'This is not a decision to be taken lightly as I explained at your consultation yesterday. Lots of women change their minds at this stage.'

She cleared her throat. 'I'm fine, truly. I'm just a bit afraid. I do want to go ahead; I must; my mind's made up. This is what I have to do.'

'If you're really sure, then there are papers to sign but I want to carry out an ultrasound scan first.'

'Why do you need to do that?'

'To confirm how many weeks pregnant you are.'

She looked surprised. 'I've already told you and you poked and prodded me yesterday.'

'I know, but this is a requirement...for the paper-work,' he explained, glancing furtively at Jake who nodded knowingly.

'Will I be able to see anything?' she asked.

'Of course, if that's what you want.'

'Come here,' she told Jake. 'I can't do this alone.'

He sat down close to Paige as the equipment was being set up and she fixed her eyes on the monitor where a blurred image appeared. Dr Ainsworth told her what he could see and only then did she understand the enormity of what she was about to do. She was shaking with fear. That was her baby, her own flesh and blood, and filled with remorse she cried, 'What am I doing Jake? That's my baby. It's alive.' She burst into tears as Jake grasped her hands. 'I'm here for you Paige. You must do what you believe is right for you. Take your time. Be sure about what you're about to do. No one is judging you.'

'I don't know what I want anymore. I'm confused and I feel so guilty. Help me to decide...please. You have to guide me Jake...I'm pleading with you.'

Dr Ainsworth met Jake's eye, nodding to confirm the earlier suspicion he'd discussed with him at the previous day's clinic.

'Dr Ainsworth has something to tell you darling,' Jake said softly. 'It might help with your decision.'

'Tell me…tell me what?' Paige cried. 'What's the matter? Is there something wrong with my baby?'

With a broad smile Dr Ainsworth shook his head. 'Everything looks fine with *both* your babies Paige. You're pregnant with twins.'

Paige looked from one to the other, not knowing whether to laugh or cry, her face contorted into an expression of total disbelief. 'Twins?' she shrieked. 'Really...I'm having twins? How amazing is that?'

With relief in his eyes Jake smiled at her reaction. 'Does this mean you'd like to reconsider?'

'Can I? Can we? Oh Jake I'm going to need your help with *two* babies. You said you always wanted children and in time I wanted children too, my own flesh and blood. Can we do this...together...please?' she gabbled, tears coursing down her cheeks.

He brushed his lips against her brow. 'Nothing in the world would give me greater pleasure Paige.'

Dr Ainsworth was overjoyed too. 'I take it you'll be going home to talk things through with Jake?'

Through her tears a relieved smile illuminated her face. 'I'm very grateful to you Dr Ainsworth and to you too Jake. I was really scared but between you, you've helped me make the right decision. I could never give up my baby...correction, *babies*. Twins! Wow! I'm the luckiest girl alive.'

10

'I thought we might go out to eat later if you're up to it,' Jake suggested. 'What do you say?'

'That'd be great. I can't tell you how much better I feel now. It wasn't that I *wanted* a termination. It just seemed the only option with no job, no money and a car on its last legs but now, with your support I can stop worrying, not that I intend sponging off you. When my rent comes in I'll pay my way.'

'Now you're being silly. Work out what I'd have paid in child support to your mum. I've nobody else to spend my money on, so now I want to spoil you and pamper my grandchildren. Is that so wrong?'

'No, not in moderation but I'm independent and I like fair play, so I'll pay my way… no argument.'

It was time for him to drop the matter. Paige was very principled and that was an excellent quality he had to admire. Her mother had raised her well.

'Is it alright for me to call Emma?'

'Mi casa es su casa. You don't have to ask. Help yourself to whatever you want.'

'*Bloody hell!*' Emma screeched to learn Paige was having twins. 'That bugger never does anything by halves, does he? How will you cope and where will you live? How will you manage financially?'

With a half-truth Paige replied that she'd continue to stay with her mother's friend who lived alone but Emma was concerned. 'What if it doesn't work out and she asks you to leave? It's a lot to expect of an old friend of your mum's.'

'I'll cross that bridge when I come to it,' she said philosophically, feeling guilty at her deceit. 'Listen, I've decided to drive up for the weekend to get my house emptied, the personal stuff I mean and then I can clean up. How do you fancy giving me a hand?'

Eagerly she agreed to help and Paige promised to call her once she arrived.

'Have you much to bring back?' Jake asked when Paige told him. 'I could come too, to help transport it. My car's bigger and more reliable than yours.'

'And how do I explain who you are to Emma?'

Jake frowned quizzically. 'What's to explain? I'm your dad. Are you ashamed of me?'

'*No.* I haven't told her about you yet. Emma has a loose tongue and it might get back to Richard.'

He was more confused. 'So? What's your point?'

'If Richard thinks I'm *living* with you...you know what I mean, which he obviously does because you said he recognised you, he'll keep well away from me. Besides, he'll think I've had the abortion now.'

'Let me get this right. Are you saying you don't *ever* intend telling Richard he has two children?'

She nodded. 'Got it in one.'

Jake was shocked by her heartlessness. 'That is *so* wrong Paige. That's exactly what your grandad did. I know you've had your differences but he still has a right to know. I can't condone that.'

She turned on her heels. 'It isn't your decision to make; it's mine, so can we drop it please? I'll *never* tell him. He made it absolutely clear he didn't want children so I won't put my children at risk of feeling abandoned like I believed I'd been. You've no idea how demoralised I felt when I was growing up to think I'd been rejected by my father. I always put on a brave face and acted as if it didn't matter when people asked but it did. It mattered very much.'

This was an argument that was not going away. If it caused ill feeling, so be it, but Jake was likewise determined to have his say. 'Do you have any idea how I felt to suddenly learn I had a daughter I knew nothing about? Well?'

'*Yes I have* because the same day I also learned I had a father who cared. We were both duped Jake, both victims of an appalling, senseless act and...'

'And which *you're* perpetuating through the next generation. You must really hate Richard to behave in such a contemptible way, that's all I can say.'

'I don't hate him. That's the problem Jake. I love him; I always will.'

He was confounded. 'I'm thankful you aren't my patient because I can't follow your logic at all. Is it perhaps an issue of, "hell hath no fury..."?'

'Maybe...I don't know. I'd find it very hard to be in Richard's company and it'd keep happening if he knew about the children. He might want access.'

He sighed. 'The time will come when the children start to ask questions about him and those questions will have to be answered. I sincerely hope you'll be ready for all the ramifications when that time comes because it *will* come and there could be a high price to pay. Be forewarned. I've said my piece now. I'll not mention it again.'

'Good. I've decided I'll go on my own this weekend. I need to be there on Monday to see my agent, so I'll be back Tuesday. Don't worry about my car. I have breakdown cover should I need it.'

Cautiously Jake asked, 'Are we still going out?'

'Of course. We're allowed to have our differences Jake and I'm sure there'll be plenty more. It hasn't taken me long to discover I'm my father's daughter. We both hold strong views. That's healthy isn't it?'

Jake laughed and gave her a squeeze. 'Go and get ready. I'm ravenous.'

'Look at you,' Emma cried, giving her a hug. 'You look to have piled loads more weight on.'

'I only saw you last week. You always know how to wind me up don't you? Get lost.'

Emma grinned. 'How long are you staying?'

'I'll probably go back Tuesday. That's the plan if I get through everything here in time.'

'Andy's coming round to give us a hand with the heavy stuff. I'm making us a meal tonight.'

Paige smiled. 'That's kind of you. Thank you.'

Emma picked up a pile of clothes and put them in a bag. 'So, tell me about this friend of your mum's. Are you sure she's keen to have you there? Did you know her before you turned up on her doorstep?'

It was time to tell the truth. She couldn't continue with the deception any longer. 'I have something to tell you but you must promise you'll not repeat this to anyone and I mean *anyone*, not even Andy, or I won't tell you.'

'I swear,' she said wide-eyed. 'What is it Paige?'

She took a deep breath. 'I lied to you. There is no old lady. I've found my dad. I'm staying with him.'

'*Bloody hell! Your dad?*' she cried. 'How did that come about? Are you sure he's your dad?'

'I'm positive but I haven't known very long and I kept it to myself because when I found out who he was, I didn't know what to do.'

'Why...who is he? Is he someone famous?'

'No, you clown. I meant I didn't know if I'd ever contact him, but when Richard and I broke up and I was pregnant, I didn't know which way to turn so I went to see him the other day. He didn't even know I existed. It seems Grandad told him a pack of lies. He told him Mum had opted for an abortion and he sent him packing with a couple of black eyes. It's a long story so I'll tell you everything else over a cup of coffee.'

Emma was on the edge of her seat throughout the revelations. Paige had never seen her friend so quiet and attentive. Not once did she cut in or divert her gaze until Paige reached the end.

'Sounds like you've landed on your feet,' Emma sighed. 'I'm really happy for you. Your dad sounds very supportive. I can't wait to meet him.'

'He offered to come with me but I couldn't risk it. I still haven't worked out how Richard managed to find out where I'd gone. I told no one at all. I didn't even know where Jake lived until he took me to his house. I know Richard had been sniffing round here because Bill next door told me when I arrived so he obviously made it his business to find me.'

'Just move on now and stuff him. He'll get over you like you'll get over him. You'll have the twins before long and you'll have no time to mither about him. Let's have another mad hour and when Andy arrives he can start humping stuff downstairs. Have you heard from Annette?'

'Yes, she was showing two couples round the day before yesterday so fingers crossed. She said one of them was hoping to move house before Christmas. Can you imagine *anyone* moving house in the run up to Christmas with little over a week to go?'

'I don't need to imagine; I'm flaming-well looking at one...you.'

Paige laughed. 'I hadn't thought of that. I'm glad I did move though; Jake's a really amazing man.'

'Don't you call him *Dad?'*

'Er...no. I can't say I'd given it any thought. We'd both feel uncomfortable I think were I to do that.'

There was a loud bang on the door. 'That's got to be Andy,' Emma said jumping up. 'He can start by bringing those bags down on the landing.'

'Any chance of a brew?' he asked the moment he walked in and Paige giggled.

'You and your brews. It's good of you to help us.'

By five o'clock the bedrooms had been cleaned and emptied and the bathroom was sparkling.

'That's enough,' Paige sighed. 'Tomorrow I'll do downstairs. Look at all that post and I've only been away for a few days. I must get my mail redirected.

There's such a lot to do. There's a few things in the freezer you can take home Emma, then I'll turn it off. Are you coming tomorrow Andy?'

'Yes. I'll clean the windows and go to the tip.'

Emma flopped down on the sofa. 'We'll murder it tomorrow,' she said confidently.

Paige sighed nostalgically. 'I'm going to miss this place after living here all my life.'

'You can come back anytime you like. You still own it. No one knows what the future holds in store and think of your new life and surroundings. You'll soon settle.'

No reference had been made to the pregnancy. It appeared Andy hadn't noticed or maybe he was just being polite. Emma had been primed to say nothing about the twins, nothing that might slip out were he to come in contact with Richard and she had given her word that she wouldn't.

There was a tearful farewell as they parted. 'Keep in touch, won't you?' Emma pleaded. 'I miss you.'

'I miss you too,' she snivelled. 'I'll call you when I get back unless I have time to call round with your Christmas presents before I leave.'

There were three important matters outstanding on Paige's 'to do' list. First she had to complete all her Christmas shopping; she had to see Annette to sign the paperwork and she had to call at Eleanor's. She doubted Richard would have given a satisfactory if indeed any explanation for her absence and she felt it better to tell Eleanor face to face, rather than over the telephone. Over the past few days, Eleanor had left messages on her answer-phone, suggesting that Richard had failed to reveal any information to his mother about their recent argument or break-up.

In less time than anticipated Paige had finished all her Christmas shopping.

It was then time to see her agent, Annette, where Paige would hopefully receive good news. It turned out that the news was *excellent* with one interested party offering thirty pounds a month more than the asking price to ward off a competitor.

That, said Annette would cover her management fee and the couple were looking for a long-term let which was an added bonus.

Later, as Paige was wrapping her Christmas gifts she realised that a heavy burden had been removed from her shoulders. Over recent days she had seen a major turn-around in her life. Desperation had now changed to elation and she had needed that so much following the recent friction and anxiety.

On Tuesday morning she gathered all the presents together and headed to her car, taking one final look at the house she wouldn't be seeing again for some time. As she made her way to Eleanor's house she was singing to her car radio, an unusual occurrence, particularly of late. For late December it was a crisp yet sunny morning and the advent of Christmas had certainly raised everyone's spirits, especially at the petrol station where she topped up her tank. There, carols boomed at full volume in a delightful grotto filled with furry wide-eyed creatures and reindeer.

Sighing, she longed for the day when her children would revel in such a heart-warming spectacle.

Cautiously Paige approached the house, her eyes warily searching for any sign of Richard's presence but to her surprise, the avenue was strangely devoid of vehicles.

She gathered the gifts together and hurried down the drive. With a wide beaming smile, Eleanor, who had seen her approach, opened the door gushing, 'I am *so* pleased to see you. I've been calling you for days. Have you been ill?' and then, glancing down, her expression immediately changed to one of joy. 'Er...is that what I think it is? Are you expecting?'

Paige giggled at her candour. 'You never miss a trick do you? Yes, I am.'

Clearly startled she stuttered, 'Come in; come in. This is such wonderful news. Richard's never said a word although we haven't spoken for a few days. I guess he must be busy, what with David and the run up to Christmas. Here, let me take your jacket. I'll put the kettle on.'

Paige followed her into the kitchen, saddened by Eleanor's joyful expectations. There'd be very few opportunities for her to see her grandchildren, given that they would be so far apart.

'So, tell me...when's your baby due?' she gabbled breathlessly. 'I bet Richard's over the moon. A new baby, it's wonderful; it really is wonderful.'

'They said the third of June at the clinic and...'

'That's the day after *my* birthday. Fancy that.'

It was time for openness so Paige came straight to the point. Taking Eleanor's hand in hers she sighed. 'I'm sorry to be the bearer of bad news but Richard and I aren't together anymore. I imagine that's why he hasn't been in touch. It was a rather acrimonious parting. He ended it. He sent me away and now I'm living near Warwick. I'm really sorry Eleanor.'

Her eyes filled with tears. 'No Paige, it isn't true. He loves you. I know he does. You're the best thing that's happened to him since he lost Jan. There has to be some mistake. Tell me this is only temporary and that you're getting back together...please.'

On a huge sigh she shook her head. 'I came here today out of a sense of duty to you. You're right to say he loves me; he does. He sent me away because he didn't want me to be burdened with his troubles, with David's care. He didn't know I was pregnant but he knows now and he came looking for me but I can't forgive him for the things he said. I told him I'd already made plans to have an abortion and...'

'Oh no!' she interrupted. 'You can't do that. You *mustn't.* It isn't that poor baby's fault. You have...'

As tears flowed from her eyes Paige cut in, 'No, I cancelled it but Richard doesn't know and that's the way I want it to stay. He's out of my life and he'll never come looking for me because he believes I'm living with somebody else. As it happens I am, but not in the way Richard thinks. The man I'm with is my father. After all those years of knowing nothing about him I finally found him and he's an amazing person who wants to take care of me and his grand-children. Yes, I'm having twins.'

There was an audible gasp as Eleanor covered her mouth with her hand and with a tremor in her voice asked, 'And you're keeping this from Richard? Do you really despise him that much Paige?'

‘I don’t despise him Eleanor. I love him; I always will but don’t you see what this would do to him, to know he had two children? Believe me, it’s better he doesn’t know. He wanted to end our relationship because of the problems with David. *He* made that decision and so I’d like to be left alone to raise my children. He hoped I’d find somebody else, somebody who would offer me a better life without the baggage he was bringing to our relationship and for that reason I don’t want him to find out I’m living with my father. I’m telling you this because I know I can trust you to keep my secret and as long as you do, I’ll make sure that you see the twins every time I’m in the area. I have no argument with you but I can’t tell Richard; I won’t. I expect you’ll need time to think about it so I’ll call you in a day or two with my new number. I’m changing my present one and I’ll give you my landline number too.’

‘So am I to act surprised when Richard tells me?’

Paige shrugged. ‘It’s up to you. You can tell him I called with your Christmas present and while I was here, I told you it was over between us. Here’s your present so you won’t be lying. I doubt he’ll mention I was pregnant as he thinks I’ve had a termination. Don’t forget Eleanor, he made it absolutely clear in front of you that he wanted no more children.’

Eleanor sighed yet again. ‘I had such high expectations for the two of you. I thought it was a match made in heaven.’

‘I never take anything for granted. I’ve had rather a tempestuous life where good things don’t happen to me, or at least they don’t last. I’d like to keep in touch Eleanor but if you decide it'd be better not to, I'll understand.' She forced a watery smile. 'I have other places to call so I'd best be on my way now.'

She gave her a warm hug and made for the door laden with beautifully wrapped parcels Eleanor had given her. 'I hope you have a lovely Christmas and I hope David continues to make progress. That'll be good for Richard, to see a marked improvement in his health. Take care. I'll be in touch soon.'

Eleanor was in tears as Paige drove away.

The setting sun was blazing through the windscreen yet cars still overtook her as if she were motionless. It had been her intent to head back sooner but after calling to see Emma at work to drop off her gifts, a five minute chat turned into lunch together and then after lunch Annette had called with further queries, requiring another visit to the Agency.

Finally Paige was on her way later than expected and being harassed by the honking horns of foolish drivers trying to beat the rush hour traffic with little or no regard for safety.

Jake was clearly relieved to see her. 'I've been so worried. You didn't call me, not once all weekend.'

'Well it's all done now. I don't have to traipse up north again. The return journey was horrendous. It never ceases to amaze me how some folk drive like maniacs and in my old car I don't have the power to get out of the way. It was really scary at times.'

He stretched out his hand and took hold of hers. 'I want you a minute. I've something to show you.'

She looked surprised. 'What?'

'Wait and see. Don't be so impatient.'

She accompanied him through the utility room to the garage. He grinned boyishly. 'How's that?'

She cast her eyes over the shiny new Peugeot. 'Is that for me?' she questioned incredulously.

He brushed his lips against her cheek. 'Yes, it is. I can't allow my daughter to take my grandchildren out in that old banger. It's your Christmas present. It was going to be a surprise on Christmas day but we need to get it taxed and insured so you can drive it. Do you like it?'

Paige threw her arms around his neck. 'That's far too expensive a present. It equates to years of child support. I don't know what to say. Thank you Jake; I absolutely love it. Blue is my favourite colour too. It's the best present I've ever had in my life.'

Jake laughed at her exuberance. 'It's simply a car to get you around. I'm told it's very reliable.'

Grinning from ear to ear, she opened the driver's door. 'It's fabulous but look how many clocks and dials there are. I'll never fathom that lot out.'

'Of course you will. It's a doddle.'

She sighed. 'I'm so lucky to have found you.'

With an introspective smile Jake murmured, 'No, I'm the lucky one Paige.'

11

'You're looking better today Grandad,' Paige said, tucking his blanket round his knees.

'He's fine. He tries it on for sympathy, isn't that right Henry?' the nurse said with a knowing wink.

'Less of the lip young woman,' Henry said with a devilish glint in his eye and Paige laughed.

She leaned over and gave him a kiss. 'How would you like to come to us for Christmas dinner? I'm a good cook though I say so myself. I've had a word with Matron and she says it's okay for you to stay overnight too so what do you think?'

Henry's face lit up. 'That'd be champion if you're sure it's no trouble. Will it be just the three of us?'

'Yes, just family.' She reflected on her words the moment they escaped her lips. Saying that had felt so natural but it was true. They *were* family. There was no one else...though soon there'd be two more.

He gave her a loving smile. 'That's something to look forward to now. When *is* Christmas?'

'It's just a few days away Grandad. Haven't you seen that lovely tree in the reception area?'

'Aye I have but I didn't know when it was. Will you help me pack my bag?'

Paige nodded caringly. 'Yes, don't worry. I'll see to everything.'

'Will we be having plum pudding? I like that. It's my favourite. Your grandma used to make a lovely brandy sauce with it. Can *you* make that?'

'I certainly can, so Brandy sauce it is Grandad if that's what you'd like but I don't want you tipsy.'

He scowled muttering, 'Spoilsport,' but there was a playful inflection in his voice.

The nurse came back to check his blood pressure. 'He perks up when you put in an appearance. Apart from his dodgy legs, he's in good health. He has his wits about him, mark my words.'

Henry glanced up. 'Aye, I need them to keep you on your toes, you naughty girl. Boy, if I had full use of my legs I'd be out of this chair in a flash and...'

'*Grandad! Behave!*' Paige squealed.

On a shrill chuckle the nurse left the room.

Paige and Jake laughed together when she disclosed Henry's risqué comment. 'Like father like son,' she commented dryly.

'Huh,' was Jake's response to that. 'I have to say though, Marjorie, my secretary, is a very agreeable lady away from the workplace.'

Paige's ears pricked up. 'Meaning?'

'I took her to lunch on Monday. I felt an explanation was warranted for your unexpected appearance in my life and we had a really nice time.'

'Is she single?'

'Yes, she's a widow. To look at her late husband, he was a picture of health. He worked out and kept fit, then suddenly died of a heart attack seven years ago. You never know what's looming,' he sighed.

Paige snorted. 'Tell me. I've had my fair share of trauma over the years. Are you seeing her again?'

'Perhaps. Do you think I should?'

'Why not if you enjoy each other's company?'

Jake shrugged. 'I don't know. I don't like mixing business with pleasure. If we fall out, it's awkward having to work together and she needs that job as a widow. She *is* very nice though,' he said dreamily.

Paige didn't answer but an idea was stirring in her mind.

It was Thursday and with only five days left before Christmas, Paige needed to do her final shopping.

She loved her new car. It was a joy to drive, easy to park and had a CD player. She had never known such luxury. Shopping was no longer a necessity; it was an absolute pleasure.

It was almost twelve o'clock as she parked in the hospital car park. Both receptionists waved affably as she scurried past towards the Psychiatric Unit to find Jake. She had persuaded him to buy her lunch as it was part of the big scheme she was planning.

Marjorie beamed as she approached. 'Jake will be out shortly. His last patient's just left. Have a seat.'

She flopped down with an audible sigh in the not-so-comfortable armchair beside the desk.

'Heavy morning?' Marjorie enquired.

Paige nodded. 'Very. I've cleaned all the upstairs today and done the windows too so I'm shattered.'

She was surprised. 'I thought Jake had a cleaner.'

With a roll of the eyes Paige smirked. 'She's useless. Blokes don't notice so she takes advantage of him. She doesn't like me because I've criticised her work a few times but not without just cause. She's persistently late, impolite and slovenly and does the absolute minimum. I find myself cleaning up after her when she's left. Can you believe that?'

She hooted with laughter. 'Have you told Jake?'

'I've tried but you know what men are like. The mere fact that she graces us with her presence satisfies him but I intend to have another go at him after Christmas in the hope he'll fire her...which reminds me, speaking of Christmas, have you any idea what I can buy Jake? I've bought all my presents except his. I can't think of anything he needs.'

'That's easy. Jake likes Gabicci V-neck sweaters and Lyle and Scott short sleeved sports shirts. He'd love one of those. Shop around though because you can pick them up a lot cheaper in some outlets. I've finished wrapping mine now. They're in the post.'

'In the post?'

'Yes, my daughter and family live in Suffolk and they're off on holiday on Christmas Eve so I won't be seeing them until the New Year.'

'So where are you going for Christmas?'

'Nowhere. I'm having a quiet Christmas at home by myself.'

She was playing right into Paige's hands. 'Right, I've ordered a huge turkey that's far too big for us so why not come to ours for Christmas dinner? I'm sure Jake would be delighted if you joined us. You can't spend Christmas alone.'

Marjorie was visibly flustered. 'Thank you, but I couldn't impose on your family Christmas. It's the first Christmas you'll ever have spent with your dad so you must enjoy it together, just the two of you.'

Changing tack Paige remarked, 'He had a lovely time he told me.'

With blushing cheeks, stumbling awkwardly over her words she croaked, 'Who...er...wh...what?'

Paige smiled. 'No need to act coy. He told me he enjoyed himself last Monday when he took you out to lunch. Did you enjoy it too?'

By this time her cheeks were crimson. 'Yes, I did, very much. Jake is quite a character away from the workplace. I...er...didn't realise he'd told you.'

'So, what about Christmas Day?' Paige persisted. 'It's only a meal, not a life-long commitment.'

Before she could reply, Jake appeared and beaming with delight asked, 'Are you ready Paige?'

Paige winked at her. 'Think about it Marjorie and give me a call. Don't forget.'

'What was that about?' Jake questioned, ushering Paige through the door.

'Marjorie's on her own at Christmas so I've asked her to join us for Christmas dinner.'

She awaited a response but none was forthcoming though his enthusiastic smile revealed his pleasure. Then he asked nonchalantly, 'Did she accept?'

'She's thinking about it. Perhaps you should ask her yourself. She probably wants your approval.'

Though he nodded in silence the faraway look in Jake's eyes spoke a thousand words. He approved.

Jake was barely visible behind the enormous bushy Christmas tree he lumbered through the front door.

Paige wiped her floury hands on a damp cloth and hurried to his assistance. 'Great, I didn't know you were buying a tree. How lovely. Do you always get one as big as this?'

'This is a first,' he panted. 'I've never bought one since I moved down here. I wanted everything to be perfect for our first Christmas together.'

Paige moved a chair aside in the spacious hallway and helped him lay the tree on its side.

'Stick the kettle on sweetheart. I feel as if I've run a marathon. I'm parched.' He followed her through to the kitchen. 'What are you making?'

'Mince pies and I've an apple pie in the oven. I'm freezing that to use over Christmas.'

He wrapped his arms around her and sighed.

'What?'

'I'm so happy we found each other. It's going to be such a brilliant Christmas isn't it?'

She leaned back and looked into his smiling eyes. 'Yes, Grandad's coming and Marjorie called while you were out; she'll be here around midday.'

At the mere mention of Marjorie's name, he was overjoyed. 'Are you sure you can cope?'

Brewing his tea, Paige smiled. 'I'm pregnant, not disabled. Have you got any baubles for the tree?'

'Of course, everything's in the car. I remembered to get lights and tinsel too. We'll get it trimmed this afternoon if you're up to it. What's for lunch?'

'Home-made quiche with salad and crusty bread.'

'Sounds scrumptious. I can't wait. I'm ravenous.'

Paige stepped back and admired the tree.

‘Happy with that?’ Jake asked.

‘Oh yes, it’s beautiful. If I had a camera I’d take a few photos to send to Emma. I might get one in the sales once I’ve got my hands on a month’s rent but my first priority is a new phone. I hate using yours all the time. I’ll pay towards the phone bill when it comes. I called Laura in New York earlier.’

‘Stop worrying about the phone bill you silly girl. Have you told her about the twins now?’

‘Yes, I have. I didn’t want to say anything until I was sure her pregnancy was stable. She’s been trying for a baby for such a while.’

‘I take it she was pleased with your news?’

She giggled. ‘She was ecstatic. Surprisingly we’re both due around the same time though I understand they often induce you earlier with twins. She knows about me and Richard too. She had to know at some point so better now than later.’

He recognised a look of sadness in her eyes. ‘It’ll get better Paige. Just give it time.’

‘I know but I miss him. I miss David too. I never thought I’d say that but it’s true. Richard and David were the closest I had to a family till I found you.’

‘Then why not call Richard?’ he suggested.

She shook her head. ‘He made his position crystal clear. He ended it so that’s how it’ll stay. Don’t you think I’ve gone over this time and time again in my head? It’d never work. He only came to find me out of a sense of duty when he learned I was pregnant. I doubt I would ever have heard from him again but for that. I’ll bounce back; I’ve recovered from a lot worse. I just have to keep busy to take my mind off him so I'm fetching all my presents down now and putting them under the tree and I'm telling you, you *don't* peek at them before Christmas...understood?'

'Yes Bossy-Boots,' he laughed.

'Don't even attempt to lift this turkey,' Jake panted as he shut the oven door. 'I bet we'll still be eating this at Easter.' He checked his watch. It was almost six a.m. and still dark outside.

'You go back to bed for an hour or so. The table's ready so I only have to prepare the veg,' Paige said. 'I'll doze in the chair if I'm tired. It's always hectic at Christmas. It'll be worse next year with the twins when Father Christmas has been.'

He laughed. 'They'll only be six months old. It's hardly likely they'll be bellowing to open their stuff before dawn.'

'But *I'll* want to open theirs early and my own as well,' she protested and he laughed once more.

He walked to the tree and removed a small parcel from the pile stacked beneath it. 'You can open this now and then I'm off to bed for an hour or so. You can have the others later.'

'Oh...others, that sounds exciting,' she gasped. 'I love Christmas.'

'Yes, I missed out on that with you at Christmas and birthdays. Tragically, Richard will miss out too with the twins but you know that, don't you?'

Paige glared at him. 'Pack it in Jake. Don't try to make out I'm the guilty one. Emotional blackmail I can well do without. *I* didn't end our relationship. *He* did so he can live with it.'

He realised he'd overstepped the mark and smiled remorsefully. 'I'm sorry. I don't want you to have any regrets when it backfires on you because someday, somehow, he *will* find out...believe me. It took me almost thirty years to find you but I did, so just remember that. That's all I'm saying.'

'Good,' she snarled. 'You've said it so let it drop. I can do without your snide comments today and...'

Hastily he cut her short. 'Right, I'm off to bed for a while and then I'll fetch my dad. Marjorie insisted she'd drive here. Wake me if you need me.'

She watched him stride from the room and close the door. Following the altercation she had lost the urge to open his present and crossing to the tree she replaced it with the others. *'Men,'* she huffed.

The earlier contretemps had been forgotten when Jake reappeared showered and dressed less than an hour later. 'I couldn't sleep and I thought I'd better give you a hand. Did you like your present?'

'I decided I'd open it later,' she commented without expounding on her reasons. 'I'll open it now.'

She retrieved it from under the tree and tore at the wrapping excitedly. She couldn't believe her eyes. 'A camera, great.' She ran across and hugged him. 'This is one of those new digital cameras isn't it?'

'It's the best and only the best is good enough for my daughter. You can take pictures of the tree now. I'm glad you mentioned it as I hadn't a clue what to buy you. I wanted it to be something you needed.'

'It's certainly that. Has it got a film in?'

'It doesn't take film. Like you were quick to point out, it's digital.'

He took it from her, pointed it at her and clicked. There was a flash and he showed her the picture.

'I'm still in my nightie,' she squealed. 'It's great though isn't it? It's so clear. Right, let me take one of you now. What do I do?'

'Just press the silver button but try to hold it still.'

Giggling nervously and with her tongue sticking out of the side of her mouth as she tried to maintain her composure, she clicked and shrieking with glee showed him the photograph. 'My very first picture of my dad,' she said. 'I'll keep this forever.'

'You like your camera then?' he grinned.

'I love it...and you too. Thank you so much Jake.'

She hurried back to the tree and returned clutching a square slim package. 'I want you to have this now before the others get here. Merry Christmas. I hope you like it.'

Unlike Paige, he opened his with care and smiled to see the lovely card inside the box. In silence he read the heart-rending words with tears pricking his eyes. Curling his arm around her shoulder he kissed her lovingly and in a broken voice he thanked her.

'How touching,' he sighed. 'I never expected I'd see the day when I received a card with *Dad* on it. I'm not easily moved Paige but your thoughtfulness has knocked me for six. It's lovely. Thank you.'

Squeezing Jake's hand she smiled fondly. 'We're going to have an amazing Christmas. I can feel it.'

The introductions had been made and Marjorie was on her second drink and feeling more relaxed when everyone transferred to the dining room.

Jake helped his father to the table and placed his napkin across his lap as he sat down.

'How lovely your table looks,' Marjorie said. 'Is this a Nottingham lace tablecloth?'

'Search me,' Paige said. 'It could be. I'm not used to expensive stuff. I came across it in the sideboard drawer and felt it was ideal for today.'

Jake joined in. 'It was my mother's favourite. She always used it on special occasions. This is the first time it's ever been used here. When Dad was taken into care and we sold his home, I brought this silver cutlery, the tureens and the fancy tablecloths here.' He sighed reflectively. 'I'm happy they're being put to good use at long last. Mum would be so pleased to know that wouldn't she Dad?'

'Aye, she would. She used to like a nice table. It set the scene for a good meal, she always said. She was a good cook too and she made lovely cakes and pies. Happy times,' he sighed nostalgically.

'Er…do you want another drink Grandad?' Paige asked to lighten the mood. 'Your glass is empty.'

He grinned. 'I don't mind if I do.'

'I'll see to it,' Jake said jumping up. 'If you need any help in the kitchen just give me a shout. I don't want you getting overtired.'

Paige carried in the soup bowls and everyone did justice to her delicious creation. The succulent roast turkey that followed was a delight as was the plum pudding served with brandy and butter sauce.

'I'm absolutely stuffed,' Jake commented. 'That was superb Paige. Well done. I'll clear up and stack the dishwasher afterwards. You've done enough.'

'I'll help too,' Marjorie added. 'Your dad's right. That's the tastiest Christmas dinner I've ever had.'

Not to be outdone Henry contributed, 'You take after your grandma. She was a damn good cook.'

Embarrassed by the compliments she blushed. 'I enjoy cooking. It's a pleasure not a chore. I'm glad you enjoyed it. I'll nip back and put the coffee on.'

As Paige left the room Marjorie remarked, 'She's quite amazing and has boundless energy. You're a lucky man. You have a wonderful daughter.'

'Don't I know it,' he stated reflectively. 'Actually she's a chip off the old block. I'm quite amazing as well when I'm in the mood.' Their eyes met and he smiled seductively, bringing a flood of colour to her cheeks as he winked at her.

Although Henry remained silent he hadn't missed the moment and smiled inwardly. She was a refined lady, this friend of Jake's, and it was obvious Jake thought so too. He had that certain look about him that his father hadn't seen for many a year.

The trio's reverie was cut short as Paige appeared with the coffee.

'I'll pour,' Marjorie offered. 'You sit down Paige. You must be exhausted in your condition.'

Henry's ears pricked up. 'Why? What's up? Are you not well lass?'

Marjorie glanced apologetically at Jake. 'I'm very sorry Paige. I assumed your grandad knew.'

'It's fine. I can't keep it a secret forever Marjorie. You're going to be a great-grandad,' she told him.

For a moment he was stunned and then he spoke. 'That's the best news I've heard in a long time. Do I take it you aren't involved with anybody presently, the baby's father I mean?'

'That's right. We're not together any longer.'

He nodded circumspectly before replying, 'That's his loss. You take proper care of yourself lass. That little baby will bring you lots of pleasure.'

She took hold of his hand. 'I'm alright Grandad. I always take proper care of myself and by the way, I'm having twins.'

He expelled a hearty laugh. 'I'll be able to cradle one in each arm then. I can hardly wait.'

Later, in the kitchen, Marjorie apologised again. 'I would never have said a word had I realised.'

'Listen, I was dreading telling Grandad. He grew up in an era when such things weren't supposed to happen. Obviously it did occasionally but it was, to put it mildly, frowned upon. You did me a favour. I couldn't have kept it from him for much longer so I should be thanking you.'

'Is this a private conversation or can anyone join in?' Jake interrupted. 'If you're worried about Dad, don't. He's very broad-minded. He's seen plenty of changes in his lifetime and very little shocks him. I want you to sit down and relax now Paige. I'm sure Marjorie and I can clear up in here and then we can open our presents.' He kissed her forehead. 'Thanks again for that delicious meal. You've been working hard for days and everything was perfect.'

Paige was more than ready for a break. 'Alright, I'm persuaded,' she said gratefully. She went back to the table, sat down beside Henry and checked her watch. It was almost three o'clock.

Mindful that Marjorie had said she would like to hear the Queen's speech, Paige hurried back to the kitchen. Finding Marjorie in Jake's arms, oblivious of her presence, she slipped away quietly, feeling a warm and satisfying glow within her.

'Come and sit down in the lounge Grandad. You can have a little snooze if you like. I'll wake you up when Dad and Marjorie have done in the kitchen.'

He needed no persuasion and when, within a few minutes he was snoring gently, Paige capitalised on the situation, using the free time to call Emma who was delighted to hear from her.

'Me and Andy have just got engaged. You should see my ring. I love it. I'd no idea he was buying me a ring. It's a big diamond with sapphires all round.'

Paige whooped with glee. 'I'm so happy for you. Does that mean the wedding's still on for May?'

'That's looking more and more unlikely. We've done the figures and we'd have to go in debt to pay for it all. It seems crazy, starting our married life in debt. We're resigned to it though because Andy is practically living here now but we haven't given up on the idea. We've simply put it on hold for now.'

'Then why doesn't Andy give up his place? He'd save the rent he's paying if he moved in with you.'

'We've talked about that too but Andy's a bit old-fashioned about couples actually *living* together.'

'What? In this day and age?'

There was a lengthy pause. 'Don't laugh but he's very principled. I'd like a baby while I've still time but he won't hear of it before we're married. How's that for being righteous?'

‘Huh, I suppose he’s had plenty to say about me.’

‘Paige...he doesn’t know you’re still pregnant. He thinks you had the abortion. You said I mustn’t tell him so I didn’t. He said his piece at the time as he’s dead against abortion so I let him drone on until he stopped. He’ll find out the truth eventually though.’

Warily Paige asked, ‘Has Andy done any jobs for Richard recently?’

‘I wondered how long it’d be before that toe-rag’s name cropped up in the conversation. No, he hasn’t, and if it were up to me he’d not work for him again after what he did to you, the bloody peasant. I gave him such a bollocking when he came to Sampson’s looking for you after you’d left.’

‘I didn’t know that. I understood you hadn’t had any dealings with him.’

‘I lied. It was in your best interest Paige. I wasn’t prepared to tell that creep anything, not that I knew where you were but then he had the audacity to turn to Andy to ask if *he* knew so he got an even bigger bollocking. He sloped off then, shame-faced.’

‘I can fight my own battles Emma. You shouldn’t have interfered. I know what you’re like; you have a right uncouth mouth on you when you start.’

Defensively she cried, ‘He came to *me* for help. I didn’t go to *him.’*

‘I still miss him like hell. I know I shouldn’t but I do. I can’t get him out of my thoughts. I shrug it off as if I don’t care when Jake mentions him but I still love him. It’ll take time I expect. We were close for quite a while,’ she sighed glumly. ‘So, on a happier note, what time are you off to your mum’s?’

‘In about half an hour. We’re both starving. I take it you’ve eaten already?’

‘Yes, we had ours at one o’clock.’

‘Mmm, I bet it was delicious if you made it.’

‘Everyone said so which reminds me, Dad’s got a lady friend, his medical secretary, so he invited her to dinner and Grandad came as well...quite a houseful. I’d best let you go or you’ll be late. Remember not to mention I’m still pregnant. You can drop that bombshell when I turn up at yours one day with the twins. Say Happy Christmas to everyone from me.’

‘Happy Christmas to you and yours too. Can I ask before you go, are you mad at me for shouting my mouth off at Richard?’

‘Don’t be daft. You were looking out for me and I’d have done the same for you. Friends forever.’

‘Yes, you can bet on it,’ she said. ‘Enjoy the rest of Christmas and thanks for the lovely presents.’

‘You too and thanks for yours.’

Henry was sleeping soundly when she returned to the lounge and with no sign of Marjorie or Jake, she assumed they were making the most of their stolen minutes.

She collapsed in an armchair and before long her thoughts were directed towards Richard as she tried to imagine the kind of festivities he’d be enjoying. No doubt with a challenging son to take care of, his day would be the same as any other. She had talked to Eleanor yesterday and there had been no notable improvement in David’s condition. Furthermore he still remained furious with his father for having sent her away. Paige sighed deeply. If only Richard had talked to her; if only he had expressed his concerns and given her the opportunity to contribute, to have her say, there might have been a happier outcome.

'Sleepy?' a calming voice came over, interrupting her thoughts. Paige looked up into Jake's eyes, eyes that forever smiled when close to his daughter.

'Sorry, I must have dozed off.'

Jake cupped his hands around her face and kissed the top of her head. 'Drink this chilled orange juice and you'll feel better. Christmas is always a thought provoking time when we reflect nostalgically about loved ones but I promise it'll pass. It's time to open the rest of our presents.'

She sipped her juice and murmured, 'Lovely. I'm fine, really. I was just resting my eyes, that's all.'

'It's little wonder you're tired,' Jake was quick to point out. 'I've noticed those platters of food in the fridge, presumably to have later today. I have to say you've really excelled with everything sweetheart.'

'It's only a few plates of cold meat and a bowl of salad. I thought, come early evening, that everyone might feel peckish. There's gateau and an apple pie too but we haven't touched the Christmas cake yet.'

'I'll definitely do it justice,' Henry, who was now wide awake, piped up with a shrill laugh. 'I eat for England. Hasn't your dad told you?'

With raised eyebrows Paige turned to Jake. 'He's kidding, right?'

'It's true,' he confirmed. 'Dad's a right glutton. I don't know where he puts it all, but it's comforting to know he has a hearty appetite. That keeps him fit and well.'

Her former melancholy quickly disappeared when they began to open their presents and she screeched with delight to find Jake had bought her a state-of-the-art mobile phone.

'It's charged and ready for use,' he said. 'You can ring your friends now without persistently hogging my house phone.'

Swiftly she rejoined, 'I rang Emma while you and Marjorie were *doing your thing* in the kitchen...and I have to say Marjorie, you're worth far more than a barnyard rooster so don't ever put yourself down.' Winking playfully at the pair of them, she grinned causing Marjorie to turn crimson once more.

On a serious note Paige added, 'Believe me, I'm glad. It's time Jake got a life outside the hospital.'

'It looks like we've been rumbled Marjorie,' Jake declared on a laugh.

'Spot on,' Paige made known. 'I was just about to wander in the kitchen to help but when I opened the door and saw...well, what I saw...I decided I'd best beat a hasty retreat.'

'Oh dear,' Marjorie sighed. 'We thought we were being discreet. Were you shocked?'

Paige tittered. 'Don't be daft. It'd take a lot more than you two in a clinch to shock me. Seriously I'm happy. Right, who's ready for party games?'

That was a welcome change of direction for Jake and Marjorie who nodded eagerly as Henry looked on mildly amused at his son's antics that were now in the public domain. Would there be further secrets in their family that hadn't surfaced in recent weeks he wondered. It had been a day full of surprises.

It was after midnight when Marjorie next looked at her watch. ‘Good heavens,’ she exclaimed. ‘It’s turned midnight.

‘Are you on a curfew?’ Jake smirked. ‘Relax and have another drink. You might as well as you can‘t drive your car. You’re well over the limit already so why not stay over tonight?’

She was horrified. ‘I couldn’t possibly do that. I’ll phone for a taxi and pick my car up tomorrow.’

She leaped up and gathered her presents together. ‘Do you know where Paige put my coat?’

Jake moved towards her. ‘If I’ve offended you I didn’t mean to. This house has five bedrooms. That was my point. I wasn’t suggesting you...’

‘Can we drop it please? This is really difficult for me. The only man I’ve ever er...*known*...was Peter, my husband. There were no other men before Peter and there’s been no one else since. I like you Jake, in fact I *more* than like you, but this is moving too quickly. Until a few days ago I was just your medical secretary and now we’re spending time together. It’s nice, very nice but I need to take it slowly. I’m really sorry if I gave the wrong impression.’

‘No, I’m the dork who should be apologising as I clearly misread the signals. This is new to me too. I thought perhaps you wanted more and I didn’t want to disappoint you nor did I want you to lose interest. I’m sorry. I hope I haven’t scared you off. I’ve enjoyed your company today as I did when we went to lunch and I don’t want to rush things either. We aren’t teenagers; we’re adults and I’d like to go on seeing you so let’s take things as they come, a day at a time. I'm more than happy with that if you are, so what do you say? Am I forgiven?'

Marjorie nodded. 'I'm sorry for the silly outburst. I think I've had a little too much to drink.'

He smiled. 'Not enough to cloud your judgement though. I really wasn't propositioning you Marjorie despite my clumsy offer of a room. That offer's still open if you'd like to stay overnight but if you want to go home, I'll come with you in your taxi, I'll get the driver to wait while I see you to your door and then I'll collect you tomorrow when you call me so you can pick up your car. It's your choice.'

'Thank you. I think I will go home. You're such a considerate person Jake and I enjoy your company too but I wouldn't want Paige to get the wrong idea about us. Where is she, by the way?'

'I imagine she's being diplomatic and keeping her distance to give us a bit of space,' he laughed. 'It's ages since Dad went to bed. She only went upstairs to say goodnight to him. So, how about that drink?'

'Okay, a small one then. You've twisted my arm.'

In the back of the taxi Jake took hold of her hand and kissed it. 'I've had a really nice day. I'm happy you came. Let's rewind and delete the last half hour or so as if it never happened. Agreed?'

'Agreed,' she said with a warm smile.

12

'Did Laura say what time they'd be arriving?'

Paige looked up from her laptop. 'Early afternoon she thought. Is that a problem?'

Jake turned up the gas fire and flopped down on the sofa with his newspaper. 'Not at all. I've nothing planned. I was thinking they might enjoy a ride out if they haven't seen the area before.'

'Good idea if Laura isn't tired. I'm really looking forward to their visit. I bet she's not as grotesque as I am though with my big fat belly,' she pouted.

Jake wandered over and stroked her hair. 'You're radiant as always so don't talk silly. Besides, your friend isn't carrying twins. Will you tell her you're having a boy and a girl?'

'Of course. I can't understand women who insist it has to be a secret till it's born. What's the point in that? Everyone wants to buy a present and it makes sense to know the sex beforehand.'

'People managed alright back in the days when it couldn't be determined,' he said matter-of-factly.

'So you're saying people shouldn't move with the times? You're saying folk should still sail the high seas even though we have aeroplanes now? Tell me Jake, how many babies have you bought gifts for? Let me make it easy; name *one.'*

When he hesitated Paige scoffed, 'I knew it; I rest my case; you can't even name *one* can you?'

His response brought a smile to her lips. 'Yes, my own, you. I bought you a car, a phone and a camera for Christmas. You're *my* baby so that counts.'

'That's cheating because I'm not a baby and you know I'm a female, not that it matters as you could have bought those things for a male too. Seriously, why the secrecy? If you're such a competent shrink, explain why so many pregnant women are hung-up about revealing the sex of an unborn baby.'

Jake grinned. 'Pass. The best shrink in the world would find it nigh impossible to get into a pregnant woman's head. It's not easy at the best of times.'

'I knew it, Freud.'

On a hearty laugh he said, 'You're hilarious when you're crotchety. Your nose starts to twitch.'

Their banter was halted by the telephone. 'I'll get that in case it's Laura,' said Paige, wriggling into a standing position. 'I can't wait to see her.'

Jake heard a squeal of delight as she replaced the receiver. 'They're here. They've just turned into the avenue. You can meet my American friends now.'

As the girls screeched and compared bumps, Jake escorted Brad to the lounge. 'While they're having hysterics I'll fix you a drink. What's your tipple?'

'I wouldn't say no to a small whisky please. You have an amazing home. It's so spacious. It's clearly a very affluent area. Have you lived here long?'

'Almost thirty years but it's strange; I still regard myself as a northerner, despite having spent most of my life here. I guess one never forgets one's roots.'

He nodded. 'I've moved about a lot in the States but it's good to go home. My folks are still there.'

'And where's home?'

'Denver, Colorado.'

Jake handed Brad his whisky and sat down beside him. 'Denver,' he repeated. 'Not a place I've ever visited but I hear it's a fast-growing city, right?'

'Yes, it is; it's one of the fastest growing cities in the States. If I can tear Laura away from New York I'd like to move back. I'm in IT and there are many more opportunities there now but she's reluctant to leave as she was raised in New York State and her family and friends are there. Don't get me wrong; I love New York but I've been a bit jittery since the 9/11 attack, especially now with a baby due soon.'

'You need to look forward Brad. You can't dwell on the past.' Jake counselled wisely. 'That terrorist attack could have happened anywhere, in any State, and any city, yes, even Denver, Colorado and given that the security in New York will now have been strengthened, it's probably a safer city to be in than any other. If you want my advice, leave for the right reasons. If you like it there then stay. Did you know many of the victims who died?'

He inhaled deeply 'Quite a lot, some very well.'

'Paige was caught up in it too. You met Richard of course who escaped with a broken arm.'

'Yes, he came across as a decent guy. I'm not too familiar with the minutiae, girl talk you understand. I simply get a précis of the main issues from Laura. I believe they had an acrimonious separation which is tragic when there are two children involved.'

Though Jake didn't answer he was in total agreement. 'What are your plans for the rest of your trip? I could give you a tour of the local surroundings for an hour or so. I've booked a table at a restaurant for seven o'clock. Paige was busy earlier making fancy cakes and sandwiches for lunch. Are you hungry?'

'Ravenous. Nothing's passed my lips today yet.'

Jake pricked up his ears. 'Listen, the hysteria has subsided. I bet Laura and Paige have gone upstairs. I'll give them a few more minutes and then check if they're ready for a bite to eat. How's the drink?'

'Superb. I'm partial to your English whisky.'

'It's Scottish actually,' he grinned. 'I have to give credit where credit's due. That's a very fine whisky and a particular favourite. It's Johnnie Walker Gold Label Special Reserve.'

'You're a man of excellent taste,' Brad answered, licking his lips as the delicious melange of flavours warmed comfortingly to his palate.

'What a pretty room,' Laura remarked. 'There's no end to that beautiful view. It's so unlike New York where the buildings are regimented like battalions of soldiers. Brad will adore this room.' She flopped down on the bed and sighed. 'I could sleep forever.'

'Do you find you tire easily?' asked Paige.

'Not at all. I don't feel any different but since we arrived in UK two days ago we've done nothing but tramp round. That's what's tired me out as there's a lot to see in London. Compared to my friends, I've had a very easy pregnancy so far. How about you? I imagine it's worse carrying twins.'

'I'm okay. I found Christmas hectic as Jake's new lady friend Marjorie and my grandad joined us for Christmas dinner. Marjorie went home that night as they aren't sleeping together yet, or so Jake would have me believe,' she sniggered sceptically, 'but he brought her back the next day to collect her car and she stayed all day resulting in yet another laborious day. To be fair, she helped clear away but it would have been lovely just to chill out. You can't though when you've got visitors, can you?'

'So shall I tell Brad we'd better be on our way?'

Paige joined in her laughter. 'No, I'm thrilled you two are staying. So much has happened since New York. We've lots to talk about that doesn't get said in emails. That reminds me, what's the significance of "drl" at the front of your email address?'

'Nothing mysterious...just "Dr Laura".'

'Oh, I didn't know you were a doctor.'

'Most dentists are and they tend to use the title in US unlike UK. The credentials are much the same I guess. Your dad's a psychiatrist isn't he?'

'Yes, who practises on me,' she hooted. 'Rarely a day passes but what I get a grilling about something but his heart's in the right place. He's saddened by my attitude towards Richard because I refuse to tell him I'm still pregnant. I can't make him understand that he's out of my life now and that's how I want it to remain. Richard made it very clear that he didn't want children but I can't get that across to Jake. He still says I should tell him but I refuse to be swayed. I won't *ever* tell him. I want no contact whatsoever nor do I want financial support for the children.'

Laura frowned. 'Oh Paige, I don't know how you can live with yourself. They're *his* children too. I'm aware of the animosity between you but he still has to be told. Give it more thought, please. I'm saying this as your true friend. What he did was wrong but what you're doing is much worse. I know it's none of my business but think of the future. It's not fair on the children. At least give him the opportunity to fulfil his role as their father. If he doesn't want any part of it, at least you'll have done the right thing.'

'And what if he doesn't want to know? I'd have to tell them at some point that their father turned his back on them, rejected them.'

'Consider your options Paige. Is it better for them to despise their father for having turned his back on them or blame *you* for never having given them the opportunity to be loved by both their parents? Can you really look your children in the eye when they pose that question, as they surely will someday and make known that you never told him about them? How did you react to discover you had a father who had been kept at bay? Weren't you irate and bitter? All the lost years because of your grandfather, were you not disappointed or hurt? Have you asked your dad how he feels about those missing years? Please don't be annoyed. I'm only trying to help you make the right decision as I'd hate you to spend a lifetime regretting a terrible mistake. Nothing can be gained by being vindictive; believe me.'

Paige glared at Laura. 'Richard made *his* decision in anger. He even made untrue allegations about me and David, saying there was something between us.

Nothing could have been further from the truth. He yelled at David most of the time, trying to get him to do things he couldn't do whereas I got results by being friendly and coaxing him to try a bit harder. I wanted him to get better to please his dad because he was so worried. I can't forgive him Laura. There was no excuse for the awful things he said. I didn't deserve such contempt.'

Laura hugged her. 'I'm sorry. I know how much you loved him; I also know how much he loved you too. He told Brad he was scared because he'd never loved anybody as much as you. He talked about his son and how difficult he could be and he went on to say that if the situation arose where he had to make a choice, it'd be you. I was close to tears when Brad told me but who am I to pass judgement? I hardly knew the guy. I was only in his company for a few hours. Er, may I use the bathroom?' she asked in an attempt at closure. More than enough had been said and she knew Paige would reflect on her comments. She didn't want to push her too far.

Paige was also thankful to end the uncomfortable atmosphere although she knew Laura was acting in her best interest. 'You have an en-suite bathroom,' she stated. 'Sort yourself out and come down when you're ready. We're eating out tonight, Jake's treat so I've made us a typically English afternoon tea.'

She smiled to show there was no ill-feeling.

Laura beamed with delight. 'I'll be putting weight on,' she giggled, patting her bump.

'Who cares? Look at me. I can't imagine what I'll look like in a couple more months.'

As Paige walked into the lounge, Jake looked up. 'I was about to come and find you. Brad's feeling a little peckish...starving, to be precise.'

Brad looked guilty. 'I'm fine, really. Is Laura on her way down?'

'She won't be long,' Paige told him. 'The food's ready to eat. How was your trip? Did you have any delays on the motorway?'

'No, there was very little traffic but I can't figure out English drivers. They're forever changing lanes so I was pleased it wasn't too busy. Back home we tend to stay in our lane unless we're pulling off. We drove through some beautiful countryside. I always imagined England to be more built up. London was hell to drive through when we arrived. Once we'd parked up at the hotel we relied on public transport until we came here today.'

'I can't blame you for that. Driving round London is an absolute nightmare,' Jake acknowledged.

Directing his eyes at Paige Brad asked, 'Are you keeping well?'

She nodded. 'Very well. I've had no problems at all. I'm hoping I don't explode prior to the due date though. Have you finished decorating the nursery?'

'More or less and it looks good. Laura has lots of ideas but her head's never out of baby books at the moment.'

'Same here,' she confessed.

'Another whisky Brad?' Jake interrupted, holding the bottle up.

Eagerly he raised his glass. 'I don't mind if I do. I could get used to this. Very palatable.'

Laura's footsteps could be heard on the stairs and Paige left the room. 'We're in here. You're washed and changed,' she remarked. 'That's a pretty dress.'

'Thanks. I thought I'd wear something more comfortable. I'm looking forward to my afternoon tea.'

'Just give me five minutes,' Paige said.

Brad's eyes lit up as they took their seats. 'A feast fit for a King,' he said rubbing his hands together.

'Get stuck in then,' Jake announced. 'There'll be plenty more food in the fridge, knowing Paige.'

'Is this a guarded secret Paige or are we permitted to know whether you're having twin boys or girls?'

'Neither,' she told Laura without elaboration.

Brad regarded Paige with a quizzical expression. 'Am I missing something here? What else is there?'

The others howled at his bewilderment. 'It's quite simple if you think about it Brad. I'm having a girl and a boy, fraternal twins,' she explained.

'Oh right,' he spluttered feeling foolish and then, in a vain attempt to redeem himself continued, 'So I take it that means they won't be identical, right?'

'Er...hardly,' Laura joined in. 'How could they be identical when they're of different sex?'

Brad's cheeks flushed. 'Put it down to the whisky Jake. I should never have had that further glass on an empty stomach. I'll not open my mouth again.'

'Rubbish. How about another?' Jake offered with a roguish glint in his eye. 'I'm thoroughly enjoying the entertainment.'

'So are you happy it's one of each?' asked Laura.

'As long as they're fit and healthy, I'll be happy. Did you have a preference?'

'No. I think Brad might have preferred a boy but he's reluctant to admit it, isn't that right?'

He shrugged. 'Maybe, for a moment, but now I'm delighted it's a girl. We can have a boy next time.'

Paige and Laura exchanged glances and repeated together, *'Next time?'* Then, with a deep sigh Paige added, 'With the highest degree of certainty I know there won't ever be a *next time* for me.'

The room fell silent as they sensed her mood.

'I vote we take a trip out and see the sights,' Jake declared. 'I'll clear away while you get ready.'

'Good idea,' said Paige. 'Take Brad to your room Laura and we'll see you back here. I take it you're okay to drive Jake?'

'I haven't had a drink,' he protested. 'I expected we'd be going out; that was the plan.'

'Alright, I'm only asking,' she huffed.

Laura was the first to reappear. After helping Jake to fold the tablecloth she plucked up the courage to talk to him about Paige. 'It's probably not my place to interfere Jake but I'm very worried about Paige. Something's not right. It's not just the matter of her being at loggerheads with Richard; there appears to be a much deeper-rooted problem. I've had friends and relatives who split with their partners but I've never come across one who would so calculatingly and bitterly refuse to disclose there were children of their relationship. It beggars belief. She can't begin to see how wrong her decision is. I just wondered if you felt the same as I do.'

'Sit down, please.' He rubbed his hands together anxiously. 'We're of the same mind but it's a very delicate balancing act for me. I don't want to drive her away. I've broached the subject many times but she gets annoyed with me. Nobody could be more concerned than I am. I know Richard; I knew him before Paige did and he's an honest chap. I'm sure he believed his actions were in Paige's best interest. I gathered from the little she said that he let her go to protect her from a life of backbiting from his son and the likely need for her to help with his care if...'

'Yes, she told me about David,' she cut in. 'Their relationship was to remain secret to avoid possible repercussions from him. Richard never came across as vindictive, quite the opposite, so it's difficult to imagine he would have ended their relationship on grounds other than those stated.'

'I only know what I've been told which isn't very much. I'm forbidden to speak to Richard. Her best friend Emma would, without doubt, be reluctant to form an alliance with me so I have no one onside.'

Laura grabbed her bag and took out a notepad. In a flash she jotted her email address on the top page and tore it off. 'I can be your ally. Paige talks to me and I don't regard this as breaking a trust; I see it as necessity. I don't think she's well, psychologically I mean, but I'm praying I'll be proved wrong.'

On hearing footsteps Laura hurriedly pressed the note in Jake's hand.

Paige bounded into the room. 'Will we have time to drive to the Cotswolds? Laura would love it there and I never tire of the lovely scenery.'

Jake checked his watch. 'Okay you excitable girl. If we leave now I don't see why not. We're eating at seven o'clock so we should be back in time to get changed. Where's Brad?' he asked Laura.

'He's outside admiring your garden.'

'Has he got his camera?'

'Yes, he never goes anywhere without it. It's such a beautiful sunny day for photographs. It's hard to believe we left a mountain of snow in New York.'

They caught up with Brad by the fish pond. 'Nice garden Jake,' he commented.

'Thanks but you're not seeing it at its best. In July it's truly amazing. I have the world's best gardener I'm sure. You'll have to come again in the summer. Bring your baby girl next time.'

Paige giggled. 'They've brought her this time but I doubt she'll remember the trip. Have you chosen a name yet?' she asked Laura.

'We like Samantha at the moment but every other day we choose a different name. How about you?'

'I've already decided on Michael and Olivia.'

Laura nodded. 'Yes, I like Olivia and Michael's a good name too. I'm not really into names like Troy, Trent and Trystan. You have to be so careful. Some names sound ridiculous when they're adults.'

Paige agreed. 'Teddy is becoming fashionable but it puts me in mind of a cuddly bear so I decided I'd stick with well used names.'

'Very wise too,' Brad contributed.

The days spent with Paige and Jake had drawn to a close much too quickly but with warm memories of English hospitality, coupled with an array of scenic photographs, Laura and Brad would have plenty to share with friends and family back home. Although brief, their visit had far exceeded their expectations.

Brad and Jake neatly packed the rental car whilst Paige clung to Laura, her eyes glistening with tears. 'We've really loved having you here and you must come again. It's been fantastic, every moment and I thoroughly enjoyed our shopping spree yesterday.'

With a humorous wink in Laura's direction Jake remarked, 'I'll decide if it was a good idea to allow you two to go shopping alone when I get my credit card statement at the end of the month.'

'Ouch, that will be *excruciating,'* Laura howled. 'I'm amazed it wasn't declined, aren't you Paige?'

'Pack it in,' Jake demanded with a hearty guffaw. 'To be fair, Paige rarely goes out so I'm happy she enjoyed herself. It's been a pleasant change to have visitors staying and I've enjoyed having time alone with Brad. To echo Paige's sentiments, you're both welcome anytime.'

He shook Brad's hand vigorously and gave Laura a hug. 'I hope you have a pleasant journey home.'

All four waved until the car was out of sight, the silence only broken when Paige, on a poignant sigh remarked, 'All good things come to an end.'

With heavy heart Jake led her indoors. Paige was a troubled young woman and he felt so helpless.

In moments of solitude, her eyes if not her tongue would utter a thousand words, words veiled in total secrecy, known only to her, and he would carefully study each and every flicker of her eyes desperately seeking the briefest glimpse into her mind...but she gave nothing away.

Over the following weeks Paige became increasingly depressed and withdrawn, causing Jake great concern. If he tried to encourage her to open up to him, she would leave the room at once.

'Are you annoyed with me about something?' he queried on one occasion after she'd spent the entire day in the kitchen without a word passing her lips.

He was met with a monosyllabic, 'No.'

Shortly afterwards she mentioned she had to go to the ante-natal clinic the following day.

'Would you like me to come too? If you'd prefer a female there, Marjorie would be more than happy to oblige. She's offered several times.'

With an insincere smile she snapped, 'I'm fine on my own thanks; it's a check-up, that's all.'

The conversation ended there and Paige attended her appointment alone the next day.

Jake was at his wits end. They couldn't continue like this. He was afraid to speak in case he said the wrong thing and Paige was either unwilling or unable to discuss her problems.

That night after they had eaten in total silence he followed her to the lounge and sitting beside her he took hold of her hand. Addressing her quietly and reassuringly he expressed his concerns, begging her to share her thoughts with him.

When she failed to respond he asked, 'Was everything alright at the ante-natal clinic?'

'Yes, everything was fine,' she told him.

'Are you worried about the birth? Do you need to talk to someone non-medical who has experience of giving birth? Is that an issue of concern to…?'

'No,' she interrupted.

'Then what is it darling? I can't help if you refuse to talk to me.'

As the soothing tone of Jake's voice touched her inner soul, no longer could she control her pent-up emotions and tears flooded freely from her eyes as she cried out, 'Jake, I don't want to lose my babies. I've lost everyone else I've ever loved.' She rested her head against him and sobbed uncontrollably.

Jake was devastated. 'What do you mean? That's not true. You haven't lost me; you haven't lost your grandad and there's no reason whatsoever to think anything will go wrong in your pregnancy. You're in excellent hands and soon you'll be giving birth to two healthy babies. Trust me, you will.'

She turned to face him. 'And when I do, Richard will find out like you said he would. Laura said that too and then he'll try and take them away from me. Look at me Jake; I'm not a fit mother; I'm shaking like a leaf. How do I know that Richard hasn't been told I'm still pregnant? He knew where to find me as soon as I left home so he must have had someone following me. How else could he have known I was here? I can't stop worrying about the twins, hoping that they'll both be fit and healthy and praying that Richard isn't just waiting to apply to the courts for custody. You've no idea how frightened I feel. I've never felt so out of control in my entire life. What kind of picture do I present to a social worker or the court? When I find I'm pregnant I threaten to have an abortion; then I run off and hide. I allow Richard to believe I'm cohabiting with you so he'll keep his distance and then when I decide I'll keep my babies I don't tell the father. It looks great that, doesn't it? The perfect mother. If I were the judge, I definitely wouldn't leave two babies in my care. I'm mentally unstable Jake; are you happy now? Is that what you wanted to hear? Is it?'

'Yes, that's exactly what I wanted to hear because now we can work on that to make you well. Having the courage to accept there's a problem is a major step forward. Since your grandfather's death you've been in denial. I recognised that some time ago but I didn't want to reap up the past. Your way of dealing with his death was to remain occupied almost to breaking point when instead you should have made time to grieve properly. I don't want to delve into it now. I prefer to discuss it calmly, starting tomorrow and I promise I'll get you through this.'

Somewhat relieved she smiled faintly. 'So you're saying I'm not loopy then?'

Jake smiled. 'I never use that word but no, you're not. You're exhausted, anxious and your pregnancy hormones are responsible for a lot of the unpleasant thoughts you're experiencing. Believe me, you'll be fine if you're willing to cooperate and don't worry about Richard for he'd never try to take your babies away, nor would he succeed if he did.'

Jake hugged her tenderly saying, 'Time for bed.'

'But I haven't tidied the kitchen yet.'

'*Bed.* I won't tell you again. *I'll* tidy the kitchen.'

13

'*A journey of a thousand miles begins with a single step,*' Jake advised her. 'I've no idea who originally uttered those wise words and I don't know the context in which they were first used but I've made use of them many times with my patients to encourage them to talk to me. I'd like you to try and forget I'm your dad. Try instead to see me as your counsellor, trying to help you come to terms with your thoughts and fears. I'm not going to write anything down. I'd just like you to express your feelings, alright?'

Paige nodded. 'What do you want to know?'

'Whatever you'd care to tell me. Let's begin with your grandad; just say whatever comes to mind.'

She paused but a moment collecting her thoughts. 'Grandad enjoyed playing Dominoes and he'd play all day with our next door neighbour. He was *very* competitive. He played to win and he did win in the main. If he lost he would curse and swear. That was the only time I heard him swear. After his stroke he became quite mild-mannered but when I was little I recall he used to scare me.'

'What was it about him that scared you?'

'I don't know. I think it was the way he looked at me with a fierce expression; at least I thought it was fierce. After he'd had his stroke he changed. I used to hop up on the bed with him then and read to him. He really enjoyed that.'

'What did you read to him?' Jake prompted.

'My short stories predominantly...the ones I wrote for magazines. He liked to hear them over and over again.' She grinned. 'Grandad was my biggest fan. He used to say he was very proud of me, especially when my first story was accepted and published. He couldn't wait to tell Bill, the next door neighbour, his doctor and the carers from Social Services who often called in. It was really embarrassing at times.'

Jake smiled. 'Carry on. Tell me about your social life after your grandad became ill.'

'Are you joking? It was non-existent. I used to get out a bit with Emma my friend and Tim, who at the time was my boyfriend but when Grandad had his stroke Tim dumped me. I know the next question so don't ask,' she said with a dry smile. 'Suffice to say I was ripping and very upset.'

'Did you resent your grandad after Tim left?'

'Of course not. He was ill. He needed me. I found other things to fill my time, what little time I had. I soon got over Tim. He was no great catch. It would never have lasted.'

With raised eyebrows he asked, 'Why was that?'

'Simple…he was an egotistical prick.'

Paige knew her words would shock him and they did. For a second or two Jake attempted to compose himself before exploding into a fit of laughter.

'Sorry Paige. That shouldn't have happened. Not very professional,' he expressed regretfully. 'Let's move on.'

'We're hardly in a professional situation are we? You're my dad and I'm your daughter. I thought we were doing quite well, considering...'

'You're right; we are. Would you like to go on?'

'Only if you would.'

'Okay...just for a little while. I'd like you to think about Tim. You told me it made you angry when he walked out on you but did you at any time consider how much you were asking him to give up?'

'How do you mean?'

'Tim was a young man and you expected him to give up his social life to be with you. Was it really fair to expect so much of him? Let me put it another way; did you ever cancel a night out with him when your mum was ill?'

'Yes at times when she couldn't be left but sometimes he'd sit in with me.'

With raised eyebrows Jake asked, 'Wasn't that a selfless act, on his part I mean?'

'I suppose so but Tim was my boyfriend. I'd have done the same for him.'

'Unconditionally and indefinitely? I'm not being critical. I'm just saying maybe it was a lot to ask.'

'You're right, it obviously was so he dumped me. I don't want to talk about Tim anymore.'

Appearing distressed, she twisted her gold bangle around her wrist and Jake felt it was time to change topic.

'So, returning to your grandad for a moment, did he deteriorate suddenly at the end?'

She nodded. 'He died in his sleep, a blessed relief because he'd become very weak. I left the room to make him a drink and when I returned he was gone. At first I thought he was sleeping but when I looked more closely he was dead. I phoned the surgery and our GP came straight round.'

'Can you remember how you felt? By that I mean did you panic or burst into tears? I'd like you to tell me what you remember about your initial reaction, your state of mind. That's very important.'

Without hesitation she answered, 'I was calm as I recall but later I started to worry about the funeral as we had very little money. I rang Social Services to tell them he'd died and they told me how I could apply for financial help towards the funeral. I felt a lot better then. I was very grateful for their advice.'

'Do you recall if you cried? Take your time.'

She gave thought to his question before saying, 'I was upset. I had no one left in my family but I don't believe I cried till the day of the funeral when I saw the lovely flowers so many people had sent.'

'Let's discuss how you felt after the funeral, how you came to terms with your loss. Try to remember if you felt depressed and if so whether you sought medical help or took any medication?'

'To be honest I didn't have time to think about it. I needed to find a job. I applied for two and got one so I went to work right away and kept very busy at home. The house was in need of renovation. It was shabby and dismal so I worked on that. I needed to occupy my time at home. I'd gone from being a full time carer to having nobody to care for but myself. I know now that I should have behaved differently. For some reason I couldn't bring myself to face the truth. Inwardly I was angry so that drove me on and soon I found a vent for my anger, David, Richard's son. I became rather aggressive verbally though not without just cause, believe me. He would have tried the patience of a saint. He was so unlike his dad.'

He paused before his next question but it seemed a natural progression as she had referred to Richard. 'Would you like to talk to me about Richard?'

'No!' Paige stated adamantly. Almost at once she added, 'Maybe another day, not now if that's okay.'

Although recognising a lack of conviction in her words, he planted a kiss on her head. 'You're such a courageous girl. Well done. How do you fancy a nice cup of tea with a slice of your delicious home-made fruit cake? I'll attend to it.'

'Are we done talking?'

He nodded. 'For now, yes.'

That was to be the first of many such sessions that continued on an almost daily basis and when, at the end of the first week she sought Jake's professional opinion, it was favourable. She had to agree she felt better. Having somebody to talk to, someone who'd pay attention without judging her faults, had helped her lay some of her demons to rest. She still had a long way to go but progress was being made.

By way of reward Jake asked, 'How do you fancy a trip to see Emma this weekend? I'll drive and you can have a few hours of girl talk. It's time I met her. What do you say?'

She was ecstatic. 'Oh yes, that'd be fantastic and probably the only chance I'll have to see her before the twins are born. I think I'd prefer to steer clear of her flat though. Heaven knows who I might bump into. I'll tell you what; we can meet at the Trafford Centre. I still need a few bits for the twins. That'd be better and I'd be more at ease there if that's okay with you. Shall I call her and see what she says?'

Her zeal made Jake smile. 'I suppose that means you'll knock hell out of my credit card again.'

'You can bet on it,' she grinned.

Emma screeched with glee to see her friend for the first time since December. 'Really, I wouldn't have known you,' she confessed when Paige tapped her on the shoulder and grinned. 'I wasn't looking for anyone with such a gargantuan er...gut. Nice shades by the way. Are you hiding from the police?'

Paige hugged her. 'You don't half know how to make a girl feel good and no I'm not, but I'd hate to bump into anyone else who might recognise me.'

Jake, hovering in Paige's shadow, inched forward towards Emma and with a friendly smile introduced himself. 'Hi, Jake Allcock, Paige's dad. It's good to meet you at last Emma. I've heard a lot about you.'

'I'm surprised you came then when I'm notorious for having such an irrepressible gob,' she chuckled.

'I'll second that,' Paige announced whimsically.

Awkwardly Jake said, 'I hadn't heard that.'

'Warra gent,' Emma squealed. 'I like you already and slipping her arm through his she quizzed, 'Will you be joining us round the shops?'

'I think not if you don't mind. Besides, I imagine the two of you have a lot of catching up to do. Shall we meet up for lunch, say around one o'clock?'

'Sounds good. I'll call you later to say where. Are you sure your mobile's turned on?' asked Paige.

He nodded. 'I'm sure. Have a good time.'

'Oh we will,' Emma said with a wink of the eye.

'Your dad's gorgeous. I bet he was a looker when he was young and he talks nice too, not like us. He seems very easy going,' Emma said as Jake went in the opposite direction. 'It's uplifting to meet a posh guy. You don't see many. I used to like Richard but he ended up being a cretin like his son.'

Heatedly Paige exclaimed, 'Don't go there! Don't even speak his name. It's ages since we've been out and I refuse to waste time talking about him.'

Emma thought better than to pursue the topic and to Paige's relief, no further mention was made.

Although exhausted by mid-afternoon, Paige had thoroughly enjoyed her day. Emma had chosen her wedding present and though Paige was unable to go to her wedding with the twins due around that time, she assured Emma she would be there in spirit.

'It's such rotten timing isn't it?' Emma grumbled. 'We'd have preferred to have it a bit later but all the decent venues were booked throughout the summer so that meant we could either get married in June or wait till next year. I'll miss having you there.'

'I'll miss being there but I'll see your photos and your DVD. Are you nervous, about the wedding I mean?'

'Bloody petrified,' Emma confessed. 'I'm having nightmares that everything's going to go wrong.'

Paige laughed. 'All brides think that you clown.'

'Are you scared about giving birth to twins?'

'Let's just say I'll be glad when that part's over. I can't wait to see my babies though. I'm glad I have Jake around to help. He's so composed and reliable but that's his job, remaining calm. He's been helping me, talking to me. He's being there at the birth.'

'Your dad?' she yelled. *'You're joking!'*

Embarrassed by her sudden outburst Paige looked round. 'Keep your voice down for heaven's sake. I need *someone* there. It's not like I have a partner.'

'But surely not your *dad!'* she exclaimed. 'Right, if they bring it forward, say by the end of next week or the week after, *I'll* come down. That's preferable to having your dad in the delivery room. Get real.'

'Seriously, would you do that for me Emma?'

'Of course and I'll make an excuse to Andy about needing something for the wedding. He'll buy that.'

Her eyes sparkled with tears. 'You're such a good friend Emma. I'm stressed out at the moment and I don't want to be a burden on Jake who's been very kind to me but I do worry I won't be a fit mother.'

'Don't talk so daft. If anyone's fit to be a mother, you are. You're the most caring person I know and once the twins are born you'll have no time to think of bad stuff. I'd trust you with my kid any day.'

'Your kid? Right lady, spit it out; why have you brought the wedding forward after you told me you couldn't afford it this year?'

With scarlet cheeks Emma spluttered, 'It was just a figure of speech, that's all. I'm not pregnant but I can't say any more. Andy will go apeshit if I do.'

'And *I* will if you don't. Anyway you just have. I can't believe you didn't tell me you were pregnant.'

'It's not that, honest. I'm not pregnant. There's a problem with Andy and if you repeat this, I'll never tell you anything again. Promise you won't tell.'

'Emma, you know you can trust me. Is he ill?'

'No, he's fine; at least we think he's fine. There's a history of testicular cancer in his family and a few weeks ago he found a lump. Luckily it was nothing to worry about but now he can't rest. He wants kids and if he did get cancer in the future it could stop us having any so we've brought the wedding forward as he believes it's wrong to have kids before you're married. He holds strong views about that.'

Haughtily she sniped, 'Well if he's been having a dig at me you can tell him I certainly didn't plan to get pregnant and...'

'No he hasn't Paige, believe me. Andy still thinks you had the abortion.'

'Yes, and he didn't approve of that either.'

'Why are we quarrelling? Andy has his own ideas about things which he's entitled to have He's not a bad person Paige; he's a good person.'

She gave thought to Emma's words. 'He is; I'm sorry. I like Andy and remember, although there's a history it doesn't mean he's inherited it. If that were the case, we'd all get everything our ancestors had.'

Emma nodded. 'I never thought about it like that. You're right. Let's drop it. Fancy a coffee?'

Paige checked her watch. 'I promised to call Jake around half-three but I could murder a drink first.'

Arm in arm they wandered to the coffee bar, their earlier dispute forgotten and when Jake appeared a short while later there was a tearful farewell.

'I'll let you know what they tell me at the clinic,' Paige said. 'It'll be great if you can come down for the birth and if you need an overnight stay I'm sure Jake will be happy to accommodate you.'

Emma patted the bump. 'It's hard to believe there are two babies in there. You take care.'

Paige watched her walk to her car and sighed inwardly. Emma's scary revelations had certainly put her problems into perspective. Andy was a kind and compassionate young guy who deserved better. No one should have to agonize about the possibility of developing cancer at his age. Life could be so cruel.

'Is something wrong?' Jake asked.

Paige forced a smile. 'Not really. I miss Emma so it's sad when we have to go our separate ways.'

'She's nice. I like uncomplicated people. She says it as she sees it and she's certainly fond of you.'

'The feeling's mutual. We go back a long way, to our childhood. Listen, are you in a rush to get home because if you can spare another hour or so there's someone else I'd like to see.'

'Who's that?'

'Eleanor. I've promised so many times I'd go and see her but I've never felt happy going on my own in case *he* happened to turn up unexpected.'

'He? Oh, right, Richard. Do you really believe he doesn't know Paige? I can't accept that her loyalties would be with you when he's her son.'

'Yes, well, we haven't really discussed him have we? Eleanor wants access to the children. That first weekend I went up north to clear my house, I called to give her my version of events. I suppose it came as no surprise to learn she had no idea Richard and I were over. He hadn't even bothered to mention it to her. She was shocked at what I had to say and I didn't embellish any part of it; I only told the truth. She could see I was pregnant so I made a deal with her. In return for her silence I promised I'd take the children to see her when I was in the area and I said she could visit us too. I told her about you, that you were my father and that I'd never move back there. She's a lovely lady. You answered her call one day when I was out shopping and when I later spoke to her, she said you'd had an interesting conversation, that you came across as a very compassionate man. She also made reference to your 'cut-glass' speaking voice…*educated*, she called it.'

With a smug smile he said, 'Did she now? I can't wait to meet the little lady. Bring it on.'

She laughed. 'Behave or I'll tell Marjorie. I know about your reputation when you were young, which reminds me, are you two sleeping together yet?'

Jake spluttered a laugh. *'Paige,* you can't ask me questions like that; I'm your father.'

'Why not? As my father, it appears to present no problem when you're investing all your energy into rifling through *my* deep and darkest secrets.'

'But that's different. It's what I do. It's my job as a psychiatrist. I have to get you to open up to me.'

Wide eyed she quipped, 'Oh right. So that makes *me* your patient then?'

'Kind of,' he answered not quite knowing how to react because he knew more was to come. Only too well did he know of her aptitude for scoring points.

She smiled sweetly. 'Then if I'm your patient, are you not required to humour me? So, let me ask you again, are you sleeping with Marjorie? Remember, it could adversely affect my recovery not to know.'

With rosy red cheeks he guffawed and spluttered, 'You are a cheeky young bugger.'

With a demure smile Paige taunted, 'I bet you say that to all your patients. Is that a *yes* then?'

'Alright, yes I am, but don't you dare breathe one word to Marjorie.'

'Why, doesn't she know?' she questioned with an innocent expression, followed by a tinkling laugh. 'I love to get the upper hand. I love you Dad.'

It was the first time she had ever called him *Dad.* He was both ecstatic and touched in equal measure. He gazed at his beautiful daughter and smiled. 'You are the best thing that's ever happened to me. I love you too Paige, more than words could ever say.'

When he stopped the car outside Eleanor's house she felt a moment's panic. Reading her thoughts in an instant Jake said comfortingly, 'You'll be fine.'

Breathing heavily she approached the front door and rang the bell. Eleanor was there in a second and throwing her arms around Paige she cried, 'It's *so* good to see you. I didn't think you'd make it so late into your pregnancy. You look a lot bigger than you did the last time I saw you.' She kissed her warmly. 'Do come in. I take it you're Paige's dad,' she said to Jake with a welcoming smile.

'Yes, Jake Allcock. We spoke once on the phone when Paige was shopping. I'm happy to make your acquaintance at last Mrs Cavendish.'

‘It’s Eleanor, please, and have a seat. I’ve rustled up a few sandwiches and cakes. I’d have made you a meal had I known earlier you were calling.’

‘No, it’s fine Eleanor,’ Paige said. ‘We didn’t call to make you any work. Sandwiches and a cup of tea will be as much as we can manage, thank you.’

‘How’s David, your grandson, coming along now Eleanor?’ Jake enquired.

With a sigh of relief she declared, ‘Much better of late thank you. He appears to have turned the corner now. He’s walking without help and thinking about returning to his flat, but he’s not driving again yet. He’s not back at work either. With a shrill titter she added, ‘David’s seeing Penny now. You remember her don’t you Paige, his physiotherapist?’

She smiled reflectively. ‘I do. She’s very good at her job and pretty too. I recall David was smitten so I’m pleased for them both.’

Thankfully no mention was made of Richard and the room fell silent for a few moments.

‘Have they given you a firm date now at the clinic Paige?’ asked Eleanor.

She shook her head. ‘It’ll most probably be about a week if nothing’s happened by then but I’ll keep you posted. I’m quite excited now. We’ve ordered a pram but I’m superstitious, so it won’t be delivered until I return home.’ Before she could stop herself, though without malicious intent, she declared, ‘I’ve had more than my share of bad luck over the years.’

Obvious from Eleanor’s reaction that she believed the remark to be directed at Richard, Paige flushed with embarrassment.

'I'm sorry Paige,' Eleanor mumbled quietly.

'No Eleanor, you misunderstand. I was referring to the loss of my mum and Grandad, nothing more.'

'It still doesn't excuse his behaviour Paige. David really misses you and always asks about you when he speaks to me. He knows we keep in touch but he would never tell his dad.'

She was shocked. 'Does he know I'm pregnant?'

'Heavens no; I'd never tell him that.'

She stood up, walked to the dresser and took out a large bag. 'A few things for my grandchildren.' She smiled. 'I've enjoyed making those. I hope you like them. Have a look while I'm fetching the drinks in.'

'Let me give you a hand,' Jake offered, following her through to the kitchen which provided the ideal opportunity for Eleanor to talk to him about Paige. 'Now we're alone, how has she been?' she asked.

'Highs and lows,' Jake sighed heavily. 'She loved Richard very much so she was devastated when she lost him so soon after losing her grandad. She has good days but there are still far too many dark days. She's lost so much in her short life.'

'Yes, but she found you. What a shock you must have had when she suddenly turned up at the hospital. She told me you'd no idea you had a daughter.'

'That's right. I was led to believe her mother had had a termination. Paige's grandfather told me that, amongst lots of other things he said and did to me.' Pointing to his crooked nose he grinned, 'I clearly wasn't what he had in mind as a future son-in-law.'

'Well I can tell you Jake that I was heartbroken to learn Richard and Paige were no longer together. It was a match made in heaven. I still don't know why he ended it. He won't discuss it but what he did was so out of character. He's normally such a kind man. If you'd ever met him you'd know that.'

'Paige obviously didn't tell you everything. I've known Richard since he was about seventeen. I was living in these parts then. I even met Paige once in a pub when Richard brought her along to meet a pal of mine. She reminded me very much of the girl I'd loved and lost but never in a million years would I have guessed that beautiful fresh-faced girl was my daughter, my own flesh and blood. Life is strange.'

She nodded. 'Do you think Paige will ever have a change of heart and let Richard see his children?'

'If you want honesty, I don't Eleanor. Leastways, not the way she feels presently. I don't believe her motives are vindictive. It's more about her dread of losing the children were Richard to go for custody. I'm pretty sure he wouldn't but she's a difficult one to convince but don't give up hope; I haven't.'

To the sound of rattling crockery they reappeared carrying the food and drink. 'Just look at this Paige. This is superb,' Jake declared hungrily.

Paige stood up and giving Eleanor an affectionate hug stated, 'The clothes for the twins are amazing. Did you really make them all yourself?'

Modestly she said, 'Yes, I love to sew and knit.'

'Just look at these Dad. Aren't they lovely?'

He looked at them closely. 'You're very talented,' he told Eleanor. 'Did you do this for a living?'

'No, I never went out to work. I learned to sew at evening classes but I don't put it to much use these days.' She poured their tea adding, 'Right, don't be shy. Help yourselves to sandwiches and cakes.'

Paige held her in a warm embrace when they had to leave. 'I'm so glad we came,' she told her. 'Once again thank you for the beautiful clothes you made. Dad will call you as soon as anything happens.'

'I'm so excited. I never thought I'd be a grandma again. I hope you have an easy time. Good luck.'

As Jake stepped forwards with outstretched hand Eleanor flung her arms around him. 'I'm so pleased to have met you Jake. Imagine, a few short months ago you didn't even know you had such a beautiful daughter and now, very soon, you're going to have two wonderful grandchildren as well.'

'Yes, life's full of little surprises,' he said dryly.

'Drive carefully,' she cautioned as she accompanied them to the gate.

Jake raised his hand and thanked her again for her hospitality. 'See you soon Eleanor,' he called out.

'What a charming lady,' he remarked as he drove away. 'She clearly thinks a great deal about you.'

A solitary tear trickled down Paige's cheek as she reflected wistfully about what might have been. She had felt Richard's ethereal presence in his mother's house despite his actual absence and the photograph on the mantelpiece of his smiling face had evoked memories of much happier times. Theirs had been a passionate relationship she would never forget.

Interrupting her reverie Jake said softly, 'A penny for them.'

'Oh it's nothing. I was miles away,' she remarked pensively.

14

Everything happened so quickly on the Saturday.

Jake left the house early after breakfast to get his weekly car wash and after tidying the kitchen Paige went upstairs to take a shower.

As she stepped in the shower she felt a twinge of pain. Within a few minutes there was a further pain, followed by a dull ache in her lower back. 'Oh my God!' she cried. 'It's really happening!'

Clutching her mobile with quivering hands, Paige selected Jake's number. It rang several times before going to voicemail. 'It's me Dad,' she yelled. 'Call me back right away. The babies are coming; at least I think they are. Something's going on. I'm scared.'

She made a second call but this time to Marjorie's number. At the second ring she answered.

'Marjorie! Thank God you're in. It's Paige. Dad's not here and I think I've started in labour. I'm very confused. I can't think straight and I'm panicking.'

'Just breathe deeply and stay calm,' Marjorie said soothingly. 'Nothing's going to happen quickly so there's no need to panic. Trust me. Are you taking deep breaths now?'

'I'm trying but I'm getting really stressed out.'

'That's normal but believe me, there's nothing to be afraid of. What time did Jake leave?'

‘I don’t know. Fifteen minutes ago I’d say. I rang and left a message for him to call me back.’

‘Tell me what’s happened so far.’

‘I’ve had two pains, well not actual *pains* but like *twinges*. The second stronger one lasted longer.’

‘How far apart were they?’

‘I’m not sure. I’m useless aren’t I? Perhaps about ten minutes. I was in the shower. It hasn’t happened again since I got out.’

‘Are you dressed?’

‘No, I’m in my robe.’

‘Alright, get dressed and call me again if you still haven’t heard from your dad. Remember to make a note of the time between pains.’

As Paige entered the bedroom to get dressed, she heard the front door slam closed, followed by heavy footsteps on the stairs. Jake barged into her room, breathing heavily. ‘Are you alright? I came straight back as soon as I got your message.’

‘Sorry, I was scared. I felt some pain but it seems to have eased off. I feel better now you’re here.’

Jake gave her a hug. ‘I’ll take care of you now. I won’t leave you again.’

‘I’d better get dressed. Will you call Marjorie and Emma needs to be told...oh, and Eleanor too. Emma promised she’d be here with me at the birth but she might not arrive in time now.’

‘I’ll stick the kettle on, make you a drink and I’ll call everyone while you’re getting ready.’

As Jake was closing her door she hollered, ‘Ring Emma first, then she can set off...and hurry before I get another pain.’

He turned back and grinned. 'Okay Bossy-Boots. Guess what...I'm going to be a grandad.'

Paige grinned back at him. 'And I'm going to be a mummy.'

'I've driven here like a maniac,' Emma spluttered, flopping breathlessly on the edge of Paige's bed. 'I thought I wouldn't make it in time.'

'Can I get you a coffee Emma?' Jake offered.

'Please and I wouldn't say *no* to summat to eat, a sandwich or a cake. I hadn't even had any breakfast when you phoned me. I'm flaming ravenous.'

'Sugar and milk?'

'Please, two sugars and a lot of milk.' Turning to Paige she said, 'You're looking a bit rough.'

'I've felt better,' she said, gripping the bedclothes tightly. 'Oh, oh...no, it's coming again.' She panted as instructed until the few seconds of agony passed. 'Never again. God, I can't understand women who go through this time after time. If blokes had to go through childbirth the world would end.'

Emma chuckled and held her hand. 'It'll soon be over and worth the pain,' she said comfortingly.

'How the hell would you know?' she snapped.

The midwife laughed. 'Ignore her. Your friend's reaction is quite normal. Once she sees her babies she'll forget all about this.'

Jake returned with a tray and placed it on Paige's side table. He handed Emma her coffee. 'These are nice sandwiches. The cook roasts her own chickens and puts a thick slice on the bread for me. For afters there's a fresh cream strawberry tart for each of us.'

'I can't wait to get my chops round that,' Emma gasped hungrily. 'What do I owe you Jake?'

'Nothing, it's on me,' he told her.

'I don't believe this,' yelled Paige. 'Here I am in agony and you two are having a bloody picnic.'

'What's up with you? D'you wanna bite?' Emma offered.

With a sigh of disgust Paige grunted, 'Definitely *not.'*

Following another strong contraction and a quick examination the midwife announced it was time for Paige to go next door to the delivery room.

'Hang on till I get there. Don't have them yet. I'll be in when I've finished my butty,' Emma said.

That comment was met with a black look.

'It'll not be long now,' the midwife said. 'Let me help you out of bed. Follow on when you're ready,' she told Emma.

'Good luck darling. Hope to see you soon,' Jake said with tears in his eyes. 'I'm very proud of you.' He kissed her fondly and she forced a smile.

Fifteen minutes later Emma, with a wide beaming smile, called Jake. 'You can meet your granddaughter now. You'll never believe how gorgeous she is.'

Cautiously he walked into the room and smiled at Paige. She looked exhausted but deliriously happy as she held the baby in her arms.

'Say hello. This is your grandad, Olivia.'

The tiny baby instantly screwed up her face and wailed loudly, causing everyone to laugh.

'I'll take her now,' the midwife said. 'It's time to get cracking again. You've a lot of work to do yet.'

Jake stroked Paige's hand devotedly. 'Well done. I'm ecstatic. She's so beautiful. I'll be outside.'

As he approached the door Paige announced, 'By the way Dad, she weighs five pounds three ounces. That's a respectable weight for a twin I'm told.'

Emma was quick to respond, 'Yes, and given the option, I'd much rather squeeze out twins weighing five pounds three each than one at ten pounds six.'

'Can you believe *her?*' Paige commented. 'Never misses an opportunity, that one. Wait until it's your turn. I'll be there giving you grief, lady.'

Smiling, Emma escorted Jake from the room. 'I'll be out for you when the next one arrives.'

He didn't have long to wait. Everyone was taken aback at the speed with which she gave birth to her baby son, Michael. Weighing in at five pounds two ounces, he made his presence known instantly.

'That's a powerful pair of lungs,' Emma laughed.

'You're right. I'm unlikely to get a wink of sleep with these two,' Paige said, cuddling Michael. 'Can my dad come in now please?'

'Just give me a minute,' the midwife said. 'Then I'll leave you together for a little while.'

Paige grinned like the proverbial Cheshire Cat. 'I did it Emma. I was scared at times but it wasn't too bad.'

Emma cooed over the babies, closely examining their tiny fingers. 'It's amazing isn't it? They're so tiny but perfect in every way. I suppose you've this to be thankful for from that lousy rat. At least he's given you two beautiful babies.'

'Do you think I'm horrible for not telling him?'

‘No! If they were mine I wouldn’t share them for a single moment with a loser like that.’

‘His mum knows I’ve come in today. You should see the gorgeous stuff she’s made for the twins. She is so gifted. You’d like Eleanor. She’s lovely. She’s no idea why Richard behaved the way he did.’

Emma was apprehensive. ‘How do you know she won’t tell him?’

‘I trust her. She promised and I agreed to take the twins to see her regularly, so she has everything to lose if she tells him but she wouldn’t do that. She’s dying to see them so I bet she’ll turn up this week-end. How long are you staying?’

‘Well, it’s Saturday today, Sunday tomorrow and the day after is bank holiday Monday, so I won’t be back in work till Tuesday. Do you want me to stay till Monday afternoon? I can square it with Andy.’

‘That’d be great but what would you tell him?’

‘I’ve only two options, the truth or a lie.’

‘There’s a third option. You could say you hadn’t seen much of me since I left and so we were having a few days together. It wouldn’t be a lie and I’d feel happier with that. At some point he has to be told. I can’t hide the twins forever but the longer I can, the less likely Richard is to find out.’

The midwife placed both babies in her arms and smiled. ‘It’s not often I deliver twins. That is such a lovely sight. Do you have a camera?’

‘Yes, in my bag. Will you take our picture please and one with my dad too?’

‘Certainly. He can come back now if you’re com-fortable...just for a few minutes mind. I don’t want visitors tiring you. You've worked very hard today. He can come again later, after you've rested.'

Emma opened the door. 'It's safe to come in now *Grandad*. Paige has finally stopped cursing.'

As Jake walked into the room the emotion of the event overwhelmed him. His daughter was smiling dazzlingly as she held her two babies. It was all too much and he cried as he held her. 'This is the most memorable day of my entire life. I could never put my feelings into words. How do you feel?'

'I'm fine now and glad it's over. How do I look?'

'Radiant, absolutely radiant.'

'Then dry your tears,' Paige said taking charge. 'I think we're about to have some pictures taken.'

The midwife held up the camera. 'Move in a little Mr Allcock. I don't want to cut your head off.'

They laughed when he joked, 'I've a fair number of patients who'd be happy if you did.'

With a quick click she captured the unforgettable moment. 'Let's have another to be sure.'

They smiled once again and then Jake took a few of Paige and her babies.

'Have you called anyone yet?' Paige asked.

'Everyone. Marjorie wants to come in later to see you; Eleanor screeched like a barn owl and I called my work buddies too. Can I get you anything?'

'I've thought of nothing but Emma's nice chicken sandwich since Michael was born. I'm ravenous.'

'Sandwich coming up,' he said.

'What a fantastic guy your dad is,' Emma sighed. 'He was very distressed when he came in. He loves you so much and the twins will be spoiled rotten.'

'I know and by Eleanor too. It's sad things turned out the way they did. Have you spoken to Dad yet about staying at ours?'

She hedged. 'I didn't like. Will you ask him? I've brought an overnight bag and a few clothes. When do you expect to be home?'

'Tomorrow, hopefully. They don't keep you long now. When I see the doctor I'll ask him.'

'Is yours a private room?'

'Yes, Dad arranged it. You know what he's like; only the best is good enough for his little girl.'

'You deserve the best. I'm happy you found your dad because you've had it rough since you were a teenager. I'm lucky too with supportive parents in good health and I also have Andy who's brilliant. I can't complain about a thing.'

'Oh yes you can, and you do. You're the world's biggest moaner,' she contradicted and they laughed.

It was then that she remembered what Emma had revealed about Andy and for a moment her joy was tinged with sadness as she prayed he'd remain well.

Paige was returning to her room when Jake came back with her sandwich. 'Betty's sent you a freshly baked egg custard. She's absolutely delighted with the news. I've heard from Eleanor too. She'll arrive sometime this afternoon so she's coming straight to the house and I'll bring her over later. I asked her to stay overnight but she was rather hesitant.'

Paige hooted with laughter. 'She's probably heard you're a womaniser but if it makes her decision any easier, tell her Emma's staying as well so she might feel there's safety in numbers.'

As Emma regarded him bemused, Paige felt some explanation was warranted. 'He's harmless, despite his reputation. It was Richard who branded Jake a lecher, long before I knew he was my dad. Richard knew him when he was seeing my mum and everybody loves to embellish a scandal to make it more interesting. Dad was married but their marriage was over in all but name. There was nothing lewd about his relationship with Mum. Dad loved her and they would undoubtedly have got married following his divorce but for my grandad's interference.'

Clearly embarrassed he spluttered, 'You have to understand *that's* merely a *miniscule* part of my CV Emma.'

Jake was soon to regret his words as she rejoined with a mischievous grin, 'Really? So you're saying there's more? Do tell.'

Paige howled with laughter. 'Give it up Dad. You have no chance against Emma.' She took a big bite of her sandwich and sighed with utter contentment.

'I think it's time you rested now,' Jake said. 'Will you come back home with me Emma? I need to call into work to rearrange my appointments next week but someone must be there when Eleanor arrives.'

'Okay,' she chirped.

Paige looked at her sternly. 'You have to promise not to say anything controversial about Richard. I'd rather his name wasn't even mentioned. Eleanor's his mum who's in an awkward position and the last thing she needs is you mouthing off about him.'

'Hey, I'm the absolute soul of discretion. I'm not a bloody idiot.'

Jake stifled a laugh when Paige retorted, 'That's debateable.'

Emma gazed at the twins. 'Aw...look, they're fast asleep now. They're gorgeous.'

'Will you tell Betty I wolfed her tasty food, Dad? If I'm sleeping when you come back later, wake me please. I'd rather sleep at night.'

It felt good to have time alone. There'd doubtless be plenty of disruption over the next hours days and weeks until she formulated her routine but that was something to look forward to, being home with her family. After smiling lovingly at her babies, she lay back and slipped into a richly deserved sleep.

'You must be Eleanor,' Emma said with a beaming smile. 'Please come in. I'm Emma, Paige's friend. I hope you had a trouble free journey. Jake's had to slip out but I'm staying till Monday. Paige timed it well having the twins at a bank holiday weekend.'

'Didn't she just. How are the babies?'

'Absolutely great. I was lucky enough to arrive in time for the birth. It was very emotional.'

'I can well imagine. Shall I leave my bags here?'

'There's a bedroom made up next door to mine if you want to stay. Jake said I'd to take you up.'

She could hardly refuse his kind hospitality. 'Yes, that'd be great thanks. I can't wait to see my grandchildren,' she gushed with an excitable smile.

'Paige told me about the clothes you'd made. She was very impressed, Jake too.' She opened the door saying, 'Right, this is your room and there's an en-suite shower room. You have a lovely view…see.'

Eleanor walked to the window and commented on the undulating countryside. 'How beautiful. Look at all those sheep and lambs and there are some lovely thoroughbred horses in the next field. I used to ride a lot when I was a girl. Do you ride Emma?'

'Me? You're joking. I'm a right gormless bugger. I'd be on my arse before I'd even got on. Oops, I'm so sorry; that just slipped out,' Emma spluttered but Eleanor was already laughing heartily.

'I can see we're going to get along fine Emma. I can't abide folk with highfalutin airs and graces.'

'Me neither,' she agreed. 'Cup of tea?'

'I'd love one.'

When Paige stirred and opened her eyes, Jake was at her bedside. 'Alright?' he asked calmly. 'Did you have a nice sleep?'

'Mmm, I was so tired. Where is everyone?'

'The twins have been taken for a feed and Emma's at the house with Eleanor. I thought it'd be nice for us to have a bit of father and daughter time.'

Paige stretched out her arm and took hold of his hand. 'Thanks Dad. You've been so supportive.'

'I think you'll find that's in the job description for a parent. Besides I like to pamper you. I've brought you some flowers.'

'They're lovely, thanks. Did you contact Laura?'

'No, I thought you'd like to tell her yourself. Why not call her now? You can use my phone.'

Eagerly she called Laura's number and when she picked up, they made small talk until Laura asked, 'What have you been up to today?'

'Oh you know, this and that...and this afternoon I was busy giving birth to twins.'

Paige held the phone at arm's length anticipating a piercing scream. She wasn't disappointed.

'Are they alright, are you alright?' Laura cried.

'We're all great. Having said that, Dad's a physical wreck but I'm unwinding now. Once I heard the babies cry I was happy and they're perfect. They're both a decent weight, over five pounds each, so that means I can take them home tomorrow, hopefully.'

Laura was thrilled. 'You've never been out of my thoughts for the past two weeks. Brad's signalling that he wants me to convey his congratulations.'

'I take it nothing's happened with you yet?'

'No, I'm still hanging on. Mum's here and she'll stay as long as I need her now. Did you have a hard time, delivering twins?'

'Quite the reverse. It was easy. There's nothing at all to worry about. One minute I was panicking and hollering like mad and the next I had a baby. Olivia was born first. Dad said that was to be expected and that she probably elbowed Michael out of the way because that's what girls are like, assertive. Michael followed a few minutes later. I felt extremely tired afterwards.'

'I can't wait for ours now. I'm so big and clumsy that I can't do anything but Brad's been an absolute treasure. *And* we've finally chosen a name we both like...Morgan.'

'Morgan,' she repeated. 'I like that; it's different.'

'We wanted one that wouldn't be abbreviated like they tend to do over here where Michael would become Mike or Mikey and Olivia would be Liv. That happens all the time.'

'Yes, it's the same here but more so in the States. I'll be thinking of you now until I hear from you. I hope you don't have to wait much longer.'

'Me too. By the way, did you give further thought to what we talked about...telling Richard I mean?'

'What's to think about? My mind's made up. I'm telling Richard nothing,' she remarked sharply. She then heard what could best be described as a heavy sigh of disapproval, though nothing more was said. 'I'll email photos of the twins once I get organised. Remember to take your camera with you.'

'Thanks. I'd not thought of that. I'll add it to my list. Good luck when you get home. Don't work too hard and remember to keep in touch.'

'Will do. Take care. Love to Brad.'

The expression on Jake's face spoke volumes.

'Don't even think of going there Dad. Richard is out of my life for good.'

Exhaling heavily he shook his head. 'You'll live to regret it, believe me.'

Grumpily she snapped, 'Fine, because then you'll be able to say, "I told you so," won't you?'

'But they're *his* babies Paige.'

His words infuriated her. *'Wrong,* they're *mine*. I carried them, gave birth to them and I'll be feeding, clothing, nursing and providing for them. Richard's contribution was to knock me up and don't look so horror-struck because afterwards he dumped me, so if I get my way, he'll never clap eyes on my babies. Do I make myself clear?'

Jake was distraught. Though she had made major inroads into combating many of her psychological issues, there still remained the biggest one of all she couldn't conquer, namely Richard Cavendish. Paige behaved as if she hated the man yet she had stated categorically in the past that she didn't, thus leaving Jake to believe she still loved him.

'I'm very sorry Paige. This is neither the time nor place for such a discussion. Please forgive me.'

'Only if you agree never to bring it up again. I left behind everything I had and everyone I loved when I moved here. I don't want your constant reminders. I'm trying to rebuild my life now and this certainly wasn't part of the deal, being psychoanalysed every day. You said you were pleased I'd found you; you also claimed you were overjoyed to be having your grandchildren around but if your so-called love and support can't be unconditional, I don't want it.'

It was time to surrender. Paige was strong willed and words alone would not suffice. There had to be another way, a different approach but how or what, he asked himself. Despite many years of experience he was beaten. 'I'll not raise it again,' he promised.

Jake stood up. 'I'll see if Eleanor and Emma are ready to visit you now. We won't stay long because they'll need something to eat. I might take them to that Italian restaurant we always enjoy.'

She nodded disinterestedly. 'Good idea.'

'Paige, listen to me. I've apologised. I was wrong. If I could take it back then I would. Let's try to put it behind us. I don't want to ruin what's been a truly amazing day.'

As he headed out of the room Paige said quietly, 'You already have.'

Within the hour Jake had returned with Eleanor and Emma and the sombre mood was quickly reversed.

'They are so *beautiful,*' Eleanor commented, tears of joy welling in her eyes. 'Can I hold them please? I won't have many opportunities living so far away. I'll be very gentle.'

'Of course,' Paige said. 'Not for too long though. I mustn't encourage attention seeking as I'll need to adhere to a strict regime once I'm at home.'

'I understand. Hello Michael,' she said lifting one of the babies from the cot. 'I'm Grandma, yes that's right, Grandma. You are such a handsome boy.'

'How do you know that's Michael?' asked Paige.

'Because he looks exactly like his brother looked when he was born, the same hair and the same little pouting lips. David was such a sweet baby too.'

With raised eyebrows Emma and Paige promptly exchanged glances, recalling their initial unpleasant encounter with David.

Anxious to suppress a throaty laugh, Emma was forced to look away but Paige had already seen the hint of devilment in her eyes. Hurriedly turning her own amusement into a smile she remarked, 'Oh? I hadn't noticed any similarity.'

'Oh yes. This little one's going to be a very good-looking young man like David. I can see it now.'

Emma jumped up, unable to contain her hysteria a moment longer. 'I need the loo,' she shrieked and bolted like a rat into Paige's en-suite bathroom.

‘Do you want to hold Olivia now?’ Paige asked in an attempt to avert her laughter. ‘I’ll take Michael.’

Jake who hadn’t yet spoken a word said, ‘May I?’

With a nod she handed him to her father who held his grandson proudly and smiled. ‘You’re so cuddly and warm Michael and you smell like a baby. We’ll have such fun before long and I can hardly wait till you’re both old enough to have bedtime stories.’

Paige couldn’t resist the temptation and quipped, ‘Yes but nothing too heavy for starters. How about “Developmental Psychoanalysis for Beginners”?’

He threw back his head and howled with laughter. ‘Okay, point taken. I’ll behave from now on.’

‘Just step out of your consulting room for a while. Work is all you ever think about Dad. Get a life.’

On a serious note he said, ‘Since I lost your mum it’s all I’ve ever done. I probably could benefit from a session or two of self-analysis.’

On hearing a tap on the door Jake placed Michael in his cot and went to open it. Marjorie, whose arms were laden with presents, screeched with delight to see the twins and placing the gifts beside Paige she remarked, ‘Well done Paige. They’re so cute.’

Jake held Marjorie in an affectionate embrace and introduced her as his friend to Eleanor and Emma.

Paige was bursting with excitement as she tore off the gift-wrap to access the contents within. ‘It’s like all my Christmases have come at once. I was really starting to believe this day would never dawn.’

She was delighted with all the gifts including the ones from Emma and displayed them on the bed for the others to see. ‘They make such beautiful things for babies nowadays,' she sighed. 'I feel very lucky to have friends and family like you. Thank you.'

When the duty nurse came to check Paige's blood pressure she was concerned. 'It's a little high,' she told her after checking it again. 'I think you should get some rest now. I'll come back in half an hour to see if it's any better. You've had more than enough excitement and stress over the past few hours so it's time your visitors left.'

Jake arose instantly. 'That sounds good to me as I need sustenance. Being a new grandad takes it out of you, you know. By way of celebration I'd like to escort you three delightful ladies to dinner. Okay? Paige can stay here and eat hospital food.'

'Charming,' she grunted as they laughed.

'Take it easy darling. I'll see you tomorrow,' Jake said giving her a hug. 'Call me at once if you need anything.'

The others gave her a squeeze. 'I'll call you later,' said Emma. 'You've done well today kid.'

The Consultant discharged Paige the next day.

Once home she was grateful for two extra pairs of hands as it didn't take long to learn how demanding two small babies could be. Eleanor and Emma were invaluable and when Eleanor went home on Sunday evening she was sorely missed.

By Monday Paige was feeling stronger, despite a continuing lack of sleep. She had planned her daily routine so she could manage alone when Emma left but it was proving impossible to fit everything she must do into one day.

Fortunately Jake had taken a few days off work, allowing her to devote sufficient time to the twins' needs and three-hourly feeds, whereas his responsibilities lay with the more mundane duties of nappy-changing and meal preparation.

It was surprising how, in just a few days, he had developed the skill to prepare and cook their meals. He had also enjoyed this new challenge.

'It's fear of the unknown,' he told her. 'I've never cooked anything apart from the odd boiled egg and believe me, some *did* turn out odd. Culinary skills were never my forte. I eat toast from an idiot proof toaster or cereal for breakfast. Anything else I eat is made by the cook at work or the chef at the restaurant I frequent. He knows my likes and dislikes and caters for me accordingly.'

Paige grinned. 'Don't you mean he indulges your every whim because you tip him so well?'

'So, what's your problem? It gets me what I want and the ladies were very impressed the other night. I really did enjoy Emma's company. I can see why you're still the best of friends after all those years. She's quite a character isn't she?'

'She's the best and I'm disappointed that I'll miss her wedding next week. It's such rotten timing. I'd have given anything to watch the ceremony.'

'Then watch it. We can drive up and stay an hour or so, certainly long enough to see her in church.'

'Yeah right and who's going to see to the twins?'

'We take them with us Paige. Babies are allowed out you know. Their carry cots will be secured with straps. It's no problem unless you choose to make it a problem. I can think of someone who'd give anything to have them for a couple of hours...Eleanor.'

She was horrified. 'They're only a few days old. I couldn't possibly leave them with anyone else.'

'Come on Paige. She isn't just *anyone else*; she's their grandma; she'd be ecstatic. Do you think I'd suggest it if I doubted her competence? They'd be out of your sight for an hour or two, that's all, and would doubtless sleep for most of the time if you fed them before we left for the wedding.'

'It's too much responsibility for an elderly lady.'

'What about me? Would you be equally afraid to leave them with me? I'm not many years younger.'

'No, that's different because I'd trust you to take proper care of them. As my dad I know you better.'

He conceded. 'You're right. It's a pity though. I'd have enjoyed watching them on such a momentous day. Still, if you have a change of heart, I'm pretty sure Eleanor would happily accommodate you.'

He left her to her thoughts and went to the kitchen to prepare their evening meal.

When they sat down to eat, impassively she said, 'I've spoken to Eleanor who was really enthusiastic when I offered to leave the twins with her for a few hours and then I called Emma who was made up to learn we'd be at the church service.'

'Eleanor will appreciate that you're putting your trust in her. She was a new mum once don't forget, so she'll know how it feels to leave a baby, in your case two, with another person. She was heartbroken yesterday when it was time to leave. She's a really nice lady and the twins will be fine there.'

'I know. I'm a compulsive worrier,' she admitted.

'I can't believe how much paraphernalia we need to take for a few hours away from home,' Paige said breathlessly as she rammed the final two bags in the already overflowing boot. 'I didn't have this much stuff when I moved house and we haven't even got the twins in yet.'

'Well, unless you know something I don't they're not going in the boot so stop flapping,' Jake panted. 'Just make sure you've got everything you need for the wedding. I'll see to everything else.'

One thing in their favour was the weather. It was a glorious day, making their journey enjoyable. The twins remained in a deep sleep until they pulled up outside Eleanor's house.

'How they've grown,' Eleanor exclaimed.

'They lost weight initially but now they've gained five ounces. I can't tell, having them day and night. They shouldn't be any trouble once I've fed them.'

She chuckled. 'How could two little sweeties like these be any trouble? They are absolutely adorable. We're going to have such a good time aren't we? I was pleased you could make it to Emma's wedding. She's a real down to earth kind of girl isn't she? We had such a laugh at your place. I really enjoyed her company. I bought a wedding present and a card for them that I'd like you to take to the wedding.'

Paige thanked her. 'She's the best friend I've ever had. She'd do anything for anybody and I intend to see a lot more of her, especially as the journey only took about an hour and forty minutes today.'

‘So will you bring the twins with you?’ she asked in anticipation. ‘If you wanted to go shopping with her, you know I’d be only too happy to have them.’

‘Yes, that’s what I was thinking but let’s see how today goes. May I use your bathroom? I must feed the twins and get ready and I’d hate to be late.’

‘Of course. I’ll put the kettle on. I made you both a snack when I realised you’d miss the reception.’

Paige hugged her. ‘You really are a star Eleanor.’

When Paige finally emerged ready for the wedding she looked radiant. After fixing Jake’s flower in his lapel she attached hers to her bag.

‘What a lovely couple you make,’ Eleanor sighed.

‘Huh, I don’t like this ugly bulge,’ Paige grunted. ‘I still look pregnant.’

‘Nonsense, it hardly shows. A bit of exercise will soon get rid of it and your loose top hides it so stop worrying; you look beautiful doesn’t she Jake?’

‘She does Eleanor. Come on, it’s time we weren’t here. Stop fussing; it’s Emma’s wedding not yours.’

Irately she retorted, ‘Thanks a bunch Dad. I don’t need reminding that no one wants me.’

‘Sorry, I didn’t mean to upset you. Come on, let’s make a move. I have to find somewhere to park.’

Jake glanced apologetically at Eleanor for having caused the minor skirmish in her home.

‘You’re sure Richard won’t call?’ Paige asked

‘I’ve already told you Paige, he only ever turns up here on a Sunday.’

‘Right...but if he does I hope you have your story ready. He must *never* be told the truth.’

She gave her a hug. 'He'll never know from me; I promise. Now go and enjoy your friend's wedding.'

The church was packed to capacity. Andy paced up and down nervously as he awaited Emma's arrival.

'You know she's always on the last minute Andy. She'll be here soon,' Paige told him forcefully and he appeared to settle down.

Suddenly there was an audible commotion at the rear of the church as the usher attempted to steer the guests into position. Beads of perspiration appeared on Andy's brow and he began to pant heavily.

'She's here now so calm yourself and go back to your best man. You can't be roaming up and down when she appears. *Now,'* she said. 'Just go Andy.'

As the organist pounded the keys Emma appeared looking demure and glorious in her beautiful gown.

Paige, fighting to contain her tears, smiled fondly as she approached on the arm of her father. 'You're so beautiful,' she whispered as she drew alongside.

Characteristically, an emotional ceremony ensued lasting close to an hour throughout which Emma's mother wept, and then a professional soprano added the finishing touch with her rendition of Ava Maria.

Afterwards the guests gathered outside, awaiting instructions from the official photographer who, by this time, had taken total control of events.

Paige wandered over to talk to Emma's mother as Emma had already been seized by the photographer who was doling out commands to all and sundry.

'It's so nice to see you again Anne,' Paige said. 'I don't think Emma has ever looked more beautiful. I love your outfit too. Blue is definitely your colour, very chic.'

'Aye and it was a very chic price too,' her father cut in with a wink of the eye, grinning at Paige.

'Shut up Trevor. You don't count the pennies at a wedding. That's vulgar.'

'Pennies? I wish,' he roared and Paige tittered.

'Ignore him Paige. He's always been tight,' Anne said. 'Hasn't it been a lovely day for the wedding?'

'Perfect. Andy looks very smart too. I want to get a few photos of the two of them so I think I'll hang about near the photographer. I'll catch you later.'

'I'd like to have a proper look at that Roller,' Jake said. 'Are you okay on your own for a bit?'

'Men and cars,' she snorted. 'Go on; take a look. I won't get lost. I'm taking some photos now.'

As Jake approached the church gates, Andy was talking to two people on the footpath but one guy in particular caught his eye as he drew nearer, the guy whose hand he was shaking vigorously.

From a distance he had looked familiar but closer, he was easily recognisable as Richard Cavendish.

Jake stopped and turned around. The last thing he wanted was an ugly scene at the wedding and worse still, Paige would be horrified to learn he was there.

He headed back towards Paige, thankful Richard hadn't caught sight of him as he approached.

After ushering her into the centre of the crowd he glanced towards the church gates from time to time until it was safe to circulate again. With no further sign of Richard or his distinctive car, it was obvious he had left the vicinity.

Jake breathed a huge sigh of relief for that could have been a most upsetting situation.

It had been Richard's intent to stay out of sight. His sole reason for attending had been to catch a brief glimpse of Paige but Andy had seen him lurking in the shadows. To mask his devious plan, he had felt obliged to give Andy a sum of money as a wedding present, describing it as the reason for his presence.

He had driven away despondently after seeing the pair of them together, Jake with his arm around her shoulder playing happy families while she, clearly three months or so pregnant, remained oblivious of his despicable behaviour, his constant womanising.

It was by chance he had seen them leaving a hotel in Manchester last month, Jake and a middle-aged woman, with matching overnight bags, their body language speaking volumes. It had troubled him to think of Paige being treated in such a contemptible way, assuming that she and Jake were still together. Their attendance at the wedding confirmed beyond doubt that they were and Richard was furious. But for it being Andy's wedding, a long-standing friend he held in high regard, he would have punched the nauseating creature, such was his contempt for Jake Allcock.

'I think we should leave now,' Paige said looking at her watch. 'It's over two hours since we arrived. It's time we were making our way to Eleanor's.'

'I think Eleanor would have called had there been a problem but you're quite right. We shouldn't take advantage of her hospitality,' Jake concurred.

'I imagine everyone will be heading for the reception soon. I'll just find Emma and wish them both a happy honeymoon.'

'Where are they off to?' asked Jake.

'They're just having a few days in Blackpool. It's all they can afford because they're broke.'

Jake was sorry to hear that. Removing his wallet from his pocket he gave Paige two hundred pounds. 'Emma's help was invaluable when she stayed with us. I know you bought her a present but please give her this and tell her how we appreciate all she did.'

Paige beamed. 'Thanks Dad. She'll be thrilled to bits with this. I won't be long.'

Holding up her train, Emma shot across the lawn and flinging her arms around Jake's neck she kissed him fondly. 'You don't know what that means Jake. We were absolutely skint, so thanks to you we can eat at a proper restaurant now rather than a crummy greasy chippy. You're such a wonderful guy and I love you as much as Paige does, I'm sure.'

'Er...thank you Emma. I'm very fond of you too,' he spluttered on a burst of laughter. 'Have a superb honeymoon and a wonderful life. God bless.'

Paige called ahead to say they were ready to leave.

'There's no need to rush back,' Eleanor said. 'The twins are fine. They're awake and very content.'

Paige was relieved to hear that. 'Their next feed is due shortly and I don't want to disrupt their routine. The wedding was amazing. I've taken a few photos to show you. You should have seen Emma's dress.'

'I hope to. Didn't you say there'd be a DVD?'

'Yes and she promised to send me a copy, so I'll let you see it next time we're here.'

'I hope I don't have to wait too long. I've enjoyed having my beautiful grandchildren here today.'

'Everything okay?' asked Jake when she hung up.

'Yes, she seems to have everything under control but I'd like to get back now. Just let me check on a missed call. It's from Laura.'

A moment or too elapsed before Paige squealed, 'Listen to this. "Morgan says, 'Hi'. She arrived two hours ago weighing eight pounds two ounces, a real bumper bundle. Hope you're well. Talk soon."'

Jake's face broke into a broad smile. 'It's been an amazing day all round hasn't it?'

'Fantastic,' she sighed. 'I'm so glad it went well.'

There was a tearful farewell at Eleanor's when they were about to leave.

'I promise we'll be back soon,' Paige said. 'Don't forget what Jake told you. You're welcome anytime at ours.'

Eleanor waved until Jake's car disappeared from view and with a heavy sigh she dried the tears from her eyes saying, 'How could you do this Richard?'

Richard paced the floor planning his revenge. The time had come for Jake to be exposed.

It still remained a mystery to him as to how Paige had moved in with Jake so soon after their parting. It was obvious there had to have been some further contact after the lunchtime meeting with Frank and Jake, but Paige had never behaved suspiciously nor had any free time to become involved with Jake, or had she? Jake was shrewd, a bare-faced opportunist who had undoubtedly groomed her well in dubious practices before seducing her. Richard nodded; that was the only possible explanation.

He poured another whisky and downed it in one. He was infuriated, but the mere thought of exposing that repugnant brute to Paige for what he really was would go some way towards exacting revenge.

He waited until Monday to make his call as Jake would presumably be at work then and Paige would be home alone. He informed his PA he had urgent business to attend to and must not be disturbed. He had thought long and hard about what he would say before calling her number but once it started to ring he was filled with diverse emotions.

Suddenly she was there, her voice loud and clear.

He paused a moment too long and she spoke for a second time, slightly louder, Hello...*hello!'* with a hint of annoyance in her voice.

'Hello Paige,' he murmured quietly. 'It's Richard. You mustn't hang up as there's something I have to talk to you about and it's very important.'

Adrenaline gushed through her body, causing her to feel weak and nauseous. He *knew*; somehow he had found out about the twins. Why else would he call her? She tried to collect her thoughts; she had to remain calm. Defensively she countered, 'Who's given you this number?'

'That's not important. I need to...'

Instantly she interrupted, 'It's important to *me* so answer me.'

He ignored her request. 'I haven't called to argue. I've called about something we need to discuss.'

Though he was confirming her worst fears, Paige was determined to stand her ground. 'I can think of nothing, nothing at all I'd want to discuss with you Richard. You have your life and I have mine.'

'But things change. Folk do underhand things and try to cover their tracks, atrocious things that cause untold heartache to others. Although we've had our differences, I never wanted to hurt you. What I did, I did out of love. Yes, I was wrong; I soon realised that but sadly too late to put it right as you'd moved on and I admit I was angry, very angry to learn that you'd moved in with Jake. I never saw that coming. I didn't even know you were involved with the guy, but that's history. It's what I've discovered recently that concerns me and I can't turn my back on it.'

Rivulets of perspiration trickled down her face as she awaited his delivery with trepidation but he was in no hurry to ruin her life. After several moments she demanded, 'Get to the point if there is one.'

She heard him clear his throat and then he spoke.

'A month ago I witnessed a disturbing incident. I saw Jake leaving a hotel with a woman. There was no doubt they'd spent the night together. They each carried an overnight bag and they were, how shall I say, all over each other. I hate telling you Paige in your condition but I thought you should know. He's playing around again. That vile lothario has never stayed true to one woman, so there you have it.'

Her mind was in turmoil. He hadn't called about the twins at all. He believed her lover was cheating on her and she laughed out loud. 'So that's it? You called to tell me Jake has a lady friend?'

He was perplexed. 'Did you know?' he asked her.

She paused momentarily. 'Whether I did or didn't know is none of your damn business but what I will say is this. Whatever Jake's faults, he would never knock up a woman then dump her like someone not a million miles away did. I'd like to get on with my housework now if you don't mind...and by the way, don't *ever* ring me again. Do I make myself clear?'

'Paige, I only thought you...'

'Yes, that's your trouble Richard. You do far too much thinking. It's a pity you never think anything through properly though for if you did, maybe once in a while, you might just get something right.'

Without affording him the opportunity to respond she slammed down the receiver and burst into tears, her nerves in tatters.

She lifted the twins from their respective cots and cuddled them, tears cascading down her cheeks.

Michael, the more sensitive of the two started to cry, seemingly cognisant of her distress. She kissed him tenderly and held him close. 'Please don't cry,' she said softly. 'Everything's going to be fine.'

Richard shook his head in disbelief. Her reaction had certainly not turned out as expected. What had he expected though? Had he anticipated a huge vote of thanks? And what had she meant when accusing him of getting everything wrong? He had seen Jake at close range. Why was she in denial?

Perhaps this wasn't the first time Jake had strayed and if that were true, what options did she have as a single mother-to-be, with nothing to live on but the rental income from her house?

On reflection he regretted his actions. His exposé, however well intended to harm Jake could only hurt Paige. That was apparently what she'd meant when accusing him of not thinking matters through.

Jake arrived home to find Paige in tears. Alarmed, he took her in his arms. 'Whatever's wrong Paige?'

'I'd like an honest answer. At Emma's wedding, did you see anyone else you recognised?'

It was obvious where this was going. 'I did Paige. I saw Richard.'

She shrugged away from his hold. 'But you didn't bother to mention that to me.'

'If you cast your mind back to when I last spoke about Richard, you'll no doubt recall that you said I should never mention his name again. Furthermore, the wedding was meant to be a happy occasion, not one to be marred by *his* presence, so when I caught sight of him, hovering by the gate, I steered you in the opposite direction, right away from him. May I ask what's brought this on?'

'He called me this morning. I thought he'd found out about the twins. I was a wreck, so traumatised I could hardly speak. At first he was evasive but then he told me why he'd called.'

'Which was?' he enquired with interest.

'To say you were cheating on me. He'd seen you with another woman, presumably Marjorie, leaving a hotel a month ago. Needless to say he called you a few obnoxious names and *then* he said he regretted having to tell me that in *my* condition. I told you I looked pregnant in that bloody awful outfit.'

He laughed. 'And that upset you, you silly girl?'

'Don't be daft; I don't give a stuff what inference Richard draws from anything. Besides, it worked to my advantage since he thinks we're a couple. No, I was terrified I'd have to fight to keep my babies.'

'That's never going to happen darling. So tell me, what were the choice names he called me today?'

That lightened the mood and she giggled. 'Er...he added *lothario* today. I think that's a new one.' He grinned as she said, 'The rest were the usual ones.'

'You have to feel sorry for the guy. He still loves you Paige. He's crazy with jealousy; that's why he hates *me* because he thinks I have what he wants.'

'Have you heard yourself? What utter rubbish.'

'Alright, have it your own way but don't forget I spend every day talking to patients so try and credit me with better insight into behavioural problems.'

Haughtily she snapped, 'Well, I don't love *him!'*

As Paige stormed from the room Jake mumbled, 'I think we both know you do.'

15

Richard made no further contact with Paige directly or indirectly thereafter.

Over the following months Paige always enquired about David's progress when she made her monthly visit to see Eleanor and thankfully it was constantly good news. He had returned to his luxury apartment where Penny spent most of her time; he was driving again and had returned to work at the factory. Many other life-changing events had also occurred.

Following a devastating miscarriage early into her first pregnancy Emma was pregnant once more and approaching her eighth month while Laura now had a six-month-old boy named Travis. Paige and Laura regularly exchanged photographs online.

Brad had started his own business of Web Design that was proving successful and they had moved to a house with a big garden, or *yard* as Laura referred to it, in the suburbs of Manhattan.

The twins were almost two years old and rather a handful, Olivia being particularly bright for her age, self-assured, loquacious and ready to argue at every opportunity.

Michael, a more subdued child was a thinker who talked only when absolutely necessary, although in cognitive development tests, they were equals.

Paige revelled in every moment spent with them.

Life had been good to Jake too. His relationship with Marjorie had flourished with talk of a wedding soon but no definite arrangements had been made. Paige believed she was responsible for the delay in fixing the date as it clearly wasn't an ideal situation for Marjorie who would be moving to Jake's home with his daughter and her boisterous twins in situ.

Jake had insisted it wasn't a problem as he would be overjoyed to have all his family living together, but Paige seriously doubted that Marjorie shared his sentiments or passion for such an arrangement.

The twins' second birthday fell on a Monday and so it was decided to bring forward the monthly visit to Eleanor's by a week so she could arrange a birthday party for them on the previous Saturday.

Paige had intended to drive to Eleanor's but Jake had offered to take them so he could spend an hour or so with Frank Jessop while Paige went shopping with Emma for her outstanding baby items.

Eleanor was always thankful to have the twins to herself for a few hours to read stories to them and play in the park where she always took a big bag of bread to feed the ducks. They enjoyed visiting their grandma and never returned home without a goody bag each, along with an array of other gifts.

Jake packed the boot of his car with the essential paraphernalia and swiftly fastened the twins in their seats while Paige made a quick call to Emma to say they were about to leave. 'Are you sure you're still fit to drive to the shops?' she asked her earnestly.

'I'm fine once I squeeze in behind the wheel,' she giggled. 'I'm expecting a sarcastic remark from you though as I'm twice the size you were and I've still a few more weeks to go. Call me when you get near and I'll be waiting at Eleanor's for you.'

Jake honked the car horn impatiently. 'I must go Emma,' she interrupted. 'Dad's getting ratty. We'll see you in a couple of hours.'

Eleanor welcomed them with open arms while the twins squealed with excitement to see Emma who turned up as they were getting out of the car

'Happy birthday Cheeky-Face,' she said to Olivia who grinned mischievously. 'You too Michael,' she added, handing them both a gift and a card.

'Say thank you to Auntie Emma,' Paige said.

Olivia hugged her and grinned. 'Thank you.'

Michael in his usual reticent manner thanked her quietly as he struggled to remove the wrapping.

Olivia grabbed Michael's gift and tore the paper off whilst making a disrespectful monkey sound.

'That will do!' Paige stated angrily. 'Do you want to go to bed and miss the party? Well?'

'No Mummy,' she answered.

'Then behave and give that back to Michael.'

Rolling her eyes, Paige glanced apologetically at Eleanor and Emma. 'She can be such a little madam at times.'

Emma nudged Jake and winked. 'I wonder where she gets that from.'

'I wonder,' he replied with a wry smile.

Paige glared stony-faced as the others laughed.

‘I’m off,’ said Jake, giving Eleanor a hug. ‘I’ll be back at three o’clock for your delicious party food. I’m looking forward to that.’

‘We’d better get off too,’ said Emma. ‘I’ve a long list of stuff I need.’

Paige fussed round the children, unbuttoning their coats. ‘Are you sure you can manage Eleanor?’

‘Do stop worrying Paige. They’ll be fine with me. First we’re going to feed the ducks aren’t we?’ she said, smiling at the twins.

‘Yes,’ Olivia screeched. She poked Michael who nodded and replied eagerly, ‘Feed the ducks...in the park...with Grandma.’

‘Right we’ll see you later then,’ said Paige.

As Emma tried to squeeze in behind the steering wheel, Paige offered to take over. ‘It’s not safe for you to drive when you’re so close to your due date.’

‘When I’m so close to the steering wheel, I think you mean. I told you I was bigger than you were. I drive every day so stop mithering. It’s not far.’

‘Has Andy been alright?’ she asked with concern. ‘There’s been no recurrence of that other business?’

‘He’s fine. He has regular checks to make sure. It seemed I was destined not to have kids a year or so ago yet now, in less than a month, I’ll have a baby boy. I can’t wait.’

She pulled into a parking space, switched off and reaching for her shoulder bag cried, ‘Come on, we don’t have all day.’

It was hot and sunny in the park and as Eleanor and the twins approached the pond, the ducks appeared to recognise them as they swam towards the edge, quacking loudly.

Eleanor opened the brown paper bag and Michael thrust his hand inside, grabbing as many pieces of bread as he could. He flung the bread into the water and the two children chuckled as the ducks fought and scrambled to capture their treat. When the bag was empty Eleanor took them to the swings.

At two o'clock it was time to wander home as the two children from next door and the adults aimed to be there shortly afterwards and there were finishing touches to add to the party food.

The twins sat in the lounge, playing quietly with their toys while Eleanor finished off in the kitchen.

'Can we play out?' Olivia pleaded when Eleanor popped her head round the door to check on them.

'You can go in the garden and take Michael's ball for a little while,' she told them. 'Lily and May will be here soon. Don't dirty your clothes.'

'Don't like girls,' Michael grumbled.

'Of course you do. They're very nice little girls so don't be silly. They're coming to your party.'

'Don't like them,' he repeated.

Eleanor chuckled. 'Go on, play nicely.'

She watched them through the kitchen window as she added two candles to their birthday cake. Olivia liked to kick the ball from one end of the garden to the other but Michael's coordination was poorer by comparison. Often he would miss the ball, fall over and cry, much to the amusement of Olivia who was much more nimble-footed.

Eleanor heard the door-bell and hurried to open it.

As expected, it was the girls from next door and while Eleanor chatted with their mother they rushed through the house and outside to join the twins.

'I'll bring them back home when the party's over, say around four o'clock,' Eleanor said. 'I expect the twins will be heading home then. Their mother has a strict regime and never deviates from it.'

'Responsible parenting I call that,' the neighbour commented. 'I'm the same. I'll see you later then.'

The moment she returned to the kitchen, Eleanor heard the door-bell again. Wiping her hands on her apron she hurried to the door once more and opened it with a beaming smile that instantly changed to a look of absolute horror. She was speechless.

'You look as if you've seen a ghost. Do you feel alright Mother?' he asked with concern.

'I...er...I thought you were in Europe until the end of the week Richard,' she stammered.

'That's right, I should have been but we needed a few bits and pieces so I decided to have a couple of days at home. I'm off back in about four days if the components have arrived. So, do you intend to keep me on the doorstep all afternoon or are you going to invite me in?'

'For a moment yes, come in,' she spluttered looking at her watch. Paige could arrive any minute and she was mortified. 'I'm having a birthday party for the children next door and two of their friends, so I have a lot to do.'

'David picked me up at the airport and as usual he was low on petrol, you know what he's like, so he's gone to fill up. He'll be back in about ten minutes.

I'll get off home then but since we were passing the end of your street I thought we might as well call to see you and then I don't have to come tomorrow.'

She stared at him blankly, disregarding his words.

'Are you sure you're okay Mum? You look rather preoccupied. Perhaps you're taking too much on at your age, having birthday parties for little children. Why couldn't the parents have their own party?'

'Well…er…' she stuttered. 'I like having children around. You know I do and they're no trouble.'

Eleanor heard a high-pitched wail but before she could investigate, Lily dashed indoors. 'Michael's fallen on the path and cut his knee. It's bleeding.'

Without a second thought, Eleanor darted through the lounge and out through the patio doors. Michael was sitting on the garden bench with tears gushing from his eyes. On inspection it was little more than a graze but a bruise was starting to appear.

'Let me,' Richard said, lifting him into his arms as Eleanor looked on in horror. He carried him into the lounge, sat him on his knee and took his handkerchief from his pocket to dab his tears. 'You're a very brave boy,' he told him caringly. 'How about we put a nice plaster on that and make it better?'

'I'll get one,' Eleanor said hurrying away.

'What's your name?' Richard asked.

Olivia answered for him. 'Michael.'

'And who are you?'

'Olivia,' she told him. 'Who are you?'

'My name's Richard.'

'Are you coming to our party Richard?'

'No Olivia, I can't. I have to go soon.'

'Why?'

'Er...because I have things to do.'

'What things?'

'Er...just things,' he smiled.

'We have a cake...a big cake.'

'That's very nice. How old are you?'

'Two.'

'You have a lot to say for a two-year-old.'

She giggled. 'Grandma says that. Michael doesn't talk a lot. Mummy tells me to shut up.'

He laughed. 'How old is Michael?'

'Two, like me.'

'I'm sorry,' Eleanor declared appearing flustered. 'I couldn't find the plasters. I'll see to him now.'

'I'll hold him while you put it on. He'll be fine.'

Michael winced as she pressed the plaster against his knee.

'Baby!' Olivia yelled.

'Let's dry your tears again,' Richard said, smiling at the small boy.

As Michael looked up at him, Richard expelled a short gasp. Just for a moment Michael brought back memories of David at that tender age. The similarities in appearance were quite remarkable.

Interrupting his thoughts, the two girls rushed in. 'Is Michael okay?' Lily the six-year-old asked.

'He is,' Eleanor told her. 'Are you hungry now?'

'Yes Grandma,' Olivia piped up in response.

Embarrassed, Eleanor tittered, 'Most of the small children who come here call me Grandma. They do so because Mrs Cavendish is such a mouthful and calling me *Eleanor* wouldn't be appropriate.'

Olivia tugged at Richard's sleeve. 'Come see our cake Richard. Grandma made it.'

'Just a quick look then because I have to go.'

Taking him by the hand she led him towards the kitchen as Eleanor watched their every move, fighting back tears. Those were her son's two children.

'Look at that Richard,' she said. 'Isn't it nice?'

'That's really lovely. Perhaps Grandma will save me a big slice. I've never seen twins before. Do you know what I mean? Twins?'

'Yes, me and Michael.' She chuckled once again, looking straight into his eyes and at that moment he knew the truth. That cute, polite, adorable child, *his daughter* had Paige's instantly recognizable almond shaped blue eyes. He sighed as everything suddenly fell into place, Michael's resemblance to David, his mother's horror to see him standing at her door and her clear desire to get him away from there.

As Richard turned to face her no amount of words could have defined his feelings more explicitly than the look of distress in his eyes as he shook his head. Quietly he said, 'Don't lie to me Mother. What time is she coming back for them?'

'Any minute now. She'll be here for the party and they'll leave around four o'clock I imagine.'

He snorted, shaking his head in contempt. 'Well, I have to hand it to you. This has to be the world's best kept secret. Well done Mother.'

She wrung her hands uneasily before explaining, 'I had no choice Richard. I was sworn to secrecy in return for access to my grandchildren. I wasn't prepared to give them up as you did when you sent that poor girl away, so I'm telling you, I do *not* want a scene in front of the children when she walks in; I mean it so it might be better were you to leave now. I feel your pain Richard; I really do but this is my home and these are my grandchildren. We can talk about this later.'

'That's one thing you've got right,' he sneered. 'I can't believe you could be so devious as to deprive me of my kids for two years. What kind of mother are you? Were you *ever* going to tell me?'

Her silence answered his question.

With a look of disgust he murmured, 'I'll wait by the door for David.'

As he made his way to the hall, the bell rang and Eleanor ran ahead of him to answer it. She prayed it would be David but sadly her prayers had not been answered; it was Paige returning with Emma.

Unable to contain her suffering a moment longer she burst into tears. 'I'm so sorry Paige. Richard's here and he knows everything,' she blurted out. 'He was supposed to be in Europe for a few more days. I wasn't expecting him, I swear.'

On a deep sigh she stated philosophically, 'It had to happen sometime I suppose. I don't blame you at all Eleanor. Where is he?'

'Right here,' he said stepping forward. 'I have no intention of upsetting the children but rest assured you'll be hearing from my solicitor and soon. How could you behave in such a despicable way? Don't bother to answer. I expect the court will determine that. Your disgraceful actions cannot fail to work in my favour.'

Olivia and Michael ran to the hall. 'Kiss Richard,' Olivia said, jumping into his arms. As he kissed her forehead his eyes were intensely focused on Paige. 'I'll see you soon sweetheart,' he said. He lifted her down and turned to Michael. 'How's the poorly leg now little soldier? No more tears?' After embracing him he set him down beside his sister.

At that precise moment David walked in through the open door. Seeing his father, Paige and Emma standing together he quipped, 'Oops...war zone.'

'David!' Olivia yelled, thrilled to see him, whilst Richard looked on with incredulity.

'Et tu, Brute?' he hollered and stormed from the house without a backward glance, closely followed by David who smiled at Paige apologetically.

Eleanor closed the door. 'Come in, come in,' she said to Paige and Emma. 'Let's not forget this was to be a happy day for the children. Richard's very annoyed and understandably so but he'll calm down I'm sure. He'd never do anything to hurt you Paige. I can't imagine how he feels to discover everyone's deceived him. I'll speak to him tomorrow and try to smooth things over and then I'll call you.'

The door-bell rang again. 'Deary me, it's just like Piccadilly Circus here today. All I've done for the past half hour is answer the door.'

This time it was Jake who had had the misfortune to bump into Richard at the end of the drive where more than a few choice words had been exchanged.

'What a day!' Eleanor exclaimed. 'Will someone find the children and fetch them to the dining room. They must be ravenous by now. Try to relax Paige.

I'll put the kettle on and we'll have a refreshing cup of tea and a bite to eat. That always helps.'

Concerned, Jake turned to Paige. 'Are you okay?'

'What do you think?' she snapped.

She couldn't fail to anticipate Jake's next remark. 'Don't dare say, "*I told you so*,"' she said irately.

Turning to Emma she spat, 'I'm surprised at you, missing such a great opportunity to mouth off.'

Emma shrugged. 'I thought there was enough antagonism without my big gob contributing more. In any case, it's nowt to do with me. Maybe it's better for everything to be in the open. At least you don't have to spend the rest of your life creeping about. I thought he was most civil considering...'

'Yes but Richard can afford to be civil, can't he? Everything's stacked in his favour,' she snarled.

Jake stepped forward. 'Enough. Let's sleep on it and see what tomorrow brings. I don't know about you but I'm here for a party so I'm joining Eleanor. It's the twins' day, not yours, so I suggest you put it behind you for now and join in.'

Eleanor looked up teary-eyed and repentant when Jake appeared. 'I'm so sorry. What have I done?'

'You've only done what any concerned grandma would have done; you kept quiet as did I. That was what Paige stipulated so now she must live with the consequences. I told her that from the outset. It isn't our problem. Paige and Richard will resolve things I'm sure,' he stated, but when uttering those words he was aware that without his intervention, matters would only get much worse. The time had come for Richard to be told the whole truth.

'Was he very angry when you met him outside?'

'No more than I'd have expected. Don't forget he doesn't know I'm Paige's father. In his eyes I'm the lecherous lover who capitalised on the situation and took her in the moment he ended their relationship. I suppose he had just cause to feel humiliated when I'm allowed in *his* mother's home at *his* children's party. In his position, I'd feel rather peeved too, and that's putting it mildly.'

When Paige, Emma and the four children joined them in the dining room, Emma was quick to break the uncomfortable silence, commenting favourably about Eleanor's culinary skills.

Despite Paige's anxiety, she joined in the games and helped the twins open all their presents. It went unnoticed by everyone except Jake that throughout the afternoon her fingers were quivering. Richard's harsh words continued to echo in her mind and she couldn't bear to dwell on the likely ramifications of her former actions. She was a nervous wreck by the time they had to leave and showed no interest in the stunning outfit Eleanor had made for Emma's baby.

'Once again, I'm very sorry,' Eleanor said.

'It's of my making so don't feel guilty about what happened. I always knew it was a possibility. Don't get involved Eleanor. Richard and I will sort it out somehow. I'll have to agree to access I suppose but I probably should have done from the outset. Thank you for a lovely party. It's definitely one we won't forget. I'll keep you informed of developments.'

'Take care of her Jake,' said Eleanor. 'She's very edgy. I do hope there's a happy outcome.'

16

'What the hell are you doing here?' Richard yelled angrily when he answered his front door, following several bouts of heavy knocking. 'I'm not changing my mind so sod off back to your girlfriend.'

Calmly Jake asked, 'May I come inside?'

'You've got some bloody nerve coming here. Did my mother give you my address? She appears hell-bent on accommodating everyone's needs but mine as does my son. Did you manage to sweet-talk *her* as well?'

'We've a lot to talk about Richard and I see little point in lining solicitors' pockets when this can be sorted out amicably between the two of us.'

'The two of us?' he bawled. 'This is bugger all to do with you! My kids are *nowt* to you. You're just the opportunist who took advantage of their mother. How long had it been going on Jake? Had you been seeing her since that meeting with Frank Jessop?'

'No, I never saw Paige before you sent her away. That's the truth. She came to me for help as she had no one else to turn to.'

'Huh! Why would Paige choose a licentious rake like you? You're a bloody liar Jake Allcock.'

'If you let me in we can discuss this in a civilised manner,' Jake persisted in a quiet tone.

'Civilised?' he scoffed. *'You?* You're nothing but a bloody animal that preys on defenceless women. You're the lowest of the low who doesn't know the meaning of the word. I saw you just the other week, coming out of a hotel with another woman on your arm and don't deny it.'

'I don't have to deny or admit anything to you as I'm the one Paige and your two children are living with, don't forget. Now if you want any part of that to change I suggest you hear me out. You have one more minute to invite me in. I don't hang about on doorsteps.'

'And if I don't?'

'Then we'll see you in court and I can match you pound for pound. It might help you decide if I say Paige has no idea I'm here. She thinks I'm looking for something for the twins. It's actually their birthday tomorrow. Yesterday's party was for Eleanor's benefit so she could spend time with them and give them their presents.'

He opened the door wider and Jake stepped in.

'Through here,' Richard said brusquely. 'Drink?'

'Thanks, just a small whisky please. I'm driving.'

'I was trying to think last night and couldn't come up with a name of anyone I hated more than you.'

'Sounds reasonable. I suppose I'd feel the same in your position were I not acquainted with the facts.'

'Facts? I know what I see. That's enough for me.'

'Sorry to contradict but *you* only know what you *choose* to see; you surmise; you don't think things through properly. I'm a Consultant Psychiatrist and I see it all the time, folk jumping to the wrong conclusion, agonising over things that don't exist but in the mind. You've been punishing yourself about the way you sent Paige away from the outset. You were in love with her but you were so riddled with guilt about David that you needed to hurt yourself. Your reasons for ending the relationship, as explained by her, don't add up. You believed you had no right to happiness because your son David was seriously ill. You felt helpless as you could do nothing to aid his recovery. By giving up Paige however, by making the ultimate sacrifice and devoting all your efforts to the well-being of David whom you loved as only a father can love his son, you hoped for a miracle in return. Thankfully you got what you wanted but it was a high price to pay, to give up the woman you loved.'

Sighing, Richard twisted the glass in his hand.

'Do you still love her Richard? Please be honest.'

He nodded. 'I always will but I blew it didn't I?'

'Maybe not. She was hurt when she came to me. I've spent many an hour counselling her. She never grieved properly after she lost her grandad. I tried hard to persuade her to contact you after she agreed to continue with the pregnancy. She came so close to having a termination. I was there when she found out she was having twins and I was relieved when she finally changed her mind. I couldn't advise her. It had to be her decision but if she had gone ahead, not only would she have aborted your children, she would have aborted my grandchildren too.'

As Richard looked at him in total disbelief, Jake nodded. 'Yes, Paige is my daughter Richard. That's why she came to me. She needed my help and I was only too happy to give it. I didn't even know I had a daughter until she turned up at the hospital with the letter her mother had written naming me but it was the best day of my life...so you see, I'm not the vile lecherous monster you make me out to be. I'm just a loving father like you are.'

The sincerity in Jake's words overwhelmed him. More than anything Richard wanted to believe him.

'You're speaking the truth aren't you?'

'I always speak the truth Richard.'

He paused to collect his thoughts. 'I don't know what to say. *Sorry* sounds so inadequate. So are you saying Paige's mother was the daughter of that guy who blacked both your eyes?'

He laughed. 'You heard about that? Yes the very one. He broke my nose too. He told me she'd had an abortion, the lying swine. All those years I'd had a lovely daughter I knew nothing about. In a way I owe you because if Paige hadn't been pregnant, I'd never have known of her existence as she wouldn't have come looking for me.'

'I'll send you my bill then,' Richard smirked. He emitted a huge sigh. 'So, what do I do now?'

'You speak to Paige and hope for the best. I can't put the right words in your mouth but just for once try to get something right. By the way, that woman I was with in Manchester is my PA. We're engaged and hope to be married soon and yes, Paige knows all about her. If you can take the day off tomorrow, why not drive down for the birthday party?'

'And how do you think Paige will react to that?'

‘That’s anybody’s guess Richard. Women can be very unpredictable so try to stay calm and reassure her you won’t take her children away. That’ll help. That’s been her main concern from the outset, that you’d find out and apply for custody.’

‘I’d never do that. Will you be there?’

‘No, not until later. You need to talk...alone. This is my mobile number should you need to call me.’

‘I meant to ask when it came up earlier, does my mother know who you are?’

‘Of course. We’re the best of friends. We’re the grandparents. I don’t think David knows but I could be wrong. He’s met the children a few times. Don’t be too hard on your mother. She only did what she had to do to see her grandchildren. You know Paige can be very headstrong at times.’

‘Tell me about it. Do you really think she still has feelings for me?’

‘She won’t admit it to me but I’m pretty sure she does. At the moment though she’s very volatile and weepy. I was worried about her last night when we got home so I went to her room to check on her. At first I couldn’t see her and then I spotted her on the floor, hiding in the darkness in her night attire, her knees under her chin, quivering and crying bitterly. I sat with her and cradled her in my arms until she stopped sobbing.’

Richard was horrified to hear that. ‘I wish I could turn the clock back. I’ve been such a bloody fool.’

‘If I had a fiver for every time I’ve heard that over the years, I’d be a very rich man. People learn from their mistakes though and it makes them stronger.’

Richard arose and shook Jake's hand vigorously. 'You're a decent bloke Jake. I should never have...'

'Forget it. Just do what's right for Paige and your children now. I won't mention I've seen you.'

He grinned. 'I thought you always told the truth?'

'I *do* but this is different. Keeping information to yourself is lying by omission, so it doesn't count.'

'So if she asks, do I say you've been to see me?'

'I suppose you'll have to now you know I'm her dad otherwise it'll restrict your dialogue somewhat. Besides, it's always better to be open.'

They shook hands again. 'Have a safe journey.'

'Thanks Richard and good luck tomorrow. Try to be patient; take it slowly and remain calm.'

Paige awoke at seven o'clock the next morning to a cacophony of noise from the children's room. They were excited at the prospect of yet another birthday party with more presents to open and they were also looking forward to seeing their great grandad they hadn't seen for a number of weeks.

Jake made his excuses to leave at ten o'clock. He had already received a call from Richard to enquire if the children owned tricycles as he intended to get them one each. He sounded anxious, Jake felt, but it was only to be expected. This was a big day with so much resting on his ability to remain calm and say the right thing.

It was just before midday when Richard pulled up outside Jake's house. He was smartly dressed; he'd had a haircut too that morning and a second shave at a service station en route.

He knocked at the door and stepped back, waiting for Paige to appear. He had briefly rehearsed what he should say but by the time she opened the door his mind was a blank.

She was surprised to see him and waited for him to speak first but he simply stared at her for several seconds before stuttering, 'I...er...haven't come here to cause trouble. I think we need to sit down quietly and talk, please Paige. I'm sorry for the aggressive way I behaved yesterday. It was a shock to discover I had...we had...two children. I'd never do anything to cause you distress. I needed to make that clear so do you think we can try to resolve matters, please?'

'You'd better come in,' she said.

Before he had removed his jacket Olivia, having recognised his voice, bounded into the hall.

'Richard,' she shrieked, tugging on his sleeve.

He bent down, lifted her up and kissed her cheek. Giggling she scurried away to tell Michael who was by his side in an instant, wanting a cuddle too.

'You seem to have made quite an impression on the children,' she remarked as the twins ran back to their toys. 'Thanks for attending to Michael's knee at the party.'

'I was happy to help. Is he alright today?'

'It would appear so. They've both been charging round the house since the crack of dawn. Michael's always falling.'

Following a lengthy pause she asked, 'Would you like a cup of coffee?'

'Thank you if you're having one. I wouldn't want to put you to any trouble.'

'This is very much *déjà vu*,' she said. 'We had similar conversation the first time you called at m house to offer me the job. You were cautious then, so how about you get straight to the point? I'm sure you haven't driven all this way for a cup of coffee and a cosy chat. There has to be an ulterior motive.'

'Please don't make this more difficult than it is. It wasn't easy coming here today. I'd really like us to be friends.'

'Friends,' she mocked with derision. 'Alright, I'll make you that cup of coffee then. That's friendly.'

Richard sighed pessimistically as she disappeared into the kitchen. This was going to be more difficult than anticipated.

When she returned with his coffee he smiled and thanked her. 'Are you still in touch with Laura?'

'Yes, by email. They came to England for several days before their daughter Morgan was born. They stayed with us for a couple of days. It was great to see them again. They also have a son now, Travis.'

'That's nice. Are they still in New York?'

Paige nodded. 'Brad has his own business now in Web Design. He's very busy. How are you doing? Is your business still flourishing?'

'Can't grumble. We get our fair share of work. As you probably know, David's back at work now. He appears to have made a complete recovery.'

'Yes, your mum told me. Now I have children of my own I can better understand the agony you must have suffered. I'm very pleased for you Richard.'

Following another awkward silence Richard said, 'I was hoping I might stay for the children's party. I have something for them. I took the liberty of buying them a toddler bike each. They're in the car.'

Paige guessed Eleanor had advised him about the twins' party. 'Thank you Richard. I'm sure they'll be thrilled. Is that why you came…for their party?'

He recalled his discussion with Jake. 'No Paige, I came to say I'm sorry again and to beg you to come back to me because life without you is meaningless. I've never stopped loving you for a moment and I'd like to spend the rest of my life with you...and our children. If you're honest you have feelings for me too for I can see it in your eyes so can we try again? I've kept away as I thought you were involved with Jake but now I know he's your father...'

Irately she glared at him. 'I don't believe it! Who the hell keeps feeding you all this information? You knew where I was living as soon as I got here. You knew the phone number too and now you know all about my father. Do you have a Private Investigator watching my every move?' she demanded to know.

He laughed uneasily. 'No, of course not.'

'So come on then, how do you know about Dad?'

Sheepishly he said, 'He told me yesterday, okay?'

'No, it is *not* okay. It is anything *but* okay. How come you were talking to Dad yesterday?'

'Don't get upset. Jake came to see me. He's very concerned about you.'

'Well he needn't be. I'm fine, just dandy. I don't need his charity and I definitely don't need yours.'

His next words shocked her.

'Look me in the eye Paige and tell me you don't love me anymore and I'll walk away forever.'

She sighed and stood up. 'That's not the point.'

'What *is* the point then?' he said, moving towards her. 'We used to be so happy, inseparable and very much in love. What went wrong?'

'You ask *that?'* she cackled. *'You* went wrong. I thought you'd have remembered how you dumped me with nothing to my name and pregnant as well.'

'That's unfair. I didn't know you were pregnant. I tried to find you as soon as I found out and begged you to come back with me but you wouldn't.'

She started to cry. 'You really hurt me Richard.'

Richard took her in his arms. 'I know darling and I'm sorry. I was out of my mind with worry and all I could see was a young woman who deserved more than I could give her. I should have asked what you wanted. If only I could turn back the clock...'

'I understood and we might have resolved that but then, when you stormed back to my office accusing me of having an improper relationship with David, your *son* for God's sake, it was over for me, much as I loved you. That was an appalling thing to even think, let alone say. It was sickening and disgusting. There was never *anything* like that between us. All I ever tried to do was help David get better, to ease your pain.'

It was Richard's turn to be angry, 'What the hell are you talking about Paige? I never made any such allegation about the two of you. Explain yourself.'

'You have a convenient memory,' Paige snorted. 'After you made me feel cheap and worthless, you stormed back into my room with the so-called truth that you were jealous. I haven't forgotten one word you said. It was horrible...vile.' She started to sob. 'Nobody had ever spoken to me like that. You said you were jealous, that you'd watched us together; you referred to our little asides, our body language, the way we looked at each other and the way David hung on my every word. You glowered at me with hatred in your eyes. I could have forgiven you for the things you'd said earlier. I knew how concerned you were about David, wondering if he'd ever walk again and make a complete recovery but to express such accusations when they were totally unfounded, well I'm sorry but I could *never* forgive that.'

Richard nodded his head repentantly. 'My God! I *did* say all those things, I don't deny it but I didn't mean it the way you interpreted it. I *was* crazy with jealousy because you achieved the things I couldn't with David. You only had to raise an eyebrow and he'd comply. I was his father and I was losing him. Can't you see how that felt? I was at my wits end. I couldn't make any headway with him. All I envisaged was an ailing invalid for ever. He was my son and I loved him very much. I wanted to be like you, of some benefit to him but he chose to comply with your wishes and ignore mine. I had to get him back and if losing you was the only way, it had to be. As it turned out, he hated me all the more for sending you away so I accomplished nothing. This has been a terrible misunderstanding darling, I swear to you. I simply wanted my healthy son back. I could never think anything bad about you. It's little wonder you wouldn't come back to me. I don't know what else to say other than I'm truly sorry for hurting you.'

She buried her head in his chest. ‘Maybe we can start afresh but I’d like to take things a day at a time for now. That’s all I can offer. I don’t just have myself to think about now; I have to be really sure that I’m doing what’s best for the children but whatever happens, I won’t stop you seeing them, ever. I don’t expect you to understand but my life has been full of distress and heartbreak. I’ve lost so many people I loved that I can’t imagine a life without pain. I do love you Richard, as much as I ever did but for now that isn’t enough. I must be really sure this time. I’ll not subject our children to the kind of disarray I’ve had in my life so far but I want you to know it isn’t a *no*; it’s a *probably,* if you’re prepared to give me time to sort myself out.’

He kissed her gently and smiled. ‘I’d wait forever for you. You’re the love of my life and if you’ll let me, I’ll prove that good things *can* happen to you.’

Paige smiled at him through her tears. ‘Who am I to criticise you? I’m not without blame, hiding your children from you. It was despicable and I’m sorry. I need your forgiveness more than you need mine. I should have listened to Dad. He’s good at what he does but I was too pigheaded to take notice. I’m not a spiteful person normally. Deep down I hated what I was doing to you. Everyone told me I was wrong, even Laura but I was so afraid you’d try to take my children away from me and I couldn’t bear to lose anyone else. Can you at least try to understand how I felt after everything that had happened to me? In my own dim-witted way, I thought that if you never knew we had children you’d leave me alone. That’s why I allowed you to believe I was living with Jake as his...' As her words trailed off he nodded.

'I'm pleased we've finally cleared the air and I'm glad you've finally met the twins. I'm sorry for the heartache I've caused. You must have been furious to discover I'd been so devious, especially when the family was complicit as well but I gave your mum and my dad no choice in the matter.'

'It's all behind us now Paige. In your situation I'd probably have done exactly the same so let's put it behind us, please, and as I've taken up a lot of your time, what can I do? Do you need any help?'

Paige shook her head. 'No, you know me; all the food's ready. I must go and get Grandad though.'

'Grandad?' he asked quizzically.

'Jake's dad. He's in a nursing home close by. He wanted to come to the twins' party. He's a likeable old chap. You'll enjoy his dry humour.'

He smiled. 'I'm happy you've found a whole new family. At least something good came out of this.'

She beamed with delight. 'Yes and Dad hopes to get married soon so then I'll have a step-mum too. Marjorie will be here later. She's perfect for Jake.'

'So, you didn't answer my earlier question. Can I stay for the party too…please?'

She grinned. 'I'll be disappointed if you don't, in fact I *insist* you do.'

'Then let me help with something.'

'Okay, you can read to the twins while I'm away. They'll enjoy that.'

'I will too.' He paused then added, 'Thank you.'

She looked puzzled. 'For what?'

'For being you, for being so understanding when I've been such a bloody idiot and for all your other unique qualities, in particular for how you've raised the twins without any support from me, financial or otherwise.'

'You have Dad to thank for that. He's been there for all of us; he's been brilliant.'

Paige called the children and Richard sat between them with their book of nursery rhymes. She leaned over him, accidentally brushing her arm against his. He nearly cried out; it was electrifying. 'Don't read that one,' she told him.

'Why not?'

'One psycho is enough in this family without the twins being scared of spiders. That's probably why so many folk suffer from arachnophobia after hearing that nursery rhyme at an early age.'

'You could have a point there,' he concurred with a nod. 'And what exactly is a tuffet?'

She giggled. 'I haven't a clue. A clump of grass I guess. I'm off for Grandad now. I won't be long.'

Richard was elated to be in charge of the children, albeit for only a short while and when Jake turned up not long after Paige had left, he was pleasantly surprised to find Richard looking composed with a book balanced on his knees as he read to the twins with an arm around each of them.

'I assume everything's going okay,' he remarked with a confident smile. 'Where's Paige?'

'She's gone to get your dad. She shouldn't be too long.' Then, swollen with pride he remarked, 'I've been left in charge of the children.'

‘Mmm, that’s quite a promising development, her leaving you in charge. How has she been?’

‘She was a bit weepy earlier but we’ve had a long talk and we’re going to try and work things out. I’m hopeful we will. She still loves me, that’s the main issue, not that I deserve it. I’d do anything for Paige but I think you know that already.’

Jake nodded. ‘Give her some space. She has quite a few dark days ahead of her yet but I’m sure, with your support, she’ll come through it.’

He sighed audibly. ‘I’m to blame for most of it.’

‘Her main concern was that you’d find out about the twins and take them away from her, despite my assurances that you’d never do that. Now you know about them, it’s less for her to worry about and the fact she’s left you alone with them is a major step towards recovery. Forgiveness is an important issue in any relationship.’

‘Yes, I’ve said and done some stupid things.’

‘So has Paige but there’s no point in dwelling on the past. It’s time to move forward now Richard.’

With annoyance in her voice, Olivia interrupted, ‘Richard, *read* to us.’

He smiled. ‘Okay, but first, do you remember my other name?’

‘Yes... Daddy,’ she squealed. ‘Now read to us.’

Richard smiled contentedly and turned to the next page as Jake looked on with approval.

Emma’s baby was born four weeks later, a healthy, chubby boy, bringing to an end the anxiety she and Andy had previously shared.

Over the next couple of months Richard spent his free time with Paige and their children. He and the twins were bonding well.

Jake was happy to note a marked improvement in Paige's mental health and emails he received from Laura about Paige's new-found state of mind were heartening. Gone were her sullen moods, replaced instead by joy and a sense of humour.

When Richard wasn't there, they talked for hours on the telephone. She missed him so much when he wasn't around. 'I've a proposition for you,' he told her one day, arousing her curiosity.

'That sounds ominous. What's wrong?'

'Nothing. I'm off to New York again in October. How do you feel about coming with me? That'd be another opportunity to see Laura and Brad and their children. What do you say?'

'Are you serious? What about the twins?'

'What do you mean? They'd come too.'

'All of us?'

'Of course. I wouldn't leave them behind.'

Flippantly she remarked, 'So would you pass me off as your PA again...or a nursery nurse perhaps?'

Cautiously he said, 'I'd hoped you might come as my wife this time Paige.'

When she didn't reply at once he was concerned. 'Paige? Answer me. Isn't that what you want?'

With a deep meaningful sigh she said, 'I always wanted to marry you but was too afraid to admit it.'

'And now?'

'If you're sure you'll cope with my psychological issues, yes, let's do it; let's get married.'

He laughed aloud. 'You, Paige Sheldon, have just made me the happiest man alive. I didn't intend for it to come out like that. I'd planned a cosy romantic proposal at the weekend once the children had gone to bed but I couldn't wait any longer for an answer. We'll have a wonderful life together, I promise. I'd give anything to be with you now. I do miss you.'

'I miss you too. I can't wait to tell Dad our news.'

'He'll be delighted. Go on, tell him and I'll talk to you tomorrow. I love you.'

Jake threw down his newspaper and peered over the top of his glasses when Paige bounded into the lounge. It was evident she had good news to impart. 'What's up?' he questioned. 'You look excited.'

'I am. Richard's just asked me to marry him.'

'And...?' he asked, eyebrows raised.

'I said I would of course. Isn't that great?'

Jake patted the cushion beside him and she threw herself down. Curling his arm around her shoulder, he kissed her lovingly. 'I'm so pleased for you. You deserve to be happy after all you've been through. There *is* one small problem though,' he said sternly.

Perturbed she asked, 'What's that?'

'There'll be lots of driving involved, coming back here every day. You insisted I must sack my useless cleaner so you'll have to carry on doing it.'

Paige chuckled. 'You clown. Anyway, I imagine Marjorie will move in before I've reached the end of the street. She's just itching for me to clear off so you can enjoy your love nest and that means she'll take over all my chores too. She thinks the world of you...*besotted* is the word.'

'And you love Richard very much don't you?'

She nodded and smiled. 'He's the best. When he ended our relationship I felt my life had ended too. I'd never have found anyone else to take his place.'

'When you next talk, tell him I'm delighted. Once you're married though I shall insist he calls me Dad rather than *that licentious rake*, so you can tell him that as well,' he quipped with a humorous snigger.

She giggled. 'You like him a lot don't you Dad?'

'Yes I do Paige. He's one of the good guys. He'll be a terrific father too. He worships the twins, as do I.' He sighed. 'I'll miss them when you leave.'

'I know but we won't be too far away.'

Her mobile rang again and it was Richard. 'I just told Mum our news.'

She tittered. 'Has she stopped screeching yet?'

'Not really. She's made up...the best news she's ever had. She's already planning our wedding and insists she's making your dress or whatever you're wearing. She sends her love…oh and I told David too. Both he and Penny are thrilled for us.'

'I knew they'd all be pleased. I've told Dad.'

'What did he say?'

On a burst of laughter she relayed Jake's amusing comments,

'I'm so embarrassed,' he said. 'I said some dreadful things to Jake and he never once lost his temper even though I was wrong about everything.'

'That's his skill Richard...his job. He must remain calm under pressure. I imagine he gets called much worse by his patients. Anyway, it's simply a case of 'sticks and stones', as the saying goes. Think of all the terrible names Emma called you and yet I know she'll be over the moon when I tell her our news. If I'm happy, Emma's happy too.'

'Are you off to bed now?'

'No, I'm going to email Laura and bring her up to speed and then I'm spending an hour on my novel. I want to finish it and send it to a couple of agents in the next few days. I can wrap it up now I know the ending.'

'What's it about?'

He heard a slight chuckle in the background. 'It's about a young woman with deep-rooted emotional issues as a result of the appalling experiences she's suffered but thankfully it all ends happily when she marries her Prince Charming.'

'I have a gut feeling it will be accepted so you see I'm already taking control of my life and learning to be optimistic.'

He needed to hear that and smiled contentedly.